Praise for A Memory of Song

"...a sweepingly epic yet intimately character-driven Norse-flavoured fantasy that will make any dark fantasy lover's heart sing with both joy and sorrow." – *Esmay, Grimdark Magazine*

"The way that Palmer has worked all this together is a brilliant feat." – *The Wulvers Library, FanFiAddict*

"Scott Palmer writes with a poetic, resonant prose that draws you in..." – *Joshua Walker, author of The Song of the Sleepers*

"...a thrilling, epic ride... a mashup of Gwynne's Bloodsworn Saga mixed with Abercrombie's First Law Series." – *Bibliotheory*

"Palmer's worldbuilding, and the depth of history and politics pulls you in like a sirens song." – *Isaac Hill, author of The Dragon Legion*

By Scott Palmer

A Memory of Song

The Sound of Starfall

A
Memory
Of
Song

First Verse of The Last Ballad

Scott Palmer

THE NYTEWOOD PRESS

First Edition

978-1-7381793-1-2

Edited by Kelley Tai, https://www.bramblecrowbooks.com/

Cover design © Stuart Bache, https://www.stuartbache.co.uk/

Chapter headings, scene break, and logo by Brian Vandevelde, https://brianvandevelde.ca/

Interior design and formatting by Scott Palmer.

Maps by Joshua Hoskins, @Noctua_Cartography

Palmer, Scott. (A Memory Of Song, The Last Ballad 1.0) Paperback edition.

For Sydney, who dared me to dream
For Indie, who showed me what real magic looks like
And for you,
Anyone who's refused to stay down

CONTENTS

A
MEMORY
OF
SONG

A Note On Maps

There are maps in this book, but you can access full colour high definition maps of the entire world at https://www.scottpalmerauthor.com/maps and follow along as you read!

You will also find a full glossary in the back of this book, but for easy reference while reading you can find it on my website at https://www.scottpalmerauthor.com/glossary.

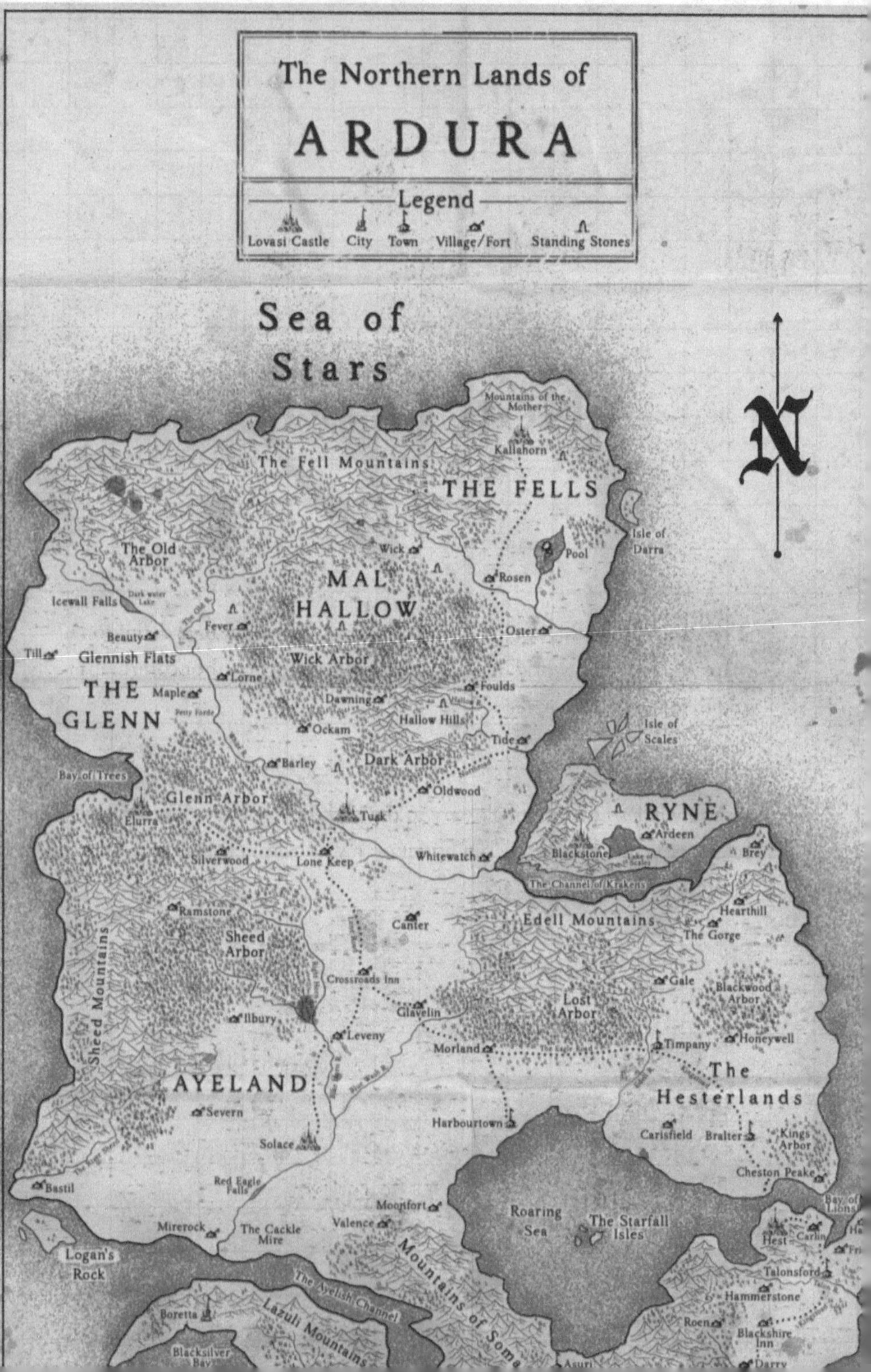

The Northern Lands of

ARDURA

— Legend —

Lovasi Castle   City   Town   Village/Fort   Standing Stones

Sea of
Stars

Mountains of the Mother

The Fell Mountains

THE FELLS

Kallahorn

Wick

Pool

Isle of Darra

The Old Arbor

MAL HALLOW

Rosen

Icewall Falls   Dark water Lake

Fever

Oster

Beauty

Wick Arbor

Till   Glennish Flats

Lorne

Foulds

THE GLENN   Maple

Dawning

Petty Fords

Ockam   Hallow Hills

Tide

Isle of Scales

Barley   Dark Arbor

Bay of Trees

Oldwood

Glenn Arbor

RYNE

Tusk

Elurra

Ardeen

Silverwood   Lone Keep

Whitewatch

Blackstone   Lake of Scales

Brey

The Channel of Krakens

Ramstone

Canter   Edell Mountains

Hearthill

Sheed Arbor   The Gorge

Sheed Mountains

Crossroads Inn

Gale   Blackwood Arbor

Ilbury

Glavelin   Lost Arbor

Leveny

Honeywell

Morland

Timpany

AYELAND   The Hesterlands

Severn

Harbourtown

Carisfield   Bralter   Kings Arbor

Solace

Cheston Peake

Red Eagle Falls

Bastil

Moonfort   Roaring Sea   The Starfall Isles   Bay of Lions

Mirerock   Valence

Hest   Carlin   Ha

The Cackle Mire

Logan's Rock

Talonsford

Mountains of Some

The Ayelish Channel

Hammerstone

Boretta   Lazuli Mountains

Roen

Blackshire Inn

Blacksilver Bay

Asuri   Fri

Uckam
Tide
Scales
Barley
Dark Arbor
Bay of Trees
Oldwood
RYNE
Glenn Arbor
Ardeen
Elurra
Blackstone
Lake of Scales
Brey
Silverwood
Lone Keep
Whitewatch
The Channel of Krakens
Hearthill
Ramstone
Canter
Edell Mountains
The Gorge
Sheed
Arbor
Gale
Blackwood
Arbor
Sheed Mountains
Crossroads Inn
Lost
Arbor
Honeywell
Ilbury
Glavelin
Leveny
Timpany
Morland
The Lost Road
The
Hesterlands
AYELAND
Severn
Harbourtown
Carisfield
Bralter
Kings
Arbor
Solace
Cheston Peake
Red Eagle
Falls
Bay of
Lions
Bastil
Moonfort
Roaring
Sea
The Starfall
Isles
Hest
Carlin
Mirerock
Valence
Haven
Logan's
Rock
The Cackle
Mire
Friars
Talonsford
The Ayelish Channel
Mountains
of Soma
Hammerstone
Boretta
Lazuli Mountains
Roen
Blackshire
Inn
Blacksilver
Bay
Odessa
Asuri
Darry
Talent
Casai
Hills of Soma
Soren
The Red R.
LAVESH
ESHER
Lysess
Behruvian Desert
Kiln
Behru
Saltsan
Saray
The
Oracle
Bay of
Bones
Jakaray
Sima
Sareen
The Bone
Sea
Kerro
Boast
The Bone
Islands
N
Tenna
The Southern Lands of
ARDURA
Legend
Lovasi Castle
City
Town
Village/Fort
Standing Stones

AUTHOR'S NOTE

This story contains graphic depictions of death and a scene of child abuse.

PART ONE

Nature has made up her mind that what cannot defend itself shall not be defended.

Ralph Waldo Emerson

THE RUN

T HE GHOST OF WINTER slipped its cold fingers around James's ankles and dug in with icy sharp nails to bleed his feet numb. He crashed into a pile of slush behind a towering pine to catch his breath. His heart threatened to tear through his ribs like a caged dog. *Go back for her!* Thundering footsteps ripped the cold earth behind him and shook the ground below his feet. The mutts were coming. The rotten stench of carnivore came with them. There was no going back.

He took off. The pine needles held a steady drip from the spring thaw, soaking him as he broke through the arbor. He was alone. He had left everyone behind when the Hawka attacked the camp. All he could do was run and hope to the gods that she ran, too. *But you can't outrun a Hawka for long...*

He stopped to listen for the river.

"Fuck," he muttered. There was nothing. He took a deep breath. He hadn't any idea where to go. And the screams of the Hawka returned. Faint, but they would chew up that distance like meat and be on him in minutes if he stopped moving. They had his tracks now.

James took off running, breaking through wet pines and ferns, upon slush and fallen needles towards what he hoped was the river. Branches sliced up his hands and face—he could taste blood on his tongue—but the Hawka would do far worse. *Careful with every step.* If he turned an ankle now, it would mean death. No question. Through sap, mud, blood, and cold, he kept running, wheezing as he barely sucked down each breath. *You're going too slow.* Pine sap tried to glue his eyelids shut—that, and exhaustion. Behind, the Hawka screamed. They picked up speed. *You can't outrun a Hawka. You're going too slow. Too slow.*

He gave into the exhaustion and looked around at the spot he would die on. *You should have gone back for her.* Rustling echoed in the woods. They had caught up. A faint snort came with the rustling. *They're sniffing you down.* A single howl, then silence. Not even a breeze crawled through the pines and bare birch. The Hawka made no sound once they found their prey. James gripped his axe with a feeble hope, like a deer that smelled the wolf pack. He wouldn't hear them when they jumped him, but the rotting stench of decay gave them away. They were slowly surrounding him. *You should have died with her by your side. You could have gone back.*

Through the brush, the soul of a dead man stood tall. His head was bludgeoned in with a nose that melted into his lips, and he stood like a man alive and beckoned James. James ran to it. The Hawka exploded out from the trees behind him. They were on his heels as he pushed through the woods. They should have caught him. *Why haven't they caught you?* He followed the dead man through the thick brush.

He ran uphill now, slowing and losing breath. Then he came to a cliff face. A chill ran down his spine as he looked up. Hundreds of dead souls stared down at him. *They love the cold arbor.* He could remember Gran's stories. *They linger there, waiting for life.*

The dead waved him up. He climbed towards them, only half sure he wasn't dead already and this was some kind of welcome. Behind him, the Hawka hooted and hooted in celebration as they scaled the cliff faster than he could believe. James gripped a smooth piece of granite and pulled himself up. When he reached the top, he was alone.

James pulled his axe around in time to meet the first Hawka as it rose from behind and jumped him. The blade sank into its snout with a warm squelch just as the Hawka opened its maw to end him. The dead Hawka fell heavy on top of him. He pushed the stinking thing off and tried to pull his axe free. The rest of them were climbing fast but James's axe had wedged itself in the Hawka's skull and wouldn't move.

There was no choice. He ran. James wheezed for air, his chest burning like a clan fire, legs knotted like they were being wrung out, ears thumping like two drums at a funeral. They were right behind him.

Maggie's knife was in his hand. He didn't even remember pulling it from his belt. *Maggie.* He thought of what they could have been. Remembered what they *were. You should have gone back for her.* The Hawka roared for the rest of the pack. They had nearly gotten their prey. *Why did the dead lead me here? Why did they want me to die on this hill?*

He followed a faint sound. A rumble in his ear quickly rose to the roar of rushing water. It was getting louder as he ran. A cold whisper in his ear told him to jump, so he jumped just before the ground disappeared below him. And he was falling, weightless. Hawka screamed from above. And then the water hit him like a cold knife and stole his breath.

The gurgling white water swept him away. He couldn't tell which way was up, but when he stopped struggling, he bobbed to the top. But his lungs weren't working—he still couldn't breathe. A hard splash echoed behind him. Another mutt had jumped. Two more plunges, and a third and fourth. *Why did you think the river would save you?* More plunges.

He choked out a strained breath, sunk his fingers into the black mud of the bank, and crawled out of the current. He felt the cold sink into his bones the moment he got out of the water. James looked behind him and saw the Hawka flailing in the white water. But one trailed behind close enough to the shore to pull itself out. It clawed at the mud and crawled out of the rushing river a few hundred yards from where he stood. James watched as the inhuman beast stood up tall on two legs and looked around and sniffed at the air with its twisted black snout. It saw him.

James turned and ran towards the arbor. His sopping wet boots slapped the ground, hard with every step, leaving prints in the cold mud. His clothes were stuck tight to his skin, heavy and cold, making every stride feel like ten. He ran until he realized it was no use. *You can't outrun a Hawka.*

He threw himself in front of a rock face in the woods. He searched for a stick heavy enough to kill a Hawka. When he found one, he pulled Maggie's knife and sharpened the stick into a spear. Every crack in the woods made him squirm. *I'm so used to you by my side, Maggie.* Slivers of pale wood piled up around him as he carved. *I'm so used to you here.* As James twirled his weapon and stabbed the air, he noticed a small cave tucked between two pine trees. He would rather risk freezing to death than the Hawka, and so he crawled inside. James sat and watched the water drip from his hair and wondered if each minute that passed would be his last minute to live. A loud crack came from close by. A rustling in the ferns and a wheezing, high-pitched snort. *It's sniffing you down. Don't move... let it kill you. Let this be over.* James closed his eyes and saw Maggie. It was far in the future. She was holding their child in her arms. They were out front of a house, by a lake. She smiled at him. *Live. You have to live...*

James opened his eyes, gripped his spear, and walked out of the cave to meet the beast. He held his spear at the ready. He could see the Hawka searching, swooping its snout this way and that. It caught his scent, looked at James, and howled. James howled back something guttural, spittle flying from the corners of his mouth just like a Hawka, and let the beast rush at him. When it lunged, he could feel power from below the earth course through him, and he thrust his spear up through the mutt's chest and skewered it into a tree trunk. James let the Hawka hang there as he studied its inhuman body; its protruding bear-like rib cage gushed dark purple blood down its mangy black fur; its crooked wolf's jaw leaked rotten green saliva through jagged teeth as it cried out in its wretched tongue. James used Maggie's knife to slit its thick throat—the veins writhed like bloated worms as they emptied. He watched the mutt slowly go limp before wiping the blade clean on his trouser leg.

You're more of a monster than this thing.

James crept back into the cave and cowered near a fire pit, still filled with charred wood and ash like it had been forgotten by another. There were logs around to sit on, but he leaned against the cold stone wall instead, hugging his knees and shivering. James held Maggie's knife tight for when the Hawka came back. *They always come back.*

It was cold. Freezing. James had never felt this kind of cold before. He could feel the ice in his bones, like they might snap. It could have been hours or minutes that he lay shivering, his teeth chattering like a woodpecker. He didn't want to die here, not without Maggie. But where was he? He heard a familiar song. Memories from another life; another person; another time. A small boy playing swords with Dad; working in the garden with Mom; visions of his time with Wulfee and her Feldarra before the Hawka came down on them. Before the world died. And he saw visions of Maggie. He saw her dancing in the rain barefoot with her head up and her tongue out to catch the drops.

In James's hand, the small opalescent stone in the hilt of her blade caught the fading sunlight, and James thought he saw her face in it. *You got her killed.*

"*Why?*" he called out to no one, but it was Alder he spoke to. "Why did you let me live if only to chase me down?"

Every sound made him squirm. Every crack and every snap. *It was Alder who sent those Hawka. He's found you.* The dead whispered to him from the night.

"*Help us. Please help us.*"

"I can't!" James screamed hoarsely. But the dead didn't hear him.

"*Help us, please,*" they begged. James went back to ignoring them, as he always had.

The sun was setting low. Its golden-red eye stared at him through the cave entrance in judgement as it disappeared below the horizon. The

Hawka came at sunrise. He'd been running all day. *You won't make it through the night. You won't.* But then the dead souls came to him. They gathered around, and the soul of an old woman knelt down beside him. Her bitter smile told him it was okay. It told him she was there to help. James opened his lungs and breathed her in. He ate what life still clung to her soul. His lungs filled with a smoky ice, and slowly, he stopped shivering. Inside, his soul warmed with magics.

The night made strange sounds, cold whispers in the wind. James murmured to the darkness like it may answer him back. The moon lit the cave with a dim grey glow. *Maggie loves the moon.* He held her knife to his chest and closed his eyes.

It was Alder sent them Hawka. Alder. You always knew he'd find you...

Soft footsteps shuffled outside his cave and a twig snapped. James tried to jump up but found himself too weak to do so. The footsteps got closer, picking up speed as they approached the cave entrance. All James could do was lie with his eyes closed and wait for whatever it was to find him. *I could have gone back...*

"Anyone alive in there?" a deep voice echoed off the cave walls like a thunderclap. James's eyes flicked open.

"Aye," James croaked. A man ran towards him with a thick cloak of fox furs. He wrapped it around James's shoulders and fumbled at his own cloak for a wineskin.

"By the gods, man, you're alive. Drink this," he said.

James took it, drank, and coughed as it warmed his body. It was shine, that old northerner's drink. He couldn't get used to the stuff no matter how often Wulfee made him drink it. The key was to just get it in ya, she'd said.

The man had a crest of greying black hair tied into a bun, a thick and tangled grey beard, and shallow blue eyes. He had the black-winged crest of the old Raven's Guild sewn into the shoulders of his cloak and black feathers down his arms to make it seem like he had wings. The man took the skin back and drank a long swig without recoil. He pulled out a hempen sack of mushrooms, picked a misshapen brown one out, and shoved it in his mouth.

"Here," he said while chewing, presenting the open sack with dirty, callused hands. "Eat."

James ate. The day had worn him bloody ragged, and he craved it. James took another drink, too, and soon had the energy to sit against a log around the firepit. A dead woman walked in from the night and sat on the log beside him. Another joined her.

"Ain't no one travelling alone since the fires went out. It's been a cold two weeks since the world died," said the bearded man. "Especially with all them Hawka about." He nodded his head towards outside. It was clear he didn't see the dead folk that had gathered around the fire pit. James could sense the man's eyes on him, studying his face and his scars.

James pulled the furs tight around himself. He didn't care to talk about the Hawka.

More and more dead gathered in from the night.

"Name's Eurick," said the man, poking around at the empty fire pit as if there was an ember buried under that white ash somewhere. "Be nice, a little fire right now, eh? Sometimes you don't know how good it all is till it's gone." Eurick took another swig from the skin and looked up, like he was cursing the gods for some old wound they had dealt him. "And sometimes you know just what you got, and it dies anyway."

"You say no one is travelling alone, but here we both are, alone," said James. Eurick laughed deeply.

"Aye, but I knew I wouldn't be alone for long," Eurick smiled. "I've been paid a great price to find you."

James sulked his head. *Alder...*

Around him, the dead hummed. Gran had sung the same tune to him as a boy. A song from long ago written deep into the soul, even in death. More came in from the night and gathered around the fireless pit, like flies to a corpse. *Since the fire is dead, maybe they see it.* They were the colour of moonlight, human-shaped whiffs of smoke. Deformed and battered, wearing the scars of their death. James had never seen so many in all his life. They hummed a song so loud James was sure that Eurick must be hearing it. He looked at the old raven, but he just stared back, curious now.

"What do you see?" he said, smiling a wide, knowing grin. "Is it *them? Are they here now*?" Eurick's eyes darted all over the cave.

"Nothing," James said.

"The Guild told me you're a seer, you know," the raven said. "Do you talk to them? The dead?" he smiled again. There were twenty or more dead folk sitting around the pit now. James looked around at them, and they stared back desperately.

"*Help,*" they begged him. "*Save us. Help us, please.*"

"No." James said. "They don't hear me."

"Oh, they will." Eurick put his hand on James's shoulder. "Come with me, and I promise you, they will."

THE RAVEN

JAMES KNEW HE WOULD need to kill the raven now. He wouldn't allow himself to become Eurick's prisoner.

The raven shared the last of his hard-bread, mushrooms, and shine with James. The raven didn't talk but studied James like a bird. James did his best to keep a distance between them as his body slowly filled with strength.

He sat amongst the dead and noted that Eurick had equipped himself well. He had good Daggland steel on his belt, sheathed blades at the hip and both ankles, a chain shirt beneath the black-winged cloak, and his warm blue eyes seemed to hide something colder beneath. James knew he would need to be careful with this one.

The raven rummaged in his bag, sorting through his maps.

James slowly picked up Maggie's knife and held it by his side, out of sight.

"Ah!" Eurick proclaimed, pulling out a map. He slammed his big finger down and poked at it. "Here's where we're going, more or less."

James had never understood the magics of maps. But he leaned in and pretended to look at what the raven was pointing at. James's fingers curled tightly around the hilt of the knife.

Eurick looked at him strangely, then down at his hand that was holding the knife.

Now.

James thrust his knife at Eurick's gut.

The raven moved with avian quickness and glided out of reach. He unsheathed his sword with the same haste and smiled.

"You wanna do this the hard way, man?" Eurick stood with his legs spread and sword at the ready and let his black-winged cloak slide off his shoulders to the ground.

James came at him slowly. He'd won sword fights with knives before—he knew he just had to close the distance.

"Why should I go with you, eh?" James said. The two men approached each other, eyes locked in a primal glare.

"The world is dying, man. The rains have stopped falling, fires won't burn, the winds have gone flat. Armies are marching. These are the days of end."

"So what am I gonna do?"

"Stop it."

James took one quick step forward and dove at Eurick. The raven swung, but his reaction was too slow, and James drove his shoulder into Eurick's sword arm and knocked him to the ground. The Daggland forged steel scraped along the stone floor of the cave and thumped into the charred logs in the dead firepit. James jumped on top of Eurick with his blade ready, but the raven just threw James off without so much of a grunt. Eurick stood back up and pulled a knife from his belt. There was a shining white diamond on the hilt, with runes and letters carved into the blade. James was fixated on it.

"I was in love once, too, man." Eurick lowered the weapon. "I know how much it hurts to lose them." It was an engagement knife, just like his for Maggie. Then he realized Eurick was only a person doing a job. It cost a king's weight in gold to hire a raven. It was whoever paid the raven that mattered.

"What does Alder plan to do with me? What makes him think I can stop all this?" James said.

"Alder? It's not Alder who sent me, man. I'm not your enemy."

"Then who?"

"The wizard."

"What?"

"He will know more about it all, man. He will give you the answers," Eurick said.

James shook his head. He didn't think he heard right.

"Wizard?"

"Maybe Warlock is more accurate. Adeqor is his name."

James didn't understand.

"All the Warlocks are dead," said James, remembering Gran's stories.

"Not all, man. Not him."

Gran had told him most died in the Starfall, thrice times a thousand years ago. And the rest killed themselves with their own power thrice times three hundred years ago.

James didn't like the sound of *Warlock*. But just then, he realized if Alder didn't send this man, then...

"The Hawka... they're after you, too?"

"Aye," said Eurick. James noticed Eurick's grip never loosened on his knife, just as his eyes never left James's. "We shouldn't fight each other, man. I'm not your enemy. But the Hawka are. And they will be back."

"You can't outrun a Hawka."

"I've got horses. They're nearby. They might do a better job at running away than us. Put that knife down, man. No need for this." Eurick studied him again. "We can ride to the setting sun, to the Old Arbor. The Hawka won't enter the deep arbors for fear of the dead."

James looked around at all the dead souls that had gathered around him. "*Help us,*" they begged him with emotionless, bloodshot eyes that seemed to stare *through* him. *They saved you from those Hawka.* He didn't want to admit it, but he trusted the dead more than himself. *They led you here so this raven would find you? So you wouldn't die?* He tucked Maggie's knife back into his belt and took a step back. Eurick tucked his knife away, too. And the dead stood up and trudged out of the cave, one by one.

"The dead are leaving." James said.

"Then we should, too," said Eurick, sheathing his sword. James still didn't trust the man. But he couldn't wait around here.

They left the cave, and the night welcomed James with a cold touch and the shadows of spindly branches for arms. He heard an owl singing and was reminded that there were more in these arbors than the Hawka. There was beauty there, Maggie had always told him, more beauty than you could ever know. He smiled, thinking of her standing barefoot in the arbor in the rain as Eurick led them to where he had two brown stallions tied up.

"I approached on foot when I saw that Hawka skewered to the tree over there," Eurick said, eyeing James suspiciously. "Takes some kinda person to do something like that."

"I found it there like that," said James.

"Uh huh." Eurick handed James the reins to one of the horses. "This one is for you," the raven said. James scratched the horse's neck.

"What's his name?" he asked.

"Name? No name. One out of the stable from the Guild. They're bred for work," Eurick answered. James didn't like that. He brushed the horse's mane with his stiff fingers and scratched its neck. *I'm going to call you Shalo.*

Eurick moved with an obsessive efficiency around the horses. He loaded bags full of star charts, brass tools, and glass eyes carefully into a padded compartment. Compasses, hourglasses, and balls of twine, he explained to James, were only in the left saddlebag. Foodstuffs, pots and pans, and extra water skins only on the right. Bedrolls and pillows were folded neatly and tucked away gently, as if disturbing them would wake them from a deep sleep. Forceps, a saw, and an assortment of small knives were the last to be packed.

"So if we have an accident on the road, they're handy." Eurick patted the bags, as if congratulating himself on a job well done.

James looked at him, and they shared a glare of mutual distrust and nodded. They rode into the night under the moon's light behind the host of dead souls.

Not two hours into the ride, the moon clouded over, and the stars disappeared. The black sky brought a bitter cold with it. James had spent many long hours in the saddle and understood the discomforts of a long and cold ride. But even being aware of the discomforts couldn't stop them from happening—but the chafe on his arse and thighs and the cold air freezing his face and hands numb left James feeling grateful. He was happy not to have been a meal for the Hawka.

James had ridden this road before with his mom and dad and a host of Hallow knights. They were on the run from King Alder, who had just risen to the Northern throne after Mal Hallow had truly lost the war to Ayeland. He remembered seeing the Old Arbor and the great thousand-foot nytewoods with their black trunks and golden luminescent blossoms rising up in the distance. He remembered the smells of peonies and honey as he stood below them, and the rush of hope he felt as looked up at the golden blossoms. The black trunk of the nytewood had writhed beneath his palm when he touched it. The ancient folk of the Hallow had one hard rule about the trees: do not spill blood beneath them, as it was a sin against the Old Gods.

It was ten years ago now that James's family had made their last stand in the Old Arbor. James's dad refused to live as a king who lost his country. He would fight until death rather than let Alder conquer him. *And you just let him die...* they had prayed to the Old Gods beneath the nytewoods, but the gods didn't hear them. James was the only person who left that arbor alive. King Calen Alder spilled blood beneath the sacred trees, and still, no sin has fallen on him.

The black trunk and golden blossoms of the nytewood were impossible to ignore. Their luminescent blooms lightly glowed below the blanket of black sky, and as he looked at them, James couldn't help but believe in their magics once more.

James and Eurick had almost travelled twenty miles before morning broke. A stiff back and a raw ass were all James had to show for it. Eurick had pulled his stallion off the road to a flat patch of grass underneath a canopy of trees.

James dismounted and his boots sank into the soggy, thawing ground; his feet soaked with cold water.

"Thanks, Shalo," he murmured, scratching his mane. Shalo neighed in response.

Eurick unpacked a heavy canvas from one of his bags and laid it under the trunk of a large fir tree where the ground was drier atop the fallen needles. James sat down and quickly flattened himself out into a lying position. His legs had turned into straw. Eurick brought him a skin of water and some more hard-bread and mushrooms. James didn't want to trust the raven, and he especially didn't like the raven's laugh, but he fed James when he was hungry, and that was someone worth sticking around for. At least at the moment. James meant to ask him something, something about the wizard, but he was completely worn ragged, and his eyes were already closed. He drifted into a strange dream where the ghost of his gran floated over him like a cold cloud and, in a broken voice that sounded like ice cracking, reminded him of an old northern saying:

"Never fall asleep first next to someone you just met."

A Sorry Lot

"**Y**OU GOT IT!" GEN yelled, then chased after the buck, following the trail of blood it left along the melted snow. Wulfee felt a pang of relief in her gut.

Nice not to be the prey this time around.

Wulfee and her crew had tracked the buck all morning, and one look at the sorry lot who followed her said they couldn't track it no more—and what had happened this morning made her want to stop more than ever. The buck had a big old rack on its head. Far more meat than they'd need and much of it would go to waste if they couldn't get the fire going, but that was the gods' fault for cursing these lands, not Wulfee's.

Wulfee stretched her back and cracked her neck side to side. She was in rough shape, roughest she had been. Her head pounded like a drum, feet were stiff and frozen, and her stomach cried for something to eat. The Hawka attack on their camp earlier that day had nearly killed her. They *did* kill many others. Folk she'd known and loved for years. The thought of it still made her sick. She had lost most of her crew. *The mutts have never come in a horde that big.*

Pike came out of the brush with a worried look under his thick grey beard.

"We'll rest here for the night. Get some meat in us. Heal our wounds," Wulfee said. "Then we carry on."

Pike nodded and led the way into a small clearing where their dinner took its last graze on soggy, yellowed grass. A stream flowed nearby, the soft trickling of it gave Wulfee a feeling of home in what had started to feel like foreign land. It had been dark in the Fells since the fires stopped burning. And Wulfee was getting thirsty for the rains—for any sign from the gods that they were still there. Gen was hollering in the distance, but Wulfee couldn't quite make out what he was saying. She figured if he really needed them, he'd start banging on something. She limped over to the stream, ignored the haggard person she saw in the water's reflection, and drank the icy cold water from cupped hands. Pike knelt down beside her and did the same. He looked over like he wanted to say something, then thought the better of it and lowered his head back down to take another drink.

"You're not done yet, old man," Wulfee said anyway.

"It should have been me," he said. "The gods know I'm ready to die. I'm ready to be with my Alissa again."

"It's not over," Wulfee said, and the old warrior looked up at her like he couldn't imagine a reason she still believed in him. "There's but one more braid to add to my hair. He's still out there, somewhere. I won't stop, not now. Not after all this," she said.

Pike stroked the long grey braids that rested on his shoulders. Each one represented a victory in single combat; each one a life. Without a sound, Pike took off the shield strapped to his back and dropped it into the soft soil beside him. The battered, knotty old thing was carved with the symbol of the Feldarra, *the nihr'el*, which meant the world tree in the northern tongue. The shield was the protector's protection. But Wulfee and her sorry crew were the only shields left in the Fells, and they failed to protect the lands from invaders when they ran from those Hawka. Wulfee's vows were piss in the wind at this point.

Then, something rustled in the branches beyond the stream, and Wulfee reached for her axe.

"It's okay, Wulfee." Pike gently touched her forearm with his age spotted hand. It was just Gen. The big lad had the deer on his shoulders, holding a set of legs in each hand. He dropped it down a few feet from the stream. The thing had soaked him in blood, and Wulfee, even after what she'd seen that day, felt bile rising at the back of her throat.

"Got this." Gen offered Wulfee a blood tipped arrow. She tucked it away, saying nothing.

"Can I go back for Maggie now?" Gen asked. "She still seems tired." The young Giy'er had grown over ten feet tall in his eighteen years—his height shocked Wulfee with every inch. But some of the Giy'er that were roaming the wild grew twenty-five feet tall and were nearly two hundred years old. So Gen was just a baby in the eyes of those massive creatures. The young lad couldn't see suffering if he stared at it all day. Wulfee supposed that was no bad thing. And he always wanted to chip in and do anything to be one of the Feldarra.

"Aye. Be careful. Don't run too fast, and do your best not to hit your head on these branches, eh?" she said. Gen looked around at the trees, then back at Wulfee, and smiled hopefully.

"Then can you tell me the story, Wulfee? Please?" Gen said.

"Not now, Gen. I've told you a hundred times already. Can't you just remember it?"

"It's better when you tell it."

"I'll tell it another time."

"Tomorrow?"

"Maybe, Gen, it's not really the time for stories. I ain't feeling alright." Gen's face turned into one big grin from ear to ear at the word maybe and skipped off into the brush. Wulfee envied his smile and his innocence. She felt like she hadn't smiled in far too long.

"T HIS *IS* FIRE ROCK, is it not?" Wulfee complained. She hadn't cursed the gods since the war with Odhran, eleven years ago down in Mal Hallow. The gods had abandoned her and let half her crew die, but she cursed the gods again now.

"I'm certain of it," Pike said. He took the rock from Wulfee and ground it between his teeth. "Tastes like fire rock."

"Let me try," said Gen, thrusting his enormous hands down to snatch the rock. He was quick for his size. He cracked the knife against the flint harder than Wulfee could, but still no spark. *The dark magics have spread, Wulf. The fires still won't burn.* They hadn't been able to get a flame with bows for weeks, but now that the fire rock wouldn't even spark, her world felt unreal, like sorcery. A chill rolled down her spine. Pike shook his head. He had just finished slicing the deer's heart out and held it out to Wulfee for the first bite. The kihl'dor always got the first bite. She sank her teeth into the tough, fleshy meat and chewed until her jaw hurt.

"Come eat some of this, Gen," Wulfee said.

"I don't want it like that," he said. Giy'er only ate their meat cooked.

"We don't know when we'll be having meat again. Now come get some of this, you haven't eaten enough," she said.

Gen shook his head and whined. "I—don't—want—it!"

Wulfee tore off another piece of the heart, blood staining her mouth. *Who are you to tell him what to do? Who are you to act like a mom again?* Her jaw burned as she chewed the thick organ.

The deer carcass lay dead beside her. The rest of it was going to go to whatever came out of the arbor and claimed it first. Seemed a damn shame after all that. To take its life for such a small return. But that was the way of nature: it wasn't pretty; it wasn't fair. This wasn't the first time she'd taken a life and left the carcass to rot, and this wouldn't be the last either.

Maggie was still struggling to move. There were long, swollen gashes down her face. One of the Hawka had pinned her down before Wulfee got there to bash the mutt's head with her axe. But the Hawka wasn't acting right. Right after it had sunk its thick claws into Maggie's cheek, the Hawka froze, as if sensing something in Maggie that scared the life out of it. Maggie was full of magics that Wulfee knew very little of. But Wulfee could tell that when the fires died and the winds and rain stopped, something died inside Maggie, too. Wulfee reckoned maybe it was Maggie's soul that died, and the loss of it was tearing her down.

Pike hadn't been able to muster the strength to treat Maggie's wounds. After a moment and a silent prayer to himself, he left Wulfee and walked into the arbor alone to find leaves of ander. Wulfee hadn't seen an ander tree in many years. Its white trunk and spindly blue leaves were sacred to the Feldarra, but she couldn't bring herself to look at one. The vinegar smell of its trunk made her sick and reminded her of how the paste failed to save her mom's life from the rot. But the paste was the best medicine they had in the Fells.

Finally, Pike came back with the leaves. Wulfee looked on as he ground them with milk of ivy, ginseng root, and honeybalm and made the medicine paste their ancestors had made for a millennium. He wasn't much of a healer, the old warrior, but he was the best they had left. The medicine paste was pungent and stung Wulfee's nose almost as bad as she reckoned it stung Maggie's wound. After the ander set, it would burn her skin like fire. Wulfee remembered that feeling and shivered. That was just the medicine eating the infection, her mom used to say. *Pain is death seeping out of you.*

"These lands are cursed as well. The gods have abandoned us," said Gen, looking back and forth at the knife and the fire rock. Wulfee wanted to disagree but found it hard. If the gods were watching over these lands still, then why did a horde of that many Hawka come down? It was sorcery that she had no time to be caught up in.

"Aye, they may well have, Gen. Those are dark skies in the north," said Pike, and he looked Wulfee in the eyes. Wulfee reckoned he knew she saw that shadow, too.

"Who summoned this sorcery, Pike? Those mutts came down in an organized way. They've never followed the word of Humans," said Wulfee.

"It's probably the same reason the fire will not burn," Gen said. Wulfee had to admit she hadn't thought of that.

"I think you may be right, Gen," Pike said, looking longingly up at the sky. Looking for advice, maybe. Wulfee looked up there herself, just to curse the gods and Father Sky. First, they took her oldest son, Tarek, from her. Now, they kept her from killing the man who took him. She had been hunting Sweyne for twelve years, and just when she thought she came within sniffing distance of him, the Hawka came down. *Why can you not let me find him? Why can you not let me rest easy?*

The sun was setting behind the great snow-capped peaks of the Fell Mountains, staining the sky blood red in its retreat.

"I must treat Maggie with the medicine paste before those wounds get the rot. But then we must be getting going, Wulfee. We cannot stay as long as we'd like to. They'll be back. You know they will be back. We must walk through the night and pray to the gods we come across a settlement," Pike said. Wulfee looked back at Maggie, lying on the yellow grass, covered with a damp wool, like she was already dead. Wulfee knelt by her side and brushed her hair. *She and James thought of you as a mother. And you did a piss poor job of it. More children you couldn't save...*

Maggie had become Wulfee's only chance at killing Sweyne. Her only chance at vengeance. The woman could crush armies with what was locked inside of her. When Wulfee had sought answers about the young woman from the soothsayers of Wick, they only called her *mage* and turned their chins down. The soothsayers had said she was from the old Druid blood of the Mal and that she should join her ancestors in death. And that was all there was to say about *mage*. Wulfee told them to fuck themselves. She didn't know what to make of all that until she first saw Maggie's magics.

And when Maggie had first told her she was different, Wulfee didn't act surprised either. She encouraged Maggie to let her magics out. Wulfee wanted to use Maggie as a weapon.

The Feldarra believed that a soul stained with vengeance couldn't rest easy in the cloud halls after death. And the only way to cleanse the soul was with the lifeblood of those who stained it. When that man killed Wulfee's son all those years ago, burning hate sucked all of the love out of her. She could only think of killing Sweyne. Only.

"We keep moving when you're done," was all she said. She looked at her wilted crew. Maggie, battered and broken. A youthful Giy'er with all the innocence of a child. And an old, grey-haired veteran, her last true karl. They were a sorry lot, no doubt. But Wulfee wasn't about to give up her vengeance that easily, and she'd need her crew alive to get it. They were Feldarra, and they would fight to death for what they believed in. She limped over to Pike, scraped some of the blue paste of ander leaf off the flat rock it was ground on, and gently patted it on Maggie's wounds. Maggie screamed and moaned, kicked and resisted, but Pike held her down.

Beneath Pike's ice-blue eyes, Wulfee saw something she had never seen in the old warrior—fear. And Wulfee knew what it was from, and it wasn't the Hawka. He was afraid that even after all of this, Wulfee still wouldn't stop until she got what was hers.

He was right.

GREENHOODS

JAMES DREAMT HE WAS back in the Fell mountains walking through Wulfee's camp. He pulled Maggie's engagement knife out, held it up to the morning sun, and admired the beauty of it. It had an ink black kraken claw handle, a treasure he'd robbed off a dead man; the bluish-silver opalescent ice stone his dad had given him when he was a boy wedged in the hilt's tip. Berend, Wulfee's smith, etched the ancient Mal words that stood for love and protection deep into the iron blade. *Ai'mair Darra.* The same words his dad whispered to his mom every morning. Everything of value James had ever collected was in that knife. *She's worth it, though. I just hope she likes it.* It had been a week now since the fires had stopped burning, and there was no wind or rain in the skies since then, either. Maggie had been ill since the last lick of flame died out. It was bleak, and James had no idea what kind of storm was coming. If he were to give the knife to her, it would have to be now. His footsteps crunched on the thin layer of hard snow as he walked towards their tent.

When he got there, he found Maggie still lying down, hardly moving. Her eyes fluttered behind closed lids. James hoped she was dreaming about better times, back when the rains and wind still danced. He gently traced her cheeks—and then she murmured, "Don't stop."

"I didn't mean to wake you." James hid the knife behind his back. "How are you feeling now?"

"Oh, you know, I've been better," said Maggie. Her voice was hoarse. She coughed until her body shook, spitting into a wooden bucket infested with phlegm and flies. "I want to go out. To the glade."

"If you're well enough, I will take you. I can carry you there if you can't walk," James said. Maggie smiled and ran a shaky hand through his hair.

"I *can't* go outside. You know that. Not without the wind. It breaks my heart not to hear it. Something is wrong, James." she cried. "Something broke inside of me when the elements stopped. I can feel the world dying, like life is leaking out of it." She reached out for James's hand. He took it and kept the engagement knife tucked behind.

"It will get better. It always gets better."

"Not always," Maggie said. "I only ever wanted to fit in somewhere, you know? I've been driven out of every home I ever had as soon as whoever takes me in finds out what I am. All I ever wanted was a family."

"I'm your family."

"You're a killer, James. And there is something *in* me I can't handle. A pain I just need to let out."

"You can let it out."

"I can't. That's why I always end up alone. I could never keep myself from letting it out. But it's like my soul is dying now. I can feel the energy seeping out of me like blood."

James didn't know how to help her, and it drove him mad. *You can give her the knife when she's feeling better.*

"Hey, you know that lake you liked? The small one, up near Wick?"

Maggie looked at him, intrigued.

"Yeah. It was beautiful there. The trees were like a green sea all around."

"I'm thinking that we should build a little place there. Like you always talked about," James said.

"I've seen you wield an axe, but never a hammer. How are you going to build a house, James?"

"It can't be that hard. Between the two of us, we'll figure it out."

Maggie closed her eyes—her old self disappearing into the sickness. She murmured, "Maybe we could be happy there." And very much unlike when James first walked in, Maggie was smiling as she slept.

"**G**ET UP!" A VOICE boomed. Then the clanging of pots and pans and the whinnies of distressed horses echoed down James's ear drums. *What is Wulfee yelling about?*

"Hurry, man!" It was Eurick.

James's reality came back—the running, the dead, a human raven. He jumped up and heard the screaming Hawka immediately. *For fuck*—he touched the knife on his belt. He looked around for the rest of his stuff, then remembered he had nothing left.

"Let's go!" Eurick held Shalo's reins out. James grabbed them, immediately pulled himself onto the horse, and kicked Shalo into a gallop. Eurick was already two dozen strides gone when James realized Eurick was leaving most of his saddlebags behind. The glowing yellow eyes of a Hawka burst out of the brush that surrounded their camp. *For fuck*—the Hawka swarmed in like ants. Their rotten breath spewed from their maws like smoke in the cold predawn air. More came, and they kept coming.

"Ride, man!" Eurick screamed over his shoulder. James dug his heels into Shalo and snapped the reins. The stallion moved like no other James had ever ridden, and he had to grip the reins tighter to keep himself from falling. It was still dark, and James was just holding on for his life.

"I can't see!" James yelled into the night, but he was pretty sure the transporter didn't hear him. "I said, I can't see shi—"

"I heard ya, man. Just follow my voice, I know the way," the raven said, humming a low note for James to follow.

It was only a few miles of riding before night began to break, and the fringes of golden light from the rising sun faded in from the blackness. A water wheel was the first thing he could make out at the end of the narrow road. He could no longer hear the Hawka screaming behind them, which meant they had gained at least five minutes. Sharp pines and jagged firs of the arbor surrounded him. The dripping sap made the smells of pine sweeter, and, like usual, James got himself covered in it as they rode past.

"That's a hamlet?" asked James.

"Aye," said Eurick. "Used to be."

"It's just more than a mile from where we camped."

"Aye."

"Well, why didn't we keep riding and sleep here last night, under one of those roofs?"

"Better to sleep out of doors, man. Better for your soul," he said as they rode into the small hamlet. *My soul?* It was positioned in a small clearing with arbor on all sides. A stream trickled through the heart of the hamlet. The mountain peaks condescendingly looked down on them from the north, reminding James of how small he felt before he ran off and hid from his problems. A water wheel sat dormant in the stream, adorned with moss and lichen. The mill beside it was a pile of rotting wood, except for a living tree growing out of the centre. *There's no one here...*

Then, two wolves trotted out from behind the mill. They stood in front of them, staring at James with human eyes. The horses whined.

Fuck.

The next second, James fell flat on his back. Pain jittered throughout his arse and into his spine.

"Don't move." The blunt end of a spear appeared an inch from his nose.

"There's been a misunderstanding!" Eurick screamed. "We are peaceful nomads." He was still mounted with his hands raised. James was a little dizzy from the fall and couldn't tell what he said that got him knocked on his arse. The man on the other end of the spear laughed.

"Hah. Peaceful. There's no peace when a Culdaine is involved," he said, and James recognized something about that voice. That voice haunted him for years. "Ask Mal Hallow what they know of peace."

"Haro?" James said it like the words were stuck in his mouth. He knew Haro would rather see him dead—the only help would be an axe to the neck.

"Not who you wanted to see, eh?" Haro smirked as a dozen folks wearing hooded green cloaks emerged from the rotting mill. Their symbol, the E'daru, a black horse with human hair and no eyes, was stitched into their cloaks and over their hearts—Rangers. Armed and as shady as an arbor. The two wolves regained their wolfish eyes, then trotted off and laid down in front of the mill, panting. Probably exhausted from having their body used by another soul, James figured. He knew the stories of E'daru and what these Rangers were.

"Men, you must listen." Eurick raised his hands. "There are Hawka—"

"We *know* there are Hawka—" Haro snapped. Somewhere above, an eagle cried. James could tell they'd been through something like hell just by looking at them. Their faces were filthy and gaunt, darkened by blood stains from weeks of fighting. They were bruised and cut up, many limping or nursing injuries beneath poultices. And James figured the cuts weren't only physical. "Nothing's been right since King Alder and the Banshee marched north to dethrone that bastard Baleth up in Kallahorn. It's been only lies and death since then."

The Banshee?

James stood still for a moment. *The Banshee...* he'd heard stories of the Banshee and none of them were happy.

"You heard me right," Haro said.

"But why would Alder dethrone Baleth?" asked James. "Baleth surrendered to him during the war. Ayeland has already conquered the north. Why would he need to do it again, and why would he need the Banshee?"

Haro spit, shaking his head.

"Baleth declared himself a king. Sacrificed his Ayelish bride, the Lady Anne of Morland, to the Old Gods. Sent her up as smoke to the moon. Folks are saying he went mad. That some dark magics from the old world possessed him. He was babbling about dead souls. Singing old songs. They're saying he awoke something. Something from deep down below. When the fires went out and the world died, Baleth convinced most folk, by the way he was acting, it was him that done it with some dark magics. By then, Calen Alder was marching on him. Folk are praising that fuck Alder as the Hero of Ages for defeating Baleth up at Kallahorn. They think he fixed the world, even though the fires still won't burn and the winds won't blow. He didn't fix shit. Now I hear Ayeland is gathering an army to re-conquer Mal Hallow, to kill off the old blood of the Mal and extinguish any future rebellions. Mercenaries of the north are marching to join the Ayelish to get on the right side of the war. I can't trust a damn soul. Especially not a Culdaine." Haro turned to his band. "I saw what happened to the folk that trusted this one's dad."

"Don't say a word of my dad," James snarled.

Haro cocked his head sideways, smiling a cocksure grin.

"See what I mean." Haro twirled his spear in circles inches from James's face. "Culdaines are known to be mad."

James felt his body tensing. He took a deep breath.

"Calm, man," Eurick said.

James wanted to be furious with Haro, kill him even, but his thoughts had drifted to what *else* Haro had said. James knew Lord Baleth. He had met him dozens of times with his dad. Baleth was one of the wisest people James had known. The folk called him Baleth Longsongs because of the sheer amount of stories the man had stored up in his head. James's dad told him that Baleth knew all the lore of the land and all the old secrets, and James's dad had often asked Baleth questions few others knew the answers to. *What would drive a man like that mad?* Just then the screams of the Hawka arose from the distance.

"Fuck. Get up, Culdaine, the mutts are coming." Haro dropped the spear and grabbed his axe. "We're going to have to squash this for now or these Hawka will get us both. I'll deal with you after."

James got up and pulled Maggie's engagement knife, his only weapon. Haro and a few other Rangers laughed out loud at him.

"By the gods..." Haro kicked the spear he'd dropped towards James. "I don't want these Hawka to get you before I can." More snickers from the Rangers, then a hand-axe landed in the dirt in front of him.

"At least give yourself a chance, eh?" said the young Ranger. He had a deep scar on his chin, and James wondered about the boy for a moment.

Do you know real pain, boy? Or only minor flesh wounds? Have you ever loved?

James grabbed the axe, ignoring the young Ranger.

On the rooftops and in the trees around the village, green hooded folk held bows. Everyone at his side held spears or axes. James gripped the axe tightly. It wasn't much of a weapon, but hoping for more wouldn't keep him alive when the Hawka came. The earth cracked violently beneath the mutts's clawed feet as they got closer. Haro whistled, and the Rangers spread out around the village, disappearing amongst the brush and decaying buildings. A blue jay landed on Haro's shoulder as he faded into the foliage.

James and Eurick hid against the crumbled old mill wall. Eurick put his fist under his chin and nodded—the old northern sign for luck—and James did the same. Eurick was more than likely safer for James to be around than the Rangers. James had never trusted the greenhoods before. The Mal of old didn't trust them—the Rangers shared their skin with animals, like the E'daru shared skin with Humans—but he had no choice now.

The ground rumbled with the weight of the charging mutts.

James glanced around for any dead that may have come to save him, but he didn't see any. *I may join them momentarily.* He lingered in that second before he saw the enemy charging. When death was only a distant sound, it was easier to deny. One of the Hawka led the charge down the road with thirty more behind. He could see their yellow eyes glowing in the dull morning light, moving as fast as falling stars towards him. Green saliva dangled from jagged teeth and blood-stained maws. Their mangy black fur soaked with greasy sweat. All of them screamed in a rabid chorus that burned James's eardrums. He gripped and re-gripped the axe.

"Loose!" Haro screamed. A line of Hawka went down. "Loose!" Snap, and Hawka fell. But they were too close now for more arrows. Haro whistled, and the Rangers poured out, surrounding the Hawka from all angles. A mangy black bear wearing human eyes came charging out of the brush. It sunk its jaws into a mutt, and the Hawka squealed a horrible sound—sharp and acidic, like iron scraping iron. Wolves howled, and a small pack ran past the black bear and tore into Hawka's flesh with a bloody maw.

James raised his axe with a wicked backswing and sunk the blade deep into the snout of the first Hawka that came his way. He pulled the blade free and braced himself for another one. At the last moment, he swung his axe in an upward arch and spilled the Hawka's innards. The weight of the impact threw him back. He stumbled and almost lost his axe, and in the momentum, the Hawka's corpse fell on top of him, covering James in sloppy gore. James pushed it off, disgusted at the Hawka's sour breath and greasy fur. He found his axe just in time to split the face of another mutt coming at him with its mouth opened, blood dripping from its jagged teeth.

His blade was stuck in the Hawka's face, but he just managed to unstick it when something smashed into the back of his head. James swallowed mud before he rolled over to wedge his left arm in the Hawka's mouth to stop it from tearing his face. Its teeth sank into his skin with a sharp burn, grinding on his bone. James busted the side of its head open with his axe. He got up, bleeding. Another Hawka lunged at him. James swung and missed, falling face-first in the mud again. He was dizzy. *Goodbye Maggie,* he thought. He waited for death's hand to hold him and take him to Hell, but nothing came. He looked up and saw the Hawka impaled by a shortsword with Eurick on the other end of it.

"AH!" Eurick screamed as he yanked his sword out of one mutt and stabbed another.

James rolled out of the way as a Ranger fell from the trees. The left side of her face had a gaping hole torn through it, and her nose was dangling off her face by a thin piece of bloody cartilage. The Hawka tore at the greenhood's chest, its mouth dripping intestines. James flung himself at it, breaking its skull open. Two more came. James swung his axe at one of them, but an arrow from above hit the mutt's eye, and it fell dead before James could touch it. James swung at the other one instead, the axe busting through the rib cage and into its heart. James fell. His head pounded like a drum. There was blood everywhere—dripping down his forehead and into his eyes, along his chest, legs... *whose blood is this?* He thought about his mom and dad, and James's vision blurred. Hawka claws suddenly pinned him to the ground. He waited for the crunch of razors in his skull, but instead, the Hawka fell to his side, dead.

"Get up, man!" Eurick reached for James. "Fight's up here. Stay on your feet!" he said, decapitating another mutt. James was really starting to think this guy was okay. Hawka were rustling in the arbor, climbing up to the treetops and roofs. The Rangers hacked, shot, and stabbed the mutts. They fought with an animalistic brutality that reminded James of a wolf hunting its prey. And they were more organized in combat than James could have ever thought possible. Behind him, the bear that had human eyes roared loudly in pain, its echo rumbling in James's chest. James watched as the Hawka tore the bear apart. The wolves had been killed, too. James saw pieces of them strewn across the bloody dirt.

"Loose!" Haro shouted somewhere behind him. But no arrows came. "I said loos— ah fuck!" There was screaming from the trees above as the Hawka made it to the high spots. Rangers splattered on the ground like the rain had once—screaming behind, beside, and below?

"Help," a broken voice croaked. James was damn near standing on him—the Hawka had trampled him into the bloody mud. James looked around. This was a job for Haro, to comfort his folk whilst they die, not him. But Haro was nowhere to be seen. It was the boy with the scar on his chin—*was,* because his limbs were now twisted like a scattered pile of twigs, his whole body a puckered scar etched in teeth marks. *Have you ever loved?* James thought before he broke the boy's head with his axe. *Rest easy.*

James's head was thumping. His arm was throbbing, bleeding, but he couldn't feel pain anymore. He couldn't feel *anything.* Was he dead now? He forgot what it felt like to be alive.

The monster in him flared up like dry tinder. Blood-soaked and sick with battle fever, he killed all that he saw. Hawka. Ranger. Hawka. They died the same beneath his axe blade. A Ranger cowered in fear, and James tore him open with sharp steel anyway. Blood and gore dripped from his hands as he tore through the flesh of another who stood too close to him. Creature or person, he couldn't tell any longer. It was flesh; it moved, and he sunk his blade into it and made it stop moving. He cried out like an animal.

"ARRRH!" Spittle dangled off his thick black beard.

You're a monster.

He knew, but couldn't stop. He hated this, but the monster only fed off that hate and kept going. It took over. He killed and let himself become numb to his demon. And in a flash, it was over. There was nothing around him but the dead. A voice came from above him, in a tree.

"They're gone, man. You need to be calm. Your arm is bleeding badly," Eurick said. The screaming had stopped, and in the quiet, the thumping in James's head was deafening. The raven came down from the tree, looked around at all the bloody corpses, then at James, and pulled his dark-winged cloak tighter.

James fell on his arse. The stem of a tiny wisp of etta was just pushing through the early spring soil. *Wulfee loved these wisps...* his arm throbbed, dripping blood. *I'm dying. Maggie, I'm so sorry...*

And then the dead souls gathered in from the morning fog and sat with him. They came in groups, and they sang. They were there to save his life.

THE WIDOW OF THE WHITE

"IS IT DEAD?" GEN poked at the bird's body with a long stick. The mother robin was on its side, as dead as dead gets.

"Just sleeping, Gen," Wulfee lied. "Come on, let's keep moving."

Gen threw the stick away and hurried along.

A lie is worth it if it gives a little hope, Wulfee reckoned. She had learned not to hope for things herself, though—she had already wasted too much time searching for the past in the now, finding notes of her sons' laughter through Gen, the way Maggie and James asked for her guidance when they needed help. Wulfee's mother taught her to take things as they came. That was the only way to get through the bitter hurt of living, one thing at a time. Wulfee was trying.

The Hawka had attacked three days ago by the time they reached the Fever Stones, and they hadn't heard the mutts since. The old Druid standing stones were like big gemstones in the moonlight. Ancient Mal had carved runes an inch deep into the stone, and they were bound with magics

Wulfee knew nothing of. A nytewood grew out of the centre, its massive canopy draping a shadow over the stones and the village and reaching out to kiss the dark clouds above. They found the village of Fever abandoned, nothing except empty barrels of barley scraped clean and a few scattered grains. A dead man lay face down in the dirt road, his body crushed and trampled over. A victim of the bloody commotion of folk abandoning the place they lived. A black and white molly cat was nibbling on its arm. Gen couldn't help himself and bent down to play with her. When the cat hissed at him, Gen looked at Wulfee with wide eyes.

"Leave the cat alone, Gen, not all of them are friendly," said Wulfee. Gen pouted.

"Let's keep moving south," Pike said, like they already hadn't been walking south for days. "There is nothing left here."

"No Hawka either. We would see signs of them," Wulfee said, remembering one of the mutts eating Colrig's insides. "But why else would these people leave?"

Pike just shook his head. He had no answers for her. So they kept walking south.

It was a long way, and walking had become almost like torture, her legs crying to rest, her spine curling in on itself—*I can't stand anymore*—but she kept going because she always kept going. She told her clan that there was no use in complaining. Complaining didn't make things right. It was good advice. Easy to give, harder to follow.

"What a fucking slog," complained Wulfee. Gen laughed.

"It's not that bad," he said. "I like walking."

"It is bad, Gen. Don't you see? People are dying. The world is dying." *And my fucking back hurts.*

"It's only just sick. It'll get better," said Gen, showing off his jagged teeth with a wide grin. Wulfee couldn't help but smile back. The big guy gave her hope, if only for a moment.

They had made it to the White River Valley. Northerners called it the Roar. It covered any bit of land where you could hear the river screaming.

Odhran Ironfist and his clan used to rule this part of the Hallow before Wulfee sent them up into the mountains during their war eleven years ago. It wasn't proper for the Feldarra to take a name and settle lands, especially lands outside of the Fells. Odhran broke the oaths by trying to settle along the White. Wulfee had no choice but to fight him.

Now, the Roar was just barren, rocky land from Lorne, to the northern Fell Mountains. Free for peasants to settle. Still, none did. *Kihl'dor Wulfee, always the peasant pleaser.* She kicked the grey dirt that couldn't even grow weeds now, not without rain. *Give them a plot of shite and think you done good.* Sending Odhran up to those mountains caused a whole wave of wars between him and the mountain clans, which left the Fells broken.

Wulfee found Pike in all of that mess. He had run from Odhran and was looking for a clean way out. A fresh start. Wulfee almost turned him away, just to spite Ironfist, but she put her pride aside and allowed Pike in. It was one of the few good choices she'd made. Pike and his shield became irreplaceable to her.

"I need a drink," said Gen. He held out his wooden goblet to Wulfee for help. She always seemed to forget the lad was terrified of running water. Wulfee nodded. The lad was severely terrified of the stuff, and it was getting worse as he got older. The 'er had a superstition that running water would eat their folk if they set foot in it. They only drink from stagnant pools, or in Gen's case, freshwater from a wooden goblet.

"Guess we're stopping," Wulfee said to Pike when she came back. He nodded. Pike looked like death. Nearly a corpse already. Not just because he looked tired, with dark bags under his eyes and pale skin, but because he smelled sour, like he and his clothes had started to decay. They hadn't had a good rest in three days, and it was starting to tear Wulfee's crew down. Pike staggered off by himself and sat on a rock. There was a small puddle of runoff beneath him. He stared into the puddle and talked to his underself. Wulfee figured it was about time she'd done the same. It had been too long. Her underself didn't much like being ignored.

After she had given Gen his water, Wulfee found her own rock near a shallow pool of runoff. The sound of white water roared. The mist gently shrouded her in dampness. It was strangely warm from the stale sunlight, like a hug from the Mother. In the shallow pool, Wulfee saw *her* reflection. A haggard bitch looked back at her from under with swollen eyes of dark blue. Her faded, curly red hair was a tangled mess. The small scar on her cheek reminded Wulfee of the bigger one on her son, Braden. He had always wanted to cover that scar up by wearing a mask or keeping his face turned away when he spoke to people. But he showed it to Wulfee without worry. He trusted her to love him no matter what. That memory was the only bit of joy Wulfee got out of seeing her underself.

"I want to know where Sweyne is," Wulfee said.

No response.

"Is Braden still alive?"

No response.

"I didn't mean to get anyone killed. Never."

Nothing. Her underself just stared back at her. The bitch didn't always talk, but she listened. And sometimes that was more important.

"I have to kill Sweyne," Wulfee said. "I'll never rest easy if I don't. Not with this hate inside. The gods won't allow me into the sky halls. My soul will fall to the Otherworld and become another. Then how will I ever see my sons again? I need to see him dead for what he did to me."

"Fate killed one son," gurgled the underself. "The other, *you* left."

Pain tingled in Wulfee's stomach, then she slammed her fist into the puddle. The underself rippled into a hundred waves. *Bitch.* Pike had hiked over, looking as disturbed as her.

"My old village of Lorne isn't far." Pike looked down in the dirt trying to find the words. "I... I remember these trees, and that rock. I used to walk with Alissa and Tess here."

"What did your underself say?" she asked. Pike had a bitter dread carved into his face. His lip was quivering and his eyes watered. Wulfee reckoned he had some cold memories waking up behind those eyes.

"Nothing nice, Wulf."

They continued to walk up the misty riverbank.

A PALE WOODEN SHACK was visible through the mist. Black ravens and blood vultures swarmed above the remnants of a village.

"By the gods…" said Pike. The clan kept walking. Dragging, more like. Wulfee had learned that no one was gonna feel sorry for her but herself, but sometimes she just needed to feel like a sad, worthless, old hag.

The village was quiet as they approached. The roadways and alleys were empty, though there were dried fish on a rack, tools lying in the dirt, and a half-starved donkey hitched up to a sad stable. Wulfee pulled the fish down for everyone to gorge.

"What are you doing, Gen?" Wulfee licked her lips. "That trout is for you."

Gen had unhooked the donkey from its stables and was now trying to feed him some of the fish. "But he's hungry."

"Donkeys don't eat fish, Gen. You'll make him sick." Wulfee took a bite of the trout and tried not to moan; it tasted so good. "Now eat."

Gen patted the donkey on his head and ate some trout.

"The people here left in a hurry," Wulfee said.

"Maybe the folk from Fever came down and warned them of something," Pike said.

They walked towards the black birds circling over the village square. Then she saw the heads impaled on spikes, missing eyeballs, missing tongues, and scalps. The severed faces of men, women, and children. When they turned into the square, they saw a hundred more, staked beneath the nytewood like a symbol of wealth. The headless bodies were piled off to the side. Being picked apart by carrion birds, torn at by wild dogs—eaten by both in the end. But the bodies weren't rotting. *There should be a stench…*

the smell of the dead would usually bite into Wulfee like the cold. *This was no Hawka attack.* Pike shook his head. Then she saw what she was looking for: wolf teeth strewn all over the place. Hundreds of them.

"This is Sweyne's mark," said Wulfee, picking a wolf's tooth up. "It was him that came through here."

"It can't be," said Pike. He kicked the Ayelish flag and the red eagle on white laid crumpled in the dirt. "They flew the Ayelish flag."

"He'd do anything for enough coin. For enough glory," said Wulfee. "It's him. He's sold his axe to the Ayelish."

Pike shrugged. She could tell he didn't want to, but the old warrior agreed with her. *Why?* The question made her sick. *The bastard wants revenge on this country for leaving him behind. Wants revenge on you...*

A soft grinding caught her ear. Wulfee followed the sound to one of the thatch-roofed shacks. She went in, the door creaking loudly, with Pike behind her. A wan old crone sat on a stump, working grain with a mortar and pestle. Pock marks scarred her face. Wulfee saw a flash of recognition in Pike's eyes as he noticed the woman. When the recognition turned to fear, Wulfee's guard flared up.

"What happened here? How did you survive?" Wulfee said. The crone answered by sticking out her chin to let Wulfee have a good look at her swollen red boils. The woman was probably used to people squirming. Wulfee had seen worse.

"Survive? Hah!" she cackled. "They came with their blood and steel, and I hid away in my magics where only my mind can find me. It is far from surviving."

Wulfee didn't know what to say.

"Where are people still living?" said Pike. "We need medicine. We need food."

"Some are making a last stand at Tusk. They will die there, though," she giggled. Pike rolled his eyes. The crone moved quickly towards him.

"You don't think I've seen it? The wise ones went south with the brigand to Ayeland. The Wolf is offering food and shelter. They say he has fire."

"No one has fire," said Wulfee.

"They say he does. And food. Lots of it."

"He's lying."

"It doesn't matter. They believe him. Who else offers such hope in these times?" said the crone. "Go die at Tusk if you don't believe."

"He's false."

"You're false, too. You don't think I've had dreams of you? I know what you've done, even if they don't," the crone snarled. "I know what you've done. You've lied. You've left folks you loved to die. You've abandoned—"

"You don't know *shit*!" Wulfee grabbed the knife at her waist, ready to shut her up permanently—but arms were pulling her back.

"Calm, Wulfee," Pike murmured.

The crone snorted.

"*You.* I know that face now that I look upon you clearly. You're the wife-killer. *You* would come back? After what you've done here?"

"I only came—" Pike started.

"For shelter? Food and medicine?" the crone snarled at Wulfee. "How did you come across that Giy'er out there? The proper story, not the made up one you tell him. What happened to the lad's parents?"

"Fuck y—"

Pike held Wulfee back. A horrible laugh came out of the old woman.

"You don't think I've seen, but I have," the crone sang. "None of them believed me he would come. The Wolf, the Wolf. And now they're all dead and without a head. And the soil's stained red. They bled, they bled!" She put the pestle to her mouth and ate what was inside. When her eyes opened again, they went bloodshot. Sweat beaded on the crone's forehead. The air in the musty shack became warm. "The Wolf, the Wolf, the wretched Wolf." The crone dropped the bowl, and Wulfee saw a diluted solution of ander. She could only imagine how strong it was from the fumes that burned her nostrils. The witch flashed a toothless smile, only blue gums, and Wulfee shivered. The legends her elders had told said that ander witches could appear as an old crone or sage, but they were as dangerous as a wolf.

Driven mad from years upon years of blurred visions and memories. They didn't know what was real and what was just a dream of ander.

"The world will die. There is no one to save it this time. There is no Hendurinn to be our hero. You don't think I've seen it? The Ailaryan Order is back. They have killed the world, and no one sees it," the crone squealed. Then her face flushed with darkness. "Leave here. Death follows you too closely." The crone flashed pointed yellow nails, as if to say she could kill them both if she felt like it. Pike backed out of the shack, and Wulfee followed without a second thought. The crone hummed a familiar tune. Wulfee thought it sounded like the one they sang to children, asking the rain to go away. *And now the rain never came back.*

"What the fuck was that?" she asked Pike.

"The Widow of the White. An ander witch. She was born out of the river long ago. Some say a hundred years or more. The elders said she drove herself mad with dreams of ander. That's what happens if you keep taking it. Your mind gets lost," he said. "She sees things. *Knows* things…"

"She remembered you."

"She remembered the man I *used* to be," Pike said stiffly. Wulfee understood, so she asked no more.

Gen was sitting on a rock by Maggie, looking out at the rushing water like he was trying to understand it. The pulse of the White River was beating beneath Wulfee's feet as she walked to join them. Pike, instead, went into one of the shacks without another word.

Maggie was lying on her back on the grass; she seemed to be swallowed by the grass as it nestled her. She often looked up at the sky, especially at night. There was always a peculiarity to her that Wulfee couldn't figure out. Like Maggie always knew more than she was telling. She had become like a daughter to Wulfee, just as James had become like a son. It made her feel sick to see Maggie in such bad shape. Wulfee had found Maggie a week before she found James and in the same way. Both were abandoned, bleeding, and near death in the arbor. She saw in them a chance to atone for her own sins, but there was nothing she could do to make up for her mistakes.

Gen seemed completely fine, even after what they'd been through. The Hawka attack had really scared the lad, but he killed more of them than any of the others. Giy'er had knuckles that were as hard as steel and thick leathery skin that was difficult to pierce. It allowed wild Giy'er to break rocks for shelters and to fell trees for fire. Wild Giy'er hunted bears and mammoths and great moose and bull elk. So, Gen flattened the mutts like flies and barely even felt it. Wulfee had grown to love him as a son, too, since she'd taken him fifteen years ago.

The proper story, not the made up one you tell him. Wulfee didn't think that Gen would like the *proper story* of what happened to his parents. He would rather hear the myth of Feldarra. She figured some things were better left unsaid. He couldn't understand the danger of wild Giy'er. Wulfee had no choice but to kill Gen's parents and their clan or risk being killed by them herself. Wild Giy'er could grow as tall as trees, and they ran faster than the fastest horse. *You had no choice but to kill them...* but Wulfee couldn't bring herself to kill the young one. Not him. *You stunted him by taking him. He'll never belong in the wild now.* She knew that. And that's why she kept the lie.

"Let's do something different, Wulfee," said Gen. "I don't feel like walking anymore. Can't we just stay here?"

"We can't stay here, Gen, it's not safe," Wulfee said. "We're not playing games out here. We don't just get to do something different when we feel like it. I need you to act like a karl and be brave, and keep going even though you don't want to." The Giy'er straightened and held his chin up high.

Pike then walked out of the shack, tucking a small object wrapped in a cloth into his chest pocket. When he saw Wulfee staring, Pike looked at her with cold eyes and said, "We should go to Tusk. It may be our last hope for salvation."

The Widow's words were sitting heavily on him. Wulfee could still hear her whistling somewhere amongst the abandoned shacks on their way out.

Wulfee's feet were mush and bone, her tongue a slab of wood. But she didn't survive this long by giving up.

"How far?" she asked.

"A good ways," he said, shaking his head as they plodded along the White River.

"Can you tell me the story, Wulfee?" Gen could hardly hold in his excitement. Wulfee was beyond tired, but when she told the story of Feldarra to Gen, she felt like everything was the way it used to be, with Braden and Tarek bundled in their blankets, waiting for Wulfee to tell of Warlocks and ghosts and the great warriors who fought them. Telling the story made everything okay.

"Alright, Gen, but come a little closer so I don't have to yell."

FUEL FOR KILLING

J AMES GOT ON ALL fours and dipped his face inside one of the soul's bodies and felt a bite of cold as he entered. He inhaled the dead. The soul resisted at first, but James's lungs were iron from long winters of smoking chuff with the clan. Death filled him and brought coldness that he'd told himself he would never put himself through again as long as he lived. But if he didn't suck the soul down, he wouldn't be alive much longer.

James swallowed once and inhaled again, deeper this time, like a big old bowl of chuff. The spirit filled him now, accepting its fate. James took two more pulls, and the spirit was nearly gone. *The whole thing.* The Hermit's words were still strong in his memory, even from so long ago. *Take the whole thing.* So James summoned his lungs to inhale. Accepted the cold like a thirsty man accepted water. One more pull, the last one, and he blew the ghost on his wound. It soaked his arm like water, and pink skin stretched over his gaping red wounds. He heaved bile; his world spun in a frenzy. James felt his insides fill with a cold nothing, but his soul warmed. He struggled for air, breathing heavily as if through frozen lungs. Then took another breath. It came easier. He breathed out again. He heard a familiar voice. *Maggie?*

"The fuck, man?" Not Maggie. It was Eurick. He looked down at James like he'd just seen him eat a ghost or something. "Your arm..."

James held it up. The pain was gone, the cold fading in his lungs.

"Yeah." James admired it. Eurick stood there with his mouth open.

"Well, can you do it on me?" he said.

"No." James remembered screaming at the dead to save his parents. But they didn't. They wouldn't...

"Well, that's too bad."

"Yeah." James wished more than anything that he could use the dead for good. Any good at all. But they only served to keep a killer like him alive.

"We better go before they come back. I'll get the horses."

"We should check the bodies first," James said.

"What?"

"The bodies, let's loot them for rations," James said. It was some of the best advice he ever got. Dead bodies had all sorts of good stuff that some brave bastard thought would bring them luck before it didn't anymore.

"Yeah, okay. Good idea. A raven needs supplies, man."

The Rangers had gold rings from Edura, silver torcs from Daggland, pearls from the Ryne Isle. Emeralds from Esher, and sapphires from the Glenn. They had rubies and rupees and lapis lazuli from Lavesh. Every precious stone and currency James had ever heard of. And he took none of it. He had no use for it. He wasn't a thief like these greenhoods. All he wanted was food.

"All of 'em dead. Seems unfortunate," said Eurick, using his knife to cut loose a wineskin from around one of the dead Ranger's necks. "What happened down here?"

"A fight happened," said James. "And they're not all dead. Haro's not here."

"You know him?" said Eurick.

"Aye," said James. "Him and his band came across me when I needed help once. I was freezing, jaw chattering like a mad squirrel. Calen Alder left me for dead after he chased me and my family down. I begged Haro for help and he spat on me. He said that he saw me leading a battle near Oster, years before. His family was killed in the crossfire. He blamed *me* for it. Said *I* killed them. Oster was my home! *My dad* was a king of those lands. Why would I choose to be in a battle there? We were being attacked. I was leading a damned resistance movement. How can any person be responsible for the folks killed in war? I was seventeen—I never even wanted to fight! I never wanted to hurt anyone."

James tried to shake out the anger brewing inside him. "And so Haro left me there. He said I was as good as dead already and the world was better for it. I carried on and lived through that night just to prove that bastard wrong. And now he's gone and left his own men, the same way he left me."

"If he left his men to die, he'll get what he deserves," Eurick said, taking a drink of whatever was in the wineskin he'd looted. Judging by his grimace, James figured it wasn't anything nice. "Let's hope the horses survived this, eh?"

When they approached the horses, they saw only Shalo. Something had spooked him, and he was squealing and trying to buck free of his restraints. Eurick's horse was missing.

"Bastard Haro must've ridden off on the other," said Eurick. James figured as much too. He walked up to Shalo calmly, made soft nickering sounds, and the brown stallion calmed. James grabbed the reins. He whispered in Shalo's ear, "I've got you, boy. It's okay."

Hawka stink was still in the air.

"Well, who's sitting on the back?" Eurick asked. James mounted. "Okay, okay." Eurick got on behind him and held on tight.

They rode up an old mining road that was carved into the thick arbor by the Lovasi many long centuries ago. James imagined the renowned Lovasi merchants, covered in amethysts and mother-of-pearl, wheeling down the same road he rode down now. He wondered what the Lovasi *really* thought of the nytewoods that sprung out of the forest canopy like gopher's heads. Gran always said that the Lovasi had the power to cut the nytewoods down, but they kept them in fear of what they would unleash from below by felling them.

To the Mal folk, the towering black trees were sacred. The nytewoods produced no seeds now, so the ones that were here would be the only ones ever to grow. The Mal believed the first trees used up all of their seeds to create a race of Humans. They believed their ancestors were born from the nytewoods's only seeding. The withering shell formed their bodies. Water seeped in and filled their veins, and the heat of the sun thickened the water into blood. When the wind provided air to bring the lungs to life, the first Mal rose and prayed to their father tree and mother earth and worshiped the elements that gave them life. The gods gave some of them gifts of magics, and the Mal called those folk Druids. The Mal lived and prayed and died under the nytewoods. It was the souls of the dead that seeded the majestic trees. And the souls of the dead that water them.

"You've got to veer off the road to the northwest up here, man, just past that big rock there."

"How can you find the way without your maps?"

"I just follow the signs. You know, the smells, the moss. The birds help too," said Eurick.

The moss?

"You know," Eurick said, "When that Ranger said *Banshee*, it reminded me of an old story I'd heard at the Guild. The Banshee's worked for the Ailaryan Order, man."

"Ailaryan Order?" James asked.

"They were a group of Warlocks from Yehven that survived the Starfall, something like a hundred-hundred years ago. They did all sorts of nasty work with their dark magics to rule. It was the Ailaryan Order that created the Raven's Guild all those years ago, man. But most of the Ailaryan Order died out when Lindis burned. At least that's what's written. No one truly knows if Lindis even existed. It's not on any map, so I say it didn't exist.

Pretty simple, if you ask me. If the ravens ain't found it, it ain't there. Anyway, the Banshees were hunters. They hunted folk down that needed killing, and they never failed. They screamed out something wretched when they'd found their prey."

Is that what you heard screaming from Wulfee's camp when the Hawka came down?

There was a moaning ahead that interrupted James's brooding. Eurick tapped his ear with one finger and pointed towards the noise. "Shh." James got off Shalo slowly and crept towards the sound until the noise became clearer—a person. The first thing James saw was the green hood. *Haro.* James walked towards him without caution now. He felt his rage boiling.

"Culdaine? That you? I need some help here. I messed my leg up," said Haro. James saw his leg and thought it was a lot more than just messed up. A bloody bone stuck out below his knee, and his leg was crooked to one side.

"Fall off a horse?" James knelt down and clenched the tip of the broken bone with his fingertips. Haro screamed.

"I had to get outta there, Culdaine. I would not stick around and die. They took down Kera and her bear. My best folk were lying dead and the Hawka just kept coming." Haro squinted. "I saw *you*... you went mad..."

James twisted Haro's bone a little. Haro blurted something guttural. *Be gentle, James. There's no need for violence. Vengeance is a silly thing with no end.* Maggie's words. *Fuck.* He knew she was right. She was always right, but Eurick nodded in approval and that was all James needed.

James twisted the bone until he heard it start to fracture, and Haro screamed, a sound that shouldn't have sounded this good to James—but James could only remember Haro leaving him to die. Vengeance was exactly how he imagined it would be, its sweet bitterness fueling the monster inside of him.

"I've imagined killing you for ten years. I imagined killing you out there in the cold arbor as I slowly froze to death. That's what got me through the night." James twisted the bone further.

"Please! Sto—" Haro cried out in agony, and James twisted.

"I lived in spite of you. I wondered if I'd ever see you again, if I'd ever have the chance to stand over you as *you* died." James clenched his axe. But now that he stood over Haro, all he could hear was Maggie. *Vengeance is a silly thing with no end.* Maggie told him that his nightmares might stop if he gave all that up. If he let go of the hate he held inside of him, maybe it would stop burning him up. He had given up on revenge because of her. Gave up on his old life and stayed in the mountains with her; James had forgotten about the king of Ayeland, Calen Alder. He forgot about his home and the faces that went with it. *You forgot about your parents, and what they died for...* James wanted to be the kind of man that a woman like Maggie could love forever—and that meant letting go of some of his fuel for killing. *She's still alive. I know she's still alive. I can feel her still.* He wanted to be that man so badly, but maybe he just wasn't yet.

James twisted Haro's bloody leg bone one last time, his knuckles dripping with blood.

"Ahhh! Fuck, Culdaine!" Haro screamed. "*You cunt!*"

"Let's play a game," said James. "Let's see if you can survive out here, alone. Let's see what kind of person you are."

Haro looked up at James with terror and disbelief in his eyes, like he was about to beg him not to leave, but instead he touched the symbol of E'daru on his green cloak, closed his eyes, and whispered a prayer to the Maw God. A blue jay fluttered down and landed beside Haro. James walked away and didn't think to look back for a second.

A Better Meaning

A WOLF HOWLED AS the last moments of evening faded into the cool darkness of twilight. The night was dimly lit by the full moon. Wulfee's stomach twisted into a hard knot. Not from hunger this time but from her damned nerves. They were in Tusk country now. The Mammoth lands. She had committed her biggest shame there and would have to face it now. They would pass right through the village of Barley, where she left her son Braden before the war with Sweyne. She abandoned him there like a dog and turned her back as he begged so he wouldn't see her crying. She had been down to two wrong choices. To leave Braden somewhere safe or risk him being killed by her side as she fought.

After Tarek died, she couldn't risk losing Braden as well. It was a hard fuckshit of a choice, and she felt like a son of a cunt for making the decision she did. The longer she was gone, the more she felt like she couldn't go back to him. That he wouldn't understand until he was older... For all she knew, Braden needed to kill her so *he* could rest easy in the cloud halls. After what she'd done, she deserved it. But she had always dreamed of seeing him again one day. She needed him to know that she only left him because she wanted to keep him safe. It was a pleasant country, Mal Hallow, safer than their home in the mountains of the Fells. He had a better chance at something good here than by her side. She hoped Braden would know that. But Wulfee knew that if they came across Braden here, he may be hostile. Pike was just as silent as Wulfee was as the thatch roofs became visible upon the small hillock.

A wolf howled again just as she felt settled. It was a big grey bitch. Wulfee had spotted her days ago, trailing behind them. Another wolf picked up the call, then the rest joined. They should have made Wulfee nervous, but they didn't. She was ready to face her son after all these years.

"By the gods, look at this," said Pike. Wulfee could hardly believe what she was looking at because she had never seen it before. It was the massive trunk of a felled nytewood stretched out for a thousand feet across the river valley. The jagged limbs swept out in a mess of splintered wood and leaf. The stump leaked a clotted, rust red sap that smelled like rotten meat. Seeing it made Wulfee's heart beat faster. Her stomach turned. This was a nytewood, felled and dying.

They kept moving along, past the sacred well of Old Lorne. Someone had filled it in with stones and gravel. They littered the loose dirt on top with yellowed skulls.

The village was ahead. Wulfee felt nervous, her stomach burning at the thought of seeing Braden. She would know him by his scar, no matter how much he'd changed. Barley was smaller than she remembered. It consisted of several once modest cabins on top of a small hillock and a desolate farm field in the flat valley below. A small stream ran through the valley, trickling off the White and pooling in a large bog in the low part of the valley. A half-dozen children ran up and down the worn dirt road that winded through the centre of the village. Sullen, pale-faced men and women stood in front of old rundown cabins, watching them. They were all staring at the Giy'er carrying the injured woman, no doubt. But Wulfee saw no scars on any of their faces. Braden wasn't there.

"We don't mean harm. We seek safe rest for the evening," Wulfee said. "Maybe food if you can spare. We've come down from the mountains of the Fells. The Hawka—"

"We don't need to talk about the Hawka or what they've done to you. Everyone has got a story these days. It's where you're headed that concerns us," said a stern-faced woman. She wore a wool dress stained with mud, and her long brown hair was in a messy bun. Wulfee could see a loving nature through her confidence. The woman stood for more than just herself. Throughout the village, gaunt men held their wives close. A few other folks stood together in bleak clusters. There were twenty or more people there, but the woman stood alone. Wulfee felt some relief that she didn't see her son, and somehow, that shamed her. The kids ran around playing goose and hop-rocks and hardly noticed the new arrivals. Gen draped Maggie over his big forearms like a baby. She coughed violently.

"We're headed for Tusk," Wulfee said. A bald man with a thick golden beard stepped forward, slapping the blunt end of his wooden axe in his open palm.

"Everyone is headed for Tusk," he scoffed. "Everyone wants to cross the river and join this Wolf that just ran his army of mercenaries through this country. They're calling themselves the Clan of the Severed Head." Voices stirred amongst the village folk. Circumstances had pushed these people to their limits. Wulfee could tell this lot would do something desperate if they felt threatened.

"We ain't joining the brigand, I promise you that. I'm more interested in killing the bastard," said Wulfee.

"That's all we've got left," Pike said. The man dropped his axe into a stump and gave the old northern sign for luck.

"We've got tack and cabbage preserve to feed you, but naught else," said the stern-faced woman.

"Tack and cabbage are more than fine," Wulfee said. "We are grateful—"

"We're also in need of ander," said Pike. "Lochweed, rosemilk, anything to treat our friend here. White willow bark or chuff for pain. One of the Hawka mauled her, but she lives. I'm afraid she has been suffering for so long she has not healed."

The woman shook her head.

"We've nothing of the sort left."

Wulfee could see the hurt in her eyes. They'd lost much here recently. Pike sighed, maybe fearing the worse for Maggie.

A man with a square chin under a thick beard stepped forward.

"I have treated scratches like that," he said. Wulfee saw jagged scars on his forearm. "Best with pollen from berg-bees. It is much like honey. Paste of ander will take longer. And of course... you'll avoid the dreams... and the fever."

"Do you have any?" Pike asked, hopefully.

"No, but I can take you to a nest come morning, before you depart. If you want to be sure she lives, you'll have to see the green man, though."

Pike took a deep breath. Wulfee knew Pike hated shamans.

The big grey howled from the arbor many miles behind them, sending most of the folks into their houses. The rest invited Wulfee and her crew to join them around a central pit of old ashes. Children continued to play their games under a sea of stars. While the villagers sat on logs and ate tack and pickled cabbage, Wulfee got to know their names. The stern-faced woman called herself Tara, and Wulfee reckoned she was someone that would do just fine in her clan. The scarred man called himself Benn and took Pike, after he had eaten, to lay Maggie down and give her their last treatment of ander paste. Wulfee didn't recognize anyone from the day she left her son here. She reckoned they had lost many friends recently.

"More people come through here every day," said Tara. "Following the river, looking for some place to make a stand. If it wasn't the Hawka that got them, it was the Wolf and his clan. They come hurt, scared, hungry, pleading. Benn arrived alone, didn't speak for three days. It was only just last week we found out he had lost his family to the Clan of the Severed

Head. They took the heads off his entire village and left him alive to tell the tale. He did the opposite and told as few people as he could. And there's more. Pregnant women are all telling the same tale. There are no babies coming out alive. Not since the fires went out."

"I'm sorry." Wulfee didn't know what else to say.

"Those are dark clouds coming. Hawka and the Banshee with them. Folk have just given up hope," said Benn.

Wulfee heard the Banshee screaming, too, the night the Hawka came down on her camp. Old kihl'dors and their karls told tales of the Banshee around the clan fires when they wanted to scare young children, but she hated that tale and never told it to anyone. The Banshee came from the old times, before the Starfall, and they liked to devour young children when they stayed up too late. At least, that was what her dad said.

"The Hawka were being led in hordes. More than fifty of them came down on our camp. Someone had organized them into ranks. Like they were being controlled," said Wulfee. "They don't seem to have come down this far south, though. We've been free of them for days. They were in the mountains for something."

Or someone...

Wulfee thought of James. She knew the boy had secrets. Things that he didn't understand about himself. She should have gotten rid of James the day the wizard stalked her in the deep arbor. She had been alone in the arbor hunting when the wizard came out of nowhere and scared the shit out of her. "*How old is he now? Can he control it yet?*" the wizard demanded. She knew James was the heir to a conquered kingdom and that someone would come looking to kill him one day because of that. But there was *more* to James than just that. He wasn't normal. She should have left him behind the first time she saw his demon come out in battle, but she had grown to love the boy, and she couldn't bring herself to do it. He refused to fight in single combat because he was afraid of himself, but he would be a weapon when it came time to fight Sweyne again. And then Maggie grew to love James, too, and theirs was a sorcerous, lightning kind of love that hung in the air like thunder. It was all too good to be true. To see that much happiness right under her own nose. And then the Hawka came... She wouldn't allow herself to blame James, though. Not yet. She could only blame herself for not letting the wizard take him.

Wulfee sat and watched the children playing. Gen had joined in with them and seemed to be in a state of pure bliss. A small boy with a tuft of thick black hair and big green eyes caught Wulfee's eye. He was as thick as a barrel of butter and seemed to be stronger and faster than the rest. He looked just like her son did at that age. Tara caught her staring.

"Big, ain't he?" Tara said. "His name is Sweyne." Wulfee felt a stabbing pain in her gut when she heard that name. "It was his grandad's name. His dad's dad. We never knew him, but Braden wasn't fond of him. He said he wanted to give the name a better meaning. He wanted to love the name instead of hate it. He made me promise that if the baby was a boy, I'd name him Sweyne. It was important to him."

Wulfee's chest quivered—she was looking at her grandson.

"Braden's his dad's name?" asked Wulfee.

"Yeh, huh."

"What happened to him? Braden?" Wulfee felt a sickness rise in her stomach, thinking of the worst.

"He left a long time ago," she said. "This one was still in my belly."

"The wars?" said Wulfee.

"Aye," said Tess. "He couldn't pull himself away from killing and ended up selling himself and his axe to a brigand. He could be anywhere now. Only the gods know. He left me and the baby the money that the brigand paid for his life. That was the only good Braden ever did for us."

Wulfee said nothing. It had been nearly fifteen years since she'd left him there. To think he had a son of his own pained her more than anything she'd felt. The boy was at least six. *Six more years you lost.*

"Does the boy have any other family?" *Do you really want to know if he ever mentioned you?* Her underself had already told her he hadn't...

"No. Both of our families are all dead. All we had was each other." Tara rubbed her eyes with thumb and finger. "I didn't want him to go. But he insisted. He's a stubborn bastard, you know the type?"

"Yes," Wulfee said. Sweyne would have done the same thing. He always made her believe he was going to make things right and bring an everlasting peace.

"He'll be back one day, though. He will. And we can put all of this behind us. The fires will come back. They *have* to," Tara said, and Wulfee knew she was trying to convince herself as much as she was Wulfee. "People are saying the Wolf has fire. And food. They're saying he's bringing people south to save them from what's coming. He's warning us all that if we don't join him now, he's going to come back to attack, and they will spare none when they do. We're praising the gods that he didn't come through here already."

"He's false," said Wulfee. "Ain't nothing gonna save us but each other."

Tara forced a smile like she knew Braden wasn't coming back as much as Wulfee knew she wasn't going to find him here. The shred of hope Wulfee clung to was enough. It was enough for both of them. The lie stopped the bleeding. It kept her going.

"We're going to leave here soon, head up into the mountains. North and west. There's folk up there hiding from war who refuse to be broken by it any longer. We're going to settle down there, away from all this heartache—somewhere safe," said Tara. Wulfee had forgotten what *safe* felt like, and the thought of it made her feel... happy.

Little Sweyne came running up to Tara, climbing into his mother's arms, panting.

"I'm tired, and I have to poop." The other kids had all found their parents, and Wulfee saw smiles on the faces of the once sullen adults. These people still had something to live for: they had love. *Her* love had been split into a hundred-hundred pieces and scattered across the cold north. But now she'd found one of them where she thought she'd find more heartache. She looked at little Sweyne and Tara as they walked off to the thatch-roofed shack. She felt that old familiar feeling of love creeping into her frozen bones and filling her with hope.

WULFEE STRETCHED ON THE cold plank and cracked her back. The popping sounds were wholly satisfying and made Gen guffaw from the corner of the room. Pike was snoring loudly and didn't budge. The Giy'er preferred to stand while he slept, so Wulfee told him to stay in the corner so she didn't wake up in the middle of the night and axe him in the chest. She saw his hands were all scratched up with red lines from playing with the cats.

"You can't let them scratch you like that, Gen. Give them a boop on the nose or blow in their face when they get you deep like that." She was no mother, not anymore, but she still did her damned best to try.

Gen looked at his hands and smiled at her.

"I don't mind. They aren't trying to hurt me. They just like to play."

Wulfee looked into his big orange eyes and pulled him into a hug. She felt Gen's big hands squeeze her back.

Outside, a wolf howled.

"It's scary here," Gen said, cowering a bit in her arms. "Can you tell the story, Wulf? Can you tell about Emmer?"

"Yeah, okay," Wulfee said, untangling herself. "Let's sit here." It was the least she could do for the lad. So Gen sat beside her and looked at her with a sparkle of joy welled in his orange eyes. Wulfee cleared her throat and told him the story.

"The Feldarra were born from the great avalanche caused by the first sky fall. The power from the stars falling chiseled frozen chunks of solid stone into human shapes and sent them tumbling down the mountain. They rolled down the Fell Mountains and into Mal Hallow where they lay for centuries, unable to move, or speak, or think. The first Druids came across them and gave them the gift of the spirits. Fire to warm their frozen, watery blood, earth to give them flesh for skin, bones, and organs, and a gust of wind to start their heart. For this gift, the Feldarra are forever indebted to the Mal and make vows beneath the world tree to always protect these lands from invaders."

"And tell about the Karls, Wulfee! Tell about Emmer." Gen was like a cat chasing its own tail, pacing up and down, and circling his shadows, too excited to sit still.

Pike stopped snoring for a moment, sat up in his cot and looked around, then laid back down and started snoring loudly again.

"Emmer was one of the first Feldarra," Wulfee continued. "Born from the rock of the Fell Mountains. She had thirty-seven children who all became a kihl'dor, and it is from them that all Feldarra descended. Emmer the Rock defeated the Epithians from Edura when their army of a hundred-hundred ships sailed here to conquer these lands. After her victory, she sang the vows of the Feldarra under the world tree, and all the men and women who fought with her sang, too. The blood of Feldarra was to be spilled on this land in its defence for all of eternity. They would never be conquered and always remain free. And so she named each one a karl, which means free in the rune tongue."

Gen grinned. Thick yellow teeth stuck out like fence posts. He went back into the corner, and in a couple of minutes, fell asleep. Wulfee rolled over and tried to get some rest herself. As she lay under the wooden struts and thatched roof, she couldn't help but feel trapped. Part of her always felt safer in the wild, and sleeping in a dead person's bed didn't make her feel better either. Soon, both Pike and Gen were snoring, and Maggie was muttering under her breath, having her dreams of ander. She had been having them much lately, and Wulfee was becoming nervous that soon she would turn mad. *If she lost control of what's inside of her, she could kill everyone around her. But what else can I do? We have to go to the green man... then I'll find Sweyne.*

Wulfee remembered the kids playing goose and hop-rocks. She never got to play those types of games when she was a little girl, not for long. Her dad used to call her Etta when she was small, like the wisp of etta flower, because of its long curly red petals that reminded him of her hair. Wulfee loved those flowers, and her mom and dad used to take her down to the Hallow Hills to pick them in the Wayk of summer. They would grow even without rain. Those were her earliest memories. But she was born into a tough clan of the Fells, and her dad was a tough kihl'dor. Her mom told her she would one day be kihl'dor and that her first-born son or daughter would be kihl'dor after her.

By the time she turned six, her dad stopped calling her Etta. They raised her to be tougher than a flower, he'd said. And she had no time to play games. Instead of playing goose, they taught her to track and hunt, to read footprints in the dirt, to smell the wind and to move as silently as a hillcat, to fletch arrows and to loose them with deadly accuracy. They made her into a great huntress of the wild. Instead of hop-rocks, they drilled her in footwork. She learned to dance around strikes and beneath swings, she learned to read the hips and the eyes, and how to time her reactions. They taught her that killing didn't require a hard blow but a soft touch. Her parents had made her into a murderer. She was a Feldarra, by blood and in practice. A descendant of the ancient peoples who defended these lands from invaders. A direct descendant of Emmer, and to kill enemies on this land was her birthright.

Her mind stirred with old memories. She had been so busy surviving; she had thought of nothing else for weeks. But Tusk country reminded her so much of her past in the Fells it hurt. Wulfee remembered when she had fallen through the ice and pulled herself onto the riverbank. She walked back to her village a few hundred yards away, freezing, teeth chattering like a mad woodpecker. She thought she would die, but when she stood half frozen and shivering before her dad, he didn't give her furs or try to warm her. He only said *endure.* And he looked at her with his dark eyes and made sure she would never forget. *"Surely, you won't die for another many minutes, hours maybe. You must learn what it's like to hurt and that you can always go farther. Endure. You need to know your limit, Wulfee. You need to learn that you're far from it,"* he had said. And inside, she was screaming. *I'm your little Etta! Help me! Why won't you help me? I'm your little girl...* And it wasn't until she convulsed that they finally warmed her with heated furs and hot tea. She slept for many long hours after that and many people thought she might not have woken up from the chill she caught. But she did. And she was no longer the little girl that fell in the frozen stream. She was a Feldarra. Bred for hunting and killing, and never meant for love. She was a damn fool to think otherwise.

The wolf howled again, breathtakingly close now. It was the big bitch that had been following Wulfee up the river. Wolves in the distance answered her call in a higher pitch, then faded farther and farther away. *She's scaring them off, not calling them in. She's protecting us...*

THE WIZARD'S TEARS

J AMES DREAMT HE WAS back in Wulfee's camp. He could feel the breeze on his face and it carried the smell of Maggie. *Peonies and honey.* It had been three days since their last battle, and Maggie hadn't been the same since. He pulled his arms around her. She had been crying again. They had been drinking all day, and the shine always made her cry.

"Have you ever killed someone by accident?" Maggie asked. Her nose scrunched up when her words embarrassed her. The shine had glazed her eyes over, one green and one blue, for the sky and the earth, she'd said.

"By accident?" James thought about all the folk he'd killed. "I get a fever sometimes, in battle. I start killing, and I can't stop. I see all of their bloodied faces in my nightmares and I wake up sick. It takes over."

"Is that why you run from the fighting?"

James nodded.

"I don't want to hurt you," he said. Maggie tucked strands of brown hair behind her ear. "Have you? Killed someone by accident?"

She nodded. Then tears fell from her eyes. James held her close. Maggie whimpered, choking on her tears.

"It's okay," James whispered, holding her even tighter—maybe the tighter he held her, the more he could take the pain away.

"Camp's moving along now," Gen hollered from the top of a grassy knoll. Behind him, a steady stream of Feldarra followed behind their kihl'dor Wulfee. They were marching out to kill another pretender of the tree. The false kihl'dor sprang up across the Fells like mushrooms.

"I'm not going," Maggie whispered.

The monster in him urged him to let her go. It needed blood to be spilled. It needed to be fed and that would be easier if he was alone. He traced her shoulders in small circles, feeling the goosebumps rise on her skin. He knew if she left, he was going with her. And if he did that, he would never go home again. "Please, don't go."

"You don't understand," Maggie cried. "I can't control it sometimes. I will wreck this family as I've wrecked every other one."

"I'll protect you," James said, and that's when the monster inside of him seemed to cower. It thought about Maggie, her rosy cheeks from chasing butterflies in the arbor, her patience when he had none, her ability to see beauty in the ugliest things—including him. She made him want to be better because she deserved someone better than who he currently was. "I'll stay by you, always. We can learn to control it together. Please, you can't leave."

"And what if I kill you?" she asked, tears falling from her bloodshot eyes. It really hit him then. Maggie was terrified of herself.

J AMES WOKE. *SHE'S STILL alive. She's out there somewhere.* The black of night had softened to a dim grey, a calm moment before colour from the rising sun splashed the sky. James and Eurick had slept on the cold, wet ground surrounded by a symphony of cicadas, burn bugs, and owls from the arbor. It was all he could do to keep going, but they got up and kept on anyway. His mind slipped back into fond memories: dancing with Maggie to the drums of the karls, walking by the river in the early morning mist and laying in the wet grass together, sleeping under old oaks and gnarled nytewoods. *She loved the foggy dew...* His mind slipped back to a less fond memory, too, Maggie's screams fading in the distance as he ran the other way.

"This isn't right. This is new moss," the raven mumbled, holding a piece of moss he'd just touched his tongue to. James didn't even respond. "We need to be moving into the old growth."

Eurick licked the moss again, picked up a handful of soggy fallen needles, and threw them to the windless air. He sniffed like a hound.

They had to leave the horses behind when the arbor got too thick. James figured Shalo was better off in the wild than underneath his arse.

There were dead children weaving in between the trees of the thick arbor, chasing each other. He remembered what the Hermit told him all those years ago, that some dead souls don't pass back into the Otherworld. They could only linger and wander, lost to this world and the next, forever.

"Where is this sum a bitch?" said Eurick under his breath.

"You're telling me you don't know?" James said.

"There was no straight answer given to the Guild," said Eurick. "Just to take *you* to the old growth of the Old Arbor."

The children gathered around James when they noticed him, and James did his best to ignore the growing assembly.

"So, how will we find the wizard?" James asked. He'd expected a wizard's tower or something.

"*Help us,*" the children whispered to him. There were twenty or more of them—all of them long dead.

"We keep looking," Eurick said and walked deeper into the arbor.

James followed the raven and paused in front of the group of dead for a moment before slowly stepping through them, one foot at a time. Then the dead followed, too.

James had always imagined that when he died, he'd be in the cloud halls, wearing fine clothing and drinking fine ale. But that musty arbor was far from what James imagined what the cloud halls would be like. *Why are there so many now? Why can't they pass?*

The children ran circles around him, playing some game that looked like goose. As James and Eurick came to the base of a nytewood, the setting sun bathed the arbor in a haunting, red glow.

The trunk of black, oily wood shone like polished steel in the sunlight; the golden flowers blossomed in limp clusters where other trees grew leaves. Their petals were withered and seemed to weep a silent sadness that James could *feel* in his body, like their pain was his own. But those flowers never fell from the tree. Even in the dead of the harsh Mal winter, the nytewoods stayed in bloom. James remembered the song *Old Red Tears,* of the battle of Old Arbor. Gran would love to sing that one when she was feeling especially bleak. It was about the Lovasi slaughter of the Mal, a thousand years ago, during the conquest of Kelson. The Lovasi conqueror led an army of a hundred-hundred folk, trained and armed, across the Old Sea to conquer Ardura. Kelson's army landed in Esher and conquered all of Ardura, from the far south of Esher to Kallahorn. It was Kelson that built the castles here. He conquered peacefully in most places, allowing locals to keep their gods and their lives in exchange for their fealty. But when the Lovasi arrived in Mal Hallow, the kings and queens of old met them with a fight. The Mal wouldn't give up their lands that easily, and Kelson butchered them for it. Longships full of Daggland warriors came down from the far north to help the Mal, sworn allies by their sacred blood oaths to the Druids. But even those formidable bastards were driven back to their cold islands. Only the Feldarra could preserve the bloodlines of the old Mal by protecting small groups of them in the mountains of the Fells. Blood from the innocent soaked the soil in those days, and it took a lifetime to wash away. It's how the trees got so big. The song ended with that. *"Blood magic,"* his dad had always whispered when the song was over. *"It was dark words that caused those deaths. And dark blood was the result. The Lovasi were only meat puppets of the Warlocks, controlled as easily as a shadow on a wall,"* Bren Culdaine would announce with disgust. James figured he was full of shite, but now, standing beneath that tree, he wasn't sure.

James rubbed some soreness from his calves and thighs and remembered his wound from that stick that he fell on. He never treated it. He should've had the rot by now, if he was normal. He had a full canvas of scars from wounds that should have killed him. It wasn't the scars on his skin that pained him, though. The painful ones became visible when he closed his eyes.

Eurick plopped down on a fallen stump by the trunk of the nytewood.

"Hawka won't bother us in here, man. This is where the dead souls live. Probably don't have to tell *you* that,"

"I've heard this legend my whole life, but I never heard why. Why can't the Hawka stand the dead?" James asked.

"The dead souls try to get *in* them. Take over their body and live inside. It drives them mad. So the mutts usually just avoid the arbors all together. Not always, but usually."

James felt something like relief. Bits of slush still clung to the shaded parts beneath the trees. He accidentally stepped in the slush and felt the cold through the holes in his worn-out boots. *Even the ghost of winter is following me.* But seeing his boots brought him comfort and sadness at the same time. His mom had made them for him, and they were all he had left of her. *Your parents died for this country, and you only hid away... All that's left of them is worn out leather and a stone in your knife... they died, and you did nothing. They needed you and you failed.* James's parents had invested their last hopes in him. His dad had gotten the Hermit to train him, and they hoped that if James could learn about his powers, they could defeat Alder. *"The war is not yet over,"* James's mom had whispered to him the night before they sent him down into the Hermit's hole. *"Ai'mair Darra, James. You remember what that means? Love and protection. It means love and protection in the old rune tongue.* He could never forget. *"I've loved and protected you for your whole life, James. And I cherished every single moment of it, I promise you that. But now I need you. I need you to do the same. Your dad and I both need you."*

But you failed her. You failed both of them. They died because you couldn't face what's inside of you and you ran...

James put his hand on the nytewood's trunk. It was as smooth and slick as a river stone, but the trunk left no residue on James's hand. The tree throbbed gently, like it was pumping blood, a soft heartbeat.

"The ancient Druids believed the souls were reborn through these trees," said Eurick. "The ones that aren't reborn just wander, like they're waiting for something. Life maybe."

The Hermit had told James the same thing. That the dead used the nytewoods to enter the Otherworld, so they could be reborn into the spirits that gave life to the world. The spirits were the wind and the rain. The fire and the heartbeat of the earth. *And now they can't live because the dead can't die.*

"I'm going to admit something to you that damn near breaks my heart, man. I'm damn well lost," Eurick said, head hung low. "Funny how all these years I've thought of myself as somewhat superior to the common traveller with all my medicines and maps. It turns out that without my supplies, I'm no better at all. I'm damn ashamed of myself. We're all the same when you take it all away, man."

But James killed—no, the monster *slaughtered*, and somehow, he still lived.

"We're not *all* equal," James said. "Some of us are monsters."

Eurick looked at him, *through* him maybe. The raven had seen that Hawka skewered to the tree with nothing but a wood tipped spear and still came into the cave to find him. *He sees you as more than just a monster.* "You gonna sit there all day, or are we going to keep looking?"

Through the arbor a ways, James broke through the thick pine brush and saw a stream trickling down the mountainside. They knelt beside it, and James filled his hands with cold water. He gulped down four handfuls and let the cold bite his throat on the way down. His hand brushed something on the bottom, buried in the slimy mud. He pulled out a handful of gold and silver coins. He reached in and found plenty more. Stamped with things he didn't recognize. Some king wearing a ridiculous crown. Letters that meant nothing to James. Shapes and symbols that meant less than nothing. Only one of them he knew. It was a Hestern coin stamped in Hest—a silver mane, stamped with the roaring head of a lion on one side and a dead king James didn't know on the other. He reached in and found gold, and silver, and jet, and pearl. Coins from all places and all times given back to the earth from which they were taken and the earth refused them homage. The coins were cold and covered in grime and forgotten, and the stream trickled on unchanged. Whatever bargain forged here was one sided. Eurick hurriedly loaded handfuls of Hestern coin into his cloak pockets as if he'd get caught if he went any slower.

"Hell of a view, eh!" a voice from behind him said.

"The fuck!" James jumped up and reached for his axe. But when he turned around, he felt a sting in his neck. His fingers reached up to a thin needle on the side of his throat. A strange, dirty man stood before him. He was barefoot, bare-chested, and wore ripped trousers tied at the waist with a hempen rope. His dark skin shimmered in the dawn light. His black pointed beard had dried clumps of mud in it. James fell to the ground limp, and Eurick fell beside him.

"Huh?" James struggled to keep his eyes open.

"We're only peaceful nomads! You've got it all wrong, man!" Eurick called out before he started snoring.

"I had to paralyze you for a moment. You'll be fine soon enough. It's just the blood of a black rattler. It's much safer this way. For me, that is. Far more dangerous for you. Haha. Yes, of course." The man bent down beside James. He smelt worse than the Hawka. "I've been waiting nearly thirty years to meet you, James. Aren't you going to say hello?" The man removed a leather wineskin from his belt and took a swig. "Alas, you probably don't know many worldly customs, being up in the mountains so long."

"Who're—"

"Adeqor, the Wizard in the Arbor, the Warlock on the Hill, the Gallant to your Gareth, you could say."

"I don't—"

"Maybe you're too young for that one. Haha." Adeqor took another long swig from his wineskin. "Sorry, not much to go around."

"Well, I—"

"Ancient songs have been sung, child. Blood magic has been called on." Adeqor pinched James's armpit and tugged his ear. James didn't feel a thing. "This might just work."

James wiggled his toes in his rotten boots. *Getting the feeling back.* The wizard put his hands on his hips and looked out to the trickling streams.

"It's—"

"It's an old prayer of the Mal to throw coins into the wizards's tears," Adeqor said. "They thought it brought them luck, to give an abstract custom like currency back to nature where it belongs. That's what they called these streams coming down the mountain— the wizard's tears. Completely inaccurate, of course. I haven't shed a single tear since Lindis burned. A genuine tragedy, that," said Adeqor. *Lindis?* "Nevertheless, luck has been lost, and no one throws coins in here any longer. These waters should run for a year or more without the rains. Most others will dry up far before then, while others will run and run, and only the gods will know where on earth all of that water has come from. It's a good place, this. You can have it all when the job is done. This can all be yours. A hundred streams filled with gold and silver. You may just be a better king than your dad."

Adeqor took another swig from the wineskin. His lips were a light blue for a moment before they faded back to pink. He mumbled something incoherent. He seemed absolutely hammered drunk. "Follow me," he said, stumbling in his steps until he faded into the distance.

James still couldn't move.

THE GREEN MAN

"T HE SPIRITS, WULFEE. THE spirits!" Maggie was stirring, shouting. "They're dying! Can't you see? But James lives. He lives..." Gen had to set her down. She had been healing well since they'd left the village. Benn had taken Pike out to a berg-bee's nest to retrieve a healthy pot full of berghoney, and her blisters had contracted and begun to scar. It was enough to get them to the Green Man, Benn said. But Maggie wasn't like others.

Mage... Wulfee thought. *The Green Man may refuse her...* The soothsayers of Wick had warned Wulfee to keep clear of her. They said she would eat the life out of the earth if she stayed alive too long. *Is that what is happening?*

"Help it rain, can't you?" Maggie said with her eyes closed. "I love the smell of rain in the spring and to taste it on my tongue. It tastes just like the river, Wulf."

"By the gods, Maggie, if I could, I would," Wulfee said, watching Maggie murmur to herself. *Mage...* A chill ran down Wulfee's spine at the thought of sorcery.

They had left Barley two days ago and were still a few days' walk from the foot of the Hallow Hills. Benn assured them that Maggie would heal quicker now, and the dreams would stop. Wulfee only hoped, for Maggie's sake, that the healing came sooner than later. The Green Man was their only hope at this point. Wulfee had no chance at defeating Sweyne without her. Maggie had been through much before she came to her. Passed from one family to the next, abandoned one time after another. She came from old Druid blood, and she knew the ways of the woods and the animals, the stars, and the moon. She knew the ways of the elements. Of all things living. She, like James, had secrets Wulfee didn't understand. Maggie scared most people with just her aura. And Wulfee could see why. Maggie was kind hearted and loving, but there was a soft light in her that wrecked the world when it glowed. And Maggie hadn't any ideas of how to dim it. Someone should have sent her across the Old Sea to train with the Abori long ago. But she wandered the Fells and Mal Hallow instead. She was dangerous in a way that was impossible to explain. Being around Maggie was like sleeping under a tree creaking hard in the wind. But Wulfee needed her. With Maggie, she was stronger.

They sat by the rushing White, eating tack and drinking raw duck eggs. Maggie stirred, opened her eyes, and stared at Wulfee. "Strange things are spoken in dreams—of spirits and the dead rising," she said, and then closed her eyes again. Wulfee felt sick seeing her like that. *Get her to the Green Man. That is all you can do.*

Gen was sitting far away from the water. When Wulfee was sure he was okay, she went to see Pike. He was alone, speaking to his underself in a nearby puddle. Wulfee had had enough of that under-bitch and didn't want to hear what she had to say, so she sat by the stream, listening to the water lap against the pebbled shore. The sun filled the world with bright golden light that only spring could give. *It must be Rise already...* Blue jays and robins sang, fat yellow rush frogs croaked, and not a wolf or Hawka was to be heard. Wulfee thought of the big grey that had howled through the night to ward off other hungry wolves outside of Barley. She almost missed her. Tara said the wolf had been following them as well, which relieved Wulfee. She reckoned little Sweyne deserved the extra protection more than Wulfee's clan did and smiled at the thought of the thick boy and his tuft of black hair.

Pike returned from his prayers, and shortly after, Maggie stopped stirring.

"Gen," Wulfee called to the Giy'er. He was chasing the yellow rush frogs in the grass and had just snagged one by its droopy leg when he looked up. "It's time to go."

Gen gently placed the frog back down. He picked up Maggie, and with big strides, caught up to her.

THE HALLOW HILLS WERE haunted. That's what Wulfee remembered from the stories her elders told around the fire. Haunted by ghosts of a hidden past and hermit folk and magics that should never be tampered with. That's what the Feldarra believed. That's what she believed and had always avoided them at any cost. Now she walked at the foot of them willingly, looking up to the dark precipices and darker valleys rolling beyond. They were nearing the Dark Arbor, a thick stretch of wooded area clustered at the south end of the hills. It was an arbor shrouded with a mysterious past, and it birthed terrible rumours of sacrifice and spirits. It was where Shaqqa Ro lived and worked. Old gnarled oaks and crusted cottonwoods grew up around the hills and covered them with a sparsely budding canopy. Black ash trees and yellow birch grew alongside silver fir and golden maple to fill out the spread. Their dying branches tangled together in a web of wood that blocked most of the sunlight from creeping into the arbor. Ferns, brambles, thorn lilies, and iced goldenrod encroached from all sides of the path they walked on. The winter flora still clung to life and lashed out at the crew's ankles as they walked through it. Dead leaves and rotten needles crunched beneath their feet with each step. They held a straight line until they came across a stream. *Follow the stream all the way to the Green Man's tent. You can't miss it.* Tara had told her. So they followed it north, deeper into the Dark Arbor.

"The medicine man shouldn't be trusted too far," said Wulfee. "They call him Shaqqa Ro along the river, but in the hills and arbors of the north, we call shamans like him death stealers. They *do* save folk with their magics. I've seen it done."

"Whatever they call him, the man is a shaman," said Pike. "Nothing more than tricks and secrets. If he can help Maggie, that's fine, but we shouldn't trust him. You know a shaman robbed me once."

"Oh, come on, Pike." Wulfee didn't have time for Pike's stubbornness. Not with Maggie sick. "I've heard the story of the shaman who robbed you enough times now. If it bothers you so much, why don't you track the old hag down and get revenge on her? If the Green Man can save Maggie, that's all that matters," said Wulfee.

"I'd sooner die than trust a shaman," Pike sneered. "You can't just kill a person and expect the pain they caused you to go away. You live forever with the scars you have inside, just as you do with the ones on the outside."

Wulfee finally said, "This is about Maggie. I'd do anything to see her well again."

"You don't think I would, too? She's family. I'd face down death for any one of you."

"It's just a shaman, Pike. You don't have to trust him."

They shared a grin.

Wulfee could see the massive tent through the thicket of branches ahead. The posts rose thirty feet through the canopy above. A heavy patched canvas was draped over massive cross-beams and made the tent look like some kind of leather-bound castle. A gaunt man with a greying black beard wearing a green hood sat outside of the tent. He was putting his boots on and looked to have a buggered leg. The symbol of E'daru was visible on the breast of his green cloak. *A Ranger.* He made eye contact with Wulfee as they passed. She didn't return his smile, but Pike did, and so did Gen. Wulfee never trusted a greenhood. Not now, not never.

A mammoth of a man with a sharp-looking spear and eyes of all white stood guarding the entrance. Pike nodded to him, and the big man held open the tent flap. Pike entered first, Gen carried Maggie in after, then Wulfee followed them. Acrid fumes spewed from a small purple flame that danced on a silver platter in the centre of the room. Various herbs and other greenstuffs hung drying from the roof of the tent. The walls were lined with cluttered shelves, and there was a thick table tucked into the corner with various glass bottles strewn all over it. The smell of vinegar tinged the back of Wulfee's nostrils. A large iron cauldron was suspended over a fireless pit.

"Fire! Wulfee, look!" Gen screamed. In his excitement, Maggie almost slipped out of his hands. "Sorry Mag."

She didn't respond.

"It's not real fire Gen," said Wulfee, unable to look away from the flame herself. "It's fool's fire."

"Sorcery," said Pike, disgusted.

An old, bald-faced man sat cross-legged on the ground in front of it. His face was leather, carved with deep wrinkles and a sadness that only years of Hell could bring. Gen laid Maggie down on the ground in front of him.

"We seek your help, Shaqqa Ro," Pike whispered.

"Did you bring payment?" said the shaman.

Pike unwrapped the item that he had taken from Lorne and presented it to Shaqqa Ro.

"A knife made from dragonbone. From the days before Kelson. It is all we have left to offer."

"Yesss. Dragonbone..." the shaman said, tasting the word as it left his tongue. His eyes flickered at the sight of the smooth bone knife. "And it's not cursed? But how?"

"It is from before the Lovasi cursed the dragons," said Pike.

"Give it here." The shaman snatched the knife from the old warrior. He licked the blade with a dry tongue, smiled strangely, then looked down at Maggie. "Show me her wounds," he said.

"She's right here," Gen interrupted. He looked between the shaman and Maggie. "Don't hurt her."

The old man knelt down to get a closer look. Wulfee didn't like the way he looked at her.

"We have treated her with ander and berghoney. Her cuts are healing well, but there is something else wrong—like she is dying because the world is dying," said Pike. The old man sniffed at the air above Maggie's wounds.

"There is no rot left in her, and the wounds have nearly closed. So, what do you ask of me, wild man?"

"Fix her. Find out what is wrong and fix it," said Wulfee.

"You would ask me to heal your friend, but you don't know what is wrong?"

"Yes," said Wulfee. "You're a death stealer, aren't you?"

"That is what we are paying for," said Pike, and eyed the dragonbone knife. The shaman quickly tucked it away when he saw Pike's gaze.

"Well then, you must give me time. Seven days. And I cannot promise that she will live," the Green Man snickered.

"We don't have seven days." snapped Wulfee. Shaqqa Ro laughed.

"You may be right!" The Green Man pulled a small pouch from his waistline and removed two yellow stained knuckle bones carved with runes. He rolled them onto the ground and watched them bounce. Then he stared at them, sighed, and quickly gathered them up again and tucked them away in his pouch.

"What is it?" said Wulfee, always curious by a reading of the runes. Shaqqa shook his head. Sighed again.

"There will be blood," he said frankly. "On this ground, we will spill blood."

Wulfee pulled her axe, and with a heavy swing, pierced it into the table.

"If she dies, so do you," she said.

"You know not what you ask for, wild woman. The runes say what they will by no influence of mine. Oh, if I could control the runes..." He laughed deeply, the tent rumbling along with him. "Oh, if I could control the runes, I would be a god. We cannot solve all things with threats. If she dies, it will not be from my lack of trying.

"Now go, and if you pull that axe out in front of me again, you'd better use it, wild woman. Seven days it will take. Seven days you will give."

As Shaqqa Ro fanned his purple flame, it grew bigger. Wulfee couldn't believe how much she craved to sit near that flame and warm herself. But fool's fire only spewed cold. From a burlap bag, Shaqqa Ro threw a handful of green dust onto the silver platter. A puff of green, acrid smoke filled the tent, and the purple flame danced wildly—swaying side to side like it was coming to life. Wulfee sneezed.

Witchcraft.

The massive man with all white eyes held the tent's flap open. Wulfee didn't want to leave Maggie behind, but this was her only choice.

"We can find a place to lie down, maybe get something to eat in the hills," said Pike.

"I could eat something," said Gen.

"We're going to Tusk," said Wulfee. "I need an audience with Claydon Coldfoot."

"Claydon won't grant you an audience, Wulfee. He has no respect for the mountain clans," said Pike. "And we don't know what kind of state Tusk is in. We could walk right into a bloody riot and never come out again. You know this."

"I need to know if it's *him*," said Wulfee. "I need to know if the Wolf is Sweyne, and then I need to kill him. It's all I've left to live for, Pike," said Wulfee. *And how do you kill a man at the back of an army?* "Claydon will know who this brigand really is. And if not him, then somebody in Tusk will."

A loud crack echoed out of the Dark Arbor and Wulfee didn't even jump. It was as if she were dead to everything, drifting in the wind like a fallen leaf. *What are you doing, Wulf? Leaving Maggie like that? How can you bring yourself to leave her? How can you still go on like this? Is it even worth it anymore?* But finding Sweyne and reeking vengeance upon him had consumed her. Giving it up would be to lose everything. She often woke up and forgot what she was doing. What her purpose was. *Your purpose is to protect your people; your children—what ones you have left.* She told herself, but it never stuck. She wasn't a leaf in the wind—she drifted like a wraith through life searching for the husk of her old self.

"Are we going hunting again, Wulfee?" Gen asked. He was swinging a stick in the air like an axe.

"Yes, Gen. We're going hunting," she said.

"Good. It's nicer out there," said Gen.

"We would need horses to get to Tusk and back in seven days. Where would you expect to find horses out here in the hills?" said Pike.

"Hey, I could get you a horse," a man's voice said. And a flock of birds scattered from the treetops. Wulfee turned around. *Pfft.* It was that Ranger they passed on the way in, sitting down with his left leg elevated on a stump. It was twisted awkwardly and covered in a poultice. The smell that came off of it stung the back of Wulfee's throat.

"You always listen in on other people talking?" asked Wulfee.

"Just trying to help is all," said the Ranger. "Name's Haro."

"I don't care what your name is. I don't go around making deals with Rangers." She couldn't help but glance at the crest of the black horse of E'daru once more. Pike nodded in agreement with her.

As Wulfee walked away, the Ranger called out, "Times like these and you'd treat a fellow offering help like that? Where else are you going to get horses?"

Damn stubborn bastard. Wulfee turned around.

"And what do you know about the times?" she said, looking at his buggered leg again. "Hawka do that to you?"

"You could say that." Haro sat up with some difficulty. "But it's the bastard who left me to die that I blame."

"We're not interested in your story, Ranger," said Pike. "What would you ask of us for these horses? We've got nothing left to give."

"Take me with you to Tusk," said Haro.

"Hah," Wulfee laughed. "We can't afford to carry a wounded man like yourself. I need answers. And I only have seven days to get them. You would slow us down too much."

"Seven days?" said Haro. "Did Shaqqa Ro's runes say that?"

"It doesn't matter what the runes said," said Wulfee. "When we return from Tusk, we can bring you gold."

Pike stared at her, and Wulfee knew he could tell she was lying and didn't like it.

Haro shook his head. "Nope. I'll get you a horse, and you take me with you. It's a price far cheaper than gold. I'll take care of myself, and if I fall behind, you can just leave me."

"Ain't no good come from following me," said Wulfee.

"Ain't no good comes from much of anything these days," said Haro.

"What are you getting out of this? I have nothing to pay you with," Wulfee said. Haro laughed.

"You'll pay me back later. We have similar motivations."

"Which are?"

"Making things right."

Wulfee didn't trust this man. She didn't like him either. But she needed a horse. If Sweyne really was this mercenary brigand called the Wolf, if his army was as big as folk are saying, Wulfee had no doubt that he would march into Tusk and then pour across the White River into Mal Hallow. The old kings and queens of the Mal would fall, the mountain clans would fall, then the Glenn. This was for conquest. It was the only reason Ayeland fought any war. They were trying to finish what they started ten years ago. That bastard Baleth made them paranoid. Everyone Wulfee has ever known would die by the hand of Sweyne and the Ayelish unless she stopped the bastard.

"Okay. So, what now?" Wulfee said.

Haro's stiff face cracked into another smile.

"Let's get some horses. Come on, it's getting late."

THE AILARYAN ORDER

"**O**H, IT'S NOT THAT bad. I needed to make sure you were the right people. A wizard can't be too safe these days, you know?" said Adeqor.

It took hours for the strength to come back to James's legs so that he could walk again.

"Urrh," croaked Eurick. James's stomach rolled. He vomited.

"Oh, that's dramatic. Come now, we're almost there," said Adeqor. The crushing sound of a waterfall filled the air. A rainbow of light danced in the mist, and James thought he smelled spring blooming.

He looked down at the pool as they walked by. The water was greenish brown, stirred up by the constant fall of water from the mountain stream above. James got a strong whiff of shit as they continued up a rocky pathway. The smell merged with the stink of dead fish as they went into a wide cave in the mountain's base.

"This ain't right," Eurick moaned.

The wizard's lair was shrouded in a layer of green moss. Water dripped from moist crevices above into stagnant puddles below. The smell of fish and shit got stronger the deeper they went. James hated that vulnerable feeling he was getting. *What have you gotten yourself into?* They came to a large flat area with colourful carpets. A long trestle table sat in the middle of the cave, and ornately carved chairs lined with fine cloth and cushions surrounded it. Sausages and smoked meat hung from hooks at the top of the cave along one wall. Shelves were stuffed with jars full of jams, relishes, and jellies, pickled vegetables, eggs, and various... animal feet, it seemed. On the other wall was rack upon rack of wine bottles. Suits of armour that sulked longingly on crooked stands were placed sparsely around the room as if for company.

"You must be hungry," said Adeqor. "Here." James grabbed the food, and he and Eurick ate like this could be their last meal. The wizard laughed, taking another swig of his wine.

When they were done, Adeqor gestured to a flat area below: a small pool of water with pieces of furniture around it. They walked down a winding stone path to chairs, a table, and a shelf full of glass bottles—wine bottles or conjurer's ingredients, or both. A small table beside it held a stack of mouldy leather-bound books. James had only seen books bound like that once before, in Kallahorn. Bones were littered everywhere—whether or not they were Human, James didn't want to know. Lumpy candles poked out of pools of hardened wax. The candles seemed to grow out of every flat surface. A beam of daylight shone through the rocks.

"Do you know what you are, James Culdaine?" asked Adeqor as he grabbed a bottle of wine off the shelf. He found a spot underneath a golden pillar of light and sat on one of the chairs. "You see them? Eh?" he scrunched up his nose. "What are you both doing standing there? Come sit next to me."

James obeyed—he didn't want to become bones on the cave floor. Eurick also obeyed without question. And as James sat, the dead souls emerged from the shadows and crowded around him.

"I know the souls are always here, but I can't see them," Adeqor hiccuped. "But you, seer, you can, can't you?"

James reached out to touch the dead souls, but his hand fell through their smoke like bodies. He hadn't told many people his secret. He'd never even told Wulfee, though he suspected she had figured it out somehow.

"I see them."

Adeqor grinned.

"The dead you see can be dangerous if you're not careful. They can haunt your dreams, take over bodies, devour living souls."

"Help us," came the cold whispers of the dead. James shivered.

"When the dead souls pass back into the Otherworld, the One Fire reignites them, and they are reborn as living spirits. The spirits are of old life. They have always been here, before anything. They live and die in the souls of every living thing for eternity. Their magics are written on the soul like a song, and when they live, the world sings with wind and rain; it dances with fire and shakes the earth with their memory. Without them, the world sits stagnant, and the dead souls cannot pass down. They're just... gathering." He took another swig. "And if the dead cannot pass down, the living cannot rise up. And vice versa."

Maggie had always told him she could see spirits dancing in the fires, feel them hanging on the wind or rain when she stood in a storm. Maggie told him she felt the rhythm of the earth, and she *moved* with it.

Adeqor said, "You will use what is inside of you to bring life back to this world, James Culdaine. You can help the dead pass down and allow them to be reborn. You can bring back the elements to the world. You are a seer of old Druid blood. A half-god World Walker. You can touch the Otherworld, and a small piece of it lives inside of you."

James had heard all of this before. It brought back sour memories that puckered his mind.

"The dead don't pay any mind to me," James said. "I have no power over them."

"It's because you don't pay mind to them. The longer you ignore them, the more they distrust you. Imagine... someone walking around in your village for years and years, pretending you don't exist. And when they finally acknowledge you, validate your existence, they're disgusted."

James had never thought of it like that. The moonsmoke bodies of the dead moved through the damp cave with motivations of their own. Aside from their gruesome injuries, they *were* kind of... beautiful. James could see how some might think it sad for them to be ignored. *Maggie thought so.* Knowing he was the only one who could see the dead made him feel guilty for ignoring them all those years. When the Hermit told him the sight was a gift, he had rejected it. When the Hermit told him he had the blood of gods, he'd denied it. James never trusted a word the Hermit said.

His dad had forced him into lessons with the Hermit when he was only nine. He and all the people of the Hallow had put their faith in James to be their saviour. To learn the Ways and fight Calen Alder for them. His dad forced him into the Hermit's stinking hole with payment of a fox's corpse to learn what was inside of himself. But the Hermit was too much—its eyes protruded out of translucent sockets, its colourful hair in shades of red, blue, green and yellow floated around its head like a thick fog. The Hermit could only screech when it spoke, an ear-cracking squeal that *hurt* James deeply. After the thing taught him to eat the life out of the dead to heal himself, he couldn't take it any longer. He couldn't save his country from conquest. He ran.

Ai'mair darra. James's mom whispered to him before Alder came, as tears welled in her warm brown eyes—they were her last words to him. *Love and protection.* He couldn't protect anything he loved. He let them die, and his country, too. He never found out what ate at him from the inside. The Ways were still only a myth to him.

"Someone has summoned a powerful song to close the Gateway to the Otherworld," Adeqor said. "A song resurfaced from four centuries of slumber. The singers of Lindis will be turning in their tombs. By re-opening the Gateway of Rebirth, the spirits of life will be reborn. The shrine of the Mother of Nature lies in the mountains, beyond Kallahorn. That is where *you* must go to open the Gateway. Only a World Walker can unlock the Otherworld."

King Alder was at Kallahorn…

Eurick coughed.

"I hate to say it, man. You'll have to send an eagle to the Raven's Guild to get a replacement. I've lost my maps," Eurick said, hanging his head. "First job I've ever failed, you know? And it's always been my dream to see the Mother's shrine."

"Relax, transporter." The wizard pointed to the shelves. "I have maps to take us there. You can use those."

Eurick's face flushed red.

"You're not going to replace me?" he asked.

Adeqor shook his head.

"No time for it. You're good for more than just maps, and you know it. I know what magics they breed into the ravens out in that Guild. We leave tomorrow. But tonight—" he uncorked a new skin of some wine that smelled like vinegar and took a long swig "—tonight, we *drink*."

Adeqor handed Eurick the skin. He took a drink and passed it to James. The smell was enough to make him gag, but he still took a big chug of it and held down his vomit.

"You are a god in the eyes of some, James. You have the blood of the Druid seers in you. A pure line back to the most ancient times, when Mal Hallow was nothing but rock and trees. Yours is the race that built the standing stones and wove magics into their runes. Your kind ruled here long before the Ailaryan Order and the Lovasi paved over it all."

People had been telling James he had the blood of old gods for longer than he could remember. *So, then why do you feel less than human?*

"Who is singing these songs?" James asked. "How is this happening?"

"The Ailaryan Order," Adeqor said bluntly.

"The Ailaryan Order?" Eurick laughed. "Come on, man."

"Baleth was using old Yehvenki blood magics before he declared himself king," Adeqor explained. "I have evidence that the Banshee travelled north with Alder. Her name is Ellorin. She was one of the most feared members of the Ailaryan Order. A reputation well earned by her need to eat life and bind the minds of others to her will. It was the Ailaryan Order's time-honoured duty to halt the spread of dark magics—the songs that brought the Starfall. They would see the whole world die to halt the spread that Baleth may have caused. Long ago, the Ailaryan Order used their magics to bind the Mother of Nature to her shrine. Like a prison of sorts. It allowed them to control her. To use the god-like deity as a tool. By forcing her to close the Gateway, the Ailaryan Order could kill the world and halt any human progress they pleased."

Adeqor twisted the bottle in his hands before taking a long drink. "As for who put the words on Baleth's tongue in the first place? I don't know, but I wouldn't be surprised to learn it was Ellorin. It's her that has led these Hawka down on the north using her mind magics, and there are more hordes of Hawka pouring out of the mountains to join them. She's binding their minds with her silver thread and weaving them like a tapestry. She's looking for you, the World Walker. Ellorin knows you are the only one who can stop them. She will stop at nothing to find you."

The Banshee... James's dad had talked of the Banshee, though he never called her Ellorin. He had said that she manipulated Alder. *Could she have manipulated Baleth in the same way? But why?* It didn't make sense. It never did to James.

"I always admired the Banshee," Adeqor said. "But she was always far too involved in human affairs. She fell in love with Alder twenty years ago and hasn't left the man's side. Even when Alder's ex-wife tried to kill her, she stayed with him. In spite of his wife, maybe. This involvement is going to get her killed one day."

"I thought the Ailaryan Order had died along with Lindis?" said Eurick.

"They unofficially still lived. And they cast me out and inflicted a curse upon me. I was no longer welcome in the group that *I* started..." Adeqor cursed under his breath.

"Why were you outcasted?" James asked.

"Jealousy—" Adeqor said, and turned his back.

Eurick cleared his throat. "We heard brigand lords are flocking out of these lands into Ayeland to serve King Alder's army over the Hallow."

"You can't beat Calen Alder." James clenched his fists. "Not with what's left. We fought him for years. We lost—everything, and now you say he has the help of the Ailaryan Order?"

This is a lost cause already.

"I think you'll find that enough ambition can kill even the heartiest of folk," said Adeqor, turning around to face James. "He's not the same king that killed your family. If he has given himself to Ellorin and her magics, he could have weakened himself. Their own hubris could distract them from us."

James thought of the horde of Hawka that attacked his village, how he abandoned Maggie, the only person who had never expected something from him that he couldn't live up to. *How many others died that day that you ran?* He remembered his dad's look of horror as Alder's army approached, and his mom's last words to him, *Ai'mair darra,* that he had failed to live up to. He couldn't even save the people he cared about.

"How would I stop them?" James murmured. "How could I do anything? I'm the son of a dead king. The blood of long dead gods. I've got nothing. No one."

"You have a power in you, Culdaine," Adeqor said. "I know you feel it in there. It's a power that flows directly from the Otherworld. It's the Ways. The same power that was inside Hendurinn, the Great World Walker from the Cycle of Dain."

Hendurinn was James's—and any child of the Hallow's—greatest hero. He touched the Otherworld and fought the Ailaryan Order. He saved the world from falling into darkness with his magics. But James was no Hendurinn. James wore ripped and rotten boots. He had an overgrown beard and tangled black hair with no braids in it. Two hazel eyes that didn't see all that well and a sore back, and a broken heart. He was nothing of what a hero should be.

"I'm no god! It will take months to reach Kallahorn. I've barely slept. I've hardly eaten. I need to find Maggie and Wulfee, and the clan. This is all non-sense."

"Months we have," said Adeqor. "But not much more. Once winter comes, most will freeze to death without fire. And whoever survives the cold will starve come spring. Then the wars will kill all but a small few who are vicious enough to fight death. The rivers will dry up and the lakes will drain. The world will die. You and Maggie won't live through the Rise of next summer if you leave now. That's *if* you find her. This task is yours. There is no one else, Culdaine. There is only you."

"Why did you make me come here, then? All this way west. Kallahorn is east."

"Because," Adeqor said smiling. "There is something else you need."

"What?" James asked.

Adeqor smacked his lips. "A weapon."

Mammoth's Head

"**S**TRANGE PLACE TO STABLE horses," said Pike. "In the Hills."

"Rangers need horses that can navigate the slopes," said Haro. "You'll need a sturdy garron to get you through the slopes."

They walked up to the run-down stable that was slowly being reclaimed by the hills.

"Hey, Lew?" Haro whispered into the darkness beyond the horse pens. A tall man draped in chainmail emerged holding what looked like a Lovasi mechanical bow. Wulfee had never seen one that worked, but she didn't want to take a chance on this one. She stood still.

"Hyuh," Lew said, muffled through a steel helm and visor. Wulfee stared at him in disbelief. Full armour to guard a stable. *Times are dark.* They heard the same stories in every hamlet they passed through. No fire. No rain. No rot. Babies were stillborn, and pregnant women were bleeding out. Wulfee shivered thinking about it.

"I need horses, Lew," Haro said. "Three will do, but you won't ever get them back. I'm sorry." He reached into the canvas sack and pulled out a clear blue stone the size of an apple. "I'm sure you understand, Lew. I can't be making any promises to return horses. May E'daru live through you."

"May E'daru live through you," Lew repeated, snatching the stone. Even in a gauntleted hand, the stone looked huge. In the clear evening, silver moonlight shone through the clear rock, revealing strands of purple and green. Wulfee thought that it might have been the most beautiful thing she had ever seen, and when Lew tucked it safely into his breaches, she felt a sadness that it was gone. The armoured man sunk silently into the dark stable.

"What was all that?" Wulfee asked.

"I promised you horses. You're going to question now how I got them for you?"

Wulfee shook her head in response.

"Don't you trust me yet?" Haro's face looked rugged in the night. The sparse grey in his beard flashed in the bleak moonlight. His stubbornness and wise ass reminded her of Sweyne, and she didn't like it. She'd trusted too easily before and suffered for it ever since. But she knew the legends of Rangers—they were body snatchers. Sorcerers who worshipped the Outcast God. They were never to be trusted.

"I don't trust you worth shit," she said and took the reins.

"Good," he smirked. "You're a wise one." His smile faded, and his voice took a more sombre tone. "It won't be safe for me to travel alone with my injury. If I get attacked, I won't stand a chance. I'm depending on you to get me to Tusk so I can tell the families of my band that one of the most important people in their lives died following me. This was our deal. Horses for escort."

Wulfee knew what it was like to break that kind of news, and it wasn't anything nice. "I know what our damn deal was."

Lew came back with three horses saddled and ready. The Ranger and the stable master shook hands and said something to each other that Wulfee couldn't hear. *Never trust a Ranger. Never. What are you doing, Wulf?* Pike mounted a brown mare and left Wulfee with a beige one. She saw Lew pointing at Gen as the stablemaster was helping Haro mount a white stallion. Haro spoke back to him in whispers. Wulfee couldn't hear anything he said. She shook her head. *God damned Rangers.*

"Come on, Gen." Wulfee shouted as she rode off. Gen followed along with big, smooth strides.

CLOUDS COVERED THE MOON, and Wulfee couldn't see shit.

"We should stop for the night," she said. "We could ride right into the river and not even know it in this dark."

"And I'm tired, Wulf," said Gen. The lad hadn't complained once, but Wulfee didn't blame him for doing so now.

"We can't stop," said Haro. "We're but a few hours out from Tusk."

Wulfee felt her inner kihl'dor boiling up.

"You go ride ahead."

Haro halted his white stallion abruptly.

"We had a deal, Wulfee. Horses for escort. If we stop, it means I'm going to need to ask one of you for help. To dismount, to get up after I lay down, and to mount again tomorrow. And to be honest with you, Wulfee, I don't trust that any of you wild folk wouldn't just take the horses and leave me to die."

"We won't betray you," said Wulfee.

"And when Wulfee says a thing," said Pike, "she means it."

"And I'm hungry," Gen moaned. Haro looked at them.

"I know who you are, Wulfee." Wulfee felt a sting of worry. *Who the fuck is this guy?* Rangers came around her camps asking questions all the time, but she didn't recognize this bastard. "You're a kihl'dor of the Feldarra, shield of the Fells. The Rangers see all from a bird's-eye, Wulfee. I know who you are and who you used to run with. And I know that if you were me, you wouldn't get off this horse. Not for any promise or kind word in all of Ardura. This horse is all that's keeping me on equal ground with you and your lot."

Wulfee stared at him in the darkness. Suddenly, she felt uncomfortable. Like maybe she didn't want to get off her horse around this fella, either. It was silent for a time as they sized each other up. The crickets and burn bugs lit up the night with their chorus, but there was no other sound as Wulfee held Haro's gaze.

Haro said, "I've got to get a word out of what happened to me and my band in the north. They have families that will wonder where they are. I owe it to them to tell them. I at least owe them that."

Then Haro turned and rode away.

"Fuck," Wulfee said under her breath. She looked at Pike, who just shrugged. *The Ranger spoke well.* Wulfee grit her teeth. He reminded her far too much of Sweyne. "Gen, we can't stop for a few more hours yet. One more tough night, then we can rest."

The Giy'er sighed, sunk his head, and sighed more, but he was obedient.

"Let me tell you about Emmer and the Feldarra before we go," she said. Gen smiled, startling the horses as he jumped up and down.

WULFEE FOLLOWED HARO ON the dark road, letting her horse guide her, trusting it to see what she could not. She was so tired she thought she might fall out of her saddle. Stuck only with thoughts of losing her sons and James, and now maybe Maggie, too. She almost wished she *would* fall to put an end to all of this chasing, to all the ache and gritting pain of it all.

Wulfee remembered one night with Sweyne so vividly it shot jolts of pain up through her whole body. Sweyne had brought Tarek out to watch a single combat. He thought bringing Braden would be a waste of time because Braden wasn't tough enough to ever fight in a single combat anyway. It was for the toughest of folk, not him. Wulfee looked on as Braden watched his dad and brother from the great arched windows of his bedchamber. He was so excited to hear about it until Sweyne stepped into the castle.

"You'll never wear the wolf mask, you hear me? Go cry to bed, you little twat!" Sweyne screamed mightily at Tarek, reeking of chuff and shine.

"Why would you yell at the boy like that? *What's wrong with you?*" Wulfee screamed back. She knew he was hammered drunk, but it was easier to match screaming with screaming. Especially with Sweyne.

"These boys will *never* live up to this!" Sweyne thrust his yellowed wolf mask in her face. It was carved from the upper half of a massive wolf's skull and fitted with a leather strap and steel buckle. It was a horror to behold, especially if Sweyne was behind it swinging an axe.

"Maybe they don't need to live up to that. Maybe none of this is what they want!" Wulfee had screamed. Tarek wanted to be a warrior, but Braden was so gentle. He only ever wanted to be a stable master or a kennel lead.

"These kids are failures," said Sweyne. Just then Braden came in and burst into tears. All the boy wanted was to hear about the single combat. "You see what I mean?" He walked over to Braden, and with his chain gauntleted fist, smacked him so hard he split the boy's face open.

Braden didn't make a sound as he fell to the ground. But Wulfee shrieked so loud and guttural it threatened to shake the entire castle down with its echo. She would have killed Sweyne right then, but when she saw the blood pouring out of Braden's face, she rushed to *him* instead. Sweyne walked past them and up the winding stone stairs. Wulfee held Braden in her arms and cried and kept crying until the salt burned her cheeks. She picked him up in her arms and walked into the mountains to find a death stealer, as they called shamans in the mountains. She walked so long she thought her knees would give out, her feet had bled into her boots, but she found the death stealer in a strange thatch roofed hut by a spring. It grew out of swampy mud on stilted, reptilian-like legs, and a fool's fire lit the windows with a purple glow from inside. Ragged wooden steps led to the hut that looked like the decrepit tail of some great beast rising out of the swamp. The shaman waited for Wulfee at the top of those steps with steaming green tea and a potion to bring strength back to her legs and feet—as if he had known exactly what ailed her. He took Braden, and Wulfee watched as the shaman closed the wound and stopped the bleeding with his green magics. He gave the boy a tea of hemp buds and ander leaf to numb the pain. And he took Wulfee's Daggland steel axe as payment. Braden had that horrible scar his whole life as a reminder of who his dad was.

Wulfee shook her head. The memories were too much for her. *Too much.* If it wasn't for Sweyne, maybe she would have let herself slip off that horse. But she couldn't stop breathing while that bastard shared the same air as her. If she couldn't ride on for her own damn self any longer, she would do it for Sweyne. For the sake of killing the bastard that ruined her life.

So she kept on, under the black, starless sky and thought of the day she'd make it right again.

WULFEE HAD NEVER SEEN a construction like this before: the massive mammoth head rising above the trees, bathing in the afternoon sun and guarding the ford at Tusk. Even the walls of Kallahorn, though almost as tall as a nytewood, were only flat, black stone.

The Mammoth's Head Castle was a marvel of Lovasi capabilities. The keep was smooth-stone carved to look like the head of the mammoths that once roamed these parts. Massive stone tusks laid on the grounds of the courtyard in front of the castle. A brawny gate of black Daggland steel came down from the upper jaw of the mammoth and bit into a drawbridge tongue. Four rounded towers crowned with battlements rose up around the mammoth where its legs would be. Its body was an ornate stone hall, with a grand arched ceiling of black slate. The Lovasi built the castle on a small rocky isle in the centre of the White River. Thick curtain walls rose up out of the water and surrounded the Mammoth. The walls were lined with turret towers and eldritch stone gargoyles whose shadows seemed to move on their own. Tusk was a maiden, the only safe crossing of the White River for hundreds of miles in either direction, and the mammoth protected her. Two massive stone bridges, one on each side of the castle, wide enough only to fit a merchant's cart, arched over the White and connected the land on both sides to the inner bailey of Mammoth's Head.

Wulfee had heard strange stories about the old Lovasi Castle—not just the ones about what magics Kelson conjured to build it or the many wars fought to defend it, but the ones about what lurked below. The myths said that the crypts beneath the river stretched down to the very inner workings of the world. The crypts were littered with the bones of some race of creatures that lived in Mal Hallow before the first Starfall, long before Yehven even existed. Some people claimed to have seen whatever lurked down there in the dark. The stories told of a creature emerging every few decades to abduct Human men for reproduction. Wulfee didn't know what to believe. But she knew these Lovasi castles weren't right. They lingered over the lands of Ardura like ghosts of something that should never have been. They were *alive* somehow and laced with sorcery. She could feel it during her time at Kallahorn. She could *see* it looking at Mammoth's Head.

The town of Tusk sat on the north side of the castle and had stone walls of its own. There were three gates—one in the north, east, and west—guarded by massive stone barbicans. Patches of wooden palisade covered weak points in the walls where time had cracked the stone. Archers sparsely covered the battlements.

Wulfee and her crew walked beneath the portcullis in the north gate. She traced the walls of the gatehouse, feeling its chipped and worn scars—scars that were much older than hers. The gatehouse gave Wulfee a false feeling of safety. She was used to doing her fighting while looking her opponent in the eye. She fed off the fear she could see, and it helped her with the killing. It was the way of the Feldarra, to kill. She reckoned they could hold the Wolf off here, even without Maggie, if they had a good lot that could all agree. She sighed. *Not bloody likely...*

After they dropped their horses off at a small stable just inside of the gates, Haro pulled Wulfee aside.

"Listen, I can help you find the answers you're looking for if you don't find them in there," said Haro. He nodded to the town.

"If you know who the Wolf is, just fucking tell me, Ranger. Don't play your games with me."

"I said I can help you *find* the answers. I don't know who he is any more than you do, but I have the tools to find out."

"I'm not interested in making any more deals with Rangers. We're tired and hungry and just ready to stay in the same place for one night."

"If you change your mind, you know where to find me. We leave for the Green Man in four days. I'll be here till then." Wulfee looked away at Pike, who only nodded. She didn't need any friends. She'd had plenty of those and seen them all dead in a field of battle somewhere. Times like these, she didn't need friends, but she needed allies. And if Pike could trust him, that was good enough for her. She shook Haro's hand, and the Ranger grinned as she did.

"I think we can really help each other, Wulfee. I respect that you're willing to go out and get vengeance on those that have wronged you. Inspires me to do the same, actually," he said.

"Four days," she said. "You better be here."

"I'm a Ranger. We don't lie," he said as a blue jay fluttered down and landed on his shoulder.

Wulfee had to believe that he would stick to his word. As they headed back to Tusk, she redirected her attention to Gen. In a slow and calm voice, she said, "Gen, you listen to me, okay? We're headed into a big town now, and I need you to be careful. You hear?"

Gen nodded.

"You can't go getting yourself all excited and stamping around. You could hurt someone from doing that. I wanna hear you say it now. I am going to be careful."

Gen smiled, like this was a kind of game.

"I am going to be careful," he said. But Wulfee knew the Giy'er was never careful. He was clumsy. He was giant. And she loved him to death. And because of that, she dragged him along to places he should never be. It was damn right irresponsible of her to bring him into a town. *You should never have taken him...* but she couldn't have left him alone. Not like she left Braden. Not like that.

They entered Tusk with caution. Dirt roads ran in neat lines, and one story, thatch-roofed shacks surrounded them. The outside walls were all that remained of a once magnificent creation—the town was rotting from the inside out. Crumbled stone statues that must have once stood taller than the walls lay scattered throughout the squares and along the roads. The town's gates were wide open. Refugees from the Hawka attacks and the Severed Head attacks were scattered throughout the dirty streets. Families sat bundled in blankets by empty fireless pits. Men and women dressed in boiled leather and armed with a variety of makeshift weapons nervously waited for something unknown. Folk eyed Wulfee wearily as she passed. And bodies. Piles of dead bodies that refused to decompose piled in corners against walls. They had all been through hell here. Pike disappeared into the crowd to ask questions.

"A morsel? Anything? Please..." A woman clutching a baby in her arms begged as they walked by. "My baby needs food!" the woman fell to her knees. *She's holding it too tight.* Wulfee felt a horrible sickness. *She's killing it...* but when Wulfee moved to do something about it, she saw the child in the woman's arms was already long dead. Wulfee turned her head and tried not to be sick. "*Please!*" The woman's shrill moan made Wulfee cringe. She felt helpless. She stepped over bodies strewn across the street, either dead or near death. Gen staggered behind. Wulfee turned and saw that he had sat to listen to the pleas of a young mother.

"Come, Gen," she yelled. The Giy'er came with tears in his eyes.

"They're all starving here, Wulfee," he said.

"I know, Gen," said Wulfee. "This is the underside of life. This is what ugly looks like."

"We're going to make it alright again, Wulf, right?" said Gen, hopeful. Innocently so. It made her stomach tingle and her eyes burn. If only it was that simple, she would have made it right ages ago.

"The gods know we're gonna bloody try, Gen. We're going to bloody try," she said. If only she believed it. She knew there wasn't a goddamned thing she could do to fix this shite. This was a game for gods. She only wanted her revenge. She only wanted Sweyne.

THE RUINS OF LINDIS

"**I**T'S THE BEST WEAPON," Adeqor boasted. "The greatest. You haven't seen a thing like it anywhere. I promise you that." James shrugged indifferently. The wizard led them into a small glade surrounded by tall pines and fir trees. Streams filled with coins flowed through the glade like shining blue veins. "This was a holy spot once, for the Ailaryan Order. The sage Warlocks of the old times gathered here for centuries to conduct their work. Corrupt, quisling bastards."

Monolithic stone pillars sat amongst the trees and rivers of the glade like dead stone Giy'er, covered in thick moss and draped with crawling lichen. Some were still standing, most had toppled and cracked under the weight of many hundreds of seasons, surrounded by their own crumbled remains—but they were all blackened with char, scorched by the fires of some great disaster from long ago. To James, these stones made the walls of Kallahorn look tiny.

"By the gods, man... This... This is Lindis..." Eurick nearly choked on the words getting them out. He was panting now.

"*Was* Lindis." Adeqor corrected him.

"This isn't on any map," Eurick said. "I didn't think it was real, man." He had his hand on his chest like he thought his heart might stop.

"The ravens of old decided it would be best to *forget* Lindis. Real shame, that. Some of us can never forget," said Adeqor. "The ravens were just another creation of the Ailaryan Order and did whatever they were bid. It's no fault of their own. They thought it better to remain a friend of the Ailaryan Order than to have their precious maps *completely* accurate." Adeqor took a drink from his wineskin. James glanced at the raven but Eurick was paying no attention. He was looking around with his jaw hanging. In an instant, Adeqor snapped out of his melancholy and smiled. "But that's not the matter! It's the weapon we need. *Essikah*! Crafted by one of the strongest Warlocks of all time, Bazal. Forging this sword was one of the last deeds in Bazal's bodily existence. The great Warlock forged it of godrock and tempered it in the blood of a hundred Human sacrifices to bring it above. He carved it with the runes of old Mal songs of power. Its connection to the Otherworld is enough to open the Gateway of Rebirth."

"This is the story of Hendurinn," James said, "from the Cycle of Dain." Gran had told him this one a hundred times. "The traitor wizard had given *Essikah* to the Great Seer, and he betrayed his own kind to do it. Together, they saved the world from the black summer and woke the spirits from darkness."

Adeqor pursed his lips.

"That is the story of Hendurinn, a story for the peasants of the Hallow. The story of Bazal is much darker," he said. "You need to understand, boy, that the Ailaryan Order has tried to kill this world, and they will try again. They locked Bazal away for helping humanity fight against them. He lost his mind before they took his body."

"The legends in the north say that the Warlocks are long dead," said James. Eurick couldn't take his eyes away from the surrounding sights.

"We lived," Adeqor said. "Though some days I wish we hadn't. Only the Ailaryan Order died all those years ago at Lindis. The Warlocks of Old Yehven still rule this world, believe me. We stand in every court and behind every map in every battle. But it's not the individual Warlocks that trouble this world. It's the Ailaryan Order. A group of Warlocks that ruled the world with their magics for three and a half millennia. They pulled the strings of the great machine called the Lovasi Empire and rid the world of those wretched dragon peoples. They wrought peace and good to every land they touched. Alas, some of them wanted more. And instead of ruling the world, they fought each other. It resulted in *this*... charred monoliths and the ashes of centuries worth of dreams.

"The Ailaryan Order rose from the dust of the Starfall and disintegrated at the burning of Lindis. And in that time, they accomplished the work of gods. Things that will go unsung by the bards and unwritten by the scholars. Things that shaped this world more than you could ever know. To see it all fall in one night, crumble under the weight of one mistake... It was crushing. Do you have any idea what it's like to live amongst the ruins of your old life?" James just shook his head. He hadn't even had the guts to *face* the ruins of his old life. "Do you have any idea what it is like to be cast aside from the only thing you ever cared for?" The wizard's mouth seemed to be stitched to the wineskin.

They came to an unnatural rock formation. Large shiny stones marbled in purple and white were chipped to jagged pieces and constructed in a neat line beneath a steep, forested ridge. The symbol of the Ailaryan Order, a flaming comet, was etched into the stone and plated with dirty gold on either side of the cave entrance. They climbed the ridge and came to another small cave. Once inside, James saw it wasn't a cave at all but a ruined hall of sorts, with flat stone floors covered over in years of dirt and grime. Light poured in from the spotted holes in the arched stone ceiling. Adeqor led him to a place that looked to have been carved out by the Mother herself. Large pillars of the purple and white stone stretched from floor to ceiling. Beneath them was a small mound of black earth.

"There it is. *Essikah*. The sword of wonder. The key to the world," said Adeqor, absolutely entranced. He rubbed his hands together.

"That old thing must be rusted to shite by now!" said James.

"Don't be a fool. That sword is forged of Godrock. Pulled from the Otherworld with a powerful song. A song so beautiful it brought entire continents to their knees in tears. You could never imagine such beauty as this. godrock is the stuff of hard magics, it doesn't rust. It doesn't break. It is perfect in every way. Bazal truly was a master." James couldn't tell if Adeqor was drunk or being serious. "Now, go. Claim it."

James frowned. He remembered that Wulfee always used to dream about some kind of weapon of magics like *Essikah*. She always told the story of *The Axe of the Moon*, the weapon wielded by the great Feldarra warrior Rianon who used it to kill the last of the mountain wyrms. Wulfee had said she imagined finding it in the mountains somewhere and using the great one-handed axe to kill Sweyne.

For a moment, James imagined telling Wulfee and the clan the story about his coming across *Essikah*. They would be sitting around on logs with flames licking at the night sky and crackling up a fury. *I found it in a wizard's cave. I also got shitfaced with him.* Wulfee would like that story. Gen would *love* that story. Pike probably wouldn't believe it, but James always found the worry on the old warrior's face amusing, especially when someone spoke of sorcery.

James walked up to the black mound of earth. *Essikah* was *growing* out of it. Thick roots snaked out of the sword's hilt and clutched the soil tightly. The blade stood as tall as James. The smell of decomposition and worms filled his nostrils and stung the back of his throat. As he looked closer, he could see that the roots were writhing. *What the fuck is this?* He truly couldn't believe what he was looking at. But he took another step forward, then paused again. *What the fuck are you doing?* The Ailaryan Order had carved the faces of long dead Warlocks into the smooth marbled stone of the pillars that grew out of the ground all around him, and James couldn't help but stare at them. Names attached to faces and laid down in stone in their memory, and they were still forgotten. *Essikah* didn't look like it belonged amongst those pillars. It looked to be closer to nature—something created by gods, not Humans.

The sword was huge. Nearly as wide as James's torso and as long as he was tall. The strange black rock had ripples of silver, emerald, and aqua swimming through it. There were old Mal runes carved into the blade running up and down each side, from tip to root, in swirls. The roots growing out of it were thin and metallic. James nudged it a bit and found that it was as sturdy as a tree. Then, the dead began to gather in.

"There are roots growing out of this thing. It's stuck in the ground," James said to Adeqor.

"Yes, of course, that is the nature of it. You just kind of, er, pull on it and jiggle it a little. Like a key that isn't quite cut right."

"What?"

"I suppose you wouldn't understand that reference," Adeqor said. "Just pull on it, guy, find out what happens."

James touched the blade and traced the cold Godrock. The dead souls poured into the ruined hall of Lindis, and their ghostly bodies glowed beneath the sprinkling of light from above.

"*Help us. Please,*" the souls begged James. "*Please.*"

James knelt down and grabbed *Essikah* as low down on the hilt as the dirt mound would allow. The roots quivered in response and pulled the sword tighter into the ground. The dead souls pressed in around him and began to chant. The song flowed through James as he gripped the hilt tighter and began to pull, and soon the roots loosened. The runes that swirled through the blade lit up and glowed a haunting blue, like the colour of the moon. The song of the dead got louder; it echoed in James's ribcage and filled him with power. And with one last pull, he tore *Essikah* free of the roots. The sword made a crunching, grating sound as James ripped it free from the dirt. And the runes danced with magics. A rush of warmth flowed through James's body, followed by a great rush of cold that didn't leave. He was holding a sword the size of a small tree, but it was weightless.

You could be great with this sword. You could really do something. You could be Hendurinn... you could save—

And then the dead stopped singing, the glow died, and the sword's true weight returned and fell out of James's hands, landing in the dirt with a soft plop. James stared at it. He felt a sickness in his stomach—like *Essikah* had stared into his soul. A feeling lingered that told him this sword would be the death of him, but at the same time would never allow him to leave it.

"So what now?" James said.

The wizard drank in response. Eurick paid little attention, still gawking at everything around him. The dead only looked on expectantly.

James picked up the heavy sword, rested the flat part of the blade on his shoulder, and walked back to his companions. It weighed as much as a dead body, and James wasn't looking forward to carrying the thing. Was even less enthusiastic about using it. He picked off dead bits of root matter that was crusted on the hilt.

"Strange," Adeqor said.

"We're good here then?" said James.

Adeqor nodded; he was already leaving the hall.

"Seems so. This makes me very happy to see *Essikah* in the hands of someone capable again. It's been many years since we planted it there in hiding. A long many years since the tragedy of Lindis."

"It's cold," he said. The sword was like ice in James's hands.

"The souls of the dead power it," Adeqor replied. "And you have no shortage of those around, now, do you? The cost of dead souls seemed a better sacrifice than living ones to Bazal. It makes little difference, really. Both remember."

James shook his head, at a loss for words. He just wanted to get this over with.

"They have come to you for help," Adeqor said. "But you are too blind to see it. Therefore, you need *me*. And I need you. You must open the door. Send the dead back down so the living can rise once more. You can bring the fires back with that sword, Culdaine. You and only you. I can be the

Bazal to your Hendurinn, James. This is your story. Bring the beauty back to this world with those hands."

James wasn't sure what to think. It reminded him all too much of those last years with his family on the run from King Alder. Mal Hallow was getting closer and closer to total defeat, so James's dad forced him to do one ritual after another to awaken the power in him. None of it worked. James had visceral nightmares of the Hermit, horrible visions of himself letting the monster out—of the people he killed. His mom begged his dad to stop, but Bren Culdaine kept forcing the rituals. Sacrifices of the living—turned to smoke and given to the moon. Bren only burned animals at first. Then an Ayelish captive. Then whoever they could hold long enough to tie up. And still James did nothing. To his dad, he was the weapon that would win the war. To the people of Mal Hallow, he was their last hope for freedom. But he was none of that. He just ended up alone in the pink snow. He couldn't protect anyone he loved then. But maybe now he could.

"So, what then?" said James.

The wizard said, "We go to Kallahorn and beyond to the Mountains of the Mother and save the Mother of Nature from whatever peril she has found herself in. Open the Gateway to the spirit world to let the spirits rise up and fill our world with life, and let the souls of the dead pass down to become fuel for the living. Very straightforward, really." He laughed and let it trail off into a sigh. "But first, let's have another drink!"

James and Eurick followed Adeqor through the ruins of Lindis and back to his abode. It was only minutes before Adeqor was passing them a drink.

THE BANSHEE HAD BEEN following James in his dreams since the Hawka came down. He could ignore her in the sunlight of wakefulness, but in the darkness of his dreams, he had no choice but to face her. Her piercing screams filled the air when the Hawka attacked their camp.

And she was there now, even as he slept, passed out from too much shine. She caressed him with a bitter touch that made his hair stand. The shadow tainted the air. It was her. Ellorin.

"You could stay here. It's safer here. Better," she said. Her voice made James's crotch move. He tried to speak but couldn't. She approached him. Long black hair draped over her shoulders, dripping oily wet. Her skin was whiter than eyes and seemed to eat all the light out of the air. Long grey fingernails curled from boney hands. She was a silhouette come to life, a shadow asking for James's hand. Her warm fingers laced around him; James hadn't felt a loving touch in so long. He leaned into her.

Who are you?

"I can be yours." She caressed his cheek. Her voice soothed his hurting heart. Her touch caused a tingle in his stomach. He had felt that way before. *With Maggie...* "Never wake up and you could stay here with me."

This isn't Maggie.

"Ellorin," James said. The name came to him like someone else had placed it on the tip of his tongue. It was the only word he could speak.

"You don't have to run anymore, Culdaine," she said. "You can stay here and be reborn into the new world. But you need to let them die. You need to let me catch you." James could see the dead souls fading away, finally leaving him alone. "You could be free from all this. The sword. The dead. Just stay here, don't fight it. I can bring you to Maggie. I can make you happy again."

"Ellorin." It was all he could say. He knew it was her name without ever hearing it.

"It won't end well for you, Culdaine," said Ellorin. "I am coming for you, and I will find you. I will tear your body into crow food after I devour your godforsaken soul. You bastard son of a bitch. I will fucking kill you for what you are." She had visited his dreams before. He didn't allow himself to become scared.

"Ellorin," he said. She scowled. Then smiled, her eyes laced with malevolence.

"I saw you run, you know. You could have saved her, but you ran," said Ellorin. James felt something evil crawling in his stomach. It begged him to come out, and he shoved it back down into the darkness. It was something that shouldn't be poked or prodded. Something he didn't want to awaken ever again. *Because you have awakened it before, yes, so many times. Too many times to remember, even. But not now, no. please, not now. Not again. Not today.* The Banshee that called herself Ellorin stalked around him in circles. Her madness was a dark shroud. "We had only come for you, Culdaine. We were only after you. If you hadn't run, she'd still be—"

JAMES SNAPPED AWAKE—COLD WATER splashed on his face. It smelled like piss. He blinked, tasted the water, and realized it was something closer to shine than to piss. James's head hurt.

"What are you dreaming, boy?" a drunk man covered in dirt yelled. "What did you see?"

"Huh?"

More water splashed his face.

"You were muttering something! What did you bloody well see?" It was Adeqor talking to him, but James was still confused about what had happened. He didn't remember falling asleep, let alone dreaming.

"It was..." He couldn't remember. Only a vague darkness. Then out of the black night came a reminder.

"SHIEEEE!"

A piercing squeal sent a chill down James's spine. Adeqor's eyes flicked open.

"No." Adeqor shook his head.

Eurick looked at James with fear in his eyes.

"No, what?"

Then, another guttural shriek from the darkness.

"SHIEEEE!"

"Oh gods, no," said Adeqor. "Hurry now, we must go." James felt a knot in his stomach, felt like he wanted to throw up. His head rushed, and he remembered his last moments with his mom and dad. *"Help us, James! Help us!"* They begged him as their killers crashed down on them, but he couldn't move. He couldn't do anything. He felt that same paralyzing fear now.

"No, what?" said Eurick. "What the hell is that?"

"It's the hunter of souls," Adeqor whispered. "The Banshee. She led the Hawka into the arbor. Ellorin's overriding a primal fear deep in the blood and minds of those creatures. She's torturing them. And she entered your dream... She is using the magics of Old Yehven to sing powerful songs. Songs that haven't been heard since... since the Starfall." He looked at James. "We cannot stay here. If she finds you, Culdaine, this is over before it even starts."

"SHIEEEE!" Another piercing shriek from the night. She was so close now James could feel the vibration in his chest. Birds flocked from the treetops.

"We have to leave. Now. She knows we're here," said Adeqor, and hurriedly filled his flask from a bottle on the shelf. Eurick packed his new maps away with his usual meticulousness. He gave Adeqor a bad look when Adeqor loaded wine bottles in with the maps.

Adeqor hurried towards the cave entrance while James and Eurick stood still. He waved his hand at them to follow. James put a fist under his chin and nodded; Eurick did the same. Together, they left the ruins of Lindis behind.

THE WOLF

"LET ME IN, YOU bastard!" Wulfee yelled. It was her last resort after knocking on the castle gates did no good.

"Out of here!" said the guard, pulling a steel sword on her. Wulfee noted how little rust it had.

"You tell Claydon that no one knows the Wolf better than I do. You tell 'em," Wulfee said. She knew he wouldn't tell him. No one ever gave her message.

"Go!" he said. She almost rushed the bastard of a guard but thought better of it and carried on. Lords and ladies were all bastards, in her experience. Not one of them was any better than the other, but all of them thought as much. Lord Claydon of Tusk, Lady Ruwen of Rosen, and even Lord Baleth of Kallahorn, who declared himself a king, sacrificed his wife, got his arse killed, and started moving southern armies north again. All of them were just as useless in bringing the fires back. All the country ever did was fight each other *or* the mountain clans. After Wulfee had beaten Sweyne and driven him and his followers into the Fell Mountains, it was only weeks before Ashan moved in with a thousand blooded folk and held Kallahorn. When he tortured the clans and their families, not one ruler came out of their castles to do a damn thing. It was Wulfee who led the Feldarra in killing the barbarian Ashan and saving the Fells from his reign. Not two years later, that bastard Baleth took the castle for himself. Wulfee refused to march on the big dark atrocity called Kallahorn again. And Baleth had held the castle for thirteen years before Calen Alder killed him. She had done more for these lands than any lord in the last fifteen years. She knew this Claydon wouldn't know none of that. None of them did. If she couldn't get in to see him, she'd have to look elsewhere for her answers.

She walked across the great stone bridge that led to the castle gates, then through the crowded streets towards the alehouse by the west gate. Folk with open, festering wounds begged her for help and grabbed at her legs as she walked by. There weren't enough death stealers in all of Mal Hallow to save this battered lot. The Clan of the Severed Head and the Hawka had left their mark on the north, and it was in the flesh of its people. Some of the folk Wulfee passed were crying, some were begging, others just sat forlornly and stared up at the sky halls where they'd be arriving soon.

"I ain't got nothing," she said to them as she kicked their grips loose. Children cried, coughing up months of heartbreak and disease; dogs barked rabidly. She knew no one could stay here. There was little food and less hope. *All those years of fighting... for this?* Wulfee had spent her entire life trying to live up to her role as a kihl'dor of the Feldarra. She stole, lied, and killed to earn it. It was hard to realize that respect was only worth a damn if the people who respected you stayed alive. She had nearly let her whole crew die.

She chose respect over love when she left Sweyne. Love was a son of a bitch, and she'd loved him something fierce. She had never felt pain like the burning that came from watching her sons' father lose his mind to madness. Wulfee should have left with her boys long before she finally got out with one of them. But there were many good years before the bad ones. Enough to convince her it could be like it was. Sweyne and Wulfee had united the north and held Kallahorn as a stronghold for the mountain clans. They did it for peace, for the oaths, to protect Mal Hallow and the Fells. But then Sweyne became restless without enemies. So he created them. He turned on the other clans. After victory, he burned the survivors on a grand pyre. He would stay up all night and watch the flames. He prayed to the Twisted God from the far south, Karaat, and turned his back on the Old Gods. The day Tarek died, Wulfee knew she couldn't do it any longer. That night Wulfee left, more than half of Sweyne's army followed her. *All I paid them with was death.* She spat. All those old thoughts left a nasty taste in her mouth.

Tanner's Alley smelled like a dead man's arsehole. Wulfee scrunched her nose up. She could never get used to the kinds of smells you found in towns. Shit and piss and that vinegar stench of far too many humans starving, fucking, and dying in one place. But there was nothing of decay. Nothing of rot, and that absence made her the sickest. The earth was dead, and it wouldn't eat.

The sun was setting as Wulfee walked through clusters of sleeping folk huddled against the walls of the street. Gone were the times when families sat and enjoyed the sunset together after a long day. She quickly found Gen, still standing. He waved to her with excitement when he saw her.

"Wulfee! Over here!" he screamed, waking a dozen people from fever induced sleep. She joined the crowd of survivors from the hill villages. Gen was keeping himself occupied by catching burn bugs and watching them light up in his palms. Pike greeted her with a small piece of tack he had saved.

"What did you find out?"

"The Wolf is a brigand lord," Pike said, "leading mercenaries from the north into Ayeland." Wulfee shook her head. "He's flying the red eagle. He's sold himself to the Ayelish and brought half of the northern country's armies with him. It might just be him, Wulfee."

"Who else would it be?"

"Anyone can call themselves the Wolf. Anyone can wear a wolf mask," said Pike.

"Not like his," Wulfee said. She remembered the hunched-back black wolf that Sweyne killed to make that mask. He carved it out of the top half of the beast's skull. It was a snarling, twisted kind of creature. Not like any wolf Wulfee had ever seen. The beast looked to have crawled out of the muddy ground. It seemed to laugh at them as it stalked them through the arbors of Kallahorn. And when Sweyne finally broke the wolf's skull open with his axe, they saw the truly haunting nature of its face. A maw that leaked shadow. Eyes of pure blood-red rolled back into its sockets. The dead creature hummed with some kind of dark magics and expunged a sour stench that burned Wulfee's nostrils and made her wretch. Sweyne couldn't wait to cut the thing open to see what was inside. But he found nothing of interest. Just blood and guts. But he made that wolf mask from its skull and ate its heart raw. After that, he would sometimes go weeks without taking the mask off. It became a part of him. It became a part of *them*. She felt the need to destroy it.

"It came from Hell, that wolf," Wulfee said. "Some kind of sorcery cursed it. And its skull held onto some of that darkness." She had only ever just thought about it before. Saying it out loud didn't make her feel any less crazy, though. Pike winced, but she knew he believed her. He was never hard to convince of sorcery.

"I need to know for sure. If it's not him, I want no part of this battle. What else did you find out?"

Pike sank his head. "They're gaining a strange reputation, the Wolf's lot. People are calling them the Clan of the Severed Head. They're leaving the heads of their victims on spikes. Some say they've gone and pulled monsters out of the hills, too, and put them in cages to fight for them."

"Not something Sweyne has done before, but I wouldn't put it past him," Wulfee said. Pike shook his head. "Severed heads… that's his kind of party trick." *He'll watch the whole world rot so he can have one more taste of glory. And he'll have an arse licking grin on his face while he does it.* Wulfee couldn't do this anymore. If she stayed here any longer, she'd be letting *him* win. "I have to leave this evening. I will be back by morning. I have to see what answers the Ranger can give me. If it's Sweyne out there, I need to end him, end my nightmares. I need it to be over, Pike."

Pike paused. "But if you find out it *is* him. Then what? How do you plan to get past this army he's leading?"

Wulfee didn't like how haggard and tired Pike looked. The old warrior had had enough, and Wulfee kept dragging him through the mud, knowing his honour would keep him by her side right until the bitter end. Maybe there was no point in feeling guilty for him—she wasn't ready to relieve him yet. She was too bloody selfish for that. She needed him.

"We've never fought against something like this, Wulfee. This is the Ayelish we're dealing with now. Not some mountain clan."

"We go get Maggie, and then we go to Pool," Wulfee said. "We get Odhran and the rest of the Feldarra to fight with us. That's how we beat him."

Pike sat up, rubbed balled-fists into his sunken eyes.

"You are not welcome at Pool, Wulfee," said Pike.

"I remember."

"You would break a sworn oath?"

"I only muttered some words before an old tree," said Wulfee. Pike stared at her. Worry filled his eyes. The only thing that scared him more than the Hawka was upsetting the gods. He didn't want to have to face the clans at Pool after his disgrace. He'd rather die in this shithole at the hands of enemies.

"The nihr'el is not just an old tree, Wulf. It's not natural. It speaks to the Inner Earth, the Great Spirits."

"*My* spirit wants to kill Sweyne. Nothing else speaks to it. If this brigand is him, he will head for Pool if he breaches the border again. He will need to make a prayer at the nihr'el before this is over. We can meet him there. Kill him there with the help of Odhran and the clans. We can fight our last battle where our ancestors fought the first. We won't win here."

"The clans may kill *us* if we return. Odhran rules there now; you know this. He has no time for the likes of you or me."

"Odhran won't kill me. He'll humiliate me, but he won't kill me."

"He'll kill *me*, Wulfee. We are brotherbound by marriage, and he still blames me for the death of his sister. The bastard thinks I killed Alissa, Wulf, my wife. He's never wanted to hear my truth. Alissa came out to stop me from leaving, and *his* guards shot her. In the dark, they thought she was a thief or spy from some other clan. It's his own fault! And he won't hear it! He'd rather blame me. He tells my daughter that I *killed* her mom!" Pike slammed his fist against his chest. "You want me to face that madman and his iron arm in single combat for my life? He hates me as much as you hate Sweyne."

The old warrior clutched his shield close to his chest. It gave him the most comfort in this world. Wulfee sat beside her old friend.

"I would never *ask* you to do that, Pike." She held out her hand.

He sighed, mouthing the words, "*nihr'el nur amo ruso.*" *World tree save my soul.*

For a heartbeat, Wulfee wondered if this was the end for them—*I've broken him now.*

But he held her hand firmly in his. "I'm with you."

No Home

J AMES DREAMT THAT THE clan fires were blazing in the camp as he and Maggie watched from the hills of Yore. Maggie nestled her head into his chest as he lightly played with her fingers. Her hair smelled like peonies and honey. Around them, speckles of orange flashed as the burn bugs danced in the silver light.

"Why aren't you afraid of me?" Maggie asked.

James kissed the fingers laced with his own. "How could I be?"

"How can you even look at me after what I did back there? Killing all these people to find someone I don't even care about. Can we just run away? I just want to walk in the woods and live by a lake off what the gods have given us."

"No," James said. "Definitely not. This is our family. *We* need a family." No one else would take in people like them. He remembered last night and what Maggie had done to those people, and part of him was still in shock... but the other part of him, the monster, gleamed at her raw murderous nature. "The killing, it wasn't your fault."

"Then whose was it? I killed an entire clan of people—including children."

"You tried to stop it. It's a curse from the gods. I have one too. It just takes over whether or not you want it to."

"When you slaughtered all those Ayelish folk, didn't part of you like that? Didn't part of you *want* it to take over?" Maggie asked.

James shook his head.

"I became numb to this. I used to wake up in a circle of corpses, broken and confused. It used to tear me up inside, but I learned to live with it. I *had* to learn to live with it. For *you*. You can learn to live with what you feel, too. We can do it together. This is our family, and it can be alright."

"No, you don't understand. I *could* have stopped myself if I tried harder. When they attacked us, I could just feel all of their energy hanging in the air like thick smoke. Wulfee was screaming at me to take them out. All of their life was like a cloud I could just inhale. And when I did, it took everything from them. When the rush of thirty people's lives had passed me by, I felt emptier than ever. The whole world died around me. Plants and animals, too. I stood in a circle of death."

"It was an accident," James insisted.

"No." A sadness stained her tears like blood as they fell from her face. "That's what I'm trying to tell you. It wasn't."

I T WAS SO DARK that when James opened his eyes, there was hardly a difference. He was on the ground, in the cold, and damp atop dead leaves and moss. They had taken rest in an old, hollow nytewood stump.

"James? You awake, man?" said Eurick.

"I ain't sure," James croaked. He had dozed off for a bit, but he hadn't a clue how long.

"Best we keep moving," Adeqor's voice came from the dark. He came into sight, black circles under his eyes. Looked like he'd been up all night drinking. When he got closer, he smelt like it, too. A rough grinding sound followed him as he dragged *Essikah* through the dirt behind him. Adeqor leaned the hilt towards James. James sighed, accepting the fact that no matter how desperately he hated his destiny, he couldn't do a bloody thing about it.

"It's been a long night, man," Eurick said.

"It's not entirely okay that a Yehvenki witch like Ellorin is using such power," Adeqor said with a grim tone to his voice. "This changes things."

"I don't know what *she* is," said James. Something cold dripped from above and splatted hard on his head.

"She's a witch of old Yehven, a survivor of the race of Warlocks that lived before the Starfall. She was a member of the Ailaryan Order. Claims to *still* be a member." Adeqor took a drink. "She was the leader of the Banshee, the group of Warlocks that hunted anyone using the magics of Yehven outside of the Ailaryan Order's jurisdiction. When the Banshee had caught up to their prey, they wailed a horrible death song to herald their coming. To let the victim know it was over. Most of the Banshees refused to use the Words to hunt. They thought that using the Words made them no better than their victims. But she... Ellorin... was different. She spun a silver thread through the minds of her enemies. Drove them mad and made them move on her whim. We hadn't ever heard a song so useful for gaining power. She could have been the High Archon of the Ailaryan Order. But we could never control her, and she hid from us for long stretches of time. She kept herself involved in petty human affairs. I should have tried harder to have killed her then, but I pitied her. She wanted to help Humans—those inferior, subservient, menial Humans. She wanted love. She didn't see the opportunity we had."

"She doesn't help *all* Humans," James said.

"Ellorin weaves her own webs, ruled by her emotions," Adeqor replied. "Before Calen Alder, there was another. And before him, another. She means to find love within the hearts of these people, but doesn't understand that the Warlocks lost their right to love when they brought the Starfall. They traded love for long lives with no consideration of what they were really doing. Something broke in the magics, and it broke the Warlock's hearts beyond the point where love was possible. Whatever Ellorin feels is not love, though she's convinced herself it is. That is why the most desperate Warlocks have turned to Humans to fill that void. But it only leads to further pain. She is singing songs that had lost their power thousands of years ago. Somehow, they are gaining strength again. Her and Alder have started a cycle of dying that can only be reversed now by *Essikah.* By you."

James felt dizzy.

"She has been stalking my dreams. Why? Why does she want me?"

"You are the World Walker, James Culdaine. A Druid half-god from ancient blood. Your coming has been told a thousand times, with a thousand different names, in the Cycle of Dain and many other songs. The story of Hendurinn was an actual event, and people have forgotten that it really happened and will happen again in the future. Life turns to legend, turns to myth, and back again. You have the power in you to open the Gateway and defeat the Ailaryan Order, just like Hendurinn."

In James's mind, he could still see himself standing in front of his mom's red corpse, ripped apart by blades. His dad's blue corpse, bashed and beaten, was lifeless and frozen solid. He woke up alone in the blood-soaked snow and found his parents like that. He failed them and his country, and he didn't have much hope that he wouldn't fail this, too. *But you could try... you could bloody try for once...*

"So, what exactly do we plan to do about this Banshee?" said Eurick.

"She is best not to be taken lightly. She's... powerful. There are things in this world that you know nothing of. Dark things being remembered. Dark songs from even darker times. It's impossible to know how far Ellorin has already gone with singing them and impossible to know how much strength the Words have gained since the elements died," Adeqor said, and scratched the back of his head. "We have to travel through Wick Arbor."

Eurick's eyes flicked open.

"That is miles out of our way."

Adeqor rested his arm on the transporter's shoulders.

"She may have led them into the Old Arbor to make us feel like we weren't safe, but that must have caused so much strain on the mutts that she won't want to keep doing it. The Hawka won't be able to handle the Wick. There are far too many dead souls in there."

"It is the most haunted arbor in all of Ardura," said James. His dad had told him that some folk lost their souls when they stayed in the Wick too long. James couldn't understand why until he travelled through the Wick. James and his mom had decided last minute they would go watch Dad perform in the stone toss at the Fell of autumn festival in Dawning. James and his mom had felt the haunting the moment they walked into the Wick. The dead souls coated every surface of the arbor like snow, marching and humming their old, melancholy songs. So many dead that James couldn't even imagine that many people living. They haunted the Wick.

"It's miles out of our way, man..." said Eurick.

Adeqor tightened his grip on Eurick's shoulder.

"Hey, man! You unhand me!"

"We *will* walk in the moonlight, and you will lead us because that is what I've hired you to do, transporter." Adeqor leaned in. "A transporter always delivers, no? Maybe I should have sent an eagle to the Guild for a replacement."

The wizard held Eurick's eyes with his. A dank stump was no place for anyone to have their last breath, and James would have prayed to the Owl that Eurick had the wisdom not to challenge the wizard any further, but James prayed to no gods—not anymore.

Eurick cracked a smile and chuckled. "Right. A raven always delivers. I'm the only living member of the Guild to have never failed a job, you know? That streak is all I've got left." He looked at James through the darkness, and James understood what he was saying. *The wizard's fucking trapped us.*

In the moonlight, Adeqor's pointed beard and dark skin had an eerie glow. He turned around and beckoned them to come out of the stump.

Eurick led. He carried the canvas sack that he had acquired from Adeqor over his shoulder. It jangled as they moved along. He cycled through the old worn maps Adeqor had given him. Held them up to the moon and tilted them at all angles.

Does he fancy to read those in the dark?

"No raven wrote these maps. Let me tell you. No structure to it at all. Thank the gods I'm pretty sure I know the way to the shrine by heart."

"By heart? You've been before?" asked James.

"Oh, no. Only ever dreamed of going there, man. *Always* dreamed of it, actually. When I got the call for this job, I could hardly believe my ears. It's damn near a dream come true."

"What has stopped you from going? Can't a map take you anywhere? That is their magics, isn't it?"

Eurick laughed. "A map can take you anywhere, man, but a raven can only fly where the job takes them. Always back to the nest when the job's done. Always."

It seemed mad to James, but he nodded along anyway. The cool night air felt good. It made him think of his twilight walks with Maggie. The songs she sang to the moon and the stars, and how she made them dance for her. Maggie had told him that the wind and fire called her name, that the rain told her the secrets of the clouds and the earth whispered to her the rhythms of the seasons. She always told him they were eating her up. Like some kind of monster. They had that in common. For so many years, he took those nights for granted. Like so many other things that meant something to him, they were gone now, and all James could do was carry on. Maggie would want him to carry on, to bring Mal Hallow back its freedom. To give peace to the people he should be protecting.

James couldn't call Mal Hallow his home anymore. Not after how long he'd been gone. When he was a boy, it never felt like home, either. All he could remember was the fighting. He was only fifteen when the Ayelish came, and they had to leave his first home near Oster. His mom promised him that when the wars were over, they could go back, but the Ayelish burned that hamlet. When James and his mom finally returned, it was only to a pile of charred logs and burnt memories. He was seventeen when his dad rose up and united the Hallow to face the Ayelish at Tusk. They slaughtered entire legions of Ayelish soldiers that tried to conquer Mal Hallow. The brown bull moose stitched on a yellow flag was waving above them. The arms of Mal Hallow.

But the Ayelish were too many. They attacked too often and from too many angles, and soon they defeated the Hallow knights and conquered Mal Hallow. In the dark of his mind or staring back at him from a shadowy corner, James still saw the eyes of some of the folk the wars made him kill. Many of the kings and queens who called James's dad a friend bowed down to Calen Alder in exchange for their lives. They burned their own flags and raised the red eagle of Ayeland. Before long, the army of the Bull Moose had dwindled to less than a hundred. King Culdaine was forced to abandon his kingdom and run north and west towards the Fell Mountains. He brought his family and every person who still followed him. But they didn't make it past the Old Arbor. Not one of them lived.

Except you.

No—James had no home. Nothing good came out of getting too comfortable at a place. Home for James was never just the bed he was sleeping in. It wasn't the smell of pinewood or maple sap. The word always seemed like a strange one to James. *Home.* All he ever did was move from one home to the next after his dad started fighting. Wulfee talked about home like it was the final destination. The place you could go to and die when you're old, grey, and less vengeful. According to that, the only place he'd ever felt anything like home was in Maggie's arms. In life or death, she was all that held him together. Their love would hold when nothing else would, Maggie told him. He had nothing else now.

"Been awhile since you been back, eh?" said Eurick.

"Ten years," said James. "Told myself I'd never come back. But here I am."

"I know people, and I know places… but you, I just can't figure out," said Eurick. "What happened to you? What happened *here* when the Ayelish conquered?" James looked at him silently for a moment. He hadn't told anyone about what happened in the wars—but Eurick was easy to talk to.

"My dad led our kingdom to their deaths and refused to surrender. His men abandoned him when it looked like there was no way to win. He took me and my mom, and what soldiers would come with us, then marched north to hide in the mountains. One last go at keeping the Mal alive."

"I know the story doesn't end there, man," Eurick murmured. "Do you remember?"

James laughed. *Remember?* He could never forget.

"The Banshee and Alder caught up. They caught up and butchered us—them. I woke up alone. Alive. The only one. I was cut up and covered in blood but alive. The snow around me was pink, and everyone I had ever known lay gutted and dismembered all around me. Mom and Dad died side by side."

Eurick gasped.

"By the gods, man," he said. "But you live?"

"A kihl'dor named Wulfee and her clan found me the very next morning after Haro and his band left me to die. The Feldarra. They saved my life. I never left her side until the Hawka came down." James looked down. He thought of Maggie and felt like shite for leaving her. He'd get to her again. Nothing would stop him but death.

But I have to do this thing, Maggie. I need to do one thing right in my life. I have to bring the fires back. I have to. Whatever it takes. My parents fought and died for this country. They believed I could help. Everyone put hope in me, and I failed them. All of them… James could practically feel Maggie's breath in his ear. *Vengeance is a silly thing with no end to it. Just let it go, James.* The smell of her hair, peonies, and honey lingered in his memory. *Why then?* He remembered asking her. *Why should I go on, if not for vengeance?* Her voice was calm. *"Go on for me. For the stars. Do the right thing because it's right, not because it settles something."*

The right thing was to be the king his parents so desperately wanted him to be. He could make the death of his family mean something. He could resurrect his dead country from the ashes and bring the world back to life with fire and wind. Let the earth feast, and the skies cry. So, James kept moving, he felt the muscles in his legs burning—the good burn that strengthened a person. He'd been feeling like he was getting weaker the past few days, cramped up in a wizard's cave. One foot in front of the other, James followed in his torn-up boots. They were the same ones that his mom had made for him. He couldn't ever bring himself to part with them. And it felt like his mom—like Nara of Oster—was still with him with every step he took.

CRICKETS AND CICADAS BUZZED, and burn bugs lit up the sky in fiery speckles. James wondered what kind of magic the burn bugs were storing in those little arses that made them spark up. Small twigs cracked underfoot of small critters, and the arbor itself seemed to vibrate under the yellow, chunky moon.

"Welcome home, Culdaine. Welcome back to Mal Hallow," said Adeqor.

James spat. "I have no home."

The Old Arbor thinned out into a valley in which a large river cut through the landscape. The water rushed down from the hills in a glistening flow of ice blue that disappeared somewhere into the night. Even in the open valley, there was no wind.

"The Scar River, the locals call it," Eurick said. "Merges with the White somewhere further down the valley. You know, there's a funny—"

"If I wanted a dialogue on this journey, transporter, I would have sent an eagle out for a bard, or a poet," Adeqor said. "I have no interest in what you have to say. Get us to the Wick."

James didn't mind much either way. He'd become used to Eurick's chatty voice by now.

They walked through most of the night before Adeqor halted them.

"Get me my wine, transporter," Adeqor said with his voice raised. Eurick scoffed and pulled out a wineskin. The wizard snatched it out of his hands before Eurick could hand it to him. "No one makes wine like they used to. It's a damn shame." He took a long, gulping pull off of the wineskin.

Then Eurick produced a hard chunk of white, crumbly cheese from the sack that they then split up and ate. James hadn't had something so rich in flavour since Wulfee's fermented goat's milk.

"What else you got in there?" asked James, nodding to the sack. Eurick used his big boot to pull it closer to him.

"Supplies. The only family a transporter has is their supplies, man. I ain't gonna lose 'em again. Not often in life you get a second chance, you know?" he said. James just nodded. Then his bowels growled. James looked around for a spot to be alone for a moment.

"Gonna take a shit," he said, and walked off toward the tree.

"Better bury it," said Eurick. James soured his face.

"Eh?"

"Bury it. Don't need to give the Hawka any help in tracking us," said Adeqor, more sternly. James shook his head in disbelief. His mouth hung open as he walked behind the tree and squatted. *Burying my shit now.*

When James returned, Eurick handed him a bottle with fruitwine in it. Adeqor was already hammered drunk. Pacing back and forth, looking out into the darkness.

"Forgiveness has given me nothing but pain," Adeqor said to the black night. "And if I get my revenge after all... what then? I always get the last laugh, and now I have no one left to laugh with. Only you, Ellorin. Only you. But you don't seem to be laughing any longer."

A tormented squeal arose in the distance and grasped everyone's attention. All three of their heads turned to look at the moonlit valley behind them. James held a mouthful of fruitwine, stiff with shock at what he was seeing. A single veiled shadow walked along the riverbank. It spewed its fetid sound through the darkness and shook the very ground. Behind her, a sea of droning Hawka marched like prisoners.

Holy fuck.

THE EYE OF OLAN

THE TOWN OF TUSK groaned as Wulfee moved through it. She reckoned few of this lot had ever felt hunger like this, and for the few who slept, far more laid awake in pain. They'd had long winters before, and times had been bleak. But they could, at least, hunt and cook meat. They could eat the horses, rats, and squirrels in soups and stews—or the dead, if nothing else, to get through hungry springs until summer and autumn brought harvest. It all tasted the same when charred up over the flame. *This is a whole new darkness. Literal darkness.* She thought, looking at the lumps of people spread across the dark streets.

The Ranger sat out in front of the stable on an overturned trough, chewing sweetbud loudly. He spat it out in a wet green wad as Wulfee walked up to him.

"Back to see me so soon? I'd almost think you missed me if you didn't look so pissed off." His lips and mouth were stained dark green, almost black from the bud.

"We found out that the Wolf is a brigand lord of the north. He's leading a pack of mercenaries hired by the King of Ayeland. Rumours are that they're re-conquering the Hallow from any lord who served Culdaine in the wars. Alder believes there are more like Baleth, who still believe themselves kings."

"The Clan of the Severed Head. I've heard," said Haro. "So you need a closer look? See if you can spot the bastard mulling about? Maybe some emblem or something that you can identify?"

"His mask. It's the only one I've seen like it," said Wulfee. "And he flies a peculiar banner. The twisted black wolf he took the mask from."

Haro reached into his canvas sack and tossed a small steel ring to Wulfee. She snatched it mid-air.

"The fuck is this?" Wulfee said, eyeing the green glass in its centre.

"The eye of Olan. Look through that, and you can see for miles. We only need to ride to the ridge a quarter mile from here, and we'll be able to see anything going on at the Wolf's camp. I mean, I could fly down there for you, but it's your eyes we need, not mine." Wulfee held it to her eye, but her vision became blurry. "It only works in open spaces." The Ranger snatched the eye back and tucked it in his pocket.

"Where'd you get that?" said Wulfee. She'd never seen treasures like that up close. They only existed in wild tales told by drunken clansfolk.

"From a necromancer I met on the roads once," said Haro. "The old fool tried to revive bones with words, a little dance, and a pitch fire. But he fed me with a strange insistence that the dried meat wasn't Human and let me sleep by his fire, so I listened to his tales, however tall. *He* told me that Olan was a cyclops who used to rule over Mal Hallow in the old times. The cyclops were thrice the size of Giy'er, though only half as vicious. But when the first Druids were born from the nytewoods, they decided cyclops were too hard to live with. Olan was a king of sorts. He had mammoths for pets and gods as mistresses. An old wise one of the Mal plucked the fellow's eye out and made this."

"It's just an old story. There is no way that's an actual eye," said Wulfee, climbing onto the horse Haro had picked for her.

"It's magic. A story to make sense of it. Whatever truth is in it doesn't mean much, really, because it *is* filled with magics, ain't it?" said Haro. "You can see farther with this than your own eyes." Wulfee supposed that was true. She lived in a world full of things she didn't understand, made in a time long gone. Magics, they called it. It was just another way of saying, "I don't fucking know."

"So how'd you get it from the necromancer?" Wulfee asked, though she already knew.

"Necromancers have a way of finding death."

They rode back through the town of Tusk to the west gates in silence.

"The nights have been long. Black as pitch and cold," Haro said as they passed a tumbledown blacksmith. A man poking at a dead forge flashed Wulfee a cadaverous smile that made her skin shake. *Was his mouth filled with worms? No... no you're going mad.* "Every morning they find more dead."

"Starving?" asked Wulfee.

"Most likely," Haro said. "Some people I spoke to came from as far north as Fever. Many seem to be giving up at this point. The choices here are to starve to death or to face the Wolf's army and have your head impaled on a spike. You sure this bastard's worth all this? You could just ride off right now. Start a new life somewhere."

"The Feldarra believe that their soul can't rest easy if vengeance has stained their heart," said Wulfee.

"Vengeance!" Haro stood up in his saddle. "So the stories of the Feldarra are true. Bloodthirsty warriors, the lot of you, eh?"

"I'm just tryin' to rest easy, and one day, no matter what happens out here, I'll see my boys again, above."

"A bastard wronged me, too. Took my son from me in the war against the Ayelish ten years past. I wasn't even running a band then. I was just trying to live with my family in peace. It was the red eagles he shoulda been killing, not innocents caught up in it all. The bastard went mad and cut down everyone in his path, *everyone*. Unfortunately for me, his path went right through our hamlet. Couldn't believe it when I saw him wandering north. Thought I had my chance to get back at him. But then the Hawka came. And in the end, he left *me* to die with this busted leg," Haro said, gestured at his mangled knee. "I crawled all the way to Shaqqa's in spite of him. I remembered what that bastard took from me. My son's smile and his laugh. The warmth of him on my chest as I held him. And I crawled through the dirt, gritting my teeth, thinking of the day I'll get my revenge. Things need to be set right. So, you see? We're both out for vengeance, Wulfee, and if it's all we've got left, let's go get it together, eh? I help you now, you help me later."

She still didn't trust the bastard, but she needed all the help she could get right now. They rode out into the dark valley beyond Tusk, towards the roaring White River.

HARO LED THEM TO a prominent ridge overlooking the southern valley beyond Tusk and Mammoth's Head, on the other side of the river. They arrived with plenty of time before sunrise. Wulfee puffed out her cheeks. She was going to have to talk to Haro until the sun came up. When she dismounted and looked out over the dark valley, she decided she'd rather sleep.

"What, you taking a nap?" said Haro, petting the mare on the back of the neck.

"Planned on it," she said, turning her back to him. "Wake me when we can see."

"Don't you know the northern saying? Don't fall asleep first around someone you just met?" said Haro.

"I'm just resting my eyes. I ain't been into talking much lately."

Some time passed, and then Haro said, "You loved this man once."

Wulfee sat up. "What did you say?" But the memories had already filled her head with song. The taste of his wet lips, his fingertips tracing her body, Braden's broken face, bleeding, crying. She was a damned fool, and she wanted to knock the shit out of her old self for believing in him.

"Love," Haro said. "This man you're after."

Wulfee looked away.

"You're wrong."

The Ranger laughed.

"There are three types of hate, Wulfee, and I know them all well. The first is the primal hate you see in a person's eyes when you're trying to kill each other. That's raw, unfiltered hate taking only the immediate present into account." He paused and allowed the cicadas to fill the silence.

"The second," he said, smiling, "is the kind bred from the great pain caused by someone who wronged you. That pain goes deep. So deep it's in your veins, flowing through you. And then there is dead love. The hate that grows from the corpse of something that was once beautiful and full of life. And that third kind, Wulfee, that's what I see in your eyes when you talk of vengeance."

A hundred things came to the tip of Wulfee's tongue before she chomped them off and swallowed them. *Who the fuck are you to imply that? What do you know of me, you body snatching bastard?* But she knew in her heart that she was only so angry because Haro was right. She loved the hell out of Sweyne once. He was the father of her children. It wasn't always madness. There were many good years, too.

"He became a mad bastard," Wulfee admitted. "Shattered me into a hundred-hundred pieces that I'm still picking up. He killed my son, Tarek."

But that was a lie, too. Tarek got himself killed. He was too much like his dad.

"Killed him? Gods, Wulfee. I didn't know. It hurts, I know."

"I could have saved him." Another thing she'd never said out loud. *Why are you saying so much to this... to this bodysnatcher.* But she'd opened a dam in her heart, and the water came rushing out of her. She couldn't stop it. "I could have stopped Tarek that day. I could have, but I didn't. He was so excited to ride under the wolf banners. He looked up to his dad and admired that wolf armour so much. I couldn't break his heart. Everyone in the Fells feared Sweyne. With his waraxe and that abnormal wolf's mask. It would have been another easy battle for him. But he dressed Tarek up in his wolf armour and sent him to fight in his place instead. The boy was only thirteen. Sweyne said that he'd won his first single combat at that age, and he wanted Tarek to prove himself." Wulfee felt the tears welling up in her eyes. She took a deep breath. "I didn't know it was going to be the last time I saw him. I would have said more..."

"We never know when it's the last time," said Haro. "Rumour in Tusk was that the Wolf is offering food and shelter to anyone willing to fight for his cause. They say he has fire. Does that sound like this madman?"

"Sounds like a lie he'd tell to convince people to kill for him," said Wulfee.

"They said it was three weeks before Claydon finally closed the gates to stop his people from joining the Wolf. Swarms of people and nearly five hundred of Claydon's blooded folk left with this Wolf, too. Claydon just let them go."

"So what chance does Claydon have to hold Mammoth's Head?" said Wulfee.

"We'll have a better idea soon enough. Something has happened in the mountains beyond Kallahorn." Haro twisted the blade in his hands. "The Hawka have never swarmed in those numbers. Something dark is leading them. Something dark is leading this brigand, and the Ayelish king, too. The wars to come will decide the fate of these lands."

Wulfee laughed dryly. "What good is land without peace, eh? When I was a girl, I knelt before the nihr'el and swore oaths to protect these lands from invaders. Oaths that meant something to my mom and dad and all of my ancestors. But somewhere, in my forty something years, they stopped meaning anything to me. It only matters that Sweyne dies. And I wanna look him in the eyes and do it myself. So he knows who killed him. So the gods know my vengeance is satisfied. If this brigand called the Wolf isn't Sweyne, then I will keep hunting him. I'll hunt him until one of us dies."

"That's the Feldarra spirit I've heard about," said Haro. "We just might be okay."

"We're far from okay," said Wulfee. "Look around. We're fucked."

T HE SUN ROSE AS a golden smudge in the pink morning sky. It was the eve of the full moon, and the souls of the dead would not be resting easy today. An army was already in marching formation across the river. Wulfee held the small steel ring up to her eye and saw the Wolf's camp as if it were a stone's throw from her. The red eagle banner was everywhere, but Wulfee saw another flag hanging limply between them—a black wolf on a midnight blue field. Sweyne's own banner. It was an ill omen to fly the wolf in these parts. Everyone knew it. The black wolf meant only one thing in the north: death. The stories said that the dead souls didn't like the beast, and the folk of the Hallow liked it less. Gods and demons cursed it alike. Wulfee knew that Sweyne was the only bastard with a big enough head to hang those wretched banners. No one had flown the wolf into battle in centuries. That was his insatiable appetite for glory on full display. Large wooden carvings of howling wolves were lined up in front of the main pavilion to form a walkway. Heads on spikes gated the entire perimeter of the camp. There was a field of tents like Wulfee had never seen before. Ranks of mercenaries from Mal Hallow and the Glenn were ready to fight against their own people at a moment's notice. The rumours, it seemed, were false. There was no fire here. But it didn't matter much. The blooded men and women that had sworn themselves to Claydon Coldfoot had gathered *here*.

Wulfee saw hundreds of them flying their own white flags, stained with their bloody handprint. A person became blooded only when they drank from their opponent's severed neck. To be blooded meant that you tasted death and spit it back out again. Each of them was proven in combat. Each of them was a cold killer. All considered lords in their own right. Derudin Deadmaker of Ockam used only blooded folk in his army, and it gave him a certain reputation of being extra bloody. Sweyne had no problem convincing folk there would be blood. He could rile up most folk to join his side. Wulfee had fallen victim to his charm herself. Wulfee couldn't help but to be impressed with this assembly. *It's bigger than anything we had ever dreamed of. An army big enough to flood the world.* She felt something brewing in her chest and stomach. Something like heartache or hatred, she reckoned. The bastard had given her plenty of that. The army was out on full display for Claydon to see, and it seemed they were getting ready to march.

Then she saw something else. She focused the eye on it. *Is that...* It looked to Wulfee like a cage. But it was far too big to be a cage. Then something moved inside of it. *It is a bloody cage... It's the size of a small castle.*

"These bastards are going to destroy everything," said Wulfee. She handed the Eye to Haro.

He looked out at the camp. "It's all gone to shit, eh?"

"Aye," said Wulfee.

"I can wait for you at the old standing stones on the hill of Tell, outside of Tusk, with the horses," said Haro. "I can wait two more days, but no more."

Wulfee nodded.

As they rode back towards Tusk, Wulfee could only think about what the fuck Sweyne put in that cage.

THE FEVER STONES

T HE BANSHEE'S WAIL ECHOED through the darkness, piercing James's soul.

"It feels like the nights are getting longer," Eurick remarked as he led them through the darkness. James agreed with him. He hadn't ever gone this long without sleep.

For two days and three nights, Eurick led them through the rocky crags of Mal Hallow from one broken and abandoned tower to the next. Crumbled stoneworks left behind by Mal rulers long gone. When they crossed the White River, James nearly slipped on a rock with his old boots and got swept away by the current. They shared chunks of crumbly white cheese and hard strips of salted mutton as they walked. They stopped only briefly to relieve bowels or bladder and always buried the remains. Adeqor became increasingly irritable towards Eurick, and James made a point not to talk much or get involved.

They came to the top of one of the many crags that looked out at the valley below. James almost shat himself at the sight of what was there. Massive grey stones stacked on each other like doorways, erected side by side in perfect concentric circles. One larger ring of stone surrounded a smaller one with an open space in the centre. It wasn't the first time he'd seen Standing Stones; he'd spotted them all throughout the north, but they still took his breath away. To one side of the structure was a small village with people mulling about. An old nytewood grew out of the middle, black and golden in full bloom, and blanketed the Stones and the village in its shadow.

"The Fever Stones," said Adeqor. "Aren't they something?" He slapped Eurick on the back. "Go ahead, raven, tell the legend of the Stones."

"Well, okay. Haven't heard that song in a while, but—" Eurick cleared his throat. "The Mal Druids of ancient times built the Stones with the magics they stole from Yehven. The Hallow kings and queens that ruled back then, before the Starfall, came here for a sacred ritual. Shamans sacrificed their lifeblood to the earth, and their souls transferred into the rock for eternity with the magics. The Daggland kings and queens later took up the same ritual using these same stones. On one day every year, the ice star and the moon align with this structure, and the Mal celebrate it. On that day, those who were sacrificed could talk to their predecessors. They could watch their families grow, generation after generation, and gather at these stones to be together."

Eurick took a deep breath. "They are always waiting for the day they would be called back by the gods to defend the Hallow. One final time."

"This was a sacred place once," added Adeqor.

"And now?" asked James. He looked down at the village of greying wood huts roofed with mouldy thatch that seemed to grow on the side of the ancient structure like a wart.

"Not so much," said Adeqor.

They walked down the crag and into the village. Stones were tipped over or chipped away, and almost every bit of them seemed to be covered in old runes that differed from the ones carved into *Essikah*. The dead souls—mostly old men and women, though James did see a few children—were everywhere. Thick black armour wrapped around their frail, bony bodies, and a scowl hung on their face.

The ghosts all had long, braided hair with dozens of knots in it. Every one of them had the same wound, a clean slit across their throats. The death of blood sacrifice. They sulked around the massive stones as if time had chained them there. James figured that whatever magics the ancient Mal Druids did here had worked. These were old souls. Their cold moonsmoke bodies were like an icy hug as he walked through them. They weren't there physically, but James could feel a heavy presence, as if there was more *life* left in them.

"They held onto their memories," said Adeqor. "Not just the faces of their families, but the faces of their enemies. Some of these souls, after living thousands of years with their hatred, are driven to find the descendants of their foes."

As the three of them approached, a few of the locals from the village whispered amongst each other, pointing dirty fingers at them as if they were the reason the fires wouldn't burn. One woman stepped forward. She was round-faced and wide hipped; she reminded James of Wulfee with her tenacity as she held her hand up and bellowed, "Name yourselves, *you fuckers*!"

James heard bowstrings stretch from somewhere he couldn't see.

"Heyo, hi," Eurick grinned, holding his arms up. "Nothing to worry about, here. We're peaceful nomads. We come from the high hills looking for other survivors."

The woman's face twisted.

"Bloody big sword for a nomad..." she spat. "The survivors are headed south, to Tusk. Folk that are passing through are saying the Ayelish are sending an army north to root out any rebellions that may have formed since the fires went out."

"Seems like they're doing a lot more than just rooting out rebellions," added a grizzly-looking man.

"They're slaughtering the whole damned country," said a comely lady who looked like she didn't quite belong amongst this lot. "In the name of their god Eralis."

"We're only looking—"

"There ain't no food for ya here," the round-faced woman barked. "No shelter, either. Best be going back to where ya come from or get moving on through to someplace else."

A man holding a blacksmith's hammer shook his head in agreement behind her. The other villagers stood in the doorways of their mud and worn wood huts, watching. Their faces were dirty, hands and knees covered in dried mud. A deer carcass sat by a dead firepit, and James felt sick at the pure lowness of it. There was no rot. Still, the flies hovered over their plunder with a piercing buzz, eating fresh meat, and left the earth empty.

James said, "We're seeking a place to make a stand against the mutts for a day. So we can alternate rest, get our strength back. They'll be on us in hours."

"I said you can't stay here," the round-faced woman scowled.

Adeqor laughed.

"I'm sorry, my friend here says it as if we're asking." It happened in a heartbeat, the wizard moved faster than a fox and grabbed her by the neck. She gasped. Choked as her face turned red.

"Get your hand off her!" James pushed Adeqor's forearm. The woman fell to her knees, wheezing. Arrows landed in the dirt around them as the villagers screamed. Adeqor exhaled slowly and held James with a repugnant glare—and suddenly Adeqor was looking *into* him.

"Stop that!" James screamed when he felt Adeqor touch his soul. Eurick's face had turned as ashen as the villagers. Adeqor pursed his lips. Closed his eyes slowly, took a deep breath, and opened them again. Then, threw his arms outwards at the round-faced woman and the man holding the hammer who had helped her stand.

A strange wind came out of his hands that flickered madly through the air in a twist of bright colours. It crushed everything in its way, the mud huts, the pack animals, the villagers, turning them into a mushy bog, staining the ground with blood. Debris fell on two people standing in the door, crushing them.

James thought he might be hallucinating—he hadn't slept in days. An arrow nicked his leg and knocked him out of it. He had to move—he wasn't going to die here. *Adeqor.* It only vaguely occurred to him as he dove behind one of the massive stones that it was Adeqor causing this. The person who would have James believe he was helping the world.

An arrow sent chips of rock soaring as it nicked the side of the stone James hid behind. Adeqor loosed his magics again and again. The men and women stood up to him with rusted rakes and short knives, firing wayward arrows.

Stop this, you fuck! James wanted to say—but he wasn't as brave as them. *Who the fuck is he really...*

The colourful wind crushed them into bloody mire, just like the others. Adeqor felled three fir trees in one of his attacks, and they hit the ground like roaring thunder cracking the earth in two. James felt a sickness boiling in his stomach. *Do something.* But all he could do was watch wide-eyed as Adeqor carried out the slaughter. *What the fuck is this?* The wizard could not be stopped. Wulfee may have done something in a situation like this, but James wasn't about to budge an inch to throw himself in the way of whatever that was. Eurick's jaw was hanging, his eyes wide. He mouthed the words: *"what the fuck, man?"* and leaned back against the stone to hide. Two Hallow queens sat between them. One was sharpening a sword, and the other was on her knees praying to the skies. They carried on as if nothing in the living world could bother them.

Adeqor's barefeet slapped the dry dirt as he walked back towards James and Eurick, and James was reminded of when Alder had trapped his family in the arbor. There was nowhere left to run. *And you have nowhere to run now, either.* The villagers fled in every direction. They carried small sacks on sticks, bowls, and buckets full of whatever food they had accumulat-ed, with young ones strewn over their shoulders. One of them, however, dragged himself through the dirt with his elbows. Pulling himself towards Adeqor like he was going to be the one to stop him.

"Let them leave. Don't hurt anymore," the man choked out. "Take what you want but let them leave."

Adeqor stood over the man and stopped his crawling with a barefoot on his forehead.

"I want *you*," said Adeqor. "Now kneel." The man whimpered, pulling himself to his knees. Adeqor grabbed the man hard by his temples and squeezed. The man squirmed, tried to force the wizard's hands off, but couldn't budge them. "I can still feel the Ways," Adeqor whispered, smiling, then opened his mouth wide as the villager writhed and screamed, his eyes rolling back.

Out of his mouth, his nose, his ears, came a blue smoke. Adeqor inhaled it with a smile. The man's face was sunken in and void of expression. Adeqor let go of him, and his body fell to the ground, bones clattering on the ground under the weight of dead skin. The wizard glowed. His beard was sharp and as black as Daggland steel. His skin shone like a river in the twilight. His eyes met James's, then slid off of him like water on a duck and found Eurick. Then he walked towards them. James came out to meet the wizard, and so did Eurick. *Essikah* felt heavy and useless in his hands. It would be no use against this wizard. *What are you doing?* He didn't know, but his legs carried him towards Adeqor while his mind shouted at him to *run.*

"The fuck was that?" James asked.

"I ate his soul," the wizard smiled, admiring his nails.

Ate it...?

"Wha... why'd you do that? Are you fucking mad?" said James. Eurick nudged James with his elbow.

"They cannot slow us down," said Adeqor. "These folk were unpredictable. Paranoid and desperate. They may have killed us in our sleep if they ended up letting us stay. Poisoned any food they sent us with. These are dark times. We don't have time for gentle negotiations."

And now there will be more orphans in the world because of you. More folk of the Hallow living without ai'mair darra; alone. But James said none of this. He was no hero.

"Oh, and Culdaine," Adeqor said. "Don't you ever lay a hand on me again."

You shouldn't have gotten involved in this. You should have killed Eurick in that cave and found Maggie. Now what choice do you have but to follow this mad man? You're a damn fool, James. A god damned fool. "Yea... I won't."

And as the sun set, Ellorin wailed the Banshee's death song behind them.

"Can you pull those magics on her?" said James.

"Maybe, but I don't want to risk my life for a maybe," Adeqor said. "Those magics only work with surety on the weakened. If I wanted to fight Ellorin to the death, I would have done it a long time ago. There is no way for us to know how much power the Words have at this point. The risk is too great."

Hundreds of Hallow kings and queens poured out of the inner circle of the Stones and gathered around James. Their cold, dead eyes studied him respectfully, as if measuring his worth. One by one, they poured out from between the stones. Scarred with the memory of their deaths and broken by too many years forgotten. *"Help us. Help. Save us. Help."* They called out to James. They were a hundred-hundred lives torn from the earth and left behind, and the weight of their pain upon James's shoulders was too much for him. Hundreds of voices, all at once, from all around him, screaming at him, crying out. *"Help us out of here. Please. Please, help us home."* James fell to his knees and covered his ears with his palms.

"It's okay, Culdaine," Adeqor said, as if he knew what was happening. "Let the dead come awake."

And they did. Hundreds more of the Hallow rulers of old walked out of the Stones like they were a doorway. And they kept coming, singing their songs and chanting loudly.

"The mutts will avoid them with all of their strength," said Adeqor. "Some of the long dead souls try to take the Hawka's bodies over because they have less resistance than Humans. It's quite disturbing. They're like parasites. Once they infect a host, they drive them into madness, so the poor victim takes their own life and finally sets the soul free. The Hawka have a crippling fear of them. Some mutts you see may actually have the soul of a dead person inside of them."

James shivered at that thought.

Eurick threw his hands up. "You're right mad, you know that? You think this is any way to be? Killing innocents and what not? It ain't right, man. This isn't how a job is supposed to go!" For a moment James feared that Eurick had said too much. And by the way the raven stroked his beard repeatedly, James figured Eurick was probably thinking the same thing.

"I would kill every person in Ardura to make sure the World Walker gets safely to the Mother's shrine," Adeqor said quietly. "You do not know what darkness is coming. You're oblivious to the power of the song that closed the Gateway. The Ailaryan Order has ruled over the world since we crawled out of the dust left by the Starfall. And I ruled over all of them before they cast me out. So, don't either of you question me about things you know nothing of."

Eurick narrowed his eyes. "It just ain't right."

"Nothing is." Adeqor traced his hands over the deep runes. "You'll learn that. It's all right fucked, actually." He went from one stone to the next, towards the towering nytewood in the centre. "Nothing we do makes it any other way. Hope is worthless, and so is goodwill. Only those who fight for what they want will make it in this world. And all the rest just live with the scars they leave us."

James couldn't disagree. The souls hummed as Adeqor studied the runes.

"This is a Druid necropolis," Adeqor said. "One of the few places where the old magics still exist openly in our world." He continued to trace the runes on different stones, looking for something. "The Mal Druids of old were taught the dark words of Yehven when the first Warlocks came to these lands. When the Druids sang them here, they left the memory of those words deep in the souls of the dead who were sacrificed." The wizard pressed his ear to one of the Stones. "I can *hear* the songs of Yehven. I can almost *taste* the words." He pulled away and licked his lips. It was as if he was trying to say something but couldn't.

The runes etched into the greatsword *Essikah* lit up in a soft crimson glow. The Fever Stones did the same. And suddenly, *Essikah* was as light as bone. Hundreds of runes and patterns of an ancient language lit up and then faded. Disappeared like a wizard's trick. James felt a strange power flowing into him from *Essikah. Or was it flowing out of him?* The sword was pulling energy from the souls of the dead.

"It's responding to you," Adeqor said, looking at *Essikah*. "We should go." His breath steamed in the sudden cold air. He sauntered away from the Fever Stones, towards the dead village and the road beyond it. James and Eurick put a fist under their chin and nodded to each other—the old northern sign for luck. There was no arguing with the wizard.

James hoisted *Essikah* over his shoulder, heavy again as the souls left him, and followed Adeqor as fast as he could. Behind them, the Banshee's death song got louder.

THAT OLD THING CALLED HOPE

T HE TOWN OF TUSK was alive as Wulfee returned through the old stone gates. Townsfolk rushed around, carrying armfuls of weapons tucked under their armpits. People carrying buckets of water, oil, or pieces of armour. Horns sounded from every direction, and Wulfee was having a hard time finding her bearings.

The bleating of it brought her back to the battlefield, the black walls of Kallahorn looming over her. Dead and dying, crying out. Her blood and gore covered hands clenched so tightly to her axe she reckoned she'd crack the handle. Half of Sweyne's army left him to join her. Then they had to turn around and fight the half that stayed. It was her own people she murdered that day. Hundreds of faces she had known for years and years turned into enemies overnight.

The horns sounded again and snapped her out of it. The horns did something to her she couldn't control. Dug into her like parasites and left her helpless. Her underself knew as much. Wulfee asked her how to make it stop, but the bitch never gave her any answers. *Everyone wants answers.* She reckoned that everyone was gonna get answers one way or another. She shouldered her way through the busy roads and headed for Tanner's Alley to find Pike.

BA-DAAAA. A horn blew a few inches from Wulfee's ear.

"Gods!" she screamed, shouldering past a cluster of would-be soldiers holding farm tools upside down. As she turned the corner to Tanner's Alley, she had to pinch her nose shut. *They ought to tan hides somewhere far off outside of town.* Gen saw her almost immediately. He was beaming with excitement and came running over. A running Giy'er was close kin to a boulder rolling down a mountainside. The ground shook beneath the weight of each step. People tried their best to make way, but one man got caught underneath his massive strides, and the Giy'er trampled him into the ground, cracking his skull, his spine, his body. Gen didn't even realize what he had done and crushed another. A violently loud snap came from below Gen's big feet as the second man broke.

"Gen!" Wulfee screamed. "For fuck's sake!"

"What'd you bring back, Wulf?" Gen grinned.

Two men laid on the ground, twisted into a jagged mess, blood seeped out in a slow, red puddle. Townsfolk rushed to them, and they cried out in horror, pointing at the massive Giy'er that killed them.

"God dammit, Gen," she said under her breath, suppressing the hot rage in her belly.

Gen turned around.

"Are they dead?"

"They're dead, Gen. You killed them." She pushed past him, ignoring his glistening orange eyes. Wulfee felt like complete dog shite for saying it, but what could she do? He needed to know what he did. *But he doesn't even know what he really is, Wulf...*

"Come on now, we're leaving this place." Wulfee stepped over one of the two men still laying on the ground. She heard a wheezy sigh come out of him. The poor bastard was still alive.

"Help him! Somebody help my husband! We were only just heartbound last week. Please, somebody help him." A woman kneeling over the dying man screamed between sobs.

"There is no help for *anyone*," Wulfee said. "Can't you see that?"

Pike sat on a sideways barrel with his knotty shield in front of him, sharpening his axe with a whetstone.

"You really didn't bring me nothing?" Gen asked. "You didn't see a nice flat stone? Or a shiny pebble?"

"I ain't got nothing for you, Gen," Wulfee said.

Gen pouted.

"It's been really *shitty* around here. I'm ready to go back to the mountains."

"We can't go back, Gen, not now. Sometimes you have to do things you don't want to do. We can't always be comfortable," she said. She didn't like being short with him, but she had too many choices to make. Gen didn't say no more.

Pike's eyes met hers as she approached.

"Well?" he said. The old warrior loved him some good old northern gossip.

"Hundreds of blooded folk, maybe more. Another thousand mercenaries just hanging about. Who knows how many Ayelish reinforcements are marching to join him right now. He's flying the Wolf banners, Pike. It's him. It's Sweyne. It has to be."

"So we get ready to fight. Sweyne is marching on Tusk," said Pike. "Doesn't seem like there are too many outstanding fighters around, but we could make do. I've led worse lots into battle, and it ain't the worst way to go out. Fighting and dying for your homeland. For the oaths." There was an awkward screeching, like a dying mouse, as he slid his axe up the whetstone.

"There's no hope of winning here, Pike. The army they have is far too great. The Wolf will keep Claydon bunkered down with steady waves. And they were getting ready to march. They could be here tomorrow if they chose. Let's leave before Claydon loses this castle." The two dead men were being dragged out of the streets by children dressed as soldiers. "It's time to return to Pool. We need the clans of Feldarra on our side if we have any chance to beat him. We need the karls of the Fells."

Gen's eyes flicked wide, and he stared at her curiously. Pike squinted and took a deep breath.

"The clans will live and die by their own swords," he said. "They won't hear what you want to say, Wulfee. They'll have no interest in helping. Odhran won't even speak to you. And you know he will kill me for what he thinks I've done. We can face death *here*. Die on the field of battle. For the oaths."

"Fuck the oaths, Pike," Wulfee sneered. "It's not our time to go yet. Not while Sweyne still breathes. Stay and fight if you need to, but I've got to see this through."

Pike shook his head.

"You've become just as bloodthirsty as him!"

Wulfee opened her mouth and let a few choice words creep up on her tongue. *Fuck you, old man*, seemed a good pairing. But she said nothing for a moment, just glared up at the sun hanging red and bloody in the sky.

"You're right," said Wulfee. "I have. I'm losing my goddamned mind, Pike. All I can do is end him and hope it gets better when it's over."

"You don't have to get revenge, Wulf. You can move on. Nothing's gonna change the past. Killing Sweyne won't make you forget what happened."

"I've failed at everything in life, Pike," Wulfee murmured. "I've failed as a mom, wife, kihl'dor, and I've failed you and many others as a friend." She wiped her eyes with the back of her sleeve—Wulfee didn't even realize she'd been crying. "This is all I've got left. Just this one thing. My revenge on that bastard. I plan to have that one thing. I need to go up to the cloud halls. I need to. It's the only way I can ever see my Tarek again. Maybe I'll find Braden there, too. I just need to find Sweyne. And when I do, I'm going to fucking kill him. Then I'll move on. Then it'll all be right. Then I can die without my soul slipping away."

The old warrior just stared at her, but Wulfee knew that he understood. The deep wrinkles around his eyes seemed to have sunk even deeper in the past weeks. He must have been as worn out as she was, ready for it all to be over.

"I don't know how many battles I've got left in me, Wulfee. I'm ready to see the gods."

"I reckon you've got a few more in you yet," she said, hopeful.

The old warrior frowned.

"Do you not remember what *you* did? Has it been so long already?" His accusing tone took Wulfee back. "How do you think this is going to work for you? Have you truly lost your mind?"

"I know what I bloody did. And I live with that," she said. "And maybe I have lost my bloody mind, but I'm not just going to lie down and die."

"You killed Odhran's family and burned his home," said Pike. "You forced him up into the mountains where he burned the homes of many more looking for you—"

"And now he leads the very clans that used to call me kihl'dor." Wulfee hated the way he was making her sound. She clenched her fists. "The very clans that followed me out of Kallahorn when Sweyne lost his mind. The only people who stayed with me are dead now. All but you, Gen, and Maggie. You don't think I fucking know that, Pike? *Are you serious?*"

"He will keep you alive, Wulfee," said Pike. "He will torture you and make a fool of you. Why in the god's eyes would you think Odhran would hear a word you try to say to him? You think he cares that the world is dying? You think he cares about Sweyne?"

"I think he knows what it's like to lose a child," Wulfee said bluntly. "And I think he wants the bards to be singing his name for hundreds of years to come. I think he wants things to be like the old times, before it all went to shite. That's why he keeps breaking his own damn oaths to settle his clan. The Feldarra don't settle. But the bastard believes in that old thing called hope. He wants something better for his people. *Our* people. And I think that's enough to get him to fight with us."

Pike took a deep breath. He seemed to have given up the argument.

"What if the Hawka got him?"

"You and I both know the Hawka didn't get Odhran Ironfist," said Wulfee.

Pike chuckled.

"You're a stubborn cunt, you know that?"

"You're an old fuckin' wank, you know *that?*" said Wulfee. The two smiled at each other.

She had treated everyone in her life with contempt, like everything was disposable. She did it all, hoping to make things right again. With her sons. With Sweyne and the clans. But life didn't work like that, and a perfect peace ain't achievable in a world like this. She was always chasing a better life. Chasing and never catching up. She had little left to hope for and less to believe in. But she could still save Maggie. She could still save Gen. And she hoped Braden was out there somewhere. She could find Braden again after she killed Sweyne, if she kept hope alive. What little of it she had left was close to her heart, and she'd protect it with her life.

"Let's go get Maggie, and we'll be on our way."

Pike's face turned to one of concern.

"We can't *get* Maggie," he said. "She is being treated. Shaqqa Ro said seven days. You cannot question Shaqqa Ro."

"Then we'll wait for her away from here," said Wulfee. "The Ranger is waiting for us with horses at the Stones nearby. We can use them to get back to the Green Man and wait in the hills for Maggie to return to health. Let's pray to the Swan that the Wolf doesn't blow through this castle and catch up with us."

"Are we going back to the arbor?" said Gen. "I'm ready to go back into the arbor."

"Yes. We're going back," said Wulfee. Gen stood up in excitement, and the surrounding townsfolk cowered in fear. The earth shook as if struck by succeeding thunder bolts when he jumped up and down. Wulfee held her hands up, as if to calm a bucking horse. "Easy, Gen. Don't you remember what happened back there? You'll hurt someone bouncing around like that." He nodded, but she could tell by the look on his face that he didn't remember. "Just sit back down, Gen."

"Can you tell about the—"

BA-DAAAA.

"By the gods!" she yelped at the war horn bleating out a few feet from her.

"To the castle!" shouts echoed. "To the castle!" The townsfolk rushed around with the feel of panic about them.

"Could it be him already?" asked Pike. Wulfee didn't think so. He would have had to have left moments after she and Haro left.

"It's midafternoon. That's not like him," she said. Sweyne always attacked either at dusk or dawn, like a wolf. He loved fighting in the dim light betwixt night and day.

"Maybe he's changed his tactics?" said Pike. Wulfee didn't think so. It didn't matter; she still didn't feel like sticking around in this rotten place to find out. "Let's get out of here."

The three of them headed towards the northern gate of Tusk that led back out to the Northroad. As Wulfee approached, she noticed the massive oak gates sealing shut with a heavy bang. Claydon Coldfoot's men stood in front of it, armed with spears and armoured heavily. The grey mammoth of Tusk was stitched on their green cloaks.

"No one leaves. Now turn around!" a guard shouted.

Another said, "Every person here will fight to defend this castle with their lives, or we'll kill you ourselves. An army is at our doorstep. Can't you bloody well see that? Turn around!"

Wulfee peered at Pike, who was glaring back at her.

Claydon had trapped them. *Well, fuck.*

FOOL'S FIRE

J AMES COULDN'T QUITE SEEM to get warm. He rubbed his hands together as they approached a broken stone tower that would be their shelter for the next few hours.

The structure was jagged rock walls surrounded by crumbled debris of the top half of the tower. They sat in the centre room, which seemed to have been some sort of armoury and mess hall once. Rusty brown racks lined three of the walls, and a cold stone hearth sat dead and empty on the other. A large gnarled trestle table stretched out in front. The dead followed him like a cold shadow into the tower. They came out of the arbors, down from the hills, and off the road. One had a small hatchet wedged into his left ear. Two women brooded around solemnly with twisted necks from a hanging. A group of a dozen or more were burnt to a crisp. They looked at him with blank stares, some without eyeballs. *Help us,* they begged.

"This tower is Lovasi built," Eurick said. "You can tell by the precision with which they cut their bricks." He picked one up. "Look at this. It's not clay brick fired in a kiln or river stones stacked on top of each other and slopped with mortar. This here is solid stone. It's cut and placed so fine they used no mortar. It's incredible, I tell ya. I've travelled to every continent, man. Ardura, Edura, and Sothura. Nothing compares to what the Lovasi Empire left behind."

"Pfft." Adeqor took a drink. "The Lovasi did nothing but steal the secrets of the ancient Yehvenki. If you want to marvel at an ancient society, it should be Yehven. You would resort to bawling if you ever saw the Golden City of Ailar in its prime, before the Starfall. The Lovasi Empire was nothing more than... a failed experiment. Lessons were learned. Many, many people burned."

"The Yehvenki destroyed themselves, man. They took their dark words and magics too far. Entire nations were victim to genocide. They upset the gods, and the gods sent the Abori to bring a star down and humble them." Eurick dropped the brick. "I've heard the legends, man. Straight from the tongues of Abori folk themselves. They poured acid made from basilisk venom down their ears to deafen themselves so they couldn't hear the songs of the Warlocks. The Abori dreameaters gave the Yehvenki nightmares for half a century before they attacked. The Yehvenki had to watch themselves die every night in their dreams, victim to cannibals that came out of the Shaded Arbor, the cannibals' skin inked all over in runes of power, dressed like animals. And when the Abori *did* arrive–"

"*Enough*!" Adeqor shouted.

James braced himself to become a pile of steaming mud in the wake of Adeqor's anger. *He's a madman.*

Adeqor twisted his face into a grin. "It was far more complicated than that, Eurick, fellow, c'mon. There is always a large portion of good in anything bad. The magic Words healed people. Eased the burdens of sickness and exhaustion. War and starvation. It wasn't all bad, you know. It was beautiful, once. Wonderfully, horribly beautiful." The wizard looked up to the sky with admiration. "The power that star brought down killed the gods and left the survivors to find new ones. Only the Words of Karaat remain. His are the Words of power, and in them, He lives on."

"Do you speak them?" said James. Eurick elbowed him. Gave him a worried look, like that wasn't a question he should be asking.

"Huh?"

"The words of Yehven. Do you speak them?" James said. He was always afraid of magics. He became even more afraid when Adeqor grinned with his big white teeth gleaming. An aura flickered around him that James couldn't understand. Adeqor was what James imagined a god might look like. *What are you?*

"Nobody *speaks* them," said Adeqor. "A person can only sing the words of Yehven." He sat up when he noticed James's twitching hands. "But what if I did, boy? Would that worry you?"

"You're going to kill us all when this is over, aren't you?" James touched the hilt of his engagement knife. Part of him wanted to just kill the wizard right now, after what he'd done back at the Stones, but he was terrified of what might happen. And in truth, he was terrified that he still needed him.

Adeqor laughed. "Oh, it will not be me that kills you, Culdaine. And it's not your time for a while yet. You have many horrible, wonderful things to do. I'm certain of that."

James grunted. He felt like a fish on the end of the wizard's hook.

"Oh, relax!" Adeqor clapped James on the back. "For such a big man, you're awfully emotional. I spoke the words once, long ago, but they have since been... taken from me. I've been cursed... outcast by the same people that once looked up to me. The Ailaryan Order left me behind after Lindis. They forgot I even existed as I suffered alone from the pain *they* caused me. Only in the company of nature did I find any solace in the many long years of suffering. That is when I walked in the path of Bazal and decided to fight *against* the Ailaryan Order."

"Somebody had to teach Baleth the songs in the first place, right?" said Eurick. "He was using them for blood magics before Alder and Ellorin ever even got to Kallahorn. So doesn't that mean somebody else is fighting the Ailaryan Order, too?"

Adeqor licked his lips. "Scholars wrote the words of Yehven on countless scrolls that were lost to time. It is entirely plausible that Baleth found one of these scrolls scattered amongst a merchant's wares, and he somehow interpreted it. Then, he taught them to many other people before Alder and Ellorin hung him. This is no mystery, just quite the thorn in my side. The old songs spread like the plague when they are sung. It's one thing to have the words of Yehven in front of you. It's another to *know* them in your mind. They're *alive.* They take over and leap onto the tongues of those they've inflicted by a will of their own. It's not any one person fighting the Ailaryan Order; it's the words. The magics in them don't want to die. It is a war that has been waged for three thousand years."

Adeqor beckoned a wineskin from Eurick. The acidic smell of Adeqor's drink made James's head spin. The three of them sat in silence for a moment before leaving the broken tower and carrying on their way towards the Wick.

"**T**HIS... AIN'T RIGHT. IT'S not how it's supposed to be." Eurick held his ragged map to the sun. "I'm not supposed to be carrying around a sack of wineskins, and I'm not supposed to be using these less than mediocre maps. A failed job would be the end of me."

"You could leave when the job's through." James looked out over the craggy valley that stood between them and the Wick. He figured it wouldn't be too hard for a person to get lost somewhere in this country. *Unless it's Alder that's looking for you.* "Just never go back to the Guild, eh?"

"It's not that simple, you know. It's not easy to hide from the ravens. And I swore sacred oaths to the gods. They would track me down and hang me as an oath breaker and a heretic. Nasty stuff. I've seen it done to other transporters who thought they'd have a go at getting away."

"So you have to finish every job, no matter what?"

"Aye."

"Even if it's gone to complete shite?"

"Aye."

"So how is a job ever failed?"

"Death, man. Either the raven or the client."

"Ain't got much of a choice about anything then, eh?"

Eurick smiled.

"A person's always got choices, man. Most of the time they just ain't the one you're looking for. Up to you to decide which one's right. And you always get to decide how you react to what's in front of you. *That* choice is always yours."

James considered that and felt some old wounds open up inside. *Maggie. I should have gone back for you...*

He had been out hunting alone on the day the Hawka came. He had gotten angry that morning because he didn't know how to make Maggie stop hurting, and when he came back to camp, the Hawka were already there. They were already there, and he ran. The other way. *Was that the right choice? One of us had to live, right?* He figured he'd better make his choice to live worth it.

"Listen," Eurick said, "I don't go around advising the folk I transport, but rarely have I ever had such a job as this. You gotta figure out whatever's burning you up inside, man, or you will not make it to the mountains. I'll be here with you. I'll help to bear the load of whatever comes our way. But everyone will die if you fail. It's the hard truth of it, man, and it ain't pretty."

James felt his stomach twisting into knots. The Hermit had told him he would have to realize what he was or it would kill him from the inside. His parents had spent their lives trying to nurture what was inside of him. And they, and his whole country, died because he couldn't do it. He didn't get the choice to hide. Not anymore.

"Aye."

Eurick had a bad habit of being right a lot.

It was only a few miles before they came across the towering trees of the Wick Arbor, a massive stretch of wood that the Mal folk believed had its own pulse. The trees were russet brown and tawny, dying, but for the bits of winter flora that still clung to dark soil.

"The folk of Mal Hallow believe nobody knows the way through," said James, remembering Gran's stories. "If you go into the heart of it, you don't come out. Nobody knows what lives in there."

"This," said Eurick, "is why you hire transporters for these types of things! I know the way, man. I know all the ways to all the places by any route."

"And Rynish transporters have a reputation for being far less murderous than the Ni'anese navigators," added Adeqor.

"Right," said Eurick. "And that."

As they approached what Eurick insisted on being the safest entrance to the Wick, James felt the coldness creep in on him again. There was death in that arbor, beyond what he'd seen yet, and he'd have to face it.

The sounds hit James with a smack. Burn bugs and skitters buzzing louder than a river, foxes and puca howling back at the wolves, owls and blood bats squawking, all in a world of their own. They were surrounded by sick old trees covered with hoary cobwebs as thick as wool. James couldn't see a damn thing.

"This place isn't right," James whispered.

Eurick led them with remarkable ease through the dark arbor. James could barely see the back of his own hand after his eyes adjusted to the night. But he stayed with the raven and trusted every step behind him.

"Follow me," Eurick said. "Watch your step over this here log."

"How can you see so well?" James smashed his shin on a branch. "It's black as pitch."

"I can see in the dark," said Eurick matter-of-factly.

"Eh?"

Adeqor stumbled over a branch and fell into James. He smelt like stale shine and body odour. "The High Ravens of the Guild feed them potions from birth. Wicked stuff, that," Adeqor hiccupped. "It's some old eldritch magics that the first ravens conjured up with Warlocks of the Ailaryan Order. The spells go way back to when the transporters were first conceived, after the Starfall. The Guild kept the secrets alive and passed them down generation to generation. They can see in the dark, see for a distance, withstand freezing temperatures, and eat remarkably little. What else?"

Eurick grinned. "I can walk on ice and through snow very well, and you would think I have the bladder of a whale, haha." He coughed. "Bah! Spider web here. Watch your face."

The first hours were deeply disturbing. Every little sound was a potential threat, and there were sounds everywhere. James remembered Gran's stories about the kinds of creatures that dwelled in the arbors surrounding the Hallow Hills. The stories of the E'daru, a horse with a Human soul that would snatch and live in the body of its victims. The stories of the puca, who may appear as something as small as a fox or a hare, or something bigger, like a beautiful man or woman. The puca lured folk deeper into the darkness of the wood where it could feed on their soul in silence. A shiver traced James's spine as he remembered how Gran would always end the puca story. *"The puca shares a soul with the Hare. She brings the harvest. If it is not fed, then neither are we. That's why the sick and the old go into the arbor before winter every year—to feed the harvest."* Sometimes in the darkness, everything was a possibility. But eventually, James got used to being helpless.

"You see that?" Eurick asked.

"You know damn well we can't see shit," said Adeqor.

"You'd see this, though. I saw a flame," Eurick said. And right then James saw the flash of flame. But it was not fire that made that light.

"I saw it." James's stomach turned. It wasn't right. "It's... green."

"Fuck!" Adeqor's body hummed with magics. "It's a Ranger's trap!"

"It may not—"

A white flame ignited in front of them.

"The fuck is that?" said James, and the light changed colour. A flickering blue light had all of their attention. *Or was it purple?* It moved like fire. *But no one has fire.*

"It's a fool's fire," Eurick said. "They trap light from the sun with their green magics and use powders to make it change colour. If we walk away from it, they'll trap us. Walk towards it, they'll trap us. Sooo...we're kind of fucked."

"I'll take care of this," Adeqor said. "As long as they make themselves visible. Walk towards it."

They approached slowly.

"Why don't we go around it?" James asked, stumbling over a log.

"We're already surrounded," said Adeqor. "We're going to have to deal with the Rangers who set this trap."

They got closer to the fool's flame, dancing green and pink now. *Maggie might think that it was the prettiest thing she'd ever seen*, and that made him smile.

Adeqor sniffed the air—but it was already too late. Twigs snapped nearby, and the ground caved under James's feet.

James was in a hole with Eurick writhing on top of him.

"You've got it wrong!" Eurick screamed. "We're just peaceful nomads."

"Shut your bloody mouth," Adeqor said, sitting up. "They've got us."

A gnarly group of leather-skinned folk wearing green hoods and armed with spears and bows appeared at the top of the hole. One of them held a plate of green and pink fire. Even from above, James could feel the cold spewing off of it. He knew it wasn't real, but the sight of the flames made his heart warm, and his mouth water at the thought of cooking elk.

"Like bloody flies to a carcass, they are," said one of them. She had the same curly red hair as Wulfee but shorter and without braids.

Another clicked her teeth at James. "Can we eat them?"

"Not yet, Gulla," said the red-haired woman. "They're road worn and muscle sore. We'll take them back to Ockam first." She tucked a strand of red hair under her hood. "Maybe we can sell them to Derudin. If he doesn't want them, then we'll eat them."

The Ranger held James's eyes with her own grey eyes. James didn't like the torment he saw in them under that vile green light.

"Tell me who you are." She glared at James.

"Don't say a word to her," said Adeqor. "Fuck you."

The woman laughed.

"It doesn't matter who the other two are. I know a Warlock when I see one. Look at that beautiful skin shining. A little smaller in flesh than the statues that are erected in Hest, mind you." She addressed her band. "No one stands within eyesight of the wizard or he will turn you into a pile of mud." Murmurs of agreement lingered in the air.

James didn't know what Adeqor was planning, and it made his chest heavy.

"Tell me, wizard, where are you going? The Ranger bands are all gathering in the Hallow Hills for protection, the Feldarra clansfolk are gathering at Pool, and smallfolk are at Tusk. Seems like everyone is putting their faith in each other in these dark times. So why are you folks running the opposite way?"

"We're going to Ockam," Adeqor lied.

"Lord Derudin of Ockam doesn't much like strangers," the red-haired woman smirked. "Especially those who come sulking out of the woods. You know that as well as I do. Now, where were you *really* going?"

James almost choked on his own tongue. "Did you say Derudin?"

Derudin was the first lord to turn his back on Bren Culdaine and bend the knee to Calen Alder. He started a chain reaction that resulted in the war being lost. And he was paranoid and violent.

Eurick elbowed James.

"You know him? Well, he may know you then," said the red-haired woman. "I'm sure Derudin would like to hear the story of how you came to be travelling with a god damned wizard of the Ailaryan Order... This is worth gold." She looked at Gulla. "Put them out. Let's get them to the wagon. I want to be gone in half an hour."

"And with the wizard?" asked Gulla, leaning too close to the hole. James felt hot wind on his face, then a rumble through his whole body. Adeqor made signs with his hands, pulling magics out of the air, then threw a swirl of ruby and emerald light at Gulla. She sloshed into a pile of goopy sap in an instant. The steaming purplish-red mush dripped down into the hole with a chunky *plop, plop, plop*. The smell made James heave this morning's cheese.

"Gulla!" shouted the red-haired woman. "I told you all to stay the fuck out of sight!" She lowered her voice to a whisper. "This is what you're reduced to, Warlock? Doing your work in secret with no help. No kings or queens calling for your help. You can't sing the words; you're nothing but a mere beggar. Pathetic." James saw a tiny dart hit Adeqor's neck from seemingly out of nowhere.

"Fuck!" he said.

"Tie his wrists behind his back and he's useless," said the red-haired woman. "These wizard tricks, you see, it's all just sleight of hand. Sign language."

Eurick fell limp to the ground, then Adeqor. *Eh?* James felt a small prick in his neck, and then the ground came up fast.

HORNS OF WAR

THE GUARDS CORRALLED WULFEE and the rest of the lot to the south gates of Tusk. There, they were swept up in a throng of civilians across the bridge and into the courtyard of the great Lovasi castle of Mammoth's Head. Then, onwards, to the second bridge.

Two rounded towers shouldered the bridge where it met the south shore. It was a massive defensive barbican that looked like half a castle. Three portcullis gates lined with murder holes fortified the entrance, and thick battlements and a wide balcony crowned the barbican. Arrow slits peppered the towers, and gaunt townsfolk holding bows filled them.

The air was thick with fear and body stench. Wulfee could tell all of these people were hungry, tired, and sick of running. Fighting seemed only a sliver better than starving—Wulfee knew that feeling all too well. She gave the sign of luck to the young woman next to her; the young woman returned the gesture. She was probably still in her teen years, yet she stood as tall as most of the men. Wulfee saw herself at that age. She held her bow with confidence and walked with the swagger of a hard bitch ready to kill or be killed. Wulfee didn't doubt that the woman was more than capable of taking a life or ten. The gods knew Wulfee was as vicious as a wolf in heat when she was that age.

Soldiers in haggard, old armour wearing the mammoth chain of Claydon Coldfoot's guard about their necks ushered the swarms of people into a crowded courtyard filled with planks of wood and rusted scrap metal. Hilts, blades, pommels, fletchings, helms, gauntlets, and pauldrons scattered across the rushes for any to take. Piles of chain shirts sat crumpled on the ground like cold iron blankets. Canvas and barrels laid about like long dead soldiers. Wulfee couldn't tell who was in charge of a damn thing. It was right fucked.

She shouldered on towards one of the turret towers. The ancient stones of the curtain walls raised up around her, too high for any of her like to have dreamed of building. They felt no different from the walls of Kallahorn, and she'd seen those walls breached. The horn blew and brought with them the dark memories. The battle of Kallahorn, the slaughter in Red Valley, watching her friends die and family die. The screaming and the begging for life. The red mud and the blood-soaked steel in her hand. They were the sounds of war. The weight of those memories was enough to crush most.

Hasn't crushed you, though. Not yet.

A scream came from somewhere. One of terror or pain, Wulfee couldn't tell. Some of the townsfolk were armoured, but more weren't. All had a flimsy bow or a crooked spear in hand, but Wulfee didn't see any arrows. She had her own bow. She took the old Feldarra yew off her back. It wasn't anything too nice anymore, but it was her mom's and Wulfee felt a closeness to the weapon. It had saved her life more times than she could count. It had killed for good and for worse than that, too.

BA-DAAAAA. A horn blew from a different direction. And Wulfee remembered all the dead piled up at Kallahorn and the smell of them the next day when the winds caught hold of 'em. The horns were bellowing out then, too, when she fought Sweyne and the folk she called family. They were bleating as the swarms of carrion picked the dead apart and turned them into shit at the battle of Red Valley, too. At Lorne, the horns blended in with the cries of the wounded who were crawling amongst the dead. She took the arm off of Odhran Ironfist that day and sent him back into the mountains. *Folk die, and the horns blow on.*

"Where is Claydon?" she asked the pock-scarred soldier nearby.

"He'll be here." He was gripping his driftwood bow so hard his knuckles were white. "He always shows up. Besides, ain't no orders to give. Other n' stand up on that wall and shoot them sum bitches that come out that valley."

Wulfee gave the sign of luck. The man returned it. And the horns blew. BA-ROOOOOO.

Could be Sweyne himself blowing that thing.

The night after Sweyne had gotten Tarek killed, Wulfee thought about dropping her axe on his face. She stood over him and thought for a long while, but she couldn't do it. They'd sacrificed to the Hare together, begging for peace. She had vowed to never fight another battle, to never touch her axe again. To be *Etta* again. She left him living. *And how'd that go?* She let that moment rule the last twenty years of her life.

"Find your place on the wall!" one of Claydon's men yelled at her, pointing at the tower.

"I'm going." Wulfee waved her hand at him in dismissal.

"Holy shit, a Giy'er," Claydon's man said. "Isn't he dangerous?"

"To them fuckers, maybe," Wulfee said. "He'll help wherever he's needed. You treat him like any other." The guards smiled.

"To the portcullis, big fella, you can help hold these gates." He pointed to a group of pallid soldiers that were standing at the gates with makeshift spears. The lot of them looked like they'd just found the old northern well o' luck when they saw Gen. Wulfee thought they were damn near about to let out a cheer. The Giy'er didn't take his eyes off Wulfee and wasn't moving. She reckoned it may have been the most scared that she'd seen the young fella. Her heart *thummed* like it had fallen into her stomach.

She pulled him into a hug. "You're going to be a great damned karl after all of this, Gen. So you come back to me when the fighting is done. You hear? You make sure you come back to me, okay?"

"I will," Gen promised. "I'll be just like Emmer. Just like you tell it, Wulf." He let go with a small smile and found his place amongst the lot of soldiers at the gates.

Wulfee and Pike climbed the barbican tower.

"You shouldn't let Gen believe in all that," Pike said. "The clans would never let him take the oaths. He doesn't have the blood of Feldarra. It's absurd to let him think he can do it. The Giy'er feel more intensely than we do, and it won't sit well with him to find out."

Wulfee disagreed. She was sick of oaths and traditions.

"Maybe it's more than blood what makes a karl," Wulfee said. And Pike's face went flat for a moment, then he smiled.

The old warrior was silent the rest of the way up to the top of the barbican. It was a chaotic mess up there. People of all ages rushed in every direction, panic stricken and distraught. Claydon's soldiers yelled directions that were lost in the din, frantically thrust bundles of arrows at passersby, and directed people to line up along the parapet seemingly at random.

"They're bloody coming!" screamed a woman who looked like she'd caught battle sickness by the way her eyes stared *through* Wulfee into nothing. *Another one broken by war.* The woman drifted down the parapet. Wulfee took a handful of arrows from a barrel, tucked them under her armpits, and then took another handful. Pike did the same, and the two found a place behind one of the battlements. She gazed down from the barbican and felt a shit almost sneak out of her arsehole. An iron blanket of soldiers was marching in neat rows. Banners of black wolves and red eagles waved, horns bellowed out, and the soliders chanted war songs in a fierce holler. She studied the people lined up along the barbican. A couple hundred tired old men and women, some only teenagers. Pike caught her with those long blue eyes.

"This could be the one that finally gets us, eh?" said Pike. Wulfee stared at him blankly.

"You said that last time," she said, notching an arrow. Pike smiled.

"I'm ready for it, if this is it," he said, putting his right fist to his chin and nodding. Wulfee did the same. *The gods know I need luck.*

BA-ROOOOOO!

The enemy's horns were blaring now. A deeper, darker din than any she'd heard.

"Bloody hell," murmured Wulfee. The footsteps of the approaching army echoed in unison. Death approached, and all she had was a skinny piece of yew and a hand axe. Pike had his shield slung over his shoulder and a bow in his hand. Not at all as threatening as he was face to face.

"At the ready!" a loud voice barrelled down the length of the barbican wall. The man it belonged to yelled again. "Notch and aim! Let's send these bloody bastards back to Ayeland!" Everyone cheered and Wulfee damn near let one out herself. *Finally, someone who knows what's going on.* His thick, blond beard looked as solid as stone, and his shoulder-length hair was knotted with many braids. He looked like a king of old.

This was Claydon Coldfoot. If his stature didn't give it away, the Daggland steel chest plate certainly did. Only lords who bent the knee to Calen Alder had the power to acquire Daggland steel. Not even the folk who call Daggland home knew how to craft it. The man thrust his shining longsword into the sky. His flag bearer profusely waved the grey mammoth on green. And the soldiers cheered. Another thrust of his sword into the sky. Daggland steel gleamed black and crimson under the sun. The cheers were louder now, and Wulfee had to admit it was riling her up.

Claydon's two sons were by his side, Aron and Macts. Wulfee had seen the oldest, Aron, win a single combat at Pool three years ago, and Macts had been cheering him on in the crowd. Aron had gained two more braids since then, and Macts had gained his first. Wulfee couldn't help but imagine how things could have been if Tarek had won that single combat. If, instead of death, he was simply given a braid.

The block of soldiers was close enough for Wulfee to see their faces. All targets for her to aim at. All lives for her to end, families to destroy. *How many have you destroyed already? You even destroyed your own.* The rushing White River protected Mammoth's Head against a siege, so all they had to do was hold them here. *Hold them until he comes.* She notched an arrow. Shot her eye down the barbican and saw the whole lot waiting on Claydon's word. Pike was beside her as always, no doubt thinking something valiant. Courageous, bloody heroic. He was always calm before a battle, and Wulfee envied that.

"Notch!" Claydon shouted, big northern lungs bellowing. "Loose!"

She let go. Watched her arrow and a hundred others pierce through the sky and slowly fall into the soft bodies of the front-line soldiers. They fell like sacks of barley to the ground, never to see the ones they loved again.

"Notch!" Coldfoot yelled, and Wulfee couldn't help but listen. It felt good to be told what to do for once. Made it feel like she had someone to blame for the killing. "Loose!" he said, and she loosed another arrow. A rain of poorly fletched arrows made from old, splintered wood fell upon the Wolf's army. They came from a hundred different small hamlets in the north, but they all died the same. The screams of pain were only faint and distant. They hardly reached Wulfee at all. It made her understand why these bastards were so willing to kill for these castles. It removed them from watching their enemy die or hearing them take their last breath. "Notch!" Claydon ordered. She notched. "Loose!" She let go, and just like that, she took a life. The dead piled up, and Wulfee notched and loosed again, and again, and again. Happy not to be amongst the dying. Her arms cramped up; her fingers blistered and bled from pulling the bowstring. With every arrow, the enemy crept closer. With every arrow, she buried herself deeper in remorse. *How many are you going to kill to get to him? How many will die because you can't just turn away from this?*

Tall wooden siege ladders appeared in the mass. Wulfee had only heard about those in clanfire stories. The people around her were tired. The arrows weren't being loosed in masses now but in staggered messes, and the enemy was learning to deal with the bombardment. Closer they crept, beneath turtle shells made of layer upon layer of leather pelts, and Wulfee felt the knot in her gut. The same old knot that was there at Kallahorn, Lorne, and the Red Valley. Ladders rose against the wall, thick and gnarled as roots. The gates below were being rammed and battered. And Wulfee loosed again and again. Watched her arrow pierce the forehead of a boy. The cheekbones of a woman. The eye of an old man long due for a dirt nap.

"In death, your memory will live on through song! It will be sung from here to Esher, the day a few hundred heroes held off the Ayelish at Tusk!" Claydon screamed in a hearty voice. Aron and Macts repeated their dad's words down the lines.

Wulfee dropped her bow and grabbed one of the long-forked poles that hung on the wall below the battlements and used it to push the ladders away. She could only manage that a few times before she found herself standing between two Wolf soldiers who had successfully climbed over the wall. Wulfee pulled her axe just in time to look a young'un in the eyes and swing her blade at his shoulder. There was a smashing clang, and the boy fell off the wall. Wulfee didn't hear the splatter he surely made.

More were coming up one after the other. Some of the people on the wall were still concerned with firing arrows, and they were getting slaughtered.

"The ladders!" Wulfee yelled. "Grab those long forks and push down the bloody ladders!" She felt the words bellow out of her lungs. Been awhile since she'd yelled like that, but people responded to it. A man came at her with his axe raised. Wulfee dodged his blow and hacked the fellow's arm off with her axe. The man screamed as he stared at the blood pouring out of what was left of his arm, so she hacked at his neck to shut him up. Wulfee grabbed a forked pole, slotted the end into the thick rungs of the ladder, and pushed it backwards, sending a dozen mercenaries back down with it.

"Loose!" she shouted. "Fire on them!" And folk picked up their bows again. Soon, arrows were raining down on the Wolf's army. But they just kept coming, coming up the wall like ants. Below, the battering rams were smashing the gates with a dismal echo. Wulfee thought of Gen and hoped the lad wasn't scared.

"Loose!" Wulfee screamed. And arrows fell. "Where the fuck has Claydon gone?" No one answered her. "Loose!" And the Wolf's army was being pushed back. There were no more ladders on the wall. Wulfee looked around and didn't see Claydon anymore.

BA-ROOOO! Enemy horns sounded in unison. *Means retreat. They're retreating already?* She saw Pike through the mad scramble of bodies.

"Pike, they're retreat—" She swung her axe into the gut of a man tumbling over the wall; he must have been holding on to the ledge. She watched him die.

"Fuck!"

She was sick of all this. Tired of taking lives. She grabbed her mom's bow off the gore-soaked ground. The horns of war bust out a bloody lullaby for the dying and the wounded. Wulfee ducked under a weak swing from a tired young man who had found himself in the wrong place. She bust his face open with her axe. A woman saw it happen and tackled Wulfee to the ground, as mad as a rabid beast. Her sweat-soaked body smeared all over Wulfee.

"Fuck you," Wulfee said, smashing the woman's head open with her axe. Rust filled her mouth. Wulfee pushed her off and got up and felt the rush of blood to her head, in her veins, and through her body. She screamed like a madwoman. Possessed by adrenaline, fear, and a bit o' northern madness.

A cheer rolled down the barbican, "HEYYA!" from all who escaped death.

Lord Claydon and his sons were back. The lord of Tusk thrust his sword to the blue sky, acting as if he'd never left. He led another cheer. "HEYYAA!"

"That one was for the dead," Claydon bellowed. Saliva hung from Wulfee's mouth in tendrils as she screamed and let the madness course through her. Battle drunk and bent up. The enemy horns faded as the mass of them retreated out of fighting distance. Wulfee felt like fucking or drinking. Preferably both, but would get neither. They'd be back. The rush of the battle faded, and the stiffness in her bones crept in.

"Death escapes us, yet again." Pike walked slowly over to her. Cries and shouts echoed all around. "For now."

"Aye," she said.

"This could be the one that gets us, though," said Pike.

"May well do," said Wulfee, indulging the old warrior in his grim prayers of death.

"I'll be ready for it." Pike sliced the air twice with his axe and admired his bloody shield. A faint smile crept onto his wrinkled face. Wulfee guffawed. Pike saying he was ready for death was like saying water was wet. She took a look around. Dead, wounded, living. All mingling about the ancient stone castle in an orgy of war. She looked out to the White River flowing like a thing possessed. The sky was blue, and the clouds were crisp white. The black birds were already circling. She could always depend on those dark winged bastards to show up. A cold shiver chilled through her body.

Suddenly, she felt drained of everything. She just needed a little rest. Just a short sleep, then they would leave this place. She was so damned tired. She knew it was time to run, but it was just so much easier to stay.

"Did you hear?" said a hook-nosed man in passing.

"Hear what?" Wulfee's gut fluttered.

"They've caged a monster from the Sheed. They'll have dragged it here by tomorrow."

THE FIELDS OF OCKAM

J AMES DREAMT HE WAS back in Wulfee's camp; rain drizzled lightly on the canvas. He had just come back from a hunt. Maggie hung his wet clothes over a crackling fire and made him tea. The smell of mint, rose hips, and kesslewood bark made him smile. She caressed his shoulder with a light touch that sent a chill down his neck. The wind whistled gently through the holes in their tent.

"I love the smell of the rain," she whispered in his ear. Tingles fluttered in his stomach.

"I love *you,*" he whispered back. He touched his lips to hers and held them there as they moved together. Held *her* there close to him, where he could feel her chest rise and fall, hear her heart beating. Her hair was soft on his face, and he took in her smell. *Peonies and honey.* Her skin was coarse with goosebumps. He was short of breath just looking at her shape, her eyes. He had never seen someone so beautiful. *Anyone at all.* He had never felt so helpless. He would give up anything, *everything,* for her love—because that's what she did for him. Maggie leaned in when he touched her. Her skin was as smooth as a river stone.

"Let's go lie in the rain," Maggie said. "I want to see if the stars are still out, baby. Let's go look at the sky and lie in the rain and talk to the winds."

His clothes weren't yet dried, but James couldn't resist running outside with Maggie. They ran to the hill of Yore, splashing in puddles along the way. Maggie rolled in the long grass there, and her magics lit the mist a cool blue. Then she laid her head on James's shoulder, and he held her tight and kissed her forehead. The sky and the stars were barely visible through the light rain. Maggie twirled her finger in the air, and the stars seemed to follow it. The dead souls gathered around them, and the stars danced for them while the rain came down. James held Maggie's lips with his and whispered in her ear. "*Ai'mair darra*, baby, forever."

Maggie pulled away and held James's eyes with hers. One green and one blue.

This is what magic really is.

"You really mean it, though?" Maggie bit her lip.

"Every time."

Maggie smiled, and James pulled her back into his arms.

"I can feel the life in everything." Maggie twirled her finger in the air again. "The wind, the rain, the earth below us. Fires are so damn beautiful I could just live in one. Some days I wonder if it would even burn me, so I touch my finger to the flame until it leaves a blister. One day, I think I won't burn at all."

James grinned. "I think it will always burn as long as flesh covers your hand."

She kissed him hard—until she started to fade. The Hill of Yore blurred into a drunk-like haze. Maggie's skin began to char and peel away. James reached out for her but she backed away. She opened her mouth and maggots poured out like a river.

"You're not here," he whispered, shaking his head. "I don't know where you are."

"It's too late. I'm already dead," she said as her face melted away. Then James stood alone but for the gentle padding of rainfall.

CREAKING WHEELS AND RUSTED hinges. Hands tied and mouths gagged. An arse full of splinters. The all too familiar feeling of a cage wagon. Dizzy and lightheaded. Shortness of breath and vomiting. Mouth full of sawdust. The all too familiar feeling of waking up slightly poisoned.

James had fallen into a big convoy with four supply carts in front and as many behind. Horses and soldiers, armed and armoured, guarded both sides. At least he wasn't in the Wick Arbor any longer. It worried him that not even a band of Rangers wanted to be in the Wick for long. Eurick and Adeqor were both awake now too, also tied and gagged. Flag bearers marched in the front and back; the white flags with the red eagle of Ayeland hung limply on their poles in the dead air. James knew that was nothing more than a peace showing. His dad had always said the Rangers flew no flags of their own, they only served E'daru.

The black godrock of *Essikah* expunged a dull glisten in the sun. It said something about the sword to James, that someone wouldn't steal it given the opportunity. It still had gnarled root nubs growing out of the hilt, and the smell of peonies and honey had gone rancid. He hated the way the sword made him feel. It nipped at his soul, tasting it like it was trying to devour him. And he knew he could never be rid of it. His engagement knife was gone, though, and *that* made him angry. He stewed over it, hearing Maggie's voice telling him to let it go. But he couldn't let it go. Couldn't let *her* go.

James didn't bother trying to recognize any of his captors. The Ayelish flag was enough for him to know they were his enemies. He'd spent half his life fighting folk flying that red eagle flag. His hate wasn't for any of the men and women that had him now, his hate was for their king. Calen Alder was nearly fifty now, and many long years with complete power had turned him mad. He fought war after war for conquest. The whole north was terrified of his presence. He had bedded Warlocks and harlots and betrayed his own wife and children for glory. *So why did you let me live? Alder? Why?*

Around midday, James heard orders to halt the convoy. The red-haired Ranger came to them with her hood down, which James knew was a bad omen for Rangers, but she didn't seem to care too much. She caressed James with grey, sorrowful eyes that made him shiver.

"My name is Florence," she said. "Since we're going to be together awhile, I thought you should know. Don't mind the bondage. My girls couldn't take any chances with the wizard and his tricks, you see. Blame the company you keep." She held a wineskin through the bars of the cage. "Come, drink." Florence poured water out in a slow stream. James squirmed towards her and drank. He felt the sawdust dissolve in his mouth as he lapped up the water. *Like a bloody dog.* Eurick did the same, but Adeqor refused to face her.

"You ready to tell me about what it is that you want in Mal Hallow?" Florence said. "There's no fire here. No food. Something about this is convenient for you, but I haven't quite figured you out."

"We're not looking for fire." James gazed at Adeqor suspiciously. He had been wondering why he didn't blow them out of that cage with his magics.

"Don't say another word," Adeqor spat yellow phlegm. "We don't conduct business with skincrawlers. We'll talk to the Lord of Ockam."

"And what makes you think he'll listen to you, wizard?" Florence asked. "We've all heard the stories about you. We've all heard of Lindis and what *really* happened. Was it you that conducted the testing? Was it *your* magics that inflamed something deep down and set the sky on fire?"

The wizard growled. "The Banshee is leading a horde of Hawka that will surely catch up with us again soon. If you don't hurry and get moving, no one will be listening to any of us ever again."

Florence paused for a moment before saying, "Bloody liar." Then, she called out to the convoy. "Let's hurry this up, eh?"

Adeqor spit again as Florence disappeared. James was relieved when the wheels creaked, and the convoy moved again.

Two days passed by as James lived in that cage. He shivered throughout the cold nights and got closer than he ever thought he would with Eurick to keep from freezing. He bore the hunger pains in his roaring stomach, and his thirst turned his tongue to wood again. James figured the cage suited him for now. The wizard had him in a cage, anyway. At least James could see the bars on this one.

On the evening of James's third night in captivity, he caught Florence admiring his engagement knife. She laughed while stabbing the air with it in a mocking fashion, and her band joined her in the revel.

James clenched his fists. *I'll kill the whole world to get that back.*

"Who's the knife for?" Eurick asked.

"Oh." James sank into himself. "Maggie. She's... I had... I don't know."

"It's okay, man." Eurick put his hand on James's back.

"I'm not so sure it is." James pulled away, feeling angry with himself.

"People make mistakes."

"Well, I made more than a fucking mistake." James kicked the bars of the cage.

"Talk about it, man. Tell me what happened. You will feel better."

James thought that was bullshit.

"Florence got mine, too, man." Eurick hung his head. "I've held onto that all these years, just hoping—ah, it was stupid of me to hope." He rattled the chains on his wrists. "We were to be married seven years ago in Esher. He gave me that knife after I'd told him about our traditions up here in the north. His name was Eronel. The whole thing violated several rules of the Guild. They strictly forbid us to have any relations with our customers. But love is like the rise and fall of the sun, man, there ain't no stopping it. I knew the ravens would hunt me down if I went through with it. And I couldn't let him be killed for breaking the oaths. I would never have forgiven myself for that. On the day of our wedding, I left without saying a word to him. I knew he'd be better off without me. When I returned to the Guild, the ravens tortured me for three years. One year for each of the months I was gone," he said, looking back up with misty blue eyes.

"Sometimes you have to do the hard thing to move forward in order to save the ones you love. It's enough for me to know he's still out there, and I hope he understands why I left." Eurick put his big hand on James's shoulder. "Maggie is still alive, man. You have to believe it. Keep going so you can find your way back to her. Same as me."

Believe she's alive. He could do that. "I was out hunting," James blurted. "When I came back... The Hawka—they were already there. I ran the wrong way. I could have seen her one last time."

"You'll see her, man," Eurick said, turning his back.

James sat in the cage and felt nothing as the cold darkness swallowed the red twilight around him.

On the fourth night, the Banshee's scream wailed through the darkness behind them. James heard whips crack, and the wheels creaked a little faster. Nobody was laughing anymore.

At midday on the fifth day, the convoy broke through the thick treeline and into a valley known as the Fields of Ockam. In the early spring, the meadows usually bloomed with winter roses that looked like pale green crystals floating on the melting snow. Now, weakly budding shafts of brown-green grew sparse and stunted across an otherwise dead field. If it wasn't for the road markers, James might not have recognized the fields at all.

The convoy rolled along the deep, rutted road, past abandoned inns and ramshackle villages. Past choked out fields that should have been sowed with this year's crop but rather sat barren. It had been nearly two months without rain. *Soon the rivers will choke out. Most will be dead by winter, and the rest will die during it.* James had a horrible, sick feeling in his stomach, like he'd fucked it all up. He was headed out of the mountains, not towards them. And every single person they'd passed in the convoy was headed the other way.

"The world isn't working, can't you see?" some haggard looking folk called out to them from the road. "It's hopeless north *or* south. East or west. It matters not."

But they continued south anyway.

"We've strayed way off path now, man," said Eurick with a tone of agony in his voice. "A week, maybe two out of our way." It seemed like the thought of taking the long way really hurt the guy. "If we don't get this job done and over with before the first Rise of winter, this ain't gonna be pretty."

By twilight of that evening, the young moon lit up the wooden palisades of Ockam in ripples of silver and purple. In a field of starving flora, the palisades stood ten times the height of a person. They were made with trunks of mountain cedar treated with ancient Druid earth magics. Derudin's grandad, Durden, had the logs dragged from ruined watchtowers to Ockam, where he used them to build his walls.

At the fort's heart, a decrepit hall perched on top of the motte. An inner and outer bailey stretched out below, surrounded by two layers of protection—the palisades and ten-foot ditch filled with jagged scrapped iron and sharpened wood. Ockam was a testament to what the builders of today were capable of—cutting down trees and robbing ruins.

James *knew* what to expect—but it was something else to actually *be* in Mal Hallow again, seeing his failures manifest in red and white. Ayelish banners hung along the walls in place of the bull moose of Mal Hallow. The greenhouse where his mother and Aylee of Oldwood had kept the winter roses alive during summer, along with a rainbow of other flowers, was only a burnt wooden frame. The place in which Derudin's stone statue once stood alongside his dad's and grandad's was a pile of crumbled rock covered in moss and grime. Seeing Mal Hallow like this was the first sign to James that they had truly lost the war, and this wasn't the same home he'd left. A visual reminder that he had truly failed to uphold his parents's legacy, that they died for nothing. And it was the first real reminder that Lord Derudin was a traitor.

James's dad had spent half a decade uniting the kings and queens of Mal Hallow to defend against Ayelish conquerors. Half a decade of riding to this fort or that, to dine with that ruler or this. Bren Culdaine won some rulers with a good word, some with a threat, others with outright gold. But they united and flew the bull moose banner under their king and called themselves one country for the first time since Kelson, the Conqueror.

And it lasted less time than it took to create. As soon as it looked like they might face defeat, the rulers of the Hallow bent their knees, one by one, to Calen Alder. Derudin was the first to do it.

Now, the crystalline roses were gone, no Mom and Dad, no Maggie either. It was just him, caged in a wagon with nowhere left to run.

"Help us," the dead whispered to him. *"Please, help us home."*

James and the dead sowed nothing but sorrow in the empty Fields of Ockam.

A WOODEN GATE LOWERED with a rusty squeal, and a rush of soldiers in boiled leather and chain armour ran across a rickety bridge.

Florence called out, "Easy there, you'll rile up the dogs." But they were already snarling.

"Did you bring any fire?" a man called out.

"Does it bloody look like it?" Florence yelled.

On the inside of the bailey, a very clean woman dressed in loose white silks greeted Florence in a language that James figured to be Lovasi or something like it. He had never heard it spoken before, but he found it quite beautiful.

The woman said something mockingly, and she and Florence laughed loudly. Florence said something back to her in the same language, and the woman smiled, scribbling on parchment.

James had only seen blank parchment at his dad's table. It had an aura of importance about it.

"Where's Lord Derudin?" Florence replied in the northern tongue.

"Drinking in the hall," the woman answered. "I will take you."

"Thank you," said Florence. And to her band: "Take the horses to stables, carts to the wrights, and everything else to the smiths." The Ranger pierced James with haunting grey eyes. They held him in a sorrowful embrace that made his heart beat slower. *She's seen dark things with those eyes.*

"You three are with me," Florence said. James felt the prick of a sword at his back as soldiers unloaded him, Eurick, and Adeqor from the cage. The clean woman in white led them through an inner gate of the bailey and up a slippery set of stairs to the massive oak door to the hall. Sounds of merriment boomed from inside as the clean woman opened the door. James figured he probably wouldn't be joining along in the revelry as long as he was a prisoner.

The rickety hall that overlooked Ockam was dark, lit only by the moonlight. It was haunting. An off-key flute mixed with a weathered-out wood harp made so much racket James couldn't believe nobody was saying something about it. Derudin sat upon an oaken throne on the dais at the far end of the hall. The man looked a lot like he did the last time James saw him. A long greying black beard, a thick gut hanging over the waist of his trousers, and as drunk as a Glennishman. A topless, yellow-haired woman sat on his lap—another woman who could never replace Aylee. He nuzzled his face into the woman's neck while balancing a silver goblet in his left hand. She cackled when he whispered something to her.

All around, people drank and boasted of times past, hardly acknowledging the newcomers. The woman in white cleared her throat when they finally approached the lord. Derudin glared at them. One lazy eye stayed half the way down.

"The fuck do you want?" he said. Glazed his one good eye over the prisoners. "Who're they? That's a big, ugly sword."

James sighed.

"What I want is payment, Derudin. You should know I don't come around for any less," Florence said casually. "Returning from my trip south, I brought you something you may find of interest." She glanced at James with a clever smile. "The one with the sword is harmless. He cries at night."

Didn't think anyone heard that.

Derudin smiled. Then he bellowed out a boastful laugh.

"My sweet, red Ranger. I don't have ears for another failure. My enemies have surrounded me. I've had nothing but news of approaching famine since you've left. If it's not droughts, it's war. An army of mercenaries calling themselves the Clan of the Severed Head have caused quite the panic by, well, severing many heads. And now I'm hearing Calen Alder has been carved in Blood Words to gain the power of Karaat." Derudin raised his goblet. "All I can do is drink and whore away the pain. If I wallow long enough, the news should turn to good eventually, eh? Don't you think? Do you bring me news of fire?"

"There was no fire. However, it wasn't entirely without gain." She nodded to the soldiers, and they prodded Adeqor forward. The wizard stumbled forward clumsily. "A Warlock of the Ailaryan Order was travelling through the Wick Arbor. He most certainly knows something about what has happened to the fires and rain."

Derudin smiled again. Twisted the greasy strands of his long black hair. The clean woman scribbled something on the parchment. James couldn't quite figure her out.

"Speak, wizard," said Derudin. "What do you have to say for yourself?" A big man holding a big sword moved in beside the lord.

"Say, I could really use a drink. D'ya mind—" A soldier touched a shining blade on Adeqor's bound hands before the wizard could reach for the bottle. "Okay, we'll drink after, then. At least untie me. I am not a criminal."

Derudin nodded, and one of his men cut the ropes around Adeqor's wrists. He rubbed at the chafed skin where the ropes had been.

"I wouldn't—" Florence started, but Derudin silenced her by holding his hand up.

"I am Adeqor." He bowed. "A former wizard of the Ailaryan Order. I am travelling with the seer to the Mother's shrine to save the Mother of Nature and open the Gateway of Rebirth."

Derudin looked deadpan for a moment, then broke into laughter.

"Haha!" he snorted. "You're seeking the Mother of Nature... You come to my court and tell me a tale straight from my gran's mouth?"

Florence said, "They told us that Ellorin, the Banshee queen, has been hunting them for weeks." Derudin regarded Adeqor coldly. "I assure you, the Banshee is more than just a story, lord. Maybe they speak some truth."

Derudin studied her curiously. The wizard reached for the bottle, but again, a soldier knocked his hand away.

"What is all this, wizard? Have you gone mad up there in those mountains?"

"A man with good sense, such as yourself, should be wise enough to consider the possibility of even the most outlandish claim, sir lord," Adeqor said with remarkable patience. "I'm sure you've noticed that the fires have gone, and the rain refuses to fall."

Derudin shifted in his oaken throne and grabbed a pickled cucumber from a jar beside him. The woman scribbled away on the parchment.

"So, you're telling me," Derudin said, crunching away on the pickle, "that you're a seer?"

He pointed the pickle at James. James agreed.

"You see the dead?" Derudin said. James paused a moment then nodded.

"*Horse shit!*" yelled the big man beside him. Derudin threw his half-eaten pickle at the man, and it bounced off his big armour with a tiny thud.

"Shut your mouth, Padraig!" he yelled. "The songs say the Druid seers can heal themselves. That true?" Derudin narrowed his eyes. One lazed downwards.

"Well..." James stuttered. He didn't want to negotiate with this traitor. "Fuck you," he was about to say before Adeqor cut him off.

"It's true."

Derudin nodded to someone behind James. Out of nowhere, two big men twisted James's arm behind his back. "I don't take the word of my own kin, let alone barbarians and wizards that stumble out of the arbors."

Derudin stood up and unsheathed a gleaming iron sword. "I like to have my own proof."

He thrust the sword into James's soft gut.

Death Is Coming

I N HER DREAMS, WULFEE slowed her mare to a trot when they arrived in the small village of Barley. Braden clutched her so tightly from behind that Wulfee almost couldn't breathe.

"I don't want to stop here, Mom," Braden whispered. "Can we just keep riding?"

No village looked nice in the dark. Wulfee didn't blame him for being scared after what he'd been through.

The bitter truth that Tarek was dead was only settling into Wulfee, and her nerves were taking over her mind and body. She wasn't sure if she could go through with it now that she was here.

He'll understand when he's older. You know it's what you have to do.

"This place isn't so bad," Wulfee said. "What's not to like?"

"The river is loud. I like the mountains better."

"We can't go back to the mountains, Brae. You know that, don't you?"

"Ever?"

"Ever's a long time."

"So, yes?"

"Maybe one day," she said, stopping the horse by an empty stable. "When things are set right, but not now. It's going to be okay, though, Brae." She dismounted and carried Braden down from the horse. A few villagers had come out of their houses to see what was going on. Wulfee ignored them. She *had* to ignore them—she wouldn't be able to bear their judgement. She knelt in front of Braden and ran her dry, callused hands through his hair and down the scar on his cheek. "Listen, sometimes people have to do things they don't want to for a little while."

"Like training?" Braden said. Wulfee smiled. He hated training to be a Feldarra. When she thought of it, she realized she hated it too. Back when she was Etta.

"Aye, kind of like that," Wulfee said. Braden was a sensitive boy. Killing didn't come easy to him. He was no fan of hunting and never went fishing. Tarek's death wouldn't go over well for him once it set in. Wulfee went to the horse and untied Braden's getaway bag.

She'd given the boy only a few minutes to grab everything that was most important to him. He was crying the whole time. She never even looked at what he put in there.

She gave him the bag now, and he held it close to his chest. He studied her suspiciously.

"Why are you giving this to me?" he said, his voice trembling with fear.

Wulfee stared back at him. Into his amber eyes, at the scar on his face. She thought of all the pain she'd caused this poor boy in his ten years of life. He should be nowhere close to a clan, and especially a war. He was a sensitive boy and deserved better. Better than she could give him. Braden grabbed onto her like he knew she might leave him. He looked at her, tears welling in his eyes. More people had gathered outside now. Wulfee saw them looking.

He'll be safe here.

In one quick movement, she lept onto her horse.

"Mom!" Braden screamed, his voice cracking. "MOM!" Braden sounded terrified, completely and absolutely so.

Wulfee kicked the horse, snapped the reins. Braden tried to hold on to the horse's tail—anything to stop his mom, but it didn't work. Wulfee couldn't be stopped. His cry was like a hammer to her skull. Her heart seized in her chest, and her throat swelled. She couldn't breathe.

He'll understand when he's older.

"Don't leave me, Mom! Please! *Please!*" Braden screamed so loud and so desperate that it broke Wulfee's soul. She heard him screaming and screaming and screaming until his voice broke. She couldn't look back. Couldn't let him see her crying. Whatever it took to save him from Sweyne, she would do it. Whatever it took. She couldn't let the bastard take him, too. Not him. *Turn back, you stupid bitch! That's your boy! Turn back... please...* But she had to save Braden. She had to get him away. Away from it all. He would understand why she left him. *It's better this way. He'll be safe here. He will. Just until I kill Sweyne, and I'll be back for you, baby boy. I'll be back when it's safe. Please understand.* She rode on into the night and choked on her own tears, nearly drowned in them.

She hoped he would understand.

"To the bridge!" Claydon's guards shouted from every direction. Wulfee's eyes flung open. She was lying in the cold dirt against the back of a mud hut in the middle of Tusk. She had crept away to be alone after the battle to gain some strength. To pray to the Stag that she may see this through. If she could have found any shine, she would have drunk herself into a deep sleep last night. But she couldn't even drown in her own sorrow. There was nothing left for her. Only heartache and buried mistakes. She had struggled to fall asleep, and now she awoke far too soon to claim she felt rested.

"To the bridge!" the cries sounded more and more desperate. "They're back!" Wulfee stood, brushed herself off, and went outside. The sun dimly lit the sky pink from below the horizon. *The absolute crack of dawn...*

The people who survived the first attack were scrambling to the same spots they held hours before. They prayed to the gods for the same kinda luck. No one seemed half as confident, and it looked to Wulfee like a good chunk of folk from yesterday went to sleep and wouldn't ever wake up. She saw Gen's big old head above the crowds by the gate.

"Gen!" she shouted. The big guy looked right at her and smiled. Took one big running stride then stopped himself, a worried look on his face, and walked over slowly, smiling again.

"Wulfee!" he shouted back. "I couldn't find you last night. I didn't sleep, and I couldn't find you." Gen picked at the scab on his elbow. "Pike told about Emmer, but he didn't tell it right. He didn't say the part about the karls."

Wulfee felt a sting of guilt in her stomach. *He was looking for you...*

"I needed some time to think about some stuff, Gen. I'm sorry. I just needed to be alone." She hadn't been alone in so long.

Gen nodded, putting his big hand on her shoulder.

"Because you miss your family?"

"That, and more," said Wulfee.

"I miss my family, too," said Gen. "I know how you feel."

And that set Wulfee's heart on fire. She didn't know the lad was missing anything and she had never even asked. *What kind of person are you? You think you've done good in this world? All you do is break things.*

"We're each other's family now, Gen, okay? You hear?" she said.

He nodded in agreement.

"We're here for each other, okay? And if I leave for a while, I'll always come back. And the same to you, a karl always comes back, okay?"

Gen stood tall. "A karl always comes back."

"Death is coming," Pike said, appearing like a ghost.

Grim bastard.

"Is there another way out?" said Wulfee.

"One. A small hunting gate, but it's guarded well."

"Well, fuck."

They had no choice but to go back to the southern barbican. Wulfee and Pike made their way up to the wall, parting with Gen, who stood at the gates again. Wulfee choked on her tongue as she peered out at the valley and the enormous block of soldiers who filled it. The enemy had siege towers now; they stood tall and proud, like trees in a forest of death. In the middle of the ranks was the big black cage. It was being hauled on three wagons by dozens of soldiers using ropes as thick as a Giy'er leg. *The fuck is in that cage?* Wulfee gripped her bow and looked around to find the barrel of arrows. It was significantly less full than yesterday. She didn't see Claydon either.

"This ain't looking much like a fair fight, Pike."

"You did your ancestors proud, Wulf," Pike said. "You defended this land to the end. Broken oaths or not. You did all you could. That's all any Feldarra can dream of."

Wulfee didn't want to hear Pike's courageous bullshit. He may believe in all that shite, but Wulfee had only reaped heartbreak from heroism. She *hadn't* done all she could. She hadn't faced Odhran and asked for help. Hadn't apologized to Braden and hadn't faced Sweyne. A clean death wasn't an option for her.

A strange and awful gurgling roar came from the cage, echoing across the valley. *Good gods, what is it?*

"They've got death in that cage," said a pock-scarred man covered in dried blood and mud. His hands started shaking, and soon he was laughing. "I heard me a roar like that un' before. As a boy on the road through Ayeland. It's a field drayke. It melts folks when they see its eyes. That, or eats them whole. It scales trees and walls and has skin like steel." He shook his head back and forth. Started his mad laugh again. He seemed deeply concerned. Wulfee looked back at him and prayed to the Crow for mystery so that her face didn't show the twisted horror she was feeling. *What kind of shit have you gotten into, Sweyne?*

"You don't get away from a drayke twice. Not twice." The pock-scarred man walked backwards slowly, then another roar echoed through the valley, and he turned and ran. Two guards tackled him to the ground, but the man kept laughing. *What kind of shit have you gotten yourself into...?* Wulfee saw Pike's face and hoped she hid her fear better than he did.

"What kind of sorcery...?" Pike muttered as he shook his head. "They have brought death itself to fight us with. They mean to take this castle today." Horns bleated out in the distance.

The first row of enemy archers marched forward. Half the people on the wall didn't have shields. *It's going to be a bloody slaughter.*

"Aye. And we're not going to stay around here to greet it," said Wulfee. "You ever seen a drayke?"

"No," said Pike. "Didn't think they were real."

Wulfee blinked. Neither did she, but she'd never dreamed the fires would go out, either.

"The Ranger made a good offer," Wulfee said. "He will take us to Pool. He can lead us through the Hallow Hills, and this army won't follow us. We can get out ahead of them. Nobody knows hill and arbor like the Rangers. We can go back to the Green Man, Shaqqa Ro, to get Maggie and bring her with us. She always dreamed of Pool and the nihr'el."

"It may not go like your plan, Wulf. You know the omens about the E'daru. They are skincrawlers. They are not to be trusted. You know this," said Pike.

Horns were blowing; people scrambling everywhere. Many probably realized the same thing Wulfee had—that they weren't going to hold them off this time.

"It's not time to die yet, Pike," Wulfee said. "Our land is not lost. As long as I'm alive, I will fight for these sacred lands. But we must defend it with victory in mind. The blood of Feldarra is still warm in our veins. I cannot run from who I really am. I can't do that." Wulfee sheathed her axe. For once in her life, she was ready to run. "I can't just lay down and die. I'm getting out of here. I need to carry on."

"And what about what matters to me? To Gen?" said Pike. Wulfee wondered when the old warrior was going to let his emotion out. He'd kept pretty quiet since the Hawka came. "The lad thinks you'll make him a karl, Wulfee. You know damn well that he can never *really* be a karl. You know Odhran would see me killed if he ever laid eyes on me again." Pike thumped his fist on his shield.

"Becoming a karl is just a matter of saying some words in front of a tree. And maybe it will be different if the fires ever come back. Things can change. People can change—"

"Gen can say the words all he wants, but the Gods will never hear them. Not from the lips of a Giy'er. The other karls won't accept him. It's the way it's always been. And people don't ever change, Wulf. Only their circumstances."

"And what makes you think the gods are still listening, anyway? The world is dying, Pike. Things *do* change, and you're a damn fool to think otherwise."

"Have you lost all hope?"

"Not all. I still stand breathing on the soil of my ancestors, and the enemy does not. Braden is still alive out there, somewhere. I can *feel* him, Pike. I dreamt of him last night. After Sweyne's dead... I can look for him again." But Wulfee only half believed her own words. *If you found him, he wouldn't want you anymore.*

"What would you have us do then, kihl'dor?" Pike sneered. He sheathed his axe and tugged at his braids to calm himself down. Wulfee knew thinking about death did that for him.

"Just stay and fight, Pike. I'm not asking you to come with me."

Pike thumped his shield again. "You know damn well I'm by your side."

"If we stay here, we will die," Wulfee said. "The best chance at defending our lands is to fall back to Pool. To convince Odhran to honour his blood. Claydon has probably already taken off in that direction. The Wolf will break through those gates and cross into Mal Hallow. He will march that army straight up the Northroad."

The enemy's archers had stopped marching. They were lining up to shoot, but they were too far away. Wulfee had no idea how they were planning to shoot *that* far. But they loosed their arrows, anyway. Pike grabbed his shield, the old clunky thing that had been with him through a hundred battles, and held it above both of their heads. Wulfee watched the black shadows of the arrows, first going up, then coming down. The sound of them striking the stone wall was like a thousand masons at work. The line of archers lowered their bows and continued their march forward.

"They've got magics in their bows," Wulfee said. Pike looked shocked. "They're over five hundred feet away, Pike. What the fuck is this sorcery?"

"Why would they sacrifice all those men to charge the wall yesterday when they had these?" asked Pike. Wulfee didn't know. *A mistake? A trick?* It wasn't like Sweyne at all. It was damn right sloppy, like a child trying to figure out new toys.

"Thought he could rush us, I guess. Then realized he couldn't. It's time to go, Pike. Let's get out of here, eh?" Wulfee grabbed her axe again. Pike just nodded, shield in hand. The two of them made their way down the tower steps and found Gen. He had his big hairy hands on the wooden crossbeams of the gate as if he was holding them up.

"Gen, come with us," said Wulfee. The Giy'er smiled. The sound of a thousand bow strings snapping echoed across the valley. A black wave of arrows blanketed the sky.

"Down!" someone shouted. Wulfee ducked beneath Pike's shield, even though they were covered by the barbican. The lot that surrounded them ducked as well. The arrows reached their apex in the sky and fell. A ten-hundred black drops of steel rain. Each one landing with a hollow thud that shook the ground beneath her. Wulfee took a breath. Then the screaming started.

All were fine below. Above, on the wall, people were dying.

"Now, Gen. Pike, let's go!" Wulfee shouted. Blood tip-tapped on the ground beside her, leaking down from the dying above. She felt ill. The Giy'er ran, and the old warrior followed. A group of would-be escapees joined them. They moved towards the inner northern gate to cross the bridge back into Mammoth's Head. Many others continued to join so that they now formed a large group.

And then the mad scramble began. Pushing and shoving all around her. Screaming and yelling in every direction. Suffering and dying atop the battlements. Another snap of bowstrings echoed.

"Down, Gen!" Wulfee said crouching down. Pike knelt beside her with his shield held tight above them. Arrows rained down on them, piercing Pike's shield with a *thwump* as they wedged into the old wood. More screaming. Death cries. Suffering and panic all around. Gen had no cover. When Wulfee stood up, the Giy'er was standing before her, completely unharmed. *The lad has luck on his side. The most loyal kind of luck I've seen.*

They ran across the bridge with the throng of people. More arrows fell. Fewer screams now. More dead.

A row of Claydon's men stood armed at the gate. Spears thrust out in a phalanx formation.

One of them screamed, "Back to the barbican, you dodgy bastards!" He pointed his spear at them, but the lad looked half-starved and the spear was rusty.

"The battle is all but lost already!" someone screamed from behind Wulfee. More shoving started. The throng pushed each other closer to the guards.

"Get back, you fucks!" one guard screamed. And then, "Kill them!"

Before Wulfee could get herself out of the mass, one guard stabbed his spear into someone's gut.

Then the fighting started. Bashing with fists and elbows, kicks and heels, anything to move away from the spears. The guards killed more and more, and behind them, arrows rained down. Everyone was going to die here. Wulfee had to bash a few heads and take a few elbows to the face and body herself. Then she felt big hands around her neck. Squeezing, choking the life out of her. Some bastard was strangling her. She kicked at him, clawed at him with dirty, broken nails, but the bloke just squeezed tighter. He didn't bother restraining her hands, though. Those wandered to her belt and found the knife she'd sheathed there. She jabbed the knife into the man's chest with everything she had. He backed off of her with a look of horror on his face.

"You stabbed me..." he gurgled.

"You were strangling me!" Wulfee said between breaths. "Are you fucking mad?"

His eyes bulged, mouth hanging open. He drooled a little, then fell over, dead.

As Wulfee pulled herself up, she watched a man die. A guard was pulling his spear out of the man's stomach when he saw Wulfee. As the man charged her, she whispered a prayer to the Bluebirds for luck, and they must have heard her. A loud splintering crack from behind them made the guard look up. That was enough time for Wulfee to slip under the spear and stab him in the small space between chestplate and helm. She held her weapon there and felt the warm blood flow down her hand, up her arm, dripping down her torso. She listened to the guard take his last gurgling breath. Flipped open his helm to see his eyes. They were already staring at something off in the middle distance. Some angel, perhaps, though Wulfee hardly believed in that kind of thing anymore. *Bastards in the Fells know better than to get in my way.* Another loud crack made Wulfee look this time. The blooded folk were battering down the gates. *And how long 'till they open that cage... how long till Sweyne is sitting on the throne at Mammoth's Head?*

She felt a big, soft hand on her shoulder.

"Time to go, Wulfee," said Gen. Thick, fleshy blood covered the young Giy'er's hands as if he was a baker and their bodies were dough.

She and Gen hurried through the gate. A rush of people had already made it past the guards and were running out to the fields beyond Tusk. Pike was waiting on the other side of the bridge, cleaning his bloodied shield with a cloth.

"We're off, Pike," Wulfee said in a rush. "Let's go." He agreed. She looked over her shoulder one last time and saw gnarled ladders erected along the walls. *They'll have the castle within the hour.*

It wasn't always easy for Wulfee to run from her honour. She had taken the oaths of Feldarra as a girl, under the thick branches of the nihr'el at Pool, in front of the kihl'dors of every clan. And she had meant what she said when she promised to protect her homeland with everything and her life. She had taken those oaths seriously and killed many would-be conquerors and pretenders of the tree. She went against her own morals to kill folk who might have been more innocent than she was, all for her honour. She fell in love with and heartbound a madman, then bore his children, and abandoned one of those children when she turned back to face the madman. All of it was for the oaths. For the Feldarra. For Mal Hallow. She'd been chasing some kind of normal life for herself. A place to sit back, smoke her chuff pipe, and watch her grandkids grow. Always chasing and never quite getting there. The oaths came first, always. Her dad had told her she needed to learn that sometimes running was the only option if you were keen on living. She was keen on that now. Keen to see her sons one day in the cloud halls to tell them she was sorry. Keen on killing Sweyne and cleansing her soul so she can die and rest easy.

It was good to hope. She was just so damn short on it these days.

"They're going to pour into this country like a river," said Pike.

"Ain't nothing going to stop a river that wants to flood," said Wulfee.

Pike smiled.

"Might be a time the whole world is flooded with their pale arses." Pike looked up at the sky, and in a lighter voice, said, "Reckon, I'll be dead by then." He seemed to relish the thought.

"Aye," said Wulfee. Maybe she would be too. She wasn't quite ready to lie down yet, though. She still had some chasing to do. "We better hurry before they open that bloody cage."

SLEIGHT OF HAND

I T WAS THAT GODDAMN cold again. Even when bleeding out hot blood, James couldn't escape it. In his veins, under his skin, in the very depths of his mind. It was freezing when the souls gathered around him, and it was about to get colder. He opened his lungs and inhaled, filled them with the souls of the dead. Ate the life from them so they would exist no longer. The wound was red and angry, gushing pulses of sticky blood onto his hand that held the gash closed. He inhaled deeper, panting through raw, chortled breaths. The souls resisted, but his lungs were iron. When he felt the life in them, he took it. All of it, like the Hermit had taught him all those years ago. He choked on a frozen breath. Still, it was better than dying, though, and James embraced the cold now—it was the only thing that had never left him.

Slowly, he felt the dead soul give him a new life. Replacing old flesh and blood with new. He screamed to mask the pain, but the pain was too ugly to cover. He heaved the contents of his empty stomach. His bowels cramped like they were being rung out. And when the pain subsided and his head cleared, he looked up to see the man who had once been his dad's closest ally gawking at him. James knew it took a real sight for both of Derudin's eyes to focus in, and they were both locked on James now.

"By the gods," Derudin murmured. "You're Bren Culdaine's son, ain't ya?" James shrugged. "You are. You are him! It must be. Bren Culdaine told us about this. He told us about you, and we thought Bren had lost his mind. But it is true, isn't it? You're Hendurinn reborn... You learned the power your dad claimed you could... I- I. By the gods... The mad bastard got you to that hermit after all..." Derudin sat back in his throne and pushed the woman off his lap. "You've grown... I–I didn't recognize..." Maybe Derudin didn't take a good enough look at James in the dark hall to notice him under the beard. James didn't answer, then Derudin pointed a dirty finger at James's stomach. "Your gut...it stopped bleeding..."

"Yeah." James lifted his tunic and rubbed a hand over clean pink flesh, still stained with blood. *But you ran from the Hermit before you learned everything you needed to learn, didn't you? You failed your dad and let him die thinking he'd failed his country and his family.* Padraig stared with his jaw hanging. The topless woman did the same. The flutist and the harpist had both stopped playing, and the clean woman scribbled madly on her parchment. Derudin smiled and raised his goblet towards the ceiling.

"AYE!" Derudin proclaimed, and the hall erupted in a bellow of merriment. Adeqor reached for the bottle and was successful this time. The flute and harp started up again, completely out of time with each other.

Derudin yelled, amused, "He's a bloody seer! A World Walker of the old times, like Hendurinn. Can you believe it? Like from your gran's stories! He's come to bring the fire back. The bloody mad bastard was right!"

More cheers. James felt sick.

"Padraig," Derudin said with a slur again, "wake Eridan, tell him Hendurinn has walked straight out of a song and into our hall. And get my equipment together. We leave in the morning!" The big man nodded and left the hall in a hurry. Adeqor stopped drinking mid swig.

"What do you mean *we?*" Eurick asked. "This is no job for the likes of an army." James cringed. "It'll be hard going, and the fewer people there are, the better for that sort of trek."

"Ah, it will be okay, raven." Derudin reached over to the topless woman and started fondling her again. "Lighten up. If what you tell me is true, it will be a fine journey! The seer here will save the Mother, and I will take the glory. Maybe take Kallahorn as my new home. I always fancied myself living in one of those Lovasi castles. Brinley will shit himself when he hears that, the smug bastard. And if what you tell me is a lie, I'll kill the lot of you and be done with it!" said Derudin. "Problem solved!"

Adeqor laughed.

"Great!" He took a swig from the wineskin. Derudin gave a curious nod to a guard, who then whispered something to the two big men who had been holding James earlier. They crept closer to Adeqor. "A bit of an escort is all we need! This will be a fine journey indeed."

Adeqor took another drink, and at that moment, the three big men seized the wizard and forced him face down onto one of the wooden dining tables. Drinks spilled and clay plates crashed to make room for Adeqor's face. The noisy music ceased. Derudin unsheathed his sword that was still covered in James's blood. Adeqor's body hummed with magics.

The lord called out, "His hands! Hold his bloody hands." But a brightly coloured spiral burst out of Adeqor's hands. Then there was a cracking smash as splintering wood blew out into the night sky, leaving behind a large hole in the roof. The wizard launched another beam of his magics and blasted two soldiers out into the dark. Just as quickly, there was a sharp thump, like a blade piercing into solid wood. And then another. Then Adeqor was screaming. Derudin stood on the table and put his scuffed leather boot on Adeqor's neck. A severed hand and pieces of fingers bled out on the table.

"I am your saviour!" Derudin called out. "I have crippled the wizard, and now I will bring fire back to our kingdom using our new seer!" The hall erupted into cheering bellows. The music started again. A woman came out of nowhere, gave James a sloppy kiss on the lips, and then, just as quickly, disappeared into the crowd cheering. James was stunned. Derudin took his foot off of Adeqor's neck. The wizard was screaming in a harsh rune tongue. "Get this wizard to our shaman to close those wounds. We don't want him to die now."

When Derudin's guards swooped in to grab Adeqor, the wizard started to fight them with his bloody stump. He headbutted one before they tackled him to the ground and seized him. The wizard screamed his jagged, foreign words as the guards carried him out of the hall.

The lord of Ockam, who James knew all his life as Derudin Deadmaker, a name he'd well earned, took his leave of the hall, which was now a mess of blood and dust and wood. Eurick looked at James with that same ashen look he had at the Fever Stones. James glared at Adeqor. Both his hands had been severed. One was completely gone at the wrist, the other Derudin had only severed from the thumb knuckle to the pinky knuckle. *Bloody wizard got what he deserved.* As much as he thought Derudin was a bloody twat, it made James feel good to see someone stand up to the wizard.

James said, "Guess we're leaving in the morning then."

"The morning it is." Eurick nudged the man who was falling asleep in the chair next to him and said, "Hey where can a guy get a drink around here, man?" The man only hiccupped.

"We should at least be safe here if the Hawka attack," James said. "There's enough of us here."

Eurick sighed and leaned back. "I guess, man. Transportin's thirsty work, though."

Then the door creaked open, and a head poked inside the room. James thought he was ten years old again, waiting for Eridan at the stables to go riding, chasing him out to the grove where they fought with swords, away from their parents while they played their own games of power in the court of childhood. Derudin's son was his closest friend for many years. James stood beside Eridan as his dead mom burned on a pyre, and that kind of bond lasted a lifetime.

Eridan walked in, looked around, and whistled.

"Holy shit, I missed all this?" He put his hands on his hips. James knew he recognized him. Eridan smiled. "You guys wanna get drunk?"

MORNING CAME, AND THE Lord of Ockam was ready early. James rubbed his eyes as Derudin walked into the courtyard guiding a large white destrier cloaked in steel barding. On a mount behind him, Adeqor was chained around the neck. He was swaying back and forth, like he might fall off were he not shackled upright. Derudin's death stealer had wrapped both of his hands in white cloth, now stained rusty red. His dark skin had lost its glow, and he almost looked Human. Beaten, hurt, and with little hope. James couldn't believe that someone had gotten the better of him.

Derudin had only a few dozen soldiers on horse with him. All assembled in the courtyard of the inner bailey. He had two brown mares set aside for James and Eurick.

"I've considered what I saw last night," Derudin said, handing the reins of his horse to one of his guards. "And I have considered the possibility that my gran's tales may stem from some long-forgotten truths. Eridan will stay at Ockam with the army to defend our gates from whatever may come around the Wick from the north." Derudin held his arms up in the air as Padraig draped a chainmail shirt over his lord's body. Other servants and guards rushed around the courtyard loading provisions and making last minute adjustments to the horses and gear. "I've advised my steward to send an eagle to Lord Richard Brynmor at Elurra, in the Glenn. He has proven a worthy ally before. I will tell him I'm leaving for a few fortnights and ask him for support should the Clan of the Severed Head breach Mammoth's Head." James considered that. He had a look up at the massive hole in the side of the decrepit hall from Adeqor. *Would this place be enough? Even with an army to defend it?* James didn't think so.

"The last I saw, she had a sea of Hawka behind her," James said.

"And my army *will* be sufficient," Derudin said. "These are blooded folk here. Each one is a proven killer in combat. My son Eridan has sixteen braids in his hair, and these folk would follow either of us into death. We've dealt with Hawka come down before and plenty else." James looked around at the rotting log walls and the rickety wooden platforms built on broken stone watchtowers.

"I bloody hope so," James said.

"Only thing you should hope for is that you live through whatever this is. If I wasn't..." Derudin turned to the clean woman who was scribbling. "What is that word you say that means really very interested?"

"Intrigued?" The woman looked up from her parchments. Derudin clapped.

"Ah yes, intrigued." He looked back at James. "If I wasn't so intrigued by this situation, I'd have killed you for good, Culdaine. I don't think souls of the dead could fix a severed head."

"Don't you have other allies to call on?" James said. "Knights to raise? Richard Brynmor has got to be a hundred miles away or more. The Banshee ain't nothing to take lightly."

"The kingdom is full of cheats, liars, and traitors. Thanks to your dad. We all hang the red eagle banners from our castle walls, but not one of us is looking out for anyone but themselves. Especially now that the fires have gone. And Brynmor breeds those big, beautiful horses in the Glennish Flats. He has a horse for every person and more to spare. He can move faster than any army in Ardura." Derudin smiled when he saw James clench his fists. "What? You think I've forgotten what your dad did to this kingdom? Do you think any of us forgot?"

Derudin was poking at the wrong spots.

"You spit on my dad's grave by flying that flag."

Derudin spit at James's feet. "Your dad has no grave. But I'll spit at the feet of the one who got him killed."

"You're a fucking traitor!" James exploded. He ran at Derudin with his hands restrained, but Padraig tackled him. The big man pounded his big fist into James's jaw, and James stopped fighting. He forgot where he was for a moment before he heard a voice.

"Let him go." Derudin helped James stand. "There's things you need to know, kid. You've been gone too long." *I know that you would have died in that arbor defending your king if you had any honour.* "It was your dad who was the bloody traitor. He went mad, kid, you remember that. Said he went looking for magics in the hills, babbling of hermits, and half-gods. Babbling about *you!* He left us all with no choice but to bend our knee to the Ayelish, or to burn alive on their pyres." Derudin stepped into a stirrup and mounted his warhorse. "What would you do to save your family from death?" *I did nothing...* The Lord of Ockam scowled at an Ayelish flag. The red eagle on white sat dead in the wind and didn't care what anyone thought of it.

"If you want to call me a traitor for saving my people, you go on ahead. I won't lose any sleep over it. I fly those flags and collect the taxes, and the Ayelish bring us food, weapons, and horses. They give me everything. Your dad left *nothing!*" Derudin spat at James's feet again. James scowled at the wet dollop in front of him. Inside, he felt broken. He had never wanted his dad by his side more. Bren would explain how Derudin was wrong. "You're lucky I've chosen to let you live. And you'll bloody remember that I own your life now, Culdaine. I can do with it as I will. You are my prisoner. If this wizard is full of shit and there is no Mother of Nature, I'll chop all three of your heads off. I'll have my revenge on your dad through you if I choose to take it." To the gatekeepers, he yelled, "Open the goddamned gates!"

He cursed some more under his breath, but James stopped listening. He wasn't there anymore. He was waking up in the snow and finding everyone he had ever known slaughtered, laying frozen in pink snow. His dad *had* gone chasing magics. But he did it all trying to save the Hallow. He didn't die for nothing. He couldn't let his family die for nothing.

"It's Calen Alder to blame, not my dad," James finally said. "He's our enemy, not each other." Derudin's hard face softened a bit. Then silence. Then the lord smiled.

"If it is Alder that has done all this, he's a damn fool for thinking he can pull it off." Derudin looked at *Essikah* on James's back. "You really are full of magics, ain't ya? Just like old Bren used to say you were." He laughed. "Let's see what the Mother will do with you. I always did like my gran's stories, Culdaine. I must know how this one ends. We'll only be making a few stops along the way. I treat my prisoners with respect, mostly. So you'll have nothing to fret over," he said.

Alongside Eurick, Derudin led the fellowship out of the gates and into the forsaken country of Mal Hallow that James once called home.

From the front of the convoy, Eurick said, "To get to Kallahorn, we must take a route that eventually won't allow for horse travel. It is a very peculiar path through the Mountains of the Mother."

"We'll deal with the horses when the time comes, transporter," said Derudin. "For now, let's keep our feet soft, eh? Take us to Dawning!"

As they rode on, James noticed the Lovasi woman in a white robe scribbling on a parchment while steering her horse at the same time.

"Who is she?" James asked Padraig, who was riding close by. "Why is she always scratching on that parchment?"

"She writes a thing called books. About *things* and stuff. Calls herself a *Sko-lar*," Padraig said confidently.

The Lovasi woman turned around in her saddle.

"I can speak for myself, gentleman. And it is impolite to call a professional by their job title. I have a name. It is Mineera Mori. I'm a *scholar* of New Lovas. I'm composing an account of life amongst the barbarian kingdoms of northern Ardura to be displayed at the Library of Vasanti, across the Old Sea in Edura."

"Barbarian?" James said, feeling insulted in a way he couldn't understand.

"She says things like that," said Padraig.

James shrugged and rode up beside Florence. He glared at her and felt hate bleed from his eye sockets.

"You know I can't give you this knife back as a prisoner," she said, unbothered. "You're too slow with that sword, and it's so heavy no one else wants to carry it, but a knife is too easy."

James lowered his voice and softly said, "I can't promise I won't kill you to get it back."

Florence's smile slowly faded when she realized there was no jest in James's voice. She looked at Padraig, who had been assigned to guard James.

"You keep an eye on him, eh?" she said.

Padraig nodded confidently.

"I've got him," he said and touched a hand to the sword on his belt. James just kept riding, saying nothing. He didn't have much of a choice at the moment. Then Eurick's words rang in his head. *A man's always got choices.* He put a hand over the spot where Derudin stabbed him and smiled. *You're a damn hard man to kill...* Maybe he had more choices than he could see, and he'd just been making the wrong ones. For now, he rode on behind Eurick, under the flag of his enemy. He needed to get to the Mother one way or another, and part of him felt safer with Derudin than he had with Adeqor. At least Derudin was damn well predictable. *You're actually going to try this thing, ain't ya? You're going to bloody try and save the world...* James would do it for Maggie and for the memory of his family. He was going to bring back the fire and send the dead back home. That was the only choice worth making.

"*Help us,*" they whispered. James hoped to Hell he could.

PART TWO

No one can keep you from living as your nature requires.
Nothing can happen to you that isn't required by Nature.

Marcus Aurelius

OLD HAUNTS

J AMES FELT A WET coldness as he walked through oceans of dead folk to get away for a piss break. The things just seemed to be in the damn way all the time now. They'd been clinging to him tighter since he'd started paying mind to them. But they were still useless for anything but to eat life from them. But the closer James got to them, the more he felt the warmth that lingered in their souls. He understood these dead weren't much different from the living. They held memories, joy, and sorrow. They were alive once, and they only want to pass through to the Otherworld so they could be alive once more.

"*Help us. Please. Let us home,*" they begged him.

"I don't know how," James said to the empty air.

"Stop talking to your willy and hurry on then," said Padraig. James figured he had convinced him he was a madman the first time a week ago when Padraig saw James talking to nothing.

"Yeah, yeah," James said, draining his bladder onto a gnarled old maple. He could tell they had passed the first Rise of summer by now from the thick and dried maple sap. Padraig tightened the ropes back around James's wrists and tied him to the other end of his horse. He gave him enough slack so that James could fall back behind and not have to talk to the bastard. They called themselves the Blood Company, Derudin's personal guard. A weathered old bunch who had fought together for two decades. The only constant in their lives were each other. They flew Derudin's flag of dirty white with a bloody red hand print and draped it over each horse beside the red eagle flag of Ayeland. It was the same banner Derudin flew before he bent the knee, and apparently he only had the bones to hang it while walking through the arbor.

Derudin Deadmaker's warriors had a reputation for being fierce. Every one of them was blooded. There were troves of teenagers at Ockam itching to get into the fighting pits so they could earn their braid and a place in Derudin's army. The Blood Company was well known for making slaves of their victims of war and forcing them to fight in the pits against young warriors who wanted nothing more than to kill any slave in single combat to earn their braid. James never understood that fierce ambition to kill. He'd wished that he could *stop* killing. For James, killing wasn't a choice, it wasn't for honour, it was for survival. And it was something dark and otherworldly—like a possession. He had sliced his own braids off a long time ago. He hated the reminder of the bloody killer he was. *Is... You haven't changed as much as you think you have, have you? Without the braids to mark your kills, you've lost count.*

James ended up walking alongside Derudin's bard. He sang for the Company as they travelled through the haunted Wick, with the Hallow Hills tight on one side. He was the lad who had played in the hall of Ockam and made an awful racket.

"Name's Itchy," he said to James one day as they were walking.

"You're not too good at that thing, eh?" James chuckled. "Aren't bards supposed to be *good?*" Itchy's eyes fell to the ground.

"Well, not when you're first starting out. I mean... I only picked it up because our last bard, Sara, died," Itchy explained. "War, you see. I only just learned what a 'c' chord was last week. I'm going on forty, for the gods's sake, it ain't easy, guy! So I just need some practice. And time."

"Lots of time," James said, laughing to himself.

"Okay, that's just mean," said Itchy. He had his black hair cut short at the front and long at the back, in the bardic tradition of the Mal. Hard lines creased the skin around his brown eyes, and they got even harder when he sang. He wore a loose-fitting shirt that showed his hairy chest, where everyone else wore leather and chainmail. And though his name was Itchy, James rarely saw him scratching.

"How do you get a name like Itchy?" James asked. The bard only laughed and plucked a rather flat sounding note.

"Same way as you, my friend. From the mouth of my parents," Itchy said. James only stared at him. He thought bards made up their own names. "They had a sense of humour," Itchy added.

The bard sang old songs that James knew and newer ones he didn't. But the lot of it was shite. He strummed his wood harp clunkily and cleared his throat in the middle of verses. But he was the only person in the Blood Company who treated James with any respect. The rest of the lot were afraid of him. All James could do was keep riding.

How long till Ellorin comes over those hills behind you? How long until she's got you on a stake, bleeding out, with your soul in her mouth?

It had been three days since they left Ockam for Dawning and entered the Wick. Three days since Derudin severed the hands and fingers of the wizard. James had one eye stuck on Adeqor, anticipating him to do something with his magics. He was full of ideas James couldn't understand. Full of forces that nobody understood. But the wizard sat still. Looking defeated. Not saying a word. Adeqor gave James the odd feeling he'd strike out when it was least expected, and they'd have to run. He hadn't trusted Adeqor since the moment he met him. And after what the wizard did at Fever, James had been waiting for the right opportunity to slip away from the mad bastard.

But they moved along steadily, and James never saw a good chance. This lot had marched together many times, and they had made no delays. Along the way, they talked and ate dried fruits, salted meats, and hard cheese, and hardly worried that the world was dead and brown all around them.

"Look at this," Eurick muttered one day as they approached a shallow stream. He pointed at the watermarks on the banks. They were at least four feet higher than the trickling water flowing below. "The streams are draining fast. Soon they will stop flowing completely."

"The Hare will not allow it," Florence said.

"Seems like it's being allowed..." said Derudin. "The gods have betrayed us yet again." Itchy plucked a grim sounding note. Derudin gave him a grim look.

"*Gods*. Are you kidding me? You think those divine lunatics could do something like *this?*" scoffed Adeqor. "This is the work of something bigger than gods."

"Sorry," said Itchy. They all stopped to take a drink from the dying stream, and the bard played no more songs.

The further they went, the more memories came to James. Like they were caught up in his old haunts and jumped out at him as he passed by. They went by small farms, furrowed on tiny strips of land between clusters of crusted cottonwoods and maples. Past wells and small hamlets that he remembered from his youth when he and his dad would take this route. It didn't quite feel the same as being completely immersed in the Wick. As long as they had the Hallow Hills on one side of them, James felt the protection of the Old Gods. The Mal believed they live below the Hills.

The Father Tree, god of justice and judge of the souls of the dead. The Hare, goddess of mercy, peace, and fertility who brought the harvest. The Owl, god of wisdom and foresight. The Stag, god of courage, strength, and fortitude, the fighter god, and the god of war. The Crow, goddess of death, decay, and mystery. The Swan, goddess of innocence, love, and all things beautiful. And the Bluebird Twins: Ayla, goddess of arts and music, and Nox, god of crafting—together, the Bluebirds brought luck. The pantheon of the Old Gods was still strong in James's mind, and each one gave him what he needed when he prayed to them. But James had turned his back on them since the Hermit tried to force him to go *down* to their world. He didn't want to have to face what was inside of himself down there. It terrified him more than anything.

I was only a child, alone, with the Hermit in a rotten hole. I had been there for days already... How could I have gone through with it? Anyone would have run.

After he had gotten out of the Hermit hole, James prayed to the Maw God for help. The Maw was the eighth god. It wore the body of a lupin, a mountainous wolf-like animal and was also known as the Outcast. A god blessed thrice by names. A god of three dominions: darkness, the moon, and the unknown workings of nature. And a god thrice cursed by the other gods. The Maw was always roaming the Otherworld and so praying to it was difficult because it was never in the same place. James could only sit under a nytewood each night and pray for the Lupin to show up. Finally, one night, it appeared to him in a dream, standing on two feet with a blood-soaked maw dripping black saliva. James asked for it to help get rid of his curse, and the Lupin only snarled and laughed an inhuman laugh that still haunted his dreams now. *"Your curse will eat you,"* it had barked at him and continued to snort and laugh. James never prayed to the Maw God again, or any other god, either.

James looked at the nytewoods they passed with unease. They made him remember the gods he turned his back on. He could see the ghosts of dead folk hanging about in swarms beneath the towering black trunks as they passed. Hundreds upon hundreds of them, doing what the dead do—waiting, he figured, for life to catch up with them. Many of them waved as he walked by. James waved back. Itchy looked at him strangely, over to the arbor, then back at James and smiled politely.

The land of his birth brought James back and made him remember. The good and the bad. It wasn't right what happened here. Generations of families that had spent hundreds of years here were killed or forced out in just a few months. They'd spent their whole lives on one plot of land. James spat. He just shook his head, but inside, he was screaming.

I had a whole life here. Love, happiness, belonging. All of those memories. I remember feeling like there could never be another way of life. I thought about this place all the time I was away... Now, nothing but the birdsong is like I remembered. Mal Hallow may as well be a different country on the far side of the sea that I've never been to before. I'm a stranger here.

New red and white flags with the Ayelish eagle hung in place of brown and yellow ones, with the Hallow bull moose. Roads and watchtowers sprung up in places where there was nothing but brush and trees before. New people replaced the ones James had grown up with. The faces he remembered from his childhood had vanished, and new ones filled their places as if the ones James knew had never existed. As if *he* had never existed. It made him want to cry out, thinking about his parents. *They died for this country, and you only ran. It's like they were never here. You made their deaths worthless. Time moves forward always. It leaves everything behind. Only the songs remember.*

He shifted his arse in the saddle and carried on riding.

The sun was falling low in the sky. James rubbed his horse under the chin, let the stallion feel some love. *Everyone needs a little love.* He had changed this horse's name to Bren, after his dad. And in a way, it felt like they were doing this walk together again, like the old days. He needed that bit of extra support to keep on.

They arrived at a crossroads, where the main dirt road was blocked by a massive felled cottonwood. Derudin wanted to go the other way, but Eurick had heard enough, and they broke out into a heated argument.

"Let's just go the other way!" Derudin shouted.

"We don't have the time for your detours, Lord. The Banshee will be on us again before we know it. Do you know how long *just going the other way* will take? We must complete the job in a timely fashion. For the sake of the gods, man! We must move the tree," said Eurick.

"Who said we weren't completing the job?" Derudin smirked. "We just need to make a stop at Dawning to show old Brinley this fresh development in our potential futures. *Me.* The Lord of Kallahorn. You think that bastard ever imagined that? You think he's ever captured a Warlock? Of course he hasn't. He'll bow down to me."

"It is a more direct route to the Mountains of the Mother along this road, Lord," Eurick slammed his finger on a map. "Please, we have to move that tree. Tell the Company to start chopping."

Derudin grinned. "We're not going down that road, transporter. We're going *my* way. To Dawning. I'll have you remember that you're a prisoner of mine. The mountains aren't going anywhere, fellow! But these schemers are always scheming. Brinley has looked down on me for decades. Best to keep him on his heels by showing him my Warlock and Culdaine's son. Show that bastard that someone is actually trying to do something about all this." Deruin gestured at the sky. "And soon, I'll have Brynmor of the Glenn protecting Ockam for me alongside my boy, Eridan. It's foolproof!"

Your Warlock? Nobody owns that wizard, thought James. Eurick sighed.

"It will add weeks to our journey," the raven said.

"I have seen enough of suffering, transporter. The war for Mal Hallow still lives in the darkness of my dreams, and its screams are endless. I have to live with this forever, but I will not subject my people to more suffering," Derudin boomed. "I need to show Brinley my strength so he will join me when the Ayelish march north again." His lazy eye drooped as he stroked his beard and looked up to the sky again. James wanted to punch him. "Sun has just about had it for the day and so have I." Derudin dismounted and found a wineskin, taking a long swig. "We'll camp here for the evening. You can drink with me tonight, raven. I'll have plenty of time to tell you why old Brinley is worth rousing up. He won't believe his eyes when he sees that wizard. Not to mention that bloody sword the seer is carrying around." To the Company he said, "Not one of you touches an axe or goes near that tree unless it's to piss on it!"

Loud cheers echoed through the arbor and sent birds flying. *Great way to attract the god damned Banshee.*

Derudin pressed the wineskin into Eurick's chest. The transporter took a long swig. Derudin looked at James. "Isn't that sword heavy?"

"Yes," said James. Derudin nodded, seemingly amazed.

"I'll have a drink," said Adeqor. The first words James had heard him speak in many hours. "Pass that here."

"Nothing for him. Wizards get crafty when they've got some shine in 'em," barked Derudin, and grabbed the skin back from Eurick.

"You wouldn't know crafty if you saw it, barbarian," said Adeqor. He hopped off his horse without using his arms, bare feet landing deftly on the dirt. His neck was still tied to the reins. He led the horse with ease, using his yoke. Itchy, the bard, stopped mid-strum, Mineera started scribbling something on her parchment, Padraig reached for his sword belt. The rest of the couple dozen crowded in, too: Florence and her band of Rangers, Tam the road smith, Gerdey the cook, and many blooded stood up with axe in hand. Derudin glared at the wizard, studying him. James remembered what his dad had said of Derudin behind his back. That he always suspected an ulterior motive to any situation. That he was untrustworthy, and that was made obvious by the fact that he couldn't trust anyone.

"And what would you call crafty, wizard? Getting yourself captured wandering in the Wick? Having your hands severed by a Human? Is that crafty?" Derudin pulled his axe and bared his teeth. Adeqor's horse squealed, snorted in a frenzy. The wizard suddenly sprang to life and calmed it in an instant with a soft word. His dark skin glowed as if some magics were flowing through his veins instead of blood. Brown blood crusted the old bandages around his wrists. His pointed black beard shone wonderfully under the fleeting light of day.

"Crafty is preparing for the end of things. Culling my energy and calling the dead," said Adeqor. Derudin's lips flattened over his teeth.

"What?" Padraig blurted. Adeqor chuckled under his breath and walked closer to Derudin.

"You ever seen a horde of Hawka? Ever had one of your friends eaten alive, torn apart? You will tonight. This fat one will probably be the first to die." Padraig gripped his axe tighter, and after a moment, James heard him gulp. "You ever seen the Banshee? Ellorin, the Queen of Shadow? You will tonight. She may eat your soul, child." Adeqor snatched the wineskin between his two shackled, bandaged hands. Took a long swig. Then another. "Set up camp. But get ready to fight. She's coming. More appropriately, get ready to run."

Derudin looked around at his crew, back at Adeqor. The wizard walked up to a tree and took a piss on it. The horse nickered softly at his side.

"Well, I told you to set up camp, didn't I?" Derudin yelled, and the lot of them scurried. "And shackle the damn wizard to a tree or something."

T HEY SAT AROUND A dead fire pit.

"And what's a smith without a forge, anyway? Eh?" said Tam, the road smith, and sulked. He was rather drunk.

"Hey, man, don't talk like that," Eurick said, also drunk. "Wasn't two weeks past that I lost my maps, my horses, and all of my supplies. What kind of transporter has no maps of the Raven's Guild, eh? No horses to transport with? I found my way back. I got different maps, fresh supplies. And here I am, transporting again. You don't need your forge, Tam. You're more than just your forge." Tam's eyes were welling; Eurick put his fist to his chin and nodded, and Tam did the same back. Then the two embraced, both crying a little.

The blooded folk sat around and sharpened their knives and axes. James recognized many of them from his dad's council meetings. Karillin Three Thumbs, a massive man with a bald head tattooed with braids. For each victory in single combat, he added a tattoo braid instead of a real one. He said an ex-lover had cut his pointer finger on his thick right hand down to the nub and gave him his third thumb. He'd taught James how to use an axe just as well with both hands. Berra Coldblood, a madwoman who spoke no words and killed on demand. She'd cut out her own tongue to keep from talking to the voices in her head. But that didn't stop her from teaching James how to keep his blade sharp by storing it in a leather sheathe and rubbing it with burn bug oil. Logan TooTall was a little person who could throw a knife into an apple placed on top of a person's head from thirty yards away. He had tried to teach James how to throw knives with the same accuracy, but James failed at that, and instead, unintentionally, taught James not to underestimate anyone. And Arda Honeytongue, whose tongue was as long as a serpent and split down the middle like one, too. She'd taught James how to spit farther than anyone he'd ever come across besides her.

They were all folk his dad feared being on the wrong side of. This was a mean lot, shrouded in boiled leather and chainmail, and each of them as solid as a gnarled oak. Padraig sharpened his sword and tried to talk with James, but James wasn't paying any attention to what the guy was saying. The big man had untied James, overconfident in his own ability to stop him should he try anything. James laid *Essikah* down in the dirt beside him. It had been chafing his lower back all day.

"That's a gigantic sword, eh?" Padraig crunched into an apple. "You know how to fight with that thing?"

"I'll find out when it's time to fight, I guess." James's stomach growled at the sweet smell of the apple.

"That seems like an awful idea. Can't you take a few practice swings or something?" Padraig tossed the apple core and screeched a whetstone up his sword blade. James shrugged. He didn't think a few practice swings were too bad an idea. The Lord of Ockam seemed wary that they had untied James and didn't take his eyes off him. James knew that Derudin didn't trust any prophecy and despised any sort of ancient knowledge. He remembered Derudin's arguments with his dad about exactly that. The runes on *Essikah* held secrets that none of them knew the answers to, save maybe the wizard, and that *would* make Derudin uneasy.

Across from Derudin, Adeqor was still shackled to a large elm and staring up at the stars through the branches. James looked up there himself and hoped to see the stars moving as if Maggie was looking at the same sky somewhere. But the stars stayed where they were, and James found he couldn't keep his eyes off Adeqor for long. *What is he planning? What kind of trick is he conjuring?* Itchy saw James and nudged him.

"You don't see it at all, do ya?" Itchy said.

James rubbed the back of his head. He *hadn't* seen much of anything since Eurick found him. He followed blindly, like a stray dog hoping to find one more scrap of food. "What do you mean?"

"The wizard has kept you in the dark like a rat. Led you astray. Pulled the wool over your eyes, as the Ayelish sing. Haven't you heard that song, *Never Trust A Warlock*?"

James hadn't.

"What's this about?" James said. In his experience, bards had always tried to use too many words to explain things.

"Still got problems with Calen Alder and the Ayelish, too, eh?"

"He took our lands and killed our people. He hunted us down and slaughtered my family and everyone I had ever known."

"And what have you done about that?" Itchy plucked a rather dissonant note and raised his chin as if waiting for a reply. James wanted to punch him.

"I lived," James replied.

"And hid away up in those mountains. Who are you really afraid of, Culdaine? King Alder or yourself?"

James felt something tingle in his stomach. Some itch of realization that he'd long subdued. *You stayed up there for Maggie. She was worth forgetting everything else.* But James didn't know how to explain that. He didn't want to talk about it.

"The Ayelish want to kill our culture, our gods, and the memory of our people," James finally said. "Doesn't that scare you?"

"Aye. But they let Derudin live if he promised to do away with the old ways and recognize their One God Eralis as the only. Better than death and torture. Better than being hunted down and slaughtered. But your dad, the mad old dog, spoke of all this nonsense. He said the fires would die, he said the earth would dry up and the crops would not grow. He said the prophecy of Hendurinn from the Cycle of Dain was coming to pass." Itchy plucked a lonely, grim sounding note. "Seems he was right. I've never really been a gambler, but I'd bet the Mother isn't doing too well, either."

"My dad never spoke of anything but drink and vengeance," James spat.

"He spoke much of that, yes. But to others, when you weren't around, your dad would speak of darker things around the fire. When he was long drunk and sure that most ears had fallen deaf with sleep, he told his stories of magics and legend. The Blood Company still tells these tales.

"When it was clear we would lose, he got desperate and sought the help of hermits and Warlocks. Invested in his greatest weapon. You. That is when Derudin, Ruwen, and Brinley got out. Many followed, including me and Sara. I'd rather pray to a false god than die young with full balls, a black beard, and songs left to sing."

"The lot of you are cowards and traitors."

"So much hate." Itchy plucked a few more notes. "They were dark times, those, and many people made some dark choices, but I've moved on. Can you, Culdaine?" James ignored him. "We all get what nature sets out for us, one way or another."

"So what's this got to do with the wizard?" said James. Itchy smirked.

"There's always more to what's going on than what he tells you. He knows more than he says."

James considered that. He hadn't trusted the wizard much at all, but he hadn't considered the wizard was leading James somewhere other than where he promised. *You put too much trust in that Warlock. You don't need him anymore.*

"Just watch yourself, is all," Itchy said. "I enjoy fucking whores, drinking too much, and playing my songs. I ain't ready to go up yet. And it seems like you may be our best chance to live."

"Alright," said James. He was just no good with words.

Itchy stood up and started strumming and singing along to *I Need A Drink In The Morning*. Soon, the lot of Derudin's crew were singing along and passing around skins of shine. James didn't much like shine and enjoyed drinking with his enemies even less, so he passed up the drink when it came to him. Instead, he watched the ghosts of dead folk move about in the dark arbor behind them, glowing like hundreds of human-shaped moons against the black night.

Itchy had exhausted the few good songs he had in the first ten minutes, and James was about ready to close his eyes. Seemed as good a time as any, with all the people about. There was a comfort in falling asleep while you could still hear voices around you. James stood up, and Itchy grabbed his arm.

"Hold on," said the bard. "I haven't got to the one about the whore and the ram yet."

"I'll be able to hear you from where I'm lying," said James.

"Come on, man. Have a drink with me." Eurick had come over from his argument, raven's cloak wide open and flapping. His breath reeked of shine as he spoke. "Let's have a song or three together, eh?" The transporter pressed the wineskin into his chest. Derudin was hammered, James could hear his voice booming over everyone elses. *A drink wouldn't hurt...*

"Come on, big man." Itchy did an enthusiastic strum. "You're one of the Blood Company tonight."

"Ah, alright. Couple songs," said James, taking a long swig. The sour, creamy taste stuck to his mouth, and he almost vomited. When he was sure he wasn't going to, he took another long swallow. Wulfee said the key was to just get it in ya. Eurick did a little jig. And James joined. The dead souls were all around him, moving to the same rhythm. He could feel them reaching out to him.

Itchy played his wooden harp, and Florence played a flute. Eurick belted out the words he knew, and James joined in where he could. Mineera watched and scribbled on her papers even in the dark of night. Derudin sat quietly and stared at Adeqor. Everyone else was up and dancing, or at least tried to. And the music loosened him up. And James moved and danced like he had with Maggie. He remembered a night with her, when Colrig held a drum ceremony for the birth of his first daughter, Deri, and they danced and drank shine till the morning sun came up. He had touched the souls of the dead then and didn't know how he did it. He felt the rhythm, and the souls moved to it, and he moved to them. And he did the same now, as he jigged his leg this way and that, hopped side to side, and sang out a word or two that he knew was coming. And the souls were with him. He took them in as they filled him up. *I will help you*, James said, and they all seemed to smile at him. He could hear their song, and it was deep inside of his soul, like a memory. He remembered dancing with Maggie to the drums and smiled. The souls filled him with raw power and welled his emotions to overflow. A tear trickled down James's cheek. He quickly wiped it away. It was the first time he had felt anything like happy since the Hawka came.

Since Maggie.

MORE

WULFEE WATCHED A BLUE jay swoop up and disappear into the ring of standing stones on top of the hill known as Tell. She saw Haro from below, waiting for them at the top. The Druid's ancient stones surrounded him like great big stone teeth. Moss and lichen covered them like fuzzy green skin, and they were carved with runes smoothed by time. How those ancient bastards moved 'em there was a mystery that she didn't care to know the answer to. She probably wouldn't believe it, anyway.

"They say the Daggland king, Harald the Great, had the Druids build him the Tell Stones to line up with the sunset on his wedding night," said Pike. "An opposing clan killed his wife in an ambush during the ceremony."

"I heard it was his tomb now." Wulfee crushed a rock beneath her boot and thought that it could have been a bone once. "And that he ain't resting easy. I've heard he and his wife still haunt these Stones." Pike cringed. For all his talk about dying, he certainly hated talking about what came after death. They climbed the hill in the shadow of the stones, and there was

Haro, leaning against one of them with his bad leg stretched out, toes up. His crutch leaned beside him. There were birds twittering around him, and Wulfee thought, for a moment, that he was whispering something to them in a strange tongue. When the birds flew away, Haro looked at Wulfee and smiled. His green hood was covered in twigs, odd-shaped leaves, and other debris. There was a calm aura about Haro, like he'd been over here sleeping during the whole battle. The horses grazed in the patch of grass in the middle of the obelisk circle. Some animal scurried away down the bushy side of the hill, and Gen stared longingly at the bushes like he wanted nothing more than to run alongside it.

"Thought I'd see you here last night." Haro grabbed his crutch and limped towards them. "I was just packing up to leave."

"Thought we had a chance," said Wulfee. "Thought I'd get a shot at Sweyne."

"Thought wrong?" Haro asked.

"Aye."

"Those horses ready to ride?" Pike asked. "They look worn out, the way they're grazing."

"Good as gold, those. Always been a bit tired, but ain't we all? They'll serve us just fine," said Haro, looking past Pike to Gen, who was throwing one of his rocks in the air and catching it again, over and over.

"You up for a big run, lad?" said Haro. Gen threw the rock in the air, staring at Haro indifferently. The rock slapped down in Gen's big palm with a loud smack. The Giy'er's glare never left Haro, and the Ranger shifted his feet. Gen threw the rock in the air, and again, it landed in his palm with a loud smack.

"We should be able to get to Pool before an army of that size," Wulfee said. "We can make peace with Odhran, warn him of the attack and fight with the full strength of the Feldarra behind us. He will sack every town along the way. This is the power he has always dreamed of. The bastard is going to use it. Time is on our side for once."

"The Green Man said seven days," said Haro. "It's been but three. When Shaqqa Ro says a thing, he means a thing. He does not negotiate with the roll of the runes."

"Not much of a choice, as it stands." Wulfee gestured behind her at Tusk and Mammoth's Head, and the flood of soldiers flowing in from the south. "I'm pretty damn hard-up and low-down."

"Shaqqa Ro's camp won't even be there in four more days," Pike said. "The Ayelish bastards are going to flood the damned world."

"Shaqqa Ro isn't one for arguing," said Haro.

"Neither am I," said Wulfee.

"Right!" Haro said. "We shouldn't waste our time, then. On our way. Shaqqa Ro's, then through the hills to Pool. And I hope you know how lucky you are. I know the Hallow Hills better than any living person. Hold me to it. I'll have us to Pool faster than you could dream possible."

They rode off, stopping at the crest of the hill to have a look with the Eye of Olan at the Ayelish bastards crossing the bridge into Mal Hallow. Sweyne would be mounted at its rear, no doubt. She spat, thinking of him left a bad taste in her mouth, but she'd never be able to forget that haunted bloody wolf mask on his head. The bastard always wanted more. It had been fifteen years of chasing him. Fifteen years since she left his bed in the night and took his son and most of his clan with her. She should have killed him then, that night in the candlelight of the master's chamber in Kallahorn. She stood over him, naked as her birth day and dripping wet from her bath, with an axe in her hand. He was passed out drunk, sleeping, his throat exposed. The blade was shaking as she held it to the gorge on his neck, her hand trembling something fierce. She couldn't bring herself to do it. Somewhere deep down, she had still loved him. Wanted him to be a dad to their only remaining son. It was time to stop fighting. Time to stop chasing glory. They needed to be together, the three of them. But all he wanted was more. More land. More gold. More people under his control. Even when he held Kallahorn, it wasn't enough. Big, ugly, disgustingly beautiful Kallahorn. The prize of the Fells. The scorn of Mal Hallow. She looked out at the army and spat once more before riding off. *I'm not done with you, Sweyne.*

T HE CHANTING CAME FIRST, then the jeering, whistling, and finally, a strange, yet oddly pretty cooing that Wulfee thought must have been some kind of bird. The ground shook with feet stomping, and the air smelled like burning flesh and vinegar. They were on the edge of the Dark Arbor, where the Green Man called home.

"Look at this," said Haro, pointing at a muddy ditch that wormed its way down one of the hills. "By the gods, I almost didn't believe it would happen."

"This was a stream," said Pike. "They're drying up. By the gods..." Wulfee took a good look and shook her head.

The Hallow Hills were barren behind them. Lumps of russet grass clung to rocky crags and outlets. Branches, mud, and leaves covered Shaqqa Ro's tent. The large man with all-white eyes stood at the sealed entrance, gently swaying a spear.

"Reckon he's working some spirit magics in there," said Haro.

"Hope he's got more than that," said Wulfee. "Reckon the spirits ain't cooperating too much anymore."

Gen said, "I don't want to go to that place again, Wulfee."

"You don't have to, Gen." said Wulfee. "You can keep watch for Ayelish folk."

"I could play Emmer! If they come, I'll smash them down like a karl."

"That's right. Just like Emmer," said Wulfee.

Then, Wulfee noticed a pale, sickly man sitting up against a tree. He was chewing on a piece of horse grass. He said, "Don't go near that tent. My daughter is in there. Shaqqa Ro is talking to the moon for us. He's asking it to pull out her tumour with its force."

"She's not the only one in that tent," Wulfee said. "I left my friend here three days past."

The pale man looked confused.

"Only my daughter is there. I came last night and saw no one. But the moon wasn't strong enough last night, so we had to stay. Pray tonight it is stronger." He pointed at the man standing in front of the door. "We've been alone, except for him, the whole time." The man guarding the tent locked his strange albino eyes on them. Wulfee meekly waved.

"What's he talking about, Haro?" said Pike.

"How should I know?" Haro spread his arms. "Maybe she's close by."

"We will talk to Shaqqa Ro," said Wulfee. "That is what we'll do."

She stomped towards the tent. The white-eyed man raised his spear. Then she felt a weak hand on her shoulder, and old traumas awoke. Losing control, she smacked the pale man who grabbed her and felt his flesh tear under her fist.

"Don't go near the tent." He dropped to his knees, holding his face as it bled. "*Please*, my daughter needs this!" Suddenly, she saw her son's face instead of the pale man's. Bleeding from the deep scar that Sweyne left there with *his* fist. She was horrified. Her gut twisted. A rush of blood to her head. She felt like she might be sick. *You're no different from him...*

"I need to speak to Shaqqa Ro," said Wulfee, suppressing the anger. She had become so good at that over the years.

Pike said, "We paid a great price for his service—" the old warrior thumped a fist on his shield, "—and some repaying needs done if bargains weren't kept."

Wulfee heard Gen gasp silently from the brush in the distance at the sight of Pike readying his weapon. The white-eyed man was waiting and ready. Calm. Too calm. The chanting coming from Shaqqa's tent was very loud now, and the thumping under Wulfee's feet felt stronger. Wulfee thought about her sons. If one of them was sick, she'd kill any bastard who got in the way of fixin' them up. She put her hand on Pike's arm.

"Why don't we speak with Shaqqa when he's done with this one?" Wulfee said. She felt horrible for hitting the man. She put a fist to her chin and nodded at the pale man for luck, though she meant it for his daughter. All the luck in the world couldn't save that pale bastard, judging by his sickly nature. He didn't return the old northern gesture, he was busy pressing down his bloody wound. "I'm sorry. We won't harm you anymore," she said.

"Thank you. Oh, the gods, thank you," the man said, down on his knees.

Maggie couldn't be far. *He probably has her closeby, in a different tent.*

"You'll wait around while Maggie could be in harm's way?" said Pike. "What if he's done something with her? We paid him in dragonbone, Wulfee. My dead—"

"Dead wife's parents' knife. I know, Pike." Wulfee rolled her eyes. "We've all got loved ones lost and hearts aching something heavy and hard. We've all paid prices greater than we wished to pay."

Haro cleared his throat, pulling a hunting knife from his belt. "We're all chasing something that means the world to us. I have as much patience as the next person, but I don't know how long that army is going to stay put at Tusk. The lot of them can't all fit, and I'd guess the Wolf got at least some of them marching through these hills." Wulfee silently gasped when he pulled down his green hood, revealing greasy, greying black hair, thick and full. "I know you have great honour regarding your children and a soft spot for others with the same. The thing about Rangers is..." Haro threw the hunting knife into the white-eyed man's neck from more than twenty yards. "...we have no honour. When it comes to killing a person that needs killing or questioning a person that needs questioning. We do what needs doing."

The big man with albino eyes dropped his spear and held both hands to his neck as he fell to the ground, gurgling through his last few breaths.

"No! No, what are you doing?" The pale man came running over. Haro pulled an axe, dropped his crutch, and sank the blade into the pale man's gut as he lunged at him. The pale man fell, murmured something about the moon and his daughter, then died.

"The fuck did you do, Ranger?" said Wulfee, frozen from what she just saw.

"What needed doing," said Haro. He touched a finger to his crest of E'daru, then touched the finger to the ground. "You wanted answers. I'm going to get you answers. We can't stay here, Wulfee. We can't wait. If you want your friend, we need to ask Shaqqa what the fuck he did with her. And now."

Pike said, "If we wait around here too much longer, we'll find out what a drayke looks like."

Fuck!

Haro hobbled towards the mess of mud and stick and tent, and poked at it with his crutch. He looked back at Pike and Wulfee.

"Gonna need some help with this one," he said, seeming slightly embarrassed that he could kill a man easier than he could break something. Wulfee walked over and kicked her foot through the dried mud and heard twigs snap under foot. She kicked enough of it off so they could peel the canvas flap open. Wulfee poked her head in first and saw the Green Man dancing around in circles. The young girl laid flat in the centre of the tent, covered in sopping wet blankets; the acrid, vile stench of the purple fool's fire danced in the corner. The daylight creeping in pulled the green man out of his trance.

"The fuck is wrong with you!" he screamed, rushing towards Wulfee with his arms stretched as if to choke her. "Out! Out!" Wulfee dropped her shoulder into his chest as he came at her, staggered him back a step. By then Pike had come in behind her, tackling the Green Man with all his weight to the ground. Gripped his neck and dropped his own face close to Shaqqa's. The shaman's headdress fell off, and the purple fire went out.

"Where the fuck is Maggie?" screamed Pike. Wulfee hadn't seen the old warrior so fired up in a long while. It made her feel good to see that the old dog still had it.

"Let me go, wild man, and I'll tell you!" gurgled Shaqqa Ro. Pike eased off slightly, allowing him to sit up. Shaqqa's lips were stained blue from whatever he had been drinking to perform his ritual, his eyes bloodshot and stained red. He had painted his brown skin with stripes of red ochre and black coal. His ribs protruded through his skinny torso as he breathed heavily to catch wind. He lifted his head towards the tent's entrance. "Did you kill Yule?" Wulfee just nodded. "Well fuck, guys." Shaqqa reached for his runes, and Wulfee kicked him in the kidney.

"Arrrfff," Shaqqa collapsed.

"No more runes!"

"You don't understand—"

"Where the fuck is Maggie!" shouted Wulfee.

"I sold her," cried the shaman. Wulfee's face sunk.

"The fuck do you mean *sold*?"

"A band of Rangers came by. Threatened to kill me if I didn't sell her to them. You can't just leave a *mage* lying around and not expect someone to be after her. You know what she is, don't you? The E'daru may come back to life with a sacrifice that powerful."

Rangers... Wulfee ignored Shaqqa and glared at Haro, projecting the violent things she might do to him.

Haro held up his hands. "Woah, woah. You say Rangers came through here? And what band was it? Surely they told you the name of their band," said Haro.

Shaqqa shook his head.

"No names given. Shaqqa Ro never asks for names. I serve all who can pay," said the shaman.

"If there's one thing I can do, it's find a band of Rangers," said Haro. "How long since they've been gone?"

"Yesterday's sunset, before the moon," said Shaqqa. Pike reached out and tightened his hands around the shaman's neck once more.

"I want my dragonbone back," he said. The shaman smiled a twisted grin through blue lips.

"It's gone, old man. Ground to dust and used in a ritual to save *this* girl from her tumour. That's not so bad, is it?" he said. Pike squeezed tighter, making the shaman croak as he gasped for breath. "You think I'm afraid of death?" Shaqqa choked. "I have seen death and come back again. I am not afraid to face it. Now or later, it will wait for me just the same."

"Killing him won't bring it back," said Haro. Pike glanced back at him.

"The fuck do you know, Ranger? It's your fellowship done this to us." He stood up and held the blade to Haro's face. "And why shouldn't I kill you right now?"

Haro was calm.

"You'll never find her without me. The good news is we have at least until the next full moon to find her. If we leave now, we have a good chance."

"Why the full moon?" said Wulfee.

"A practice that the Rangers borrowed from old Lovas. Sacrifice."

"What?" said Pike.

"Death," said Haro vaguely. *That* Pike understood. Shaqqa Ro sat up on his elbows, panting for breath. He smiled an awful grin.

Haro left the tent, then Pike and Wulfee followed. She saw Gen peeking out from behind a tree.

"You can come out now, Gen." Wulfee called, but the Giy'er stayed put. Haro was studying the ground, sniffing at the air like some kind of dog. A blue jay came down out of the trees and landed on his shoulder. A big smile traced its way across his face that made Wulfee want to punch him.

"They went into the hills," he said, gazing up at the rocky green lumps like they were an old lover come back to greet him. He mounted his horse and started off towards them. Wulfee, Pike, and Gen hurried after him. Wulfee looked back at Shaqqa Ro's wide-opened tent flap and the two corpses out front. *Chasing men off into the hills again. How many times, Wulf? Always chasing and never catching...*

She had it all, once. Sitting easy atop Kallahorn with Sweyne, the castle, and her boys chasing each other, playing with invisible axes, and still she wanted more. She was no different from Sweyne, really. She had wound up spending her life chasing what she once had. *Why do we always want more?* She reckoned that if she made it out alive, she'd learn to be happy with whatever she had left. She'd found herself thinking more and more of her grandson Sweyne since they'd left Tusk. Hoped the boy was safe up there in the mountains where they were headed. She reckoned she'd do her best to rest easy when it was over. *But not yet. No, not yet. Still chasing.*

Full Dark

JAMES SMACKED A SKITTER off his cheek.

"Fuck!" he said. The bugs were a relentless foe in the nighttime. Deep grey clouds covered the moon and the stars, and there was nothing but darkness, and yet James couldn't sleep. Despite his throbbing feet and tired bones, he found no rest. The shine had all but worn off, but he still stood slowly so as not to fall over. The whole crew seemed to be out. Snores and heavy breathing filled the silence, but James preferred the sounds of nature. It reminded him of Maggie. She used to go out and walk in the night, barefoot in the grasses, and sing songs to the stars. He used to love going out and just listening to her.

Still unable to see a thing, he walked into the night. He swatted at the skitters and dodged the stings of the burn bugs. The dead were with him, though, and they urged him towards something he couldn't quite understand. They moved with him, and he felt their rhythms. He couldn't deny that.

He thought of the Hermit and its mouldering hole. Tried to remember what it told him about the dead spirits, but all he could remember was the stinking Hermit. Its pale, slippery skin and beady grey eyes. Whiffs of smokey hair shining the colour of a greasy rainbow. He shook his head to put an end to that memory. Nothing nice about that. He peered out to the darkness, yawning as he pissed. *You could just do away into the dark right now. Nobody would know you were gone until morning.* He almost pissed on himself when he heard something moving out there. He squinted his eyes but couldn't see a thing. Out of the blackness came a distant screech. A whining, guttural sound that was unlike anything in nature. He had almost forgotten about *her.* The Banshee's death song rang out, and James cut his piss short. Then all around him were the rabid screams of the Hawka closing in. The carnivorous wail of hungry predators pierced James's ears violently. *They're coming down from the hills...* He considered running. Realized he had no place left to run.

"They're in the bloody hills!" James called out to whoever would hear.

"For fuck! Weapons. Up. Attack!" blurted Derudin with more than a slight drunken slur. They scrambled to get up, their armour and weapons clinking, limbs flailing. James had never feared death; it was the only thing he had never run from because death would be the sure way to run from everything else. But now, as the Banshee closed in, he had never felt more fear.

There were cracking sounds from the hills above them. There was snorting and heavy breathing. The smell of blood and urine rolled down the hill and hit the back of James's throat. The Banshee howled, and the Hawka with her.

Then silence—until they burst down the hill. Their yellow eyes lit up the black like stars in the night sky. *Essikah* lit up with its own light. Magics flowing through the runes flared up in orange and red before glowing blue on the black metal and lighting up a small area around James. The greatsword had turned as light as bone. He held it with one hand.

"I'm here, man," Eurick said from the dark. "Stay close. I can see the mutts."

He came to James's side and pulled out his sword. Then he heard a loud crack, someone tumbling, and the droning of sad, broken harp strings beside him.

"Noooo!" Itchy cried out dramatically. "My harp!" The bard disappeared into the night behind them.

Derudin's Blood Company was making death cries of their own to match the Hawka. Banging their swords on shields and hollering a mad holler. The mad scattering continued around James as he swung at nothing. *A practice swing.* There was an energy in that sword that he couldn't explain. But he liked it. The Hawka were screaming right on top of them now. James heard the earth ripping beneath their claws as they pulled themselves closer, making the snort of a hungry carnivore about to feed.

"Stay by my side," said Eurick.

"How many?" James swung around as human and beast clashed, screamed, and thumped in the darkness.

"Too many!" Eurick squelched his sword into a Hawka. "Over here, man."

As James followed Eurick's voice, he felt something close to him, watching him.

"She's here, man," said Eurick. James felt a breeze at his back. A chill went up his spine. James spun around and swung *Essikah* at nothing. Felt a whiff by his other side. Spun and swung at nothing but darkness. *For fuck!* The sword was too big, too awkward.

"Come out, Banshee!" James screamed into the blackness. "Come and fight me face to face, the old northern way." Clenched his grip around the glowing hilt of *Essikah*, and grit his teeth. Felt the old animal rising from its dark place inside of him. *Gods, let her fight me face to face and I will tear her bloody head off. Just let this be over with.*

"Here!" Eurick cried out, and James ran towards his voice. Felt something grab him; he swung *Essikah* where he thought the head would be and hit nothing.

"Stop! It's me, Itchy." Itchy ducked down, clinging to James desperately. James kept moving towards Eurick's voice. Itchy dragged on him, pulled at his clothes, his legs. James tried shaking him loose with no luck. He felt something in front of him. Heard it coming. Swung *Essikah* into the face of a Hawka. The momentum of it took James to the ground, and the bloody, dead thing smacked down on top of him and stole the breath from his lungs. The reek of meat-eater filled his world, and he turned his face to vomit. Itchy had disappeared again. Horses squealed, galloped, cried out in pain and confusion. James felt the ground shake as one of the horses galloped right beside him. There was screaming from horseback. The screams of folk dying. James caught his breath. *But where am I?* The weight of the dead Hawka was suddenly off him. A hand pierced the darkness.

"Come on, man," said Eurick. "Deeper into the arbor where they won't follow."

The transporter seemed to be everywhere at once. James took his hand, but then a violent tackle took Eurick down.

"Fuck, man!" Eurck groaned. The grinding of iron on iron echoed through the night. James heard the Banshee cry out her death song; she was looking for him. James spun around, and a Hawka pounced on him. Teeth sunk into his raw flesh. James screamed like his body was on fire as the Hawka gnawed on James's ribs. The burn of its teeth gnawing, grinding, chewing made him scream out again. Pain filled him and he burst out, blubbering, flailing, crying. "*Please,* gods, save me. Maggie, oh, I love—" All around him people screamed in their deaths, but the Banshee loudest of all, gleamed in life. *I tried, Maggie, I tried. I'm sorry.* James tried to force the stinking mutt off him, but it sunk its jaws deeper. He felt its teeth tearing muscles between his ribs.

And there was the wizard, shackled to a tree. He was glowing.

"The sword! Use the bloody sword," he seemed to say, but James couldn't hear much besides the ringing in his head. But he remembered the dead. James called to them, not with words, but using the cold ground beneath them. He breathed in their souls and ate the lingering life inside of them. He let them fill his lungs, heal him, and keep him alive. *But for what?* He felt sorcery at his fingertips as strength filled him. *Oh gods.* The chill of a thousand corpses knocked James's senses awake as the old dead rose from the cold earth and lit his soul on fire. *Father Tree save me.* But it was too late for prayers. His eyes bled with warm tears as the demon that was him ate up everything of *James* and stole his body.

The thing that was James pounded on the rock-hard skull of the mutt, its thick damp fur. He tore at its floppy ears, but the Hawka was relentless in sinking its jaws deeper. James flailed his hand through the dirt, looking for *Essikah.* He found nothing.

"Help!" James screamed at the dead around him. They glared at him with sunken heads and twisted necks. "Please." James ripped the Hawka's mange but it didn't move. And the dead rose out of the forest like the tide. The Hawka on top of him scurried off as lost souls clung to it. Every Hawka fled, squealing like scared dogs as they ran back into the Hallow Hills.

James found the cold godrock of *Essikah* and felt its power surging from below. It begged to be used and like the servant he had become, James obeyed his new goddess. His arms and legs moved by no will of his own as he chased down the mutts. Anyone who got in the way fell with pieces of their bodies missing, holding their throats, their stomachs, their chest. He heard Ellorin screaming her death song. Some of the Hawka stopped to spit words at him in their vile tongue before running off again. A thin silver thread dangling from each Hawka's head caught James's eye like dull moonlight. Ellorin moved the beasts like string puppets. The Hawka clawed up the hill in a frenzy—but James didn't mind the chase. The dead were marching with him now.

He caught the mutts. *Essikah* spewed icy rage, and it burned deep down inside of him. He cut through flesh and fur, and everything tried to get away. He walked them down, killing the fallen, screaming and screaming until his throat begged him to stop—because there was nothing human left to give. The rage burned him up, but it was good. *Oh yes.* It felt so good; he let it flow through him and didn't even try to stop it this time. *The power of the gods.* James heard the Banshee's song fading into the Hills.

Even after the Hawka were dead, carved up, he couldn't stop himself. He slashed anything that moved into pieces. Left them brutally butchered and never to be buried. And the burning in him turned into pleasure, and he was alive with it. He killed and could never *be* killed. He breathed the dead in to heal his wounds that bled like rivers. And *Essikah* became a part of him, or he a part of it, and together they could not be stopped.

He felt the cold earth below, and the gods below it. Blood poured out of anything that he touched his sword to. The Blood Company was nothing beneath the blade of *Essikah.* Arda Honeytongue saw him coming, and he cut her down in one swing. He became aware that he couldn't stop himself. *You're a fucking monster.* He hated himself. He hated *this.* But he couldn't stop. The dead souls moved all around him. They seemed to chitter madly as James turned the living into *them.* Above, below, and all around, the dead swarmed him. And he killed, even as his victims begged him to stop. *A monster...* Then he found himself *looking* for someone. And he found her even in the darkness. Florence begged him not to kill her. She threw the engagement knives on the ground before him. His and Eurick's most valuable possessions. James knelt down and picked them up, tucked them away in his belt. Suddenly, it felt like he had a piece of Maggie with him again. He raised *Essikah* into the sky above Florence to cut her down...

...then, all at once, the demon was out of him, and there was nothing but exhaustion and corpses. James pitied Florence, who was crumbled into a ball of submission; he lowered his sword.

"Please," the red-haired Ranger begged, sobbing. James felt like there was no air left to breathe, and he collapsed to the ground. Footsteps crunched away from him in a hurry.

The living Hawka scattered like mice, squealing like swine. *The dead are stealing their bodies.* The Banshee screamed from even farther now.

James struggled, reaching out for each breath. One of his lungs didn't seem to work. Foamy bile filled his mouth. *Essikah* was lying there in the dirt, and the runes were still alight with magics. Orange, red, purple, until blue. All flowing through the runes like a song. James realized his jaw was hanging. *Maggie would have thought it beautiful.* And then the magics faded, and the sword was just the same old heavy lump of godrock.

James vomited. Tried to roll over but screamed in pain. Tried to call out, but his voice didn't seem to work. *You're about to die. This is it.*

Then the dead came back to him like carrion to a corpse. They filled his lungs with their bitter life, and James took all of it despite the wrenching pain in his side, his gut, everywhere. And slowly, the clouds in his mind cleared, and the straining of his breath faded. He shivered, convulsed, then vomited black again. He screamed. Heard moaning. *Please, gods, let it be Eurick.* He felt the ground rumbling. Heard galloping.

"*Naaay.*" It was Bren.

The stallion nudged at James with its long face. James reached his bloody hand up to Bren's muzzle and pulled himself up.

"That's a good lad," said James. Looked around but couldn't see a thing. "Eurick?" he called out.

"Here, man. You alright?"

James followed his voice.

"I'm okay," said James.

Eurick grabbed hold of Bren.

"You sure, man? Something came over you."

"Are you coming?" James said.

"Job's not done yet," Eurick said with a strained smile. "I've taken a hit to my head, and I'm quite dazed." James helped him up. Eurick's arm was dripping blood beneath his chain shirt. Then, behind him, he saw a red fool's fire light up from the hills. Ellorin stood behind it, and she held the cold crimson flame up to her face, revealing wild, oily hair that glowed a purplish silver under the starless sky. It trailed down her long body all the way to the ground. Her eyes were glowing blue, pulsating as she stared down her prey. Her pale, slippery skin was radiant in the darkness. Then she turned and walked away. Slowly, the crimson red flame faded to nothing, and they were left in full dark once again.

With a grunt, James lifted *Essikah* off the ground and tied it to Bren. Another grunt to get himself mounted into the saddle. Then he helped Eurick. They both moaned. The two had been in better shape. Bren was remarkably calm, considering the chaos.

"I can't see a thing," said James.

"That's okay, our horse can. And I can. We will find solace in Dawning, a few miles from here. Let's take the long route, through the Wick, though, eh? Avoid those hills. Derudin got his way after all."

James remembered Adeqor shackled to the tree.

"The wizard is—"

"Don't worry about the wizard," said Eurick. "It's you that needs to wake the Mother. You are the seer. This is our chance to get away from him, man."

James snapped the reins, and they rode off into full darkness. *The dead saved me. They really saved me.* He thought and figured he owed them something.

They rode for a time. James held on tight and readied himself for a fall at any moment from the exhaustion that seized him.

"Hold up," said Eurick. "There's someone here." James slowed Bren to a trot. Rubbed the stallion's muzzle.

"Who's there?" said a panicked voice from the darkness. It was Derudin.

"Who do you think?" James sneered.

"Are they coming?" he said, voice dripping with terror.

"Yes," Eurick said. "We must ride on."

"No! No, you can't leave me. Please. Don't leave me out here with the mutts. Don't leave me out here," Derudin begged. "Oh gods, Culdaine, I've never been so damn afraid. What the fuck was that?"

James hesitated. There was a time, when rumours of Derudin's treason were going around, that James would have killed him on sight. But these were different times, darker. He needed folk like Derudin alive. And he was starting to think he needed folk willing to stand up to Adeqor.

"I'll be back for you." James felt Bren's heartbeat, his body warm on James's cold hand, and his own heartbeat slowed to match it.

"Culdaine, the mutts will be back. They'll be back before you. I'll die out here. Fuck, Culdaine, we can all pile on that horse." Derudin made a move to hop onto Bren, but the horse shifted away. Almost throwing James and Eurick off.

"*Naaaay,*" said Bren.

"I will take Eurick to Dawning and tell Brinley of the coming attack. And I will come back for you."

"Please, Culdaine. Gods, don't leave me! How do I know you'll come back?" Derudin said, but James was already gone.

"Don't tell Brinley I was afraid!" he shouted after them.

THE SKY BLED CRIMSON as morning came. The red sun pierced through the sparsely budded trees of the Wick as they approached Dawning. James thought how he might have sat with Maggie, smiling at its beauty once. At *her* beauty.

"You really gonna go back for him?" said Eurick. James nodded.

"Aye. The Hallow needs every one of its men right now. Even traitors."

"He still flies the Ayelish red eagle."

"He flew the flag of the Blood Company when we travelled with him. In his heart, he's no Ayelishman." James fumbled at his belt to retrieve Eurick's knife. "I got this back for you."

The raven looked at him suspiciously as he reached for it.

"How'd you get this back?" he asked.

"Found it." James said, and Eurick said nothing.

There was still silence behind them. Only the dead followed James now.

Long Chances

IT WAS IN THE wild where Wulfee felt most at home. It used to be the place where life met death with a gentle caress that went unnoticed but to herself. She used to see it everywhere: mould nestling against moss, spindly skeletons of dead trees hugging the lush branches of living ones, the dead carcass feeding the living, the dirt growing the new year's life with the energy of last year's death. But there was none of that now. Now, there was only stagnant death. Only feeble remains of mulled and broken life beneath their feet. It tore at something inside of Wulfee and left her feeling uneasy. *Ain't nothing like it should be...*

The Hallow Hills were jagged, mossy rocks and rolling hills of brown grass spattered with lifeless pine and ash and birch. Old land infested with the memories of old life. The smells of dead leaves and mud filled the air.

They had been riding now for most of the day, and the horses didn't much care for the hills, despite Haro's claim that Rangers had bred them for these treks.

Gen pretended to balance on a log as he walked, holding his arms out to balance himself. "If the fires haven't come back, what will we have for the feast at my karl ceremony?"

"I'm sure we could come by some forage, maybe cabbage preserve from a nearby village," said Wulfee.

Gen pouted.

"I don't really like eating cabbage. I'd rather have something roasted over the fire."

"Wouldn't we all." Wulfee's stomach growled. They'd eaten like stray dogs for too long.

"What drums will be played, you think?" Gen asked. "Will you play the drums for me, Pike?"

"These arms are for swinging axes, boy." Pike flexed his fingers and his knuckles cracked like snapping branches. "Rangers have been known to beat many a drum, though. What about it, Haro?"

"These hills are no place for drums," said Haro. "The earth magics have slept in these barrows for a hundred-hundred years. You wouldn't want to wake them."

"Can we have earth magics at my ceremony?" Gen was now hopping along on one foot.

"No, Gen. Earth magics have no place in front of the nihr'el. The world tree is full of its own magics." Wulfee's horse nayed. She patted it for comfort. She laughed internally at the realization that her horse and Pike shared a fear of sorcery. Pike glared at her, as if he read her thoughts. She wondered if he could sometimes, with how well the old warrior knew her. "But I'll tell you what, Gen. I believe the fires will be back by then. I think we'll have roast boar and roast apples and roast corn, too. The harvest will be in full, and the lands will be at peace. It will be great, Gen. You will be great."

The Giy'er blushed.

"I just want to make you proud, kihl'dor." Gen chased a white hare into the brush ahead.

"The Hallow Hills were a sacred barrow," Haro said as they crossed a stream barely trickling. "The last resting places of a hundred generations of Mal Druids."

"How do you know all of this?" Wulfee grimaced, the drying mud of the stream bed looked like flaking skin. "I heard the Mal didn't write a damned thing down, just tried to remember it all. Then they all died."

"Their bones do plenty of talking," said Pike.

"*Grim bastard,*" Wulfee murmured as they passed another cairn. She felt a sickening urge to push the cairn's stones over and dig up whatever was laid to rest below, but she knew that was just the Druid's death magics seeping into her thoughts. Whatever still lived in the body buried under the stone grave was best left in the dirt. Pike frowned towards the cairn like he might be having the same urge. When their eyes met, his gaze quickly slipped away. She remembered why she had paid mind to keep out of the Hills. Death lived there.

"The stories live on through song, and the Rangers love to sing, Wulf." Haro smiled. "The Druids believed there were earth fairies that guarded portals to another world in these hills. And all who passed to the Otherworld could never return with their life. It was a form of ritualistic suicide for the old."

"And what do you believe?" said Wulfee.

"More than you, less than others. Bout as much as most, I reckon."

"And you believe in sacrifice? Like your fellowship does?" said Wulfee in a bitter tone.

Haro looked at her, completely serene.

"I did once," he said. Wulfee couldn't tell if he was lying or not. She hated liars. "Now I'm not so sure what I believe in. But I won't let them harm your Maggie. We'll find them. There are tracks everywhere. Look at this." Haro pointed to a cluster of boot prints. "They're not even trying to hide. They have no idea that someone is after them. That will be our advantage."

"If there's something you're not telling us, I'll gut you myself," Wulfee said, smiling. *You fucking prick son of a—*

"Seems there's something you're not telling *me*. Shaqqa seemed to think there was something special about Maggie. He said *mage*. The soothsayers say a mage will bring the end of things. Just like a mage brought the Starfall."

"There *is* something special about her. And I don't know nothing about mages."

"Mmhmm." Haro scooped a sopping green hunk of sweetbud from his pouch and placed it in his mouth. Wulfee wacthed him suspiciously. *What does this bastard think he knows?*

They chased hunches and followed dead ends for three days before Wulfee got frustrated. Every minute that went by was a minute closer to Maggie's death. And if she was honest with herself, that wasn't the worst thing on her mind. She thought of Sweyne's army catching up with them. Cutting down the nihr'el and filling Pool with stones. It wasn't a world she'd care to live in, that. But she walked on, slept in the dirt, ate what little food they could forage, and kept her worries to herself. All of them had worries, and talking about hers wouldn't make them go away. Through the hills that she trusted so little and behind the Ranger who she trusted less. Dark times called for some shady acquaintances and long chances. It would all be worth it when she was standing over Sweyne's dead body.

Haro had promised Wulfee he knew what he was doing, that he had the band's tracks. But she was convinced otherwise. *He's a liar.* Wulfee was relying too heavily on Haro now. When he crept off into the bushes, Wulfee followed him.

"Where are they?" Wulfee spat. "How far?"

"Don't bother me. I'll find them," he said as he disappeared into the brush. Wulfee crept up on him anyway.

He was sat cross-legged in the dirt, leaning against a tree. His eyes were rolled back into his skull, pulsating rapidly, and his mouth was muttering strange sounds.

Skincrawler... A sick feeling filled her stomach, and she turned away, disgusted.

"Pike," she said. The old warrior looked up at her. "What do you remember of the Rangers from the clanfires?"

Pike looked uncomfortable.

"The legend of the E'daru. I remember it well; it stuck with me. It's twisted, Wulf," he said, showing concern.

"Tell me."

"They say the E'daru is a black horse with long black Human hair and has no eyes in its glowing black sockets. It was once a Ranger who had crawled into the soul of a horse and found that after spending too much time in its skin, it couldn't leave. Over time, the E'daru became as much a horse as Human. It rides in the dark arbors of the north, looking for victims to bodysnatch so it can feel a Human life again, if only for a short time. The Rangers claim the E'daru was the first skincrawler, and they are all descendants of it. The E'daru is their god of life, their blood mother. And the Outcast is their god of death, giving inner peace and acceptance with the maw of its virtue. Only the Maw god hears the prayers from half-beasts, and so the Rangers have no other choice but to pray to it."

"And they sacrifice to please the Maw..." Wulfee said. Pike only nodded. Wulfee shook her head. *Madness...*

When Haro came back, he knew exactly where to go. He led them to an especially high hill that had a particularly low valley on the arse end of it. Wulfee marvelled at how much it looked like the curves of a woman. They crept into that valley with hills on all sides of them, and Wulfee felt like she may as well have been in a trench. Through the trench was a sharp, rocky crag covered in runes. She had a bad feeling about this place. She could sense life here, but it was shrouded over the coldness of lingering decay. Almost like someone or something was watching them. A dozen carved and weathered stones in a perfect circle stood crumbling beneath the crag. Druid works of old. A nytewood stump grew in the centre like a wart.

"They passed through here. Recently. We're getting close." Haro pointed at more footprints in the dirt.

"And when we *do* get close, what's the plan?" Wulfee studied the prints for herself. Hoof and paw alongside Human prints. They were skinchanger prints alright.

"Ambush. It's the only way, with the numbers greatly on their side." Haro packed a hunk of sweetbud into his mouth.

"How would a good band not plan for ambush?" Pike held his arms out. "Do you not call yourselves masters of the wild?"

"Listen. Any idiot born with the blood of a Ranger can survive a winter in the arbor to pass the training and earn themselves a greenhood. Any greenhood can follow their band leader, and any band leader can follow the old wood lore of the Rangers to do good work. It's only once every hundred years they get someone like me. Someone with an eye for nature so keen, so precise, to re-invent tracking, hunting, and arbor warfare. Someone who the E'daru has blessed with its presence thrice." Haro spat green into the bushes. "I know things other Rangers couldn't even dream of." A blue jay fluttered down and landed on his shoulder. *That damned bird...* Wulfee's stomach twisted. Something wasn't right. "They're absolutely set up for ambush, and I know exactly how."

"Then why'd you run off?" Wulfee accused. "You say you're such a great Ranger. Why'd you give it all up?"

They were all standing in the centre of the crumbled stone ring, blue sky and chunky white clouds above, the sun watching over them like a glowing yellow eye.

"Because some bastard killed my band," said Haro bluntly. "James Culdaine and the mutts that tracked him killed all of them. Then, he left me to die with a busted leg."

Wulfee's eyes flicked open. *James?* She heard movement behind one of the crumbled stones.

"Did you hear that?" Pike unsheathed his axe. *The bastard walked us right into a trap.*

"Nothing to worry about," said Haro. He stuck two fingers in his mouth and whistled. A band of a couple dozen greenhoods appeared from one side of the hill and flowed down into the trench like a fleshy green waterfall. A large mangy bear and a procession of wolves came behind them. Then a few dozen more Rangers from the other side, all of them armed with axe and bow and only the gods knew what else. *God damned bastard of a Ranger. This is what you get for blind trust, you dumb old braud. This is what you get for taking long chances.* "Right on time, folks. These are our prizes."

"The fuck is this, Ranger?" Wulfee pulled her axe but didn't think she'd get much done with it.

"Like I said before. You and I ain't so different. A man wronged me, almost took my life from me. Brought death upon my band, my family, and left me crippled and dying in the wild. I crawled, no... I dug my fingers into the earth and *dragged* myself twenty miles to Shaqqa Ro's. The whole time I had one thing on my mind, to get my revenge. To kill James Culdaine. Just gut the smug son of a bitch and leave his innards for the crows and the gods."

James... he's alive...

"How? How did you do this?" Wulfee choked out.

"The blessings of E'daru." Haro said. The blue jay on his shoulder chirped as Haro fed it a chunk of sweetbud. His lips twisted into a wicked, ungodly smile as he twittered something to the bird.

"I don't like these people, Wulfee," said Gen, twitching nervously.

"It's okay, Gen." Wulfee put her hand on the big guy's forearm to settle him, but it didn't do much.

"Don't like us?" Haro wagged a finger at him. "C'mon, Gen. You don't even know us."

In an instant, they tripped the Giy'er up with a rope around his ankles. He fell to the ground with a loud thud. He pounded his fists and tugged at the ropes, crying.

"Wulfee! Help me!"

She took a step before three Rangers surrounded her with axes, another with rope.

"Calm, Wulfee," said the old warrior as Gen thrashed behind him. "We can't win this one." The Rangers who struggled to steady Gen were sent flying.

"You should have nothing to worry about if you believe in James," Haro grinned, his teeth stained blackish-green. "We'll have the word spread across the entire north that I have James Culdaine's lover and kihl'dor tied up in the hills. If he wants you to live, he can come and trade his life for yours."

"Help me, Wulfee!" Gen shouted.

"Let him go!" Wulfee said and made a move towards him, but the Rangers surrounding her closed the gap. She glared at one who was younger than her Tarek would be, beard all sparse and sad, his eyes distant. Another as old as Pike and twice as grizzled. A third took her knees out from behind and tied her up as surely as you'd expect a Ranger to work a knot.

"Wulfee!" Gen screamed. Kicked and flailed. For every greenhood who got pummelled, another was standing by to take their place.

"Let the damned Giy'er go, you cunt!" Pike spat. He preferred fighting folk rather than tying them up. Wulfee knew that well enough.

"Stop it!" screamed Haro. "We will set the Giy'er free. We have no use for the thing, and the poor lad has been through enough. The boy belongs in the wild, with the other Giy'er."

"The big fucker could come back for that red-haired bitch, Haro," said one Ranger. "It thinks she's its mom. Why would we set the thing free? Let's just kill it."

"We're not going to kill him. And we can't keep the lad imprisoned like this lot. He's a liability. And I don't think he will come back once he finds out that Wulfee has lied to him his whole life about what really happened to his family," said Haro.

Wulfee's blood boiled.

"They will kill him," said Pike. "The Giy'er don't like others from different tribes than their own."

"Yes. Better they kill him than me." Haro smirked. "And I think it's time we finally let the boy know what happened to his *own* tribe? I think he's been in the dark long enough, don't you?"

"You fucking bastard," she muttered through trembling lips.

"What's he talking about, Wulf?" Gen asked softly.

"Tell him, Wulfee," Haro cooed. "Tell him what I'm talking about."

Wulfee stared down at the cold dirt. Ashamed at herself for getting the kid caught up in her shite.

"It's complicated, Gen. You know I have to look out for the safety of the clan. All karls know that," she said. Gen rubbed at the ropes around his wrists and ankles. He writhed like a wounded snake. The Rangers pressed Gen's face flat against the dirt. His panicked breaths rose puffs of dust.

"What's complicated? What!" he shouted. A Ranger twisted his boot on Gen's face in an attempt to keep him quiet, but the Giy'er just screamed louder. "What!"

"Let him go!" Wulfee screamed. "Let him go, and I'll tell him."

Haro smirked. "Off him." The Rangers untied Gen's ankles and let him stand.

"I just didn't want to hurt you, Gen, so I never told you," Wulfee said and got to her knees while Gen sobbed. She'd made some tough decisions and came out of them feeling like she'd made the wrong one more often than not. Saving Gen when she took him all those years ago, though, she knew that was wrong. She had a big hole in her soul that only Gen could fill. She told herself it would be easier to take him with her than to kill him. Easier to lead the boy on and let him believe he had some kind of normal life than to tell him she'd stolen his old one. Pike was right. Some dreams just don't come true. She had to let Gen know the truth about what she did.

"Wulfee stole you away, Gen," Haro said. "Killed your family and took you away so you could fight for her." The Giy'er fanned his head around, first at Haro, then to Wulfee. A big line of snot hung from his nose.

"That's not really how it happened, right Wulfee? You tried to save them but—"

"I killed them, Gen. I'm sorry. It was the only way to protect the clan. Giy'er are a danger to us. I couldn't have them that close to us. I never would have done it if I knew what I know now… if I knew *who* you were. What your parents might have been. But when I saw you, just an innocent child, I couldn't do it. I couldn't kill a child. I saw too much of my own children in you. So I took you. I thought I could give you a good life, Gen. But you don't belong with us. With all of this violence. You deserve to live in peace, Gen. War is no place for Giy'er." *War is no place for any of your children…*

"No!" Gen flailed his arms and sent a couple of greenhoods on a trajectory. Stomped around looking for a way to run. Rangers prodded at him with axes and spears until he ran off through the Hills by himself.

Wulfee stood up with the urge to run after the lad. She felt that old, heavy feeling in her heart. Like it had been drained of blood and filled with molten iron. It burned and hissed in her chest as Gen slowly disappeared. She took a few kicks to the ribs from a Ranger and didn't even resist when they tied her wrists up. But when the young one stuck a greasy hand in her pockets to see what he could steal, she kneed him in the balls. It wasn't the best idea, considering the position she was in, but she rarely missed a good opportunity to knee a man in the balls who deserved it. The man paid her back with a fist to her temple, and she fell over, dazed.

"Put them in the barrows with that witch," said Haro, smugly. She grit her teeth with half a mind to just chase after Gen and *let* the Rangers slay her. Pike's hand on her forearm stopped her.

"Calm, Wulfee," Pike whispered. "It's not our time to go yet. One more braid, remember?" Wulfee remembered. They nodded to each other.

God damned long chances never pay off.

THE OLD WAYS

"**D**IDN'T THINK YOU'D COME back," said Derudin. The Lord of Ockam was sitting up against a large boulder on the side of the old road looking gaunt and feverish. Still dressed in his nightclothes and covered in dirt, blood, and twigs. James stopped Bren in front of him and helped him up. Derudin's grip was weak, and his hands were cold and clammy. "Really didn't think you'd come back," he said.

"I told you I would," said James. Derudin just nodded. James knew Derudin was a man short on trust, and earning a bit with him might go a long way. He knew Ellorin would come for him tonight, and that the Banshee would throw everything she had at him this time. But Dawning was the safest place they could be, surrounded by arbor and the dead.

"What kind of king unleashes that kind of darkness upon his own people?" Derudin asked.

"The same king that killed my family."

"Times are dark, Culdaine."

"Aye," said James, and they rode the rest of the way in silence.

The fort at Dawning stood on a tall hill overlooking the Dawn Fields. The Wick Arbor surrounded the fort and field. The scarlet light of the red sun poured over Fort Dawning, and it almost seemed peaceful. Four square watchtowers of stone, connected by wooden palisades, surrounded a sturdy motte at the centre of the village. Outside of the wall, a deep ditch was carved into the earth, circling the entire village.

Dawning was a small valley cut into the Wick, and the folk here were one with the haunts of the wood. But there weren't nearly enough people to fight Ellorin's Hawka. It seemed like Brinley had taken the warning of the coming attack seriously, though. James could see armed soldiers in the watchtowers and more at the bottom of the hill digging trenches and placing sharpened pikes in the moat.

James and Derudin rode up to the fort, returning nods from folk as they went past. All of them looked different shades of pallid through their iron helms. Some recognized Derudin and looked frightened. Guards in chain and boiled leather, draped in cloaks of yellow wool stitched with the black crow of Dawning, greeted them at the bottom of the hill. When they saw the Lord of Ockam, they let them ride up to the palisades without a word.

They crossed the moat bridge and passed beneath the open gate. James spit when he saw the red eagle of Ayeland hanging from the watchtowers. The courtyard was confined and busy. Folk were moving weapons, food-stores, and water-buckets like they'd been attacked many times before and come out the better. Watching the folk of Dawning was like watching a beehive. *It's what a good leader can do.* James's dad had taught him that. And his dad had always respected Brinley Scareye. He was one of his best. *What kind of person are you now, Brinley? Just as paranoid as Derudin?*

There was a row of pitched tents on both sides of the inner bailey, and refugees from all over the country were taking shelter there. Some looked ready to fight, some less so. Dawning was in far better shape than Ockam, but James wasn't convinced everything was okay. He noticed folk bent over gathering grain that had scattered around the base of the large granaries. *Are they empty already? It's going to be a long winter.* James knew that if folk didn't get their crop sowed by the thirty-first Wayk of summer, there would be no harvest. And no harvest meant death if the granaries were empty.

Eurick was laid up in one of the tents that lined the palisades from the inside, and a wise one from the Hesterlands was treating his wounds. He told James that he would come find him after he'd gotten some mellow tea from the wise one.

James hitched Bren on a post outside of Brinley's Hall. It was a modest hall, made of oak, mud, and a thatched roof. It used to be such a grand and eloquent building for him as a boy.

"You didn't say anything to him about, you know—" Derudin chewed his nails, "—how I got a bit upset about the Hawka and the Banshee?"

"I didn't say a thing," said James. "But I don't know about Eurick. He does a lot of talking."

Derudin took a deep breath. Exhaled. And they entered the hall. Brinley stood at the far end, staring quietly into a grand, fireless pit. They'd pushed long banquet tables to either side of the room. Large tapestries were strewn across the tables seemingly in haste, torn apart and wrinkled. Brinley had laid out a map of northern Ardura in the centre of the hall. He placed coloured stones all over it in patterns that James didn't understand. Guards held tight to their hilts and rested the tip of their shining swords on the ground in front of them. *Brinley's men used to wield iron axes. Perks of bending the knee, I guess: shiny steel swords.*

"Brinley, good to see you again, old boy," said Derudin in a light tone, not at all the grand entrance he'd imagined. "Seems we're in the thick of it again, eh?"

Brinley turned to face them. He stared at them with one real eye. A black steel eye filled the socket of the other one, and a black scar streaked out from both sides like oil.

Folk wear scars proudly in the Hallow, and so Brinley coloured his scar black with ink to make it stand out. Black hair full of braids rested on his shoulders, and he studied Derudin disapprovingly.

"Heard you had some problems on the road," said Brinley, his voice low and raspy.

"Seems our new king has loosed the Clan of the Severed Head to maraud his new kingdom. Taking our taxes and half our grain ain't good enough anymore. Seems like Baleth really did it in for all of us when he declared himself a king and killed his bride." Derudin pushed his lazy eye back to centre.

"So what is it you would ask of me?" Brinley crossed his arms behind his back.

"Some shelter and a bit of food for who's left."

"And what would you do, Lord of Ockam, if I came to your hall begging for help? After all these years?" Brinley paced, his boots shooting echoes off the walls. Derudin furrowed a brow, took a few steps forward, and stood up straight. James had almost forgotten how damned big he was.

"Let's get it straight, old boy. I'm not begging for a damned thing." Derudin thrust a thick finger at James. "He came through my door the same as he came through yours. This is Culdaine's boy. He is the seer, just like that mad old bastard Bren had tried to tell us. I saw his magics with my own two eyes. He is going to bring back the fire. Bren was right about all of this. He wasn't just a madman."

Your dad died with his best people believing him a madman. That is what you did to protect your family's memory...

James saw the red eagle flag waving in his mind. The bull moose buried in the mud. "I can just gather a few supplies and be on my way. The Banshee is after *me*. There is no need for any of your folk to get caught up in this. The Hallow doesn't need to suffer anymore from the likes of me or mine."

"I've been caught up in it for ten years, boy." Brinley held James's gaze, like he was trying to see Bren in there somewhere. "Would have been better to have died fighting, like your dad." *He didn't die fighting. He died running.* James felt the need to make things right for his people.

Derudin said, "We did what we did so our people could live. It didn't matter a damn about my life back then, in the days of the Hallow."

"Those were the fighting days. The Bull Moose days," said Brinley. Then a thought came to him, and he looked upset by it. "I need to tell you something, Din. I don't know how it slipped my mind. I've had word that Ockam was sacked last night."

"But Ellorin and her Hawka were in the hills last night." Then a realization crept onto Derudin's face. "The Ayelish? Did they split their force from Tusk?"

"My scouts swear to me it was Humans who stormed the walls, but there was no red eagle and no black wolf. They said they saw the silver owl on grey waving."

"Brynmor? The Glennish bastard knew I had left Ockam because I asked him for help to defend it. I'm a goddamned fool. He must have swept in right away. Eridan probably opened the damn gates for him. Why would Brynmor do this?"

"Thought he was on the wrong side of this war, maybe," Brinley said. "Maybe Ellorin got to him with a deal he couldn't resist. Never could trust the Glennish. The Glennish are fish on land that will flop to whoever offers them the best chance of water."

Derudin put his head down into his hands and rubbed at his temples with his thumbs.

"Were there survivors?" he croaked out, his lazy eye drooping. "My son, Eridan, surely he escaped..."

"I don't know," said Brinley. James could feel the weight in the air. The heaviness that war brought and death delivered. He would have done anything to take that burden away when he was a boy.

"I can leave here, go to the Mother on my own. Ellorin won't attack Dawning if I'm not here," James protested.

Brinley smiled at that, and James got the impression that Brinley thought he was smiling at a child.

"You think it's all about you? This is about life and death in the most basic sense. Whatever part you think you play serves some other, bigger purpose. But this is a war for basic survival. There is more to worry about than the Banshee. Richard Brynmor sees what I see. There's going to be a lot of people starving to death soon, freezing to death come winter. Brynmor doesn't plan on being one of them. They're coming for what food we have left, too. The Glennish will attack Dawning whether you're here or not. Calen Alder won't stop until he's wiped out the old blood of the Hallow. Go run off and let the Banshee chase you. It makes little difference; we still face war," said Brinley. "Calen Alder marched north last summer with his retinue to meet with the lords he'd annexed ten years past. He ate my food and drank my shine in this very hall."

"Aye, mine, too," said Derudin.

"I said the words of Alder's One God Eralis and prayed with him. He told me that all who see the One God Eralis as their only will survive into the new world. Spitting lies off his tongue. He was judging our strength. Now his brigands and mercenaries can sweep in and do the job for him while he sits in Kallahorn with the Ailaryan Order and watches the world die."

"I had word from my heralds just last week that the Banshee carved Alder with Blood Words," said Derudin. "I've got no time to waste. I need to go back for my people."

Brinley looked horrified. "Blood Words? Are you sure your heralds heard correctly?"

"They told me what they heard, and I didn't question their word. Someone carved Calen Alder with Blood Words. He is serving darker gods than Eralis now. He's lost his mind to madness. I need to go find my people. There must be survivors."

"I'll help you find them, Din, but let's think about this. The Blood Words can't actually *work,* can they?" Brinley ran a finger up his arm as if imagining the Words on his own flesh.

"More than one legend says they can. Lovas never conquered Daggland for a reason. And the Abori..." said Derudin, and Brinley agreed.

"So what would you suggest we do?"

"We find my people, band together, and march on Kallahorn. Kill the bastard. We should have done it years ago."

"Calen Alder is not like normal folk," Brinley said dismissively. "The man wields a sword better than anyone in Ardura, and he openly fights in combat to prove it. Nobody can beat him in single combat. No one can lead an army like him. That is why we bent the knee. We didn't stand a chance against him. With Blood Words carved into his skin, he will be like a god. No one can defeat him."

"We could," insisted Derudin. "Us and a few hundred blooded fighters. A grand escort of Hallow knights. Think of the songs they'll sing of us."

"You may have abandoned your people to make songs for yourself, Derudin, but I won't leave mine. I will stay here and fight until I die. And I will worship my own gods as I do it," said Brinley, and he mouthed a silent prayer to the Stag for courage.

"I *didn't* abandon my people" Derudin stuck his dirty finger up to Brinley's face. "Culdaine here is the seer. I've seen his magics with my own eyes, Brinley. It's real. The stories of Hendurinn, it's all real. The Old Ways don't have to die. We could have our kingdom back. The Mal Hallow. Like the old days. I left my people hoping to save them, and now I've lost them. He looked down, but James saw tears welling in his eyes.

Brinley looked deep into the fireless pit. At the cindered logs and the charred brick, the dust white ash and the chalky black soot. His fists clenched and un-clenched. His jaw twisted. He stroked his short beard with calloused hands. James wouldn't have guessed what he was thinking if he had a hundred tries at it.

Brinley said, "And how can we fight a force so strong with our broken dominion? Half the Hallow lords who bent the knee to the Ayelish are dead now. The other lords who sit in the forts of the Hallow are Ayelish born. There are a dozen mountain clans that refuse to fight for any side but their own, hiding out in the mountains and at Pool." He cast a brooding eye at the map. "Calen Alder and the Banshee will wipe all lands clear, from Mal Hallow to Esher, to make way for their new world."

He pointed to the floor of the hall where he had coloured stones laid out on a map. "You see this. King Alder has taken Kallahorn as his stronghold. Some say he's got a thousand folks there, some say it's more like fifty. It's impossible to know how many he is hiding behind those walls. The red stones up here are Calen Alder. Then, he has given command to some brigand from right here in the Hallow and promised him kingship when they win the war. The mad bastard is calling himself the Wolf. Already, thousands of wild folk and mercenaries have flocked to join his pack, and now thousands more Ayelish reserves have backed him. A large force, enough blooded folk to make my scout shite himself. They sacked Tusk a couple of weeks ago in a single day. Claydon Coldfoot and a rebel group of survivors from the Hawka attacks held out there, but they retreated nearly as soon as the fighting started. The black stones represent the Wolf, down here. The white stones here are the Ayelish force commanded by King Alder's daughter, the Lady Hellen. They are garrisoned at Lone Keep, ready to pour into the Hallow once the brigands clear the way. I reckon they will start pouring in behind the brigand lord once he's progressed far enough up the Northroad. The green ones here are the Banshee and her hordes of mutts. Right on top of us and all around in the Hallow Hills. And now—" Brinley grabbed a handful of blue stones from a small wooden box and slammed them down on top of Ockam, "—we've got the Glennish pushing in. Don't you see we've got nowhere to run? Nothing to do but stand and fight. King Alder is preparing for battle, a large one. He's going to be pleased as a fucking pheasant when he finds out we have little fight to give him."

"Each one of us is worth ten of them," said Derudin.

"That's really cute and all, but it's a load of shite." said Brinley. "You've been sitting your arse on that throne and hearing the word *yes* an awful lot the past few years, eh?"

"I've been enjoying the fruits of many long years at war," said Derudin. "What have you done that's so great? You bent the knee to that bastard just like I did. You've just hid up here in your valley and feasted, haven't you?

Prayed to a tyrannical god and betrayed your own. What kind of god could claim to be the only one? Claim to make all of this?"

Brinley stepped forward, meeting Derudin nose to nose.

"I did what I had to do to *survive!*" Brinley boomed. "And I'm doing the same now."

"Then we are the same, Brinley. Can't you see? We both did what we had to do, and Alder has divided us. He's taken away what made the Hallow strong. We were bound, soul to soul, person to person. Our people were one. We were alive. And our king was powerful. And now his son has returned with magics and legend, and we can be a part of that song," said Derudin. He pointed at James, and his lazy eye made it hard to take him seriously. "I've got nothing left now but to fight."

Suddenly, James felt self-conscious. He wasn't anything that a hero should be. Just a ragged, old nobody.

You're somebody to me. Maggie would always tell him. Sometimes he even believed her.

The two lords gawked at James, expecting some great saviour. He wasn't that, at least he didn't feel it. He never understood what Maggie had seen in him that was so great, didn't get why she was always trying to make him see he could be better. In his mind, he just couldn't be. *And that's why you ran when the Hawka came. You were afraid she'd make you face yourself.* But that wasn't true. He was afraid that together, they would both *become* their true selves and have to face the consequences. James decided he couldn't be a hero, not on his own. He just wasn't one. But he could go back to the Hermit and beg forgiveness. He could face himself and learn to speak with the dead. Then he could go to the Mother alone.

Brinley spread his arms wide. "We will feast tonight, in honour of the Summer Moon. Just like any other year. It's the First Wayk of summer, for the gods' sake, and I mean to celebrate that. If that bastard takes my fort, I want nothing here for him. And if we live through the night, we will brace to fight again tomorrow. Our song is yet to be sung."

"Now, I need to go find my people." Derudin slammed his fist on his chest.

"My scout should be back before sunset. I sent him this morning to look for them," said Brinley. "Let us ride out together. I will bring my best folk. If anyone is out there alive, we will find them." Brinley and Derudin joined their hands and made a single fist.

"The Hallow still lives on this day. It will be on us to determine if it lives till the morrow," said Brinley. And the two exchanged the old northern sign for luck. Brinley spoke to one of his guards. "Have every banner of the red eagle taken down and buried. I want the black crow of Dawning flying over us as we take what could be our last supper."

Golden spears of sunlight shone in through large, oval topped windows, and dust danced in their light. James smiled. Mal Hallow wasn't dead, not yet.

OAK AND THORN AND ASH

J AMES HADN'T REMEMBERED A time since he'd been so damned hungry. For weeks, each meal comprised just enough food to keep from starving. So when he'd heard that Lord Brinley had already ordered a large assortment of foodstuffs for the evening's festivities, he didn't waste a damned minute getting his arse in front of that spread. The Great Hall of Dawning was alive with merriment. Bards were singing and telling stories, women were laughing, men were gossiping, kids were screaming, and babies were crying.

There were links of smoked sausage the length of a spear, wheels of white crumbly cheese the size of a man's head, cracker cakes, and hard barley bread. Pickled onion and carrot and cucumber and turnip with dill, rosemary, and fennel. Jams of brambleberry and apple and pear. Kegs of barley beer and malt cider, and pewter cups full of them went around. Brinley's eldest daughter, Tilda, was handing out the food and talking with each person alongside her mother, Lady Sessely. Tilda was only a couple of years James's elder. The two younger daughters, Brigid and Aione, were filling up cups of barley beer and cider and handing them out. Together, the sisters were known as the Three Black Crows of Dawning. Their black hair was full of braids, and their milky white skin was full of scars.

"Good to see you again, James," Tilda said, and offered him a wooden trencher. Lady Sessely smiled at him and stared for longer than was comfortable. It felt like she, too, was trying to see Bren in him.

"Thank you." James accepted. He couldn't help but shove the food down his gullet like a feral dog.

And it tasted like dirt in his mouth.

Rotten and sour. *How can you eat after what you did back there? How can you expect anything to taste sweet after that darkness?* James had been doing his best to avoid his memories of last night, but with some food in his belly, he couldn't avoid it any longer. *You killed Derudin's folk last night. You let the monster out. Let it out, and it will not go back easily.* Seeing everyone around him acting so cheerful made him sick. *Don't they know how close they are to death? Don't they know what I am?* He spat, then took a sip of sour tasting cider. He hadn't seen a feast like this, where they had just eaten all day since the black sun came all those years ago. That was close to his tenth winter, when all the Hallow came together for a party. Some of the soothsayers had predicted the world would end when the black sun happened, so everyone got hammered drunk. But when the moon slid in front of the sun and the world went black, nothing happened. Brinley was at that party, James remembered. Maybe he thought the world was ending now. James couldn't blame him; it probably was.

Black clouds rolled in and turned the sky to overcast. It would have pissed down a cold rain in a living world, James reckoned. Still, folk were dancing about and actually seemed happy. They didn't seem concerned that it hadn't rained in over two months or that none of them had seen a lick of fire in just as long. People surrounded him, and he still felt completely alone. He couldn't say a damned thing to a single one of them. *How could I? How could anyone understand this?* Wulfee would have told him it was just the way of things. The gods weave as the gods will. But she was gone, too. Everyone was gone. He was completely alone. Just as he was when he woke up in the pink snow all those years ago.

He cursed Father Sky, but the clouds made him forget all that. They were the blackest of black. Death was hanging over them all, and it was just a matter of time before it started pissing down.

A loud roar came from down the hill. A horn bellowed out a sombre note. The horn of mourning. Lord Brinley was back, and he had dead folk with him. James made his way towards the gates. The horn of mourning sounded again, and the lord and his convoy came through the gates mounted on horseback, trailed by a small convoy of Hallow knights and wagons. The black crow on gold and the bloody red hand on white waved proudly above them. Brinley and Derudin were up front, and James thought Derudin looked rather morose. Itchy, the bard, sat up in the front of one of the wagons and looked as forlorn as James had ever seen a person. Mineera was there, too. She seemed to still have parchment clutched in her hand. *Probably had a whole wack of shite to scribble about all that.* He didn't see too many others from the Blood Company. Not until the trailing wagon passed, stacked high with bodies. Some butchered to pieces, others half eaten, none of them intact. James knew he had probably killed a good amount of them.

James watched the convoy roll by from the crowd. Folk were already rushing about to prepare a funeral. Men carried long beams of oak for the pyre that they could never light. Women and children wrapped bundles of kindling and strung thorn wreaths that would never burn.

When they're laid to rest
for their final pass
The Hallow folk ascend
From Oak, and thorn, and ash

It was an old poem from the Cycle of Dain. Gran had told him stories from that old cycle of songs and poems his whole life, and that was his least favourite one. Folk only ever recited it at funerals. James had seen enough of his own die to know the ceremony that was about to occur. He had watched his childhood friends burn on a pyre of oak and thorn during the war, and in the end, it was only ash. And the soil would eat that. It was a sacred death ritual of the ancient Mal to release the soul to the nytewoods. It made sure they wouldn't linger. *So what good is a pyre with no fire? Cold corpses dumped upon cold logs...*

These folk had all lost their minds. No one was sure of what to do without the fires, so they carried on with their usual chores, hoping everything would just work out for them. They truly hadn't a clue what to do about it all. They were well and truly hopeless.

And you could save them. You could bring back hope to this country...

A man stinking of ale staggered by and gave James a big old nod.

"To our last supper, eh? Or to the gods for saving my arse if it ain't," he slurred. James nodded back.

"Aye," he said. The man handed him a cup full of ale. James took it, and they clinked their cups together before he downed it in one long swallow.

A shaman walked by, hammered drunk.

"I will call the fire," he said. He was barefoot, wearing a dress of mountain lion furs, his skin painted with the yellow paint from tusslehawk egg yolk. A bone necklace made from ram's teeth clicked and clacked around his neck, and a crown of thorns hung loosely on his brow. Long, greasy brown hair sat knotted and tangled on top of his head. The shaman raised a staff of black nytewood painted with runes. "Dagdora!" he screamed. Nothing happened. The shaman glanced around, looked at his staff like something had jammed it, then shrugged and kept walking.

James took one look at the death stealer and made his mind up. He decided he would not wait around in this place to die. He was nothing but a killer, a monster. It was all he'd been good for, to be used as a weapon. That was what he told himself when he wondered what he was doing it all for. He was doing it because it was all he was good for. Maggie thought he could be better than that. And James even believed her. Maybe he could. But if he was being honest with himself, it all scared him. Thinking of Ellorin coming for him chilled him to the bone. She would pull his little wisp of a soul right out of him. If being better meant facing that fear, he didn't know if he could do it. Not without Maggie to be there when it was all over with. And what scared him more than all that, even than death, was that after all of this time, he was just a lesser man himself.

He left the courtyard to find Eurick.

Brinley's folk had set up a sea of tents at the bottom of the hill, on the east side facing the Hills. James poked his head in two dozen tents before he found Eurick. They had laid the transporter in a cot with his mangled arm in a sling. His black raven's cloak hung on a pole beside him. Others were in the tent, too, in similar cots with similar ailments. The transporter grinned when he saw James's head pop in.

"It's the seer! Man, come in here," Eurick said. A few of the others in the small tent stirred and stared. "This is him, the one I told you about."

"Can you bring the fire here, to us?" asked a rather gaunt and skeletal-looking man with a bandage wrapped around his head.

"With your magics?" said a hopeful, hollow-eyed boy who then coughed up half his lung. James shook his head.

"No." He scratched the back of his head, embarrassed. James looked at Eurick's arm. There were a few deep gashes that were stitched together. "You okay?"

"Chain shirt saved my arse, surely," said Eurick. "Otherwise, they'd have torn the thing right off me."

"Luckier than some others…" James felt a sting of guilt stab his gut.

"You're James Culdaine," came a gravelly voice from one of the cots. "Are you really him?"

James suddenly felt like he was being watched from some unknown place. He thought of the wizard for some reason. "Who's asking?"

"I'm surprised you're still here after the dark message that came for you," said the woman with the gravelly voice.

James stood up.

"What message?" *Who is this?* James glanced around the tent. He lied to himself that he wasn't looking for the wizard.

The woman's eyes went wide with realization.

"They didn't tell you? The bastards didn't tell you…"

"Tell me what!" James felt the monster waking, stretching out its limbs and cracking its neck.

"I'm a herald in the service of Brinley. Overheard a message that came in last night from a band of Rangers in the hills. Some Ranger named Haro is looking for a man named James Culdaine. Said he has his lover and his kihl'dor tied up in the Hallow Hills, at the standing stones there." That shocked James still for a moment. *Maggie… that bastard Haro lived… This is what you get for choosing mercy. This is what you get for turning your back instead of doing what needs doing.* He clenched his fists. *Maggie.*

James's legs were moving on their own.

"Hey!" Eurick called after him. James stopped in the entranceway but didn't turn. "I know it's hard, man. Terrifying even. But we haven't finished this yet. Go get her and come back, eh? We can face this thing together. Surely you'll be back to finish this."

"Heal well, Eurick," said James. He would have said more. *Thank you for saving my arse in that valley. Thank you for pulling those mutts off of me. Thank you for being a friend.* But he said nothing. He was never good with words.

"I've never failed a job, you know. I'm the only living member of the Raven's Guild who can still say that truthfully. What I'm saying is that I'm not going to chase you, James. And if the wizard is truly gone and you leave, I'll have failed the job. We should finish this thing together. You're the only one who can open that Gateway, and I'm the only one who can take you there. Go get her and come back. I understand your need to save her. But don't get yourself killed, man. Don't forget about the rest of us."

IN THE COURTYARD, JAMES leaned against the gnarled wooden palisades as the sun went down. The fort slowly quieted and became still. He waited until there were only two guards by the gates. He kept his head down as he passed. *Don't look back.* He walked up into the hills, and when he had walked a fair distance and felt pretty sure nobody was going to stop him from leaving, he ran. He ran like he did when he was a boy. Just full on, as hard as he could. He used to run when his dad told him they needed to move again, that the war had caught up with them. He'd get himself lost up a tree and laugh to himself as he heard his dad's out riders calling his name below, never thinking to look up. He would run when it was all just too much for him. He only wanted to live like the other boys and girls. He didn't want to be a monster. Never wanted to kill people or see the dead, or be forced down a hole to learn magics. He only ever wanted love. He only ever really wanted what he had in Maggie. The two of them weren't afraid of each other. He needed to get back to her.

Essikah was on his back, slapping against his skin. The crickets wailed along with the droning of his footsteps. The burn bugs lit up in flashes as he passed. *If you slow down, the skitters will get ya.* His dad used to tell him. So he ran without slowing down. His heart smashed in his chest, feet pounding off the dirt in his worn-out boots. His legs were burning from the weight of *Essikah*, and still he ran. He was running to Maggie. To Wulfee. He had absolutely nothing left but them.

Ahead of him, something glowed under the moonlight. Glowed like... *the wizard.* He stood in the middle of the road as if he was waiting. His skin exuded an oily sheen in the pitch-black night.

He said, "I've waited for you."

"How did you know I'd be here?" James thought about reaching for *Essikah* but didn't think it would be of much use to him.

Adeqor's lips curled into a horrible, malevolent smile.

"I overheard the scout. When you're as old as I am, you learn who to listen to. I knew you'd run to her when you got the message."

James pulled *Essikah* anyway, but the souls weren't with him, and it weighed too much to use effectively.

"Save that energy for the journey you have ahead of you, boy."

"I'm going to get Maggie."

"Of course you are. Right after we make a quick stop," said Adeqor. The wizard held his bare stumps up, bandages stripped away as if to show them off. They had completely healed already.

"What are you?" said James. He was equally terrified and amazed by Adeqor.

"I'm a goddamned wizard, boy," said Adeqor. "And that cunt of a Banshee is a Warlock of the same blood. You have to kill her, or you will never make it to the Mountains of the Mother. Face her."

"Why can't you do it? What am I going to do to stop her?"

"I told you, if I wanted to fight her to the death, I would have risked it a long time ago. And besides, I've had some reversals recently... Without my hands, it will be rather difficult to pull magics with sign language. And my tongue has been cursed, and I can no longer speak the old Words of Yehven. I could not stand up to her. You, however, the seer reborn, a half-god amongst Humans, the World Walker. You will eat her soul."

"I won't."

"You will. Or she will eat yours. She won't stop, boy. Understand this. Ellorin outlived every single one of her enemies. She comes out on top, always. If you don't face her head on before the Words gain full power again, it will be the same with you."

"I'm going to get Maggie and Wulfee," said James. Adeqor flung himself out of the darkness and clubbed James across the face with his stump.

"The fuck, man?" said James. He felt oddly condescended.

"Don't be a damned fool. You know as well as I do that if the world dies, Maggie dies too," said Adeqor. "If you do what I tell you and you can defeat Ellorin, you can live and save your precious love and your country."

"What do I care if King Alder keeps this land? He's had it for ten years already. Let him and the Banshee have it. He's taken everything else from me, too. Why would I risk more? I'm not a bloody hero. And I'm no damned king. I want what family I have left by my side. That is it," said James.

"It's not about the land, it's about the people. These people need you. This bastard Calen Alder will kill the world to stop you from getting up there to Kallahorn and opening that Gateway. The Ailaryan Order is behind him. What don't you understand? Only you can stop him. You can have revenge for all he's done to you. You just need to go back and face *her*. Calen Alder is weaker without her."

"But how?" James yelled. "How can I stand up to her magics? I'll die, like all those folk you killed in Fever."

Adeqor clicked his tongue. "Ellorin's power comes directly from the Words, boy, and the Words are weakened. What I used on those people at Fever is something else entirely. Something of my *own* creation."

James couldn't comprehend. Magics were magics. "They say someone has carved Alder with Blood Words. That he is no different from a god. Even if somehow I beat Ellorin, we can't beat him."

"The Blood Words are more a curse than a gift. They destroyed the Dagglandic Empire and left them primitive for centuries. I tell you this as a fact. If you can kill Ellorin, you can do anything."

"I can't fight the Ayelish. I can't win the folk of the Hallow their land back. I don't know how to lead. I'm only good for killing," said James.

"You don't have to fight them. It's not your land anymore, anyway. But they are your people. And they need their king to bring them back to a life worth living." Adeqor stroked his pointy black beard. James smelled peonies and honey. *Do it for her. You can still be the man she deserves. You can find her again one day and live a happy life in that shack by the lake. You can follow this madman for a while longer, yet. You can face the Hermit again. Do it for your parents and for your country. Make their deaths mean something... You have to do* something—*anything. You can kill the monster. Yes. I can kill it. You can make things right. For you, for everyone. There isn't any other choice. Not one you could live with. This is what your life has led towards. You have to face this task—you have to or die trying.*

"Tell me how. Tell me how to do it, and I'll do it," said James. Adeqor's mouth curled up into a cheerful grin. He put his arm around James as they turned around and walked back. The moon lit the hillfort of Dawning a glistening cold silver against the night sky.

"You must learn the Ways," said Adeqor. "Druid death magics." James felt something tighten around his neck, almost like fingers. But there were no fingers, it was magics. And James knew that the wizard still had tricks he wasn't revealing. "I'm taking you to see an old friend."

The grip tightened around his neck. And then James couldn't breathe. And then he couldn't see.

THE BARROW

WULFEE WOKE UP TO a rat nipping at her stomach. She swatted it away, cursing the gods. She was hungry and sore, surrounded by bones turned to dust and grime by time. The Rangers had thrown them in the barrow three days ago, and the only solace down in the dank cavern was that Maggie was there. Wulfee felt comfort in being near her. She'd rather be thrown in a hole with Maggie than see her killed. Wulfee tried to sit up, but the knot in her back fired a jolt of pain up her spine and made her reconsider.

"Fuck," she heard herself say, though the words just fell out of her mouth.

"You alright, Wulf?" said Pike from somewhere in the dark.

"I've laid in cleaner beds." She felt her body for rat bites.

"Aye," said Pike.

"You really think James'll find us here?" Wulfee's hand traced her torso, protruding rib bones marked her emaciation.

Maggie said, "In my dreams, he finds us. *Where* he finds us and if we're still living when he does is not so clear." She was too calm. "The nytewood roots from the stump above run through this place. They still live. I can feel their life pulsing in me. They go deep, deep. There is still water down there, I feel that, too." The dirt on the ground rose to swirl and move in the air. The air was tight, like all the life was being sucked out of it—and Maggie seemed to breathe it in. Wulfee shook her head.

"Don't do it, Maggie," Wulfee whispered. She could feel her heart straining to beat, like the life in *her* was being drained.

"Why shouldn't I?" There was a carelessness in Maggie's voice that Wulfee hadn't heard before, and it made her shudder. The soothsayers had said she would lose control of her mind one day, and when that day came, she would not be able to control the magics.

"You *know* what will happen if you do." Wulfee didn't think that day was anytime soon. "We all know. And we all still love you. We're going to get out of this. We're going to find James and anyone else from our clan who survived."

Maggie released the magics. All the tension fell out of the air, and Wulfee could breathe normally again. *I need you to use this on Sweyne, not me...*

It was hard to tell days from nights in the barrow, and sleep didn't come easy when it was the only thing to do. But Maggie was much like her old self most of the time. Something about the barrow gave her strength. Her wounds had healed, and she seemed to have most of her mind back. The Rangers had shackled her up and left the rest of them free. They were afraid of her, they'd said.

"Do you not know what she is?" a Ranger named Jerrick said to her one day while bringing them a waterskin and a plank full of nuts and mushrooms. "She moves the earth, that one. Not natural. The Lovasi Warlocks hunted and killed her type for centuries. If it was up to me, I'd follow their lead." He plopped the plank of foodstuffs down in front of them and walked off.

Maggie talked often under her breath, and Wulfee often didn't understand what she was saying. When she did hear Maggie, she talked to gods and the roots of the nytewood, to the rats, and often just to herself. She was always strange, but now Wulfee wondered if she might be turning mad. When the greenhoods had offered Maggie ander, she turned it down. Wulfee begged her to accept it.

"It will help with your pain."

"I don't feel pain, Wulf, only tired. The ander dulls my senses, and then I can't smell the wonderful old dirt or hear about all the beautiful things it's eaten before. It's hungry, you know? All it does is talk about eating," Maggie had said. The Rangers had more than a few in their lot who depended on ander though, and they boasted of it proudly. Wulfee kept a keen eye and learned all kinds of things about the skinchangers. The scouts who did the mapping were all dependent on ander. They used the visions to learn about their environment and connect more deeply with the Outcast and the E'daru. They were no strangers to mind-altering. Most of the rest of them chewed chunks of dried sweetbud all day and night. She could see the green stains in their mouths and she could smell it on their breaths. Wulfee learned long ago from her father that sweetbud did nothing but cloud her reality with falsehoods. She found no enjoyment in the high it provided. The Rangers used it all day and night, though. It helped them talk with their animals and feel the earth, they said. The fellowship expected all Rangers to wear their hoods up at all times. Wulfee learned it was a great dishonour to them to have it down for any reason, including sleep. They wouldn't show their hair out of respect to the E'daru, whose hair was the only bit of human left in it. The E'daru was more likely to approach bands wearing hoods so it would feel unique amongst them. And they believed that long hair brought ill omens. They were a strange lot, and she learned more about them as each day passed. But as each day passed, she fell more and more into her doubts. *It's been too long here.*

"Sweyne and his army can't be far from Pool by now." Wulfee imagined the golden blossoms of the nihr'el, the smell of peonies and honey, the sky blue water—Pool. "It's only a month's march around the hills."

Pike found her in the dark and handed her a water skin.

"Drink, Wulfee," he said, and she did. Didn't realize how thirsty she was. "You can't worry about such things that aren't in our control. Focus on what we *can* control. We can stay alive while remaining ready to die. Nobody can break our will. We need to get out of this barrow. That is what we control at this moment. We need to find a way. It's no place to die."

"Seems about as good a place to die as any. Plenty of company around." Maggie was sitting down, holding her knees now. "The dirt would be glad to have us."

"We can still get to Pool..." Wulfee tried her best to sound hopeful. "We can bunker down there. We can defeat the Wolf there. It can still be like it was." She said the words, but the belief she had in them had faded.

"Look at me, Wulfee." Maggie pointed at the scars on her face, held her shirt up, and showed the scars from the Hawka's bite. The deep pink punctures looked like long worms along her torso. Bloody miracle she lived. "It ain't ever gonna be like it was. Not now."

Wulfee touched Maggie's scars. Looked into the eyes of the woman she put herself through so much to save, time after time. She felt like she didn't know herself or what she wanted. *How could you let this happen to her? To any of them? You should have been protecting your children. Why didn't you do better?*

"Gods, Maggie. I'm sorry," she choked out. "I'm no kihl'dor to have put you through this."

"It was written in the stars, Wulfee, ain't no stopping the stars," said Maggie.

Wulfee sobbed. She moved away to be alone in her own corner of the barrow. *Maggie, James, Gen.* They were her own little second chance at redemption for failing her own children. Something to keep her feeling fulfilled as she chased the old ways. She remembered a time when she swore to herself that she'd never leave them behind. Not *them*. She had found all of them all in need of help, brought them to health, and gave them a place amongst her clan. They needed her, and if she was honest, she needed them. It was cold in the Hallow, and the heart needed warming. Now she'd dragged Maggie through the mud and nearly gotten her killed, and she had gotten James culled into a trap. She had ripped the heart out of Gen and stomped all over it. *That poor lad is probably tired and hungry right now. Upset and scared... It'll be okay, Gen. It will. It hurts more in the beginning, but it will get better.* She just wanted to talk to him. To explain things as best she could, though she knew he would have a hard time understanding. He could never see it the way she saw it. He was too innocent.

Then she thought of her grandson, little Sweyne. In a better world, she'd be by his side. Still, she chased the desire to see Sweyne the senior killed by her own hand, to see the bastard get what he deserved after all he'd done to her. To see his face when he realized it was her that ended it for him after all of these years. *It will all be worth it. It will, it will.*

"MOM, WATCH THIS!" BRADEN screamed, wearing an iron helm that was far too big for him, before running head first into Tarek's chest. Tarek winced as Braden bowled into him, then spun his little brother over and threw him flat on his back. Both boys laughed. Wulfee smiled.

"By the gods, boys, be careful," she said. Wulfee dreamt they were in the Grotto Valley, below the Fell Mountains. It was the Wayk of summer, the wildflowers were blooming in every shade of the rainbow, and the tall grasses swayed in the light winds.

"Ah, it's good for them to get a little rough." Sweyne wrapped his firm hands around Wulfee's waist and pulled her close. He smelled her hair and kissed her neck, and Wulfee felt her heart warm, and her body glossed over with goosebumps. "I got them both a gift."

He pulled out two small wooden waraxes.

"I got Berend to cut them up for me. It's about time we start training them," said Sweyne.

"Braden is only four, surely we can hold off," said Wulfee, remembering her own training starting the day she turned six. *The day Etta died...*

"He'll be ahead." Sweyne walked towards the boys holding the small axes in the air. "Boys! Look it here!" The boys cheered and ran to him. He gave them their weapons and unsheathed his own. Sweyne showed them a few different moves, and Wulfee sat and fletched arrows as she watched them. Tarek was smooth and efficient in his movements; Braden was rash and unrelenting with his, always rushing in with all his might too soon. It wasn't long before the two boys crowded around Sweyne as he knelt to show them his wolf mask. Wulfee hated it when he showed them that cursed thing, but the boys looked up to him so much, they both dreamed of wearing it one day.

The birds were singing, and a cookfire crackled loudly with the smell of charred grouse rolling off of it. Together, the family foraged wild garlic and cooked it with onions and a cube of bear fat in the bottom of the cook-pot. The four of them sat in the mountain valley, and Wulfee watched the plume of smoke rise up to the blue sky as they ate their roast grouse with garlic and onions. She watched the beautiful faces of her children as they laughed, falling deeply into the eyes and heart of her lover as they enjoyed the life they had created. She had never been happier...

T HEN SHE OPENED HER eyes. The ferocious smell of feces and urine almost choked her. She coughed and rubbed her eyes. Still couldn't see. It was so long in the dark her eyes had convinced her they no longer worked. *How many days? Ten? Twenty?* She had no way of knowing. It had been long enough to wear her tunic to a threadbare shirt and for her to stop concerning herself that she was living amongst her own filth. So long that she'd wished for death more often than not. The time dragged on slower than a drunk in mud, and Wulfee brooded. Night ran into day into night, and it made no difference. She sat in the cold dark and felt the hope draining from her fingertips. *They'll bleed me dry of the stuff down here.* She didn't know if James would ever get the message or if he'd ever come for them. But there were two things she knew for sure. That Haro was a bastard son of a bitch and that he was dangerous. The barrow only had one way in and out, and a pack of greenhoods stood by it all day and night. Each of them armed with a bow and spear that they wielded like a butcher wields a cleaver or a weaver wields a loom. *Fucking skincrawlers...* they had worn Wulfee to the bone. She was tired, fed up, and out of hope. She barely had the energy to talk to Pike. It wasn't even being imprisoned that bothered her anymore. It was the thought of another massive failure. The thought of never getting her vengeance and her soul never resting easy. The thought of never being happy.

She'd been imprisoned her whole life, and her captors were no mere people that she could trick or persuade. She was held captive by hate and the want of revenge, fear, the need to make right what she'd wronged, regret, and a self loathing from every wrong choice she'd made. The walls of that prison were much thicker than any barrow, and she'd been scraping at the stone so long her fingers were bloody. She felt as empty as she did the moment her sons left her belly. She remembered the dark void that was left behind when the boys came forth squalling. The overwhelming loneliness of knowing that her child was no longer a *piece* of her, that an actual part of her body was taken from her. It was how she felt now. Nothing left. She was helpless. And as the time kept slipping, so did she.

"This could be it, Pike," she said.

"No, Wulf. What are you saying? We will get out of here. This is just another wall to break down, a river to cross," said Pike.

"And if we do? We'll never stop him. You saw how many folk were behind that bastard. Said it yourself, they'll flood the whole world. He's going to win… the bastard always wins in the end."

"James will come for us. We will get out of here and find Gen. Braden… we can get Tess back, too," said Pike.

"My son won't even recognize me. And I've been no mother to them, anyway. And you, Pike. You remember Tess as the baby girl who was taken from you. Not the woman that she is," Wulfee scoffed. "You've been no father, either. We've been wandering too long, Pike. We convinced ourselves we were chasing something when all we were doing was running further away from what really mattered."

And Pike was silent for a time. Wulfee hated his silence. *Say something, old man! I need you to tell me I'm wrong. For fuck's sake, tell me I'm wrong—that I didn't waste my whole damned life.*

"I've lived a life without hope, Wulfee. I've lived that life, and it ain't no easy road. You taught me to believe again. To believe in something worth living for. We were going to bring the ways of old back to the Fells. Killing bastards who called themselves kings and protecting the old ways. We were gonna make a safe place. A place to call home for our kids."

"All we made were enemies and corpses," said Wulfee.

"We did what we thought right," said Pike.

"That's what Sweyne always said… Gods, I hate him." Wulfee remembered his musk, his taste.

"You loved him once."

"And what is hate but rotten love?" said Wulfee, and Maggie cut in.

"Hate is only as strong as what breeds it," she said. "I always told James to let go of his hate, that it only made him a monster. Love is stronger. Hate is a mask that can be thrown off or thrust upon you at the will of the gods. What kind of monster have you become, Wulfee? What kind of choices have you made?"

"I made choices that needed to be made. Not one of them easy," said Wulfee.

"And that's why we followed you," Pike said. "Because you weren't afraid to make those choices when everyone else stood by, afraid to make 'em. We all knew Sweyne had gone mad. Only you said it. You did something about it. That's a true leader."

Wulfee felt a pain in her stomach, twisting knots in her gut. It welled up inside of her, and she couldn't help but to sob. She let the tears fall for Gen, for James, for almost getting Maggie killed, for making Pike stay by her side. Wulfee didn't have to leave her son. She didn't have to leave Braden, but she did. And she deserved every bit of heartache she felt because she would do it again. Between breaths, all she said was, "He didn't belong anywhere near a war. He didn't belong anywhere near a war."

Wulfee waited for the pain to come down, but it never came down, so she crawled tighter into a ball in the dank darkness, and when something touched her, she screamed.

"It's just me," Pike said softly with a hand on her shoulder. "It's time to move past it, Wulf. Maggie said it. It ain't ever going to be like it was. But we can make do with what it is."

Wulfee finally said, "I've gotten so many killed, Pike. So many."

"And every one willing," said Pike. "We're all just waiting to die in those mountains, Wulfee. You know that. Any day could be your day."

"I could have stopped years ago..." said Wulfee.

"And I could have run off," said Maggie. "All of us were caught up in the same tide. The moon pulls where it wills. We are a family."

Wulfee couldn't help but remember the old times. All the times she could have walked away. Stayed still.

There were a thousand who left Kallahorn with her. When the clan dwindled to a few hundred, it didn't make much of a difference. She could still run down any pretender that needed doing so. Sooner or later, she'd find Sweyne and she could stop chasing him across the north. Fight after fight, night after night, the clan dwindled further. Her cause became less clear. Sweyne was impossible to find. She was wandering, looking for everything and finding nothing. Odhran rose up against her and settled at

Pool where no settlement should ever be. And one morning, Wulfee woke up in the freezing cold of winter to find that her clan had dwindled to ten. And the Hawka whittled those ten further. Soon, she would be all alone. Perhaps she should have been alone all along. She left Sweyne's army with no thought that someone might follow her. *You will be alone in death when your soul falls short of the cloud halls. You will never rest easy...* She leaned back, pitying herself, and her hand touched a smooth rock. She picked it up, ran dirty fingers over it, and admired its purple-blue glow. It was moon rock. *Gen would love this.* Wulfee tucked it away in her pants pocket.

A heavy door creaked open, and a blinding beam of light shone down from somewhere above. Footsteps—or foot *step*, Wulfee knew the sound of a hobbled limp when she heard one—clacked on the old stone as someone approached. The fresh smell that wafted in was enough to make Wulfee try to get a good whiff of it. Mildew filled her lungs from weeks in the barrow.

"The Old Mal rulers have always fascinated me," Haro said, strangely nonchalant. "That's why I chose this spot to set up camp. They lived and died here for a hundred-hundred years before Kelson drove them back to the Fell Mountains. They built these great barrows to mark the dead. Great big stone structures, built with the help of Giy'er and some unknown magics. They carved their runes into them and filled them with old magics. The shamans buried the Mal in mass down in these barrows. They believed the nytewood's roots absorbed their souls and fed them into the Otherworld, where they were born again. A cycle as old as time, broken, buried, and forgotten."

"What do you want, Ranger?" said Wulfee. She'd heard all of this shite before and didn't see the point.

"Everyone is just trying to get what they want, Wulfee. Everyone is reaching in the same basket, but the basket is empty. You can't have something yourself without taking something from another. One man's hate is another's desire. One's hope is another's despair. A constant cycle of love and loss and revenge to be carried out for all of time. This is nothing new."

"Is that what this is about, Ranger? Has your revenge finally come?" Wulfee clenched her worn and dirty fists, thinking of James and the trouble she'd gotten him into. Haro continued talking as if he didn't hear her.

"Time forgets all things, and to hope for anything different is foolish. The Wolf will cut down our trees and fill the wells with stones, and we will keep living. Not even the gods are immune to the god of all gods–Father Time. We're cursed to live in a godless world, Wulfee. So be it. All folk will get what's coming to them," said Haro.

"Did you come down here just to tell us how grim it all is?" said Wulfee.

Haro chuckled.

"No, you know how damn grim it all is, Wulfee. No one needs to tell you that. I came to tell you that nobody is coming for you. My scouts have word from Dawning that Culdaine is missing. He has either left or was never there. Killed by the Banshee during a surprise attack in the hills or run down by Lord Brynmor at Ockam, most likely. You'll be coming with us when we leave on the morrow. It's over."

"*Liar!*" Maggie erupted. "He was not killed. He wasn't..." Wulfee put a hand on Maggie's shoulder, but Maggie brushed it off.

"Believe what you want. He's more than likely dead, like half this bloody country. We leave tomorrow." Haro spit green.

Maggie curled up into a ball. Muttering quietly, "*Liar.*"

Dead... Wulfee's stomach twisted. *He's dead...*

"Where would you go?" Pike asked. "There is a war down these hills."

"Aye, you speak the truth of that, old man. And when there is a war, I've always found it to my advantage to pick a side and cut my enemies in half." Haro packed another chunk of sweetbud into his mouth.

"To Rosen then?" said Pike.

"The lords of the Hallow are gathering in Rosen, yes. Maybe they'll muster up quite a good little defence, too. Those northern bastards are as surly as bears. But I'm less of a gambler and more of a sure thing kind of guy. It's important while picking sides to choose the right one. I've made arrangements for the Rangers to join the Wolf. Scouting, foraging, and, you know, ranging. King Alder has offered all of my bands their lives and the claim to the hills and arbors when the wars are done. We're riding down to meet him in Foulds come sunrise."

Wulfee sank down into herself, into the darkness, and knew that it was all over. She'd lost.

THE HERMIT

JAMES WOKE UP ON horseback, lying on his stomach. His hands and feet were tied, and his mouth was gagged with rope. *But how?* He could smell stale shine on the wizard.

"Mrrhm," said James. *Fuck you!* Adeqor turned around.

"Oh, thank the gods you're awake. I was worried I gave you too much. Nectar of the blood maw plant can be a tricky dose to get right! It's the carnivorous nature of them, you see. The big ones eat more than just flies, you know," said Adeqor. "Alas, that is not important! We're almost there now, just don't move," the wizard laughed. "Oh, that's right. You can't anyway."

James wriggled his toes. Almost shite in his pants when he realized there was another person tied onto the horse beside him, still unconscious. *The fuck is going on? Who is this other person? Where the fuck?* The wind from riding was tugging at James's tunic, playing with his hair. He tried to look around, and all he saw were trees. But it was all familiar. Then he saw the crooked trunk of a nytewood and the jagged rock formation that looked like a mountain lion's jaw, and he knew where they were. They were in the

Hallow Hills, right above Foulds, and James knew that there was only one reason the wizard would bring him here. "It's time you made your mind up, Culdaine. I know you've always needed help with that, so I've stepped in to help guide fate on its most virtuous of quests. You're going to meet with the Hermit to finish what you started all those years ago."

"Mrrrhmmm," said James. *The fuck I am!* He shivered, thinking about what lay ahead and still trying to figure out who was tied up on the horse with him.

The steed came to an abrupt stop at the word of Adeqor. James felt his body ceased by a sudden and dreadful terror. He could tell the horse felt it too. They had come to a grove of oak and nytewood. Bright nyteflowers blossomed in a sea of gold on top of oily black trunks, high above the lush oak canopy. Budding rose bushes grew in thorny patches, and peonies bloomed in pink bursts. Green butterflies and glowing blue pixie flies scattered as the wizard's steed galloped past. Even without the rains, the nytewoods provided life.

The smell of the rotten hermit hole was a defensive stench. His dad had told him it was to keep away bears and unwelcomed guests. After James had met the Hermit, he knew that thing didn't need any sort of defence. The Hermit could do earth magics beyond imagination. It could twist the land to swallow a person up if it wanted. And it wouldn't be found if it didn't want to. James remembered when his dad shot the orange fox with an arrow, disemboweled it, said a prayer to the Crow, and then decapitated it and handed James the head. Blood dripped from loose tendons hanging out of its neck like purple and blue worms. James's dad had said as long as they had payment, the Hermit would let them find it and tell James its secrets. *Oh, gods.* James felt sick. He suddenly realized why Adeqor had the other person tied up. *They're payment for the Hermit. A sacrifice... This isn't right. You need to run...*

Adeqor said, "The Hermit's grove is just ahead. It's time for you to go. I have provided payment for you. This is an Ayelish scout that I caught sleeping in the arbor last night. The nectar of the blood maw flowing through him will last for another many hours, so he shouldn't trouble you. With *this* payment and an apology from you for running away all of those years ago, the Hermit should tell you its secrets. It will show you the Ways." Adeqor took a drink from a wineskin with an Ayelish eagle carved into it. He smirked. "I saw your accident at the crossroad. Oh, gods, it was a wretched sight to see you slaughtering everyone like that. Thought you were going to die right there. You must learn to control this demon in you or all of us will die. Trust me, I'm not anymore happy about this than you are. Fate is a fickle thing, and to trust it in the hands of a barbarian is absolutely ludicrous."

"Mrrhmm," James spoke through the rope in his mouth. *I won't do it. I won't kill an innocent person for this. I won't see that thing, not again. I won't.* James tried to convince himself.

"You understand what I'm saying? Don't bother coming back until you've learned something. It will only result in death. I will keep *Essikah* here for you, wouldn't want to lose it down there. Remember, I know where Maggie is now, too. You wouldn't want anything bad to happen to her, right?" Adeqor cast a sardonic grin. James felt his blood boil.

This fucking wizard has you.

Adeqor helped James down from the mount, then untied his wrists and ankles and removed the rope gag. James rubbed at the chafe. He was thankful for the relief, but he would still rather be tied up than face the Hermit again.

"The Hermit can put fear into the mind of anything approaching," said Adeqor. "In case you forgot. It's rather uncomfortable, even for an old bloke like me being so close to an earth fairy and its mind burrow." Gran had always called the Hermit an earth fairy, too. James's dad liked to tell him that fairies didn't exist.

But he had never been down there.

James had barely escaped with his life. He broke the sacred oaths he gave to the Hermit in front of the gods and left before his training was complete. The Hermit tried to *keep* him there. It didn't even want to kill him.

"You can stand there for as long as you need to, but you know what you have to do."

"I was going to come back here on my own," said James.

"You planned on it, but you weren't going to," said Adeqor.

"I would have," said James.

Adeqor smiled and made a strange cooing sound at the sky. An eagle fluttered down from close by. James looked over his shoulder, confused. "Now I have to send an eagle to the raven to bring the folk here to Foulds. Hopefully, it reaches him before Dawning falls to the Glennish. Poor fellows don't even realize Lord Brynmor will be there by tomorrow morning with a force of two thousand horses. He'll blow the gates right off of Dawning and be feasting there by tomorrow's moon. They should all just leave right now. It'd save many hundreds of lives, no doubt. But these rulers are stubborn. Let's just hope to the gods that Eurick doesn't get tracked here by Ellorin. I'm going to owe the Guild an onerous amount of currency when this is done. The Raven's Guild always gets ya with these little things!"

Adeqor whispered something to the magnificent bird on his shoulder in a strange tongue, then the eagle picked up and swooped away. It amazed James to see. He looked around at the grove and saw scores of dead emerging from the thicket. Men, women, children all armed with axes and dressed in ancient Mal garb. They were chanting something in their rune tongue, something primal—almost animal— and instinctual.

"The dead have gathered around the nytewoods for all of time." Adeqor spread his arms. "I can sense them. Something about these hills brings the magics out. They are waiting for a god to lead them, James. Don't come out of that hermit's hole until you become the god they need."

Grizzled folk with hard faces and long, braided hair surrounded him. The kings wore thick beards, and the queens wore metal hooks in their noses. They marched and chanted and filled the grove with their cold smoke beings. Souls without bodies. Memories without lives.

James was fed up. There was too much he didn't know. Too many things that made up his world that made no sense. He had to see that bloody Hermit to get answers about the dead. He hadn't been able to understand what had happened at the crossroads a few nights past. He had never understood the demon. Thinking about it made his chest heavy and stomach turn. It had happened to him before, like that. He could still taste the blood in his mouth. Feel the power of the Otherworld on the tip of his fingertips. He was out of control when the dead filled him, and he became the monster he spent ten years hiding from. *But what is it? How do I control it?*

They were questions for the Hermit. Questions that he needed the answers to. It was difficult to gain an audience with it though. James's dad had gone to great lengths to get the Hermit to take him on before. Sacrifice and a great fortune. James looked at the near lifeless body of the scout. Picked him up and threw him over his shoulder like a sack of grain, then turned and faced the far side of the grove. He walked, one foot in front of the other, and tried not to think of how god damned terrified he was.

T HE HERMIT'S GROVE WAS gnarled, overgrown with dead, brown grass from last year. The spindly fingers of rotten oak trees reached from above to caress him. Soggy wood, moss, lichen, and dead leaves from last fall covered the ground, like something had sucked the beauty dry in the area around its hole. James saw the ghosts of many dead folk sitting on fallen logs around a fire pit. They looked like they'd been there a long time. James couldn't help but think of sitting around Wulfee's clanfires with Maggie in his arms. *Peonies, honey, and woodsmoke.* The souls saw James and gave him the old northern sign for luck. He returned the gesture and carried on. He recognized the path he was on. The jagged rock that looked like a mountain lion's face, the waterfall that had reduced to a mere trickle, and the smell of the deep arbor growth. And when it reeked like dying flesh, he knew he was close.

When James saw the Hermit's hole dug into a rise in the ground, he felt relief and terror that the Hermit had allowed him to find it. *It's expecting you.*

The hole was covered with a thin, mucous-like layer of forest slime. James's dad had told him it was something made from earth magics. The smell rising from it was sickening. James dropped the unconscious scout, stretched his lower back out a bit, and cracked his neck from side to side. He covered his nose and mouth with one arm and reached down. His other hand squelched into the slimy skin, gripping it with a fleshy squeeze and folding it back. A wave of warmth and rotting stench came up as he opened it. James dragged the body of the scout closer, then rolled him down into the dank darkness. James took a deep breath of fresh air and then went down himself. The mucous-like skin closed over the hole like a thing alive.

It was much colder down there than the wave of warmth suggested and more uncomfortable than James had remembered. It was not as dark as it should have been. The hole was lit by earth magics of many kinds. Glowing purple mushrooms sprouted from ground to ceiling, between twisted, writhing roots of nytewood and oak and pine. Wrigglemoss shed a warm, greenish light with each step he took, pulsing to the vibration of him; lichen hung damp and moldy from every crevice above. James got the feeling that it was watching him, feeling him as he moved through the Hermit's tunnels. He dragged the scout behind him like a bale of hay. *That's a man, there. Not a bloody sack of grain. Do you have no honour left in you? You wouldn't even let him fight for his life like a warrior and die a good death. Is this what it means to face your past? To kill an innocent man for your own benefit?*

He dragged him through the dank tunnels; the roots moved and slithered all around him. It felt like the tunnel could collapse at any minute. He dragged the human sacrifice deeper into the black hole. A slimy, damp dew covered James's body like sweat. He wiped his brow with the back of his hand. Then he saw the flickering pink light of the Hermit's fire playing on the cave walls ahead, and a black shadow moved across it. He dragged the body deeper, and the dirt and growth of the tunnel smoothed out into a stone cave. In the middle was a fool's fire in pink, burning out of a witch's plate and roaring madly. Bones were scattered all around the smooth stone ground. Human skulls were lined up on shelves, displayed proudly. Then he saw it slithering behind the flame. Its pale, slippery skin and beady grey eyes. Smokey rainbow slicked hair. James's dad told him it may have been a Human once, long ago. And it still resembled a Human, somewhat. It was crouched over like its spine was broken, and it walked on all fours like an animal. Its body was hairless and covered in patches of earthy brown muck. Then James heard metal clinking in the shadows. *Good fucking gods.* There was a woman and a young boy chained up in a gibbet. Both nude, and the boy was so starved his bones poked through his skin. *Bloody fucking hell...*

"Sssskl'rhosss!" The Hermit moved up on James so fast he froze in fear. It studied him with its animal grey eyes. Clicked and hissed at him. Pinched and prodded his body. Sniffed at the unconscious scout like some kind of rabid beast. He could feel it inside of his head, feeling around in his thoughts, scrolling through his memories.

"You want to know my secrets, pink man?" the Hermit said in the northern tongue this time. "Or have you come for my things?"

"I brought you payment, Hermit. I have questions," said James. Chains clinked from the shadows. The woman and young boy in shackles were suffering some unknown pain. Hunger, and only the gods knew what else. It made James feel nauseous. *If you were any kind of hero, you would save them. Any way at all.*

The woman said something James couldn't understand. She had a sad, desperate tone in her voice. He studied her closer—the red hair, the sad eyes. She reminded him of Wulfee. It could have been Wulfee in a different life.

"You gawk at my pets?" the Hermit clicked its serpent tongue. "I could make you a pet. I need a friend for the woman and boy."

James stuck the toe of his boot into the scout laying on the ground.

"Do what you want with him. Your payment." *Stay calm and be persistent. The thing will try to trick you or trip you up with words. Be careful.* He could still remember his dad's lecture.

"This is not the first time you have come to my hole. I know the smell of your memories. You are the same boy who could not handle my secrets before. The same boy who did not like the things I showed you. You ran from the truth. You stole the things I taught you and ran before you saw my secrets."

"I am a man now. I've grown. I have questions that only you can show me the answers to. I have brought you payment." James said, toeing the scout again. James's heart was thumping in his chest now. He was ready to accept whatever came of this and move on. He wanted it to be over with more than anything. "Give me another chance. I want to help the world. Teach me how to help. I need to know your secrets."

"You will run, boy. You will run from my things, and you will not like my secrets. It will be like it was before. I know this. I have seen it in my fires. You, hiding away until you are hunted down and the Banshee eats your soul. You are not brave enough. You do nothing but follow. The Ailaryan Order has come back, and you will not stop them because you do not believe you can stop them. You will never rest easy, no matter what you do. I have seen this. It is here, in my fires. You don't think I've seen it?"

"Your witch's fires and dreams of ander do not always show the truth. You know this, and I know this. I am not the same boy I was. I will hear you, and I will not run this time. This is to bring the fire back. To bring back hope. But I have questions I need answers to."

"You say you are not the same, yet you stand here before me with the same smell, the same teeth and flesh, the same eyeballs. How am I to know that your mind is not also the same?"

It doesn't believe you. Stop being a goddamned coward and make the thing believe you...

"I came back here, didn't I?" said James.

The Hermit's mouth twisted into a smile.

"Yes. Yes, you came back. So you're not afraid now, is it? And you will listen to my secrets, you say? You will see my things?"

"I will do what I need to. I am a seer, and I need to control what's inside of me to bring the fires back." James felt a chill roll through his body because he really meant it this time.

"The fires!" the Hermit yelped. "Bring them back, you say? Hah! A seer who does not want to know the secrets of the earth is no seer at all. A World Walker who has not walked between worlds is false. Why would I show my things to a barbarian? Why would I tell my secrets to a false coward?"

Make it believe you. Believe it yourself...

"Because I am a coward no longer, Hermit," said James. "I need your help."

"Convince yourself of that, not me. I already know the truth about it. You don't think I know?" It grabbed the scout's shoulders with its feet and chained him to the gibbet with the woman and boy. It produced a length of rope and tied the scout up with neat precision. Then it crawled towards a small, stagnant pool of water that sat at one end of the cave. A green slime had formed on top of it that looked like the skin of a frog. The Hermit sat on the edge and dipped its feet in, stirring the water around a bit and making the thick sludge ripple. Chains rattled, and a whisper echoed from the shadows in a rune tongue James didn't understand. The woman seemed to ask for help. James mouthed the words, "I'll come back," but he didn't think she could understand him. The woman kept rattling her chains.

"If you would know my secrets, then you must first see my things, boy. You need to understand how it is. And you must see it for yourself. Follow me." The Hermit slid into the pool and disappeared into the depths.

James wondered what Hendurinn would do. *He'd break those chains and leave with the scout, boy, and woman, now. But you're not a hero, are you? Heroes don't deal death like you do. That is what gods do. That is what you are. And gods are no one's hero. The god that grants life requires death, as well.* James looked at the gibbet, at the woman and small boy, dirty, cold, starved and exposed, and the unconscious scout tied up beside them who would never see the light of day again. He knew he couldn't save them *and* save Maggie, too. Not right at this moment. He would see the whole world die to save Maggie. He walked to the pool, turning his back on the screaming woman, the boy, and the chained scout.

James stood over the bubbling pool of dirty water. The Hermit had disappeared, swam off somewhere beneath the water. You *could leave. Get out of here, get Maggie from the hills and never come back.* But he was getting sick of running. He took a deep breath and plunged into the strangely warm water.

SORRY

At least Haro had the bones to hold the knife and do it himself. Wulfee shed no tears as she watched all twelve of *her* braids hit the earth, but watching Pike's grey strands of twisted hair fall made her outright weep. Every child of the north dreamed of having a grey head full of braids one day, and the elders who sat around the fires telling their old stories and tugging on their braids were the heroes of any clan. Pike had thirty-three. Thrice times eleven. Far more than any person Wulfee had ever known. But the Rangers wore their hair short under their green hoods and thought the braids to be barbaric. Long hair was an insult to the E'daru, whose hair only grew long because it lost its human ability to cut it. They didn't want long-haired barbarians travelling with them through the sacred hills for fear of ill omens.

He could have died for you a hundred times with all of his honour intact. Another life you've ruined. Another soul you've crushed.

Once Wulfee and Pike had their hair chopped and their wrists tied up, the Rangers started their descent out of the Hallow Hills. For all the hatred coursing through her, Wulfee couldn't even bring herself to words. She marched silently, floating like a crow's feather lost in a storm. It was dark and cloudy the whole first day. That night, she chewed on an old strip of smoked venison and listened to the Rangers sing their songs. She longed for the wolf bitch that followed her up the White to come by and take her away from this life.

Pike didn't talk either. *How could he talk? They have stripped him of the only thing he had left to comfort him—the thought of a good and honourable death. For the gods to recognize his achievements and grant his soul access to the sky halls. You've doomed him to an eternity of mockery... What kind of Feldarra would let their hair get cut?*

Later that night, Maggie whimpered.

"James and I wanted to have children, but the seed wouldn't take. Why couldn't we have a normal life, Wulfee? Why do the gods damn me from love?"

She was crying aloud, and Wulfee had a cry with her.

"Love is pain, Mag. Love is pain."

"And so is loneliness, Wulf. So, what kind of hurt is it you want to live with?"

"I want to be free of pain. For you, for all my children..."

"It can't be that way. Pain makes the good times better. Everything comes around in the end, Wulf. You can't have it all one way."

She is your daughter whether you birthed her or not. You took her in and loved her as much as your heart could love. Dust and debris danced around them with Maggie's magics, glowing moon-blue in the darkness, and made Wulfee nervous. *She's becoming more careless the closer to death she gets.*

"We're all going to die before this is over, Wulf. I've seen it. Why am I damned, Wulfee?" said Maggie. Wulfee wished she had answers for Maggie but she didn't. The sky was dancing above them, stars swirling. *Good gods, she'll bring one down on us...* Wulfee thought of her meeting with the soothsayers of Wick and shivered. *Mage.*

Rangers woke up, pointing and whispering.

"The stars are moving!" one said.

"That's the sign of Starfall," said another, and many agreed. They were all looking up.

The dust and the dead leaves were alight around Maggie, the skies above dancing. *They're not just dancing, they're performing. For Maggie.*

"It's the gods done that," said one Ranger pointing to the stars. Many agreed.

Only Wulfee knew the truth. Oft times she wasn't even sure if Maggie knew.

"I'm going to die first. He's going to have to watch me die, Wulfee, and that is when you should worry," said Maggie. She was talking non-sense.

"I'm sorry, Maggie. This is all my fault. I've gotten you into this," Wulfee said. She didn't know what else to say.

"It's been told in the tides, Wulf. There ain't no stopping the moon, you know that. We need to be strong," Maggie said, "now more than ever." Wulfee put her fist to her chin and nodded. Though, she reckoned luck had given up on her, and she was okay with that. *Look at this woman. She's stronger than you could ever hope to be. You thought you were helping her, but all this time she's been helping you.*

"You made me better, you know. You were like a child to me, Maggie. I love you," said Wulfee. "I'm sorry." All her sap was dripping out of her, along with her hope.

"You saved me, Wulfee, and more than just my life. Gave me something to believe in. When I was a girl, I imagined my life would be miserable, like my mother's. She didn't believe in love. She didn't believe in anything, really. And after her and my dad caught me making the leaves dance, they left me at the very next village. Folk passed me from one family to the next my whole life. Abandoned every time someone found me out. But you found me out and kept me *because* of that. You wanted to use my power, not get rid of me. Whatever happens, know that you saved me," said Maggie. "But my life is draining out of me, along with all the life left on earth. I can feel myself losing more and more of my soul every day."

"You're the only hope I have to kill Sweyne, Maggie. You're the only hope I have," Wulfee sobbed. It felt good to say it out loud to her. Wulfee could see the blue veins through Maggie's pale skin. Her brown hair was matted and straw-like. She was in terrible shape, and it broke Wulfee's heart because she hadn't a clue how to help her anymore. The world was dying and taking Maggie with it.

The night was cold, and Wulfee found herself missing fire more than ever. Under the din of insects, she lay brooding, shivering and half asleep. The chill was in her bones. She sat up from her half dream. Maggie slept close by. Above, the stars were still dancing. *Good gods, just let her live.*

Come morning, they were off before most of the birds had awoken. The greenhoods were remarkably efficient with their camps. Haro explained that they only set up tents in extreme weather. They slept on the ground under the stars most nights. Wulfee saw many of them speaking with birds and squirrels, and she could have sworn the creatures were conversing back in some twittering tongue lost on Wulfee's ears. When the Rangers would sit on the ground cross-legged with their eyeballs rolled back into their skull, Wulfee knew they were inside of their warg animal somewhere. She rarely knew what animal they were in and never knew where they were. Bears, wolves, hillcats, and great bull elk heeled them on their travels. As well as countless species of birds and squirrels and foxes. No doubt the familiars of the greenhoods. Each of them prayed the E'daru would find them and warg into them on their travels through the hill and arbor. What was a nightmare to most folk was an honour to the Rangers.

"To be blessed by the E'daru is to be touched by legend," Haro said with his mouth full of sweetbud.

If that kind of legend touched Wulfee, she'd shit herself.

The Rangers were far stranger than she imagined, but they knew the land intimately, and for that, she was thankful. Scouts and foraging parties came back with multiple routes to choose from and a bounty of edibles that had survived the droughts.

On the third afternoon, they stopped by a pool of mud.

"This was once a trickling waterfall and a shallow drinking pool," said a Ranger named Coal. "A glade of green grass spotted with bright yellow dandelions used to grow right here." He pointed to a patch of russet coloured dust. The Rangers ate their forage and dug a hole in the mud pool to get to the freshwater below. They pulled it up in buckets and dumped it into stew pots for the horses while some of the stewards fed them stale oats. Pike had gone off to a quiet part of the banks to speak to his underself in a muddy puddle. She could hear his soft mumbles as he said his prayers, and it reminded Wulfee of the clouds whispering in the distance before a storm. *Gods know he needs a prayer now more than ever.* Wulfee reckoned she was past due for a prayer herself, so she sat on a rock and stared into her own calm piece of water. It shocked her to see her without all that red curly hair. It always amazed her that her underself could find her in any piece of water; no matter how small or muddy, she was always there. It gave Wulfee an odd comfort. She used to long for the day when she'd look into the water and there would be no one there to judge her. No one there to make her feel ashamed for her mistakes. But she looked upon her underself with a strange empathy now. *You've been through all the same shit I have, and you're still here. Every time, without fail. You've been beaten, stabbed, left for dead, and you come back. Through love and loss, and the aching bloody pain of a broken heart, you come back. And you make me face the things I don't want to face. The guilt in those eyes is enough to break me...*

"I'm sorry I stopped talking to you... It just hurt so badly to remember it all," she said. And her underself stared back at her sagely. "It's finally over. I'm going to see Sweyne after all. Though not quite like I imagined. I can stop chasing him. In a way, I'm actually relieved. I'm going to rest, after all these years. Either it's easy, or it ain't, but it's time to find out."

Her underself remained silent. Wulfee studied the familiar face looking back at her. Those hurt eyes and tired soul. *What happened to you? You used to love, you used to laugh...* Her underself showed her the truth. How things were, not how she imagined them. The Feldarra believed the underself knew the truth of the soul. That talking to it and admitting your weaknesses to it would make a person stronger. A Feldarra had to be able to look their underself in the eyes and remember all the things they'd done. The underself reminded the Feldarra of who they were, not who they wanted to be. She was no kihl'dor and no mother. She was a grandmother to a child who would never know her and an exile lost in her own land. *The old times are gone, lady, they ain't ever coming back.* Her underself blinked and turned toward Pike. Wulfee looked up and saw her most loyal companion sitting alone, hands around his knees.

She started towards him but stopped in her tracks. She couldn't believe what she was seeing an inch from where she was about to place the sole of her boot. A wisp of etta. Scarlet and green amongst the brown and russet of the dead leaves and dirt. Its curly, glass-like petals were glowing in the sunlight. *"Look at this, sweetie, it looks just like your hair."* Her dad's words rang in her ears. The wisp of etta grew even in a drought. Its roots would just keep digging and digging, never stopping until they found water down there somewhere. Wulfee's dad had told her that some of them, long ago, dug so deep that they hit the fiery core of the world, and that's why they were so brilliantly red. Wulfee knelt and touched it with her dirty hands. The smell of honeysuckle and brambleberry hit the back of her throat as she breathed it in. Its long, skinny stem sprouted six beautiful green leaves. *One each for Tarek, Braden, little Sweyne, James, Maggie, and Gen.* Tears were falling down her cheeks, and she hadn't even noticed until they were dripping off her nose. She felt the strength inside of her building. The mere sight of the wisp ignited the old fire in her. *It still grows, even in the deepest of droughts. It's still here.*

And she knew she could keep going, too.

"Giy'er?" Wulfee overheard a scout close by, speaking with a panicked voice to Haro.

"Not just one. There is an entire pack of them following us."

"You're sure?" said Haro without a hint of fear in his voice.

"I'm sure. You don't forget thirty Giy'er when you see them," the scout said.

Gen... Gods I hope you're not caught up in this.

"What are they doing in the hills?"

"Looking for food, most like. Probably driven up out of the fields and arbors by the Wolf's army passing. They probably believe us to have dried meat they can eat."

May the Stag be with you, Gen, sweetheart...

"We *do* have some." Haro crossed his arms.

The scout puffed his cheeks. From where Wulfee stood, he looked two-thirds the size of Haro.

"Well, yeah we do. But—"

"Leave the lot of it behind us on the morrow. Maybe it'll slow them down," said Haro. "And what else?"

"The Hammer of the Glenn, Lord Brynmor, has sacked Dawning. He moved his host there from Ockam in just two days. The folk at Dawning were still digging ditches. The Glennish seem to be aligned with the Ayelish. I'm told there is a large host on the move in retreat from Dawning. Lord Brinley Scareye. It's very possible he will be coming through these hills, as well, or close to them."

Brinley... isn't he a lord of the old Hallow? Maybe there is hope yet. It didn't surprise Wulfee to hear that the Wolf had reinforcements from the Glenn. What surprised her was that so many still lived to oppose them.

"Smells like a battle brewing." Haro clapped his hands. "Let's remain vigilant from these hills, eh? We don't need to be seen until we want to be seen. Let our enemies fight each other."

Hare, please carry Gen far from here with haste.

Wulfee walked over to Pike to give him the gossip. *How long will it take him to accept that his hair is gone?* The old warrior saw her coming and turned away from her.

Wulfee stood beside him anyway. "Lord Brinley is moving through close by, in retreat. Maybe we can get our arses into his host." It wasn't much to hope for, and it was a long chance, but Wulfee reckoned if she was starting over, she had to start somewhere.

Pike looked up at her, almost cracked a smile.

"I thought you were done with long chances?"

"Reckon I've got about one left in me. Need my crew, though."

"I'm ready, Wulfee, to die," he said, peering back into the pool of mud.

The next morning, they walked down a tunnel of overgrown nytewoods on a path that led to Foulds. Every inch was overgrown with hedge, bramble, ivy, and nettle, and there were brief moments that Wulfee missed the barrow. Her ankles were scratched and swollen with rashes, and her feet were torn and blistered. There was life around the nytewoods and *that* Wulfee didn't understand.

By afternoon, they were in the hills directly above Foulds. Haro held his arm up to halt the march just short of a cliff that offered a viewpoint of the small village below. The mill wheel had been torn down, and the mill itself was falling apart. All that stood were mudbrick hovels roofed with sod, a stable, a smith, and a butcher. A single desolate well sat in a small clearing at the village centre. Haro and the scout passed the eye of Olan back and forth. Wulfee couldn't see shite but the outlines of the buildings and a few figures mulling about.

"It's that bloody wizard from the Old Arbor. The fuck is he doing out here?" said Haro. The scout shrugged.

Wizard... the fuck is the wizard doing around here? Wulfee thought of James.

Haro had another long look into the eye of Olan.

"It's a trap. It must be. We should wait in the hills until that wizard leaves or the Wolf arrives," he said. "Avoid going down there. The wizard will know a warged animal when he sees one."

"Those Giy'er are still stalking us, boss. I'm not sure I'd want to be in these hills should they attack. We'd be like bears in a snare," said the scout nervously. "And the bands have been talking, Haro. They hear the voices of gods in these hills. What if that wizard is working the earth magics of the fairies? What if—"

"The fairies died off centuries ago. Not one has been seen since the days of Kelson. That wizard is right here, right now, and if I never had to talk to him again, I would be all the happier for it," said Haro. "We stay in the hills tonight."

Wulfee remembered the clanfire stories of fairies, and they weren't anything nice.

The Rangers stayed put and set up their perimeter. Scouts returned after a few hours with baskets full of berries and roots, and nuts with mint leaves and ginseng. She drank water out of a fresh stream that was trickling from a deep reservoir in the Hills and tried to pretend like things were looking up. *At least you're not starving like some people in this country.*

The sunfell was ribbons of pink and purple, red and orange, slowly fading to black. *Reckon you're in the sunfell of your own life, old braud. Can you go out as brightly as the sun?* She felt something stir in her stomach. Gooseflesh consumed her, and the hair on her arms stood up like a hundred-hundred little soldiers, ready to give the fight another go. Maybe she could go out like the sun, with everyone looking up at her. When she glanced around at the Rangers, not one of them seemed to notice her. They had a perimeter that was impossible to break. *But maybe if I make enough noise, the wizard will notice. Then...* she didn't know what would happen then. Didn't much care to work it out either? In her experience, magics were best if she was never any near them. *But it's a chance...*

Just as the sun dipped out of sight, Wulfee found Pike and Maggie conversing by the shallow water pools in the rock.

Maggie said, "Another starless night, Wulfee. The moon and the stars can mate behind that veil, and you know what that means."

"We should run," Wulfee replied instead.

"Run? You?" said Pike.

"If we make enough of a racket, maybe that wizard will come up here." Wulfee glanced down the hill through the woods at Foulds.

"That's a great idea," Maggie grinned widely.

"That's an awful idea, Wulf." Pike hiked his shield up as if to defend himself from Wulfee's words. "Wizards are best avoided."

"I met with a wizard in the woods by Wick. He called himself Adeqor." Wulfee looked at Maggie. "He'd asked about James."

"About James?" said Maggie. "About the dead?"

Wulfee didn't know Maggie knew about that. She was worried she'd scare her.

"About dead souls, and he wanted to know where James was," she said. "Maybe that wizard found him."

"That's a long chance," said Maggie.

"It's over, Wulfee," Pike said bluntly. "Can't you bloody see it's—"

A Ranger screamed from somewhere on the perimeter. Then a body was flying past Wulfee as if the Ranger had grown wings. When he came crunching down on the far side of camp, Wulfee knew something threw him. Crashing footsteps rolling down the hillside rumbled the ground. Ten, twenty more of them, like a stampede, threw dust in the twilight sky. The Rangers were scrambling, grabbing their spears, axes, bows, flinging them, loosing arrows at the mass charging towards them. Another body landed right in front of Wulfee, greenhood off, his short black hair matted with blood. He ogled Wulfee with lifeless eyes. Then she felt a firm hand pull her into the shallow pools of water. It was Pike, and Maggie was behind him.

The Giy'er moved so fast that Wulfee thought they may have fell out of the starless sky. Massive, hulking bodies of grey flesh, muscle, and bone ran the Rangers down like a stampede. Flailing their tree trunk sized limbs as they ran, knocking the Rangers about like flies. She had been exposed to Gen and his human-stunted gentleness so long she had forgotten what wild Giy'er could do to a person.

But none of them paid any mind to the small trickling stream falling from the Hills. Wulfee waded silently behind Maggie and watched the Rangers die, wondering if they would be next.

Rangers were swinging their axes and throwing their spears, but the Giy'er brushed them aside like flies with stone hands the size of baled hay. Most of the arrows loosed had bounced off their callus-hardened skin, and the ones that stuck seemed only a minor annoyance. They swatted them off like skitters or burn bugs. The Giy'er roared, a wicked deep rolling sound that didn't let up. It sounded like a star falling. Wulfee was absolutely terrified. She cowered as low as she could in the water but couldn't help but watch. If death was coming for her, she wanted to see it coming. Horses whinnied all around, and Rangers tried to direct them away, but they got caught up in the carnage anyway. Wulfee saw a Giy'er squeeze a man so hard that his brain exploded out of the top of his green hood. She vomited, and the yellow bile floated around her on top of the water until she pulled herself out of it. The hulking giant threw the corpse and pounded its stone fists against its chest. Bears and wolves were squealing as they were bludgeoned apart by stone fists. Wulfee saw a Giy'er grab a human-eyed bull elk by the horns and toss it over the trees. The Rangers scrambled into dozens of groups, evacuating in different directions. *This is where you die...*

Not before long, the massive beasts were digging through the wagons. Wulfee could hear them talking to each other in their crude tongue. When they found the stores of smoked elk and venison jerky, they ate it by the fistful. Their twisted, hairless faces ripped at the meat with pointed fangs. *Good gods... Nihr'el nur amo ruso.* Muscles in their arms and legs writhed like snakes, sinews in their neck popped out as thick as ropes as they tore at the meat. It seemed as if the Rangers had given up the fight. Wulfee could hear horses galloping off in the distance. But plenty were still here, dying. And then she heard a hundred bow strings snap at once, echoing like a whip off the Hills surrounding them.

Arrows rained down. Piercing the top of the beast's heads, which seemed to be much softer. Wulfee remembered combing Gen's wispy hair, the curiosity in his orange eyes. Giy'er fell, heavy and dead. Another whip cracked, and more iron rain fell, followed by trees falling. The Giy'er scrambled now. Rangers poured down the hills; a more organized attack. From one side first, then the other. The Giy'er were turning this way and that as they were prodded with spears and arrows from all sides and above. Rangers caught the Giy'er in nets and killed them.

"Now's our time!" Wulfee pulled herself out of the water. "Let's go!" The last two members of her crew followed. A whip cracked somewhere behind her, and Wulfee ducked on impulse. A flinch of nervousness, and she tripped over herself. Pike reached down and pulled her up. Covered them both with his shield as the arrows pierced the ground around them.

"Well, don't go and die before me now," he said, a fist to his chin as he nodded. They ran towards Foulds. *Maybe James is there. Maybe the wizard can help...* here, she was taking long chances again. Seemed almost foolish, but she had to realize that maybe she was just a damn fool. Another whip cracked, followed by more falling trees and screaming. Wulfee reckoned there was absolutely no worse sound than suffering. Another body flew past her and crashed through the arbor and down the hill towards Foulds.

"That way!" she screamed, but Haro stood at the treeline with an axe in his hand.

He limped towards her.

"You're not getting out of this one, Wulfee. I'm not done with you yet. You're going to take me to James."

She had no weapon. *Probably can't beat this one without a—*

Pike stepped in front of her.

"My underself told me I would face death in these Hills one day." He swung his axe side to side, shining iron glinting under the moon. His shield was marked with the battered tree of the Feldarra. The nihr'el. "Ever looked death in the face, Ranger? Care to?"

Haro smiled and limped towards Pike. Wulfee wondered how he was so nimble with the bad leg.

"Let's go, old man. You and I, let one of us take the journey up tonight," he said.

But their taunts were interrupted by the sound of thunder—a Giy'er was charging at them. They had a smile on their face like a child about to crush an ant.

"*Wulfee!*" Maggie screamed, "We need to move."

"Go without me," Wulfee hissed. "I won't die crouched over like no dog." To the Crow she said, "*You can bloody wait for me.*"

Then a smaller Giy'er tackled the bigger one from the side, and they both went tumbling to the ground. Sounds of stone on flesh thundered across the arbor as they pummelled each other. The smaller Giy'er got on top and flattened the bigger one's face into a pulp. *Gen...*

"Gen!" she screamed. The young Giy'er took two more big swings, fists dripping dark blood, and looked up.

"I came back for you!" he called out with a grin. "You said that karls always come back, you remember? I came back." Then had his head knocked by a giant fist. Gen fell flat on his back, and Wulfee thought he was dead by the way his eyes disappeared into his skull for a moment, but he got up. He swung his fist into the gut of the bigger Giy'er as it charged at him. It was enough to make it stumble back into the thrust of a Ranger's spear. The iron point took it in the shoulder, and the Giy'er roared out that deep rumbling sound and, with its fist, sent the Ranger flying. Then it had its ankles sliced from behind, and two Rangers threw a net on him. Wulfee's heart skipped. She wanted to yell, but she struggled to breathe. The Rangers surrounded Gen. One Ranger stabbed him in the thigh, and he fell screaming in agony.

"Get the net on him!" Rangers yelled, scrambling to find another net. Wulfee picked up an axe and swung the blade deep into the shoulder of one of the Rangers from behind. Two more turned and swung at her, but she used the man she'd killed as a shield. Blood spattered as blades squelched into the man. Wulfee threw the body at one and her axe at the other. Blood gushed from his chest as Wulfee pulled her blade out. Gen got to his knees and crushed the other one's skull with his fist. Another Ranger thrust a spear at Gen but missed. Wulfee ran at him and tackled him to the ground. Rolled around, and then he was on top of her, sour sweat dripping on her face as he struggled to reach for the axe beside them. She held his arm back with everything she had. *Please, Stag, let it be enough.* The man's dirt laden fingers were reaching, reaching, getting closer—and he got it. Wulfee raised her arms over her face with what little strength she had left in them. *Tarek, baby, I'm coming.* And blood spattered her face. The man had his head caved in by the blunt end of Pike's axe. The old warrior smiled and held his hand out. Wulfee took it and stood up, ran over to Gen. He was strewn across the ground, crying and shaking. Touching all the different red gashes on his body and the big one on his leg.

Maggie shouted, "I can sow him up. I can fix him!" She ran towards Gen, but they had no needle and no thread. Wulfee knew they couldn't help him besides just being there. Around them, the Rangers were killing the Giy'er trapped in the nets. A group of greenhoods were walking towards them. Pike came rushing back with a look of concern.

"We have to go, Wulfee. If we would go, it has to be now," he said. "That man, Haro, wasn't like any other person I've fought. Right before I killed him, his eyes went all white, and it felt like I was fighting a dead corpse. These Rangers ain't right, Wulf."

Gen was struggling to put any weight on his leg. The blade had torn through his thigh muscle.

"We have to go, Gen. We have to go," said Wulfee. She couldn't hold in the tears now, seeing him hurt. She knew he couldn't get up right now. *He only needs a little time to heal.* She had seen Gen heal inhumanly fast before. He looked up at her, tears shining in his big orange eyes.

"I can't stand up. I can't, I can't. My leg, it really hurts, *Wulfee.* It really hurts," Gen cried.

Wulfee held his big hand.

"It's okay, Gen." She stroked hair from his eyes. "It's all okay." She wouldn't leave him.

"I came back for you, Wulfee. They were following me, but I led them here. I came back. Karls always come back, right? No matter what. Isn't that what you told me?" said Gen. Wulfee cried for both of them, and maybe for everyone else, too.

"You did, Gen. You came back." Her chest burned, throat swollen, nose running like the White River. "I'm so sorry, Gen."

"We have to go, Wulfee!" Pike screamed. The greenhoods jogged towards Wulfee and Gen when they saw Pike and Maggie scatter.

"I can be a karl now, can't I, Wulfee?" said Gen. "When we make it to the world tree?"

"The best." She put her hand on her heart. "You're going to be okay, Gen. You'll be the best karl there ever was."

"Now, Wulf!" Pike said one last time before he disappeared down the hill with Maggie. Gen whimpered.

"Don't leave me, Wulfee." Gen pleaded. "Please, I can't run. My leg is messed up, Wulfee!"

"I won't leave you." She knelt over him as tears fell on her son's wounds. Two Rangers held spears to her neck while another netted Gen.

"He needs help. He's not dying, he only needs some help! For the gods' sake, he won't hurt you. He's not like them!" she screamed, but the Rangers just tied her up, too. "Don't you hurt him!" Wulfee screamed a terrible yelp that was laced with twenty years of heartbreak and failure. "Don't you fucking touch him!" The pain seeped out of her like steam leaving a kettle. One of the Rangers took another step, and Wulfee bared her teeth like a rabid beast. "Don't you fucking touch him."

And they didn't.

"Wulfee?" Gen cried out in confusion. She put her hand on his big shin as she lay down in the dirt beside him.

"I'm here, Gen. I'm here."

THE OTHERWORLD

THE SURFACE OF THE water closed over with earth magics the second James plunged in. He couldn't swim back up. The slimy water burned his eyes. He didn't know where the hell to swim to. He was losing his breath, and faster now that he was panicking. *God damned shite.*

He brushed his hand against the bottom of the pool. *Or is it the side?* He felt around like a madman until he found a tunnel. As he swam through it, the tunnel narrowed, and James felt his stomach twist into panicked knots. His lungs were empty already. His heart started pounding, head thumping. He kept pulling himself through the water, sure he would burst out gulping for air at any moment. The tunnel closed in around his body, walls pressing him in tighter and tighter. Then he broke into a wide-open pool. He swam towards the dim light above, hoping to break through the surface. His head broke through, cold air on his face, and he gasped. *Thank the gods.* He looked around the dark cave, wondering which direction to swim to. He was miserable, and he was shivering now. Then the cave lit up with earth magics. Purple and blue and green. Moss, mushroom, and insect. Twisted roots of nytewood, oak, and ash tangled together in a mess of black and white and brown and green that hung down from the ceiling like thick, furry snakes. The cave walls grew around him on all sides but one, where the cold pool of water met a flat area of stone. The Hermit was sitting there in front of a large totem with a face carved into it. Roots and mycelium covered the totem's head and looked like mossy hair. The face had its mouth and eyes closed tightly. The Hermit seemed to pray to it, murmuring something in a foreign tongue as it swayed back and forth.

James pulled himself out of the water, dripping wet and cold, his feet squelching with every step as he walked towards the Hermit.

It said, "It is good to pray to the earth stone when Humans come for my secrets. This is one of my most adored things. I have so few things these days."

"What is it?" said James.

"A god stone. The trees breathe in the memories of the dead and drop them through the roots into the god stone's head. It filters them into the pool, and then the trees drink from the pool. Then the earth absorbs the memories of each of its children and remembers." The Hermit licked the god stone and slithered around its base. "The world is a living being. One soul, one nature. You would know this already if you were not such a coward. The memories of all who die feed into a single experience, and it all moves with a single motion. Everything helps to produce everything else. Spun and woven together into a tapestry of life, all occurring at the same time. You are nothing more than a little wisp of a soul, animating a jacket of flesh and bone. These stones are the good gods. Never changing, not even with the seasons. They live betwixt life and death for eternity."

"What? There are more of these?" said James. *Is it saying the trees are alive?* The thought made James uncomfortable. He had pissed on an awful lot of trees and figured they must be pretty upset about that. He would be. The Hermit scurried away from the stone face and towards James so fast it made him flinch. Its oily, wet skin stunk like rotting meat, its breath like rancid milk.

"Yes, there are more. And a fairy to guard each one. Confined by earth magics to guard them, yes. To protect these stones from the Creators. I was born of the mud and clay below, formed by the earth's own calloused hands, a child of the rock and wood and soil. I cannot leave this hole any more than you can fly with the ravens." The Hermit scowled. "But nevermind all of that. They are my secrets, and I've given you enough of them already. And now you've seen one of my things, too, and your dirty eyes can't unsee now, no. You need to learn the Ways, not my secrets."

James felt the violent ache in his head again. Splitting, piercing into his thoughts and memories. Searching through and scattering them this way and that. He had entered the Hermit's domain and submitted himself entirely to its magics. James had to be careful now. His dad had warned him to be so very careful. *Don't think of violence. It will know. It's always a step ahead.*

"I'm ready to learn. What would you ask of me?" James held his hands together, begging. "Please."

The Hermit chittered.

"The souls will never respect you if you seek their favour because of another. You are here for the sake of someone else, not because you want to be."

"I didn't want to come back here at first. But I know now that I have to learn the Ways. I have to do it for my people. For Maggie."

"You need to want it for yourself. You need to find what your soul craves. Is it love? Because you've had that, and you ran when trouble befell you. Is it home? Because home is not just a piece of land that someone can take from you. Home is some place inside of you." The Hermit moved in and sniffed around James's ears. He could feel it searching through his memories, culling his firsts with Maggie: when they first met, first laughed, first made love; the Hermit ran greasy fingers over those memories as it clutched them in James's mind. He was dizzy, delirious. The Hermit's magics were coming on strong, and James had little control in stopping it. He felt like something had burrowed into his mind, and he couldn't find it to stop it if he wanted to—he only knew it was there, taunting him. When the Hermit was done with Maggie, it flipped through other memories James had buried deep down. His dad, dead and blue, strewn out in the pink snow, his beard covered in frozen vomit; his mother's body, entrails hanging out like bloody ropes. Made him think of every person he'd ever killed when his demon took over. They all had loves and lives of their own, people waiting for them to come home from a war they ain't ever coming back from. The Hermit made him remember.

James tried to move away from the Hermit, but soft roots under his feet had absorbed him like a pool of mud.

"Look at all you've done. These are the things that eat your soul, pink man. These are the things you must throw away to See," the Hermit prodded. James felt something puncture his head. He thought he must have taken an axe to his skull. Something wriggled inside of his mind, beneath his brow, under his eyes. He felt it sucking and pulling on his memories. Then he saw glimpses of Maggie, at the river, by the fire, in bed, flowing by as if those visions were caught in a river. He saw fires crackling in hearths, and a boar roasting on a spit, fat dripping and hissing in the coals. He saw the stars above, but they were so close he could almost touch them. And he was hanging onto Maggie so tightly he was worried she might burst. It was raining. And he was happy. Maggie looked up at him.

"Stay here with me, James. Don't leave me again. You can never leave me for true." Then the sky fell on them like a blanket, and they lay in the blackness together, forever.

"I won't ever leave you," he said, realizing he was saying it out loud to nobody but the Hermit. It flashed something like a smile at him with its twisted mouth.

"You see now, pink man. This is what could be if you let the demon out," the Hermit chittered. "If you let it fester, it will eat you from inside and take over. You are ready. Come."

James followed it to a dark corner of the cavern. His legs moved on their own and didn't even care that he was scared shitless.

"The lack of spirits tortures the dead. The souls can only linger," the Hermit said.

"They call to me for help," said James.

"Yes. I know this. And now you will go to the darkness with them. You must see their world. It is the only way. A World Walker must Walk. You must make the passage to their world and come back. It is the gods you need council with, not me. This is my secret."

James swallowed hard. The blood was rushing to his head, and he was getting dizzy. *Why did you come here?*

He could hear running water, but the sound was wrong. It sounded heavier, like mud. The Hermit lit up the area with its earth magics and revealed a shimmering pool of metal.

"It is a wonderful thing, this. A wonderful thing to have as my own." The Hermit stood beside the strange pool and ran its boney finger through it.

"What is it?" said James. The waterfall of metal clumped down loudly so that the Hermit had to raise its voice to be heard.

"It is a quicksilver stream, flowing directly from the Otherworld. Cold steel water. It is very secret." The Hermit ran a finger through it again, looking at the quicksilver with admiration. "It is my own, to protect. You must get in. Get in, get in! It's the only way, the only way! You must go under."

The Hermit scurried around the cave walls, collecting glowing blue mushrooms, then came back to James in a hurry, reeking of fungus. It poked him towards the pool of quicksilver, picked other glowing things along the way, and ground them up in a shallow wooden bowl.

"It's the dead souls you wonder about, yes?" it said, grinding away.

"Yes," said James. "I need to guide them."

"You do not know their language," said the Hermit. "You do not even know what they are."

"So tell me," James said.

"You must learn it from *them*. First, you must eat this." The Hermit spooned a shining purple paste out of the bowl with its bare hand and smeared it in James's mouth. It was spongy and earthy, and tasted vile, but James ate it. Puckered his lips and slapped the top of his mouth with his tongue to get the sticky stuff down. Then, oddly, he remembered it tasting like maple syrup and craved more of it. He stood before the pool of liquid metal, poked his toe in, and felt like he may be able to walk on it.

"Get in," it chittered again. "I would go with you, but I haven't been in so long. In so very long. The gods do not remember me. I was different then..."

James was about to take a step when the Hermit pushed him. He fell into the pool and landed hard. The liquid felt like steel beneath him, and he was only partially submerged. He rolled over and floated on his back and felt like he was on solid ground. The quicksilver had strange fumes coming off of it, and James felt sick as it rolled down his nostrils. The quicksilver parted around him, not soaking into his tattered shirt and torn trousers. The Hermit was chanting something foreign in a deep, booming voice. It banged rocks together in a constant rhythm. James was completely weightless.

"HeyHa," the Hermit chanted in perfect unison with the banging of the rocks. James felt lightheaded. His world flickered.

"HeyHaHeyHa." The Hermit's chant got faster. The banging of the rocks grew louder. James was delirious. In a pool of liquid metal, he let the fungus take over his consciousness. The Hermit started laughing maniacally. The souls were screaming out to him in an indiscernible tongue. "*Helphelphelphelp...*"

...and then his world was a green-black sea. *Or is it the sky?* Milky lights flared up and blended into a spiral that sucked James deeper into the sea-sky. Bodiless souls scattered desperately as if his presence was of great terror to them. But he dove deeper into the spiral until his feet touched golden grass that pulled at his boots like mud. The sky was the same green-black, but now it was lit with the swirling bodies of a million souls.

Beams of light flickered and flowed. Something moved towards him. It walked in the sky like one would on flat land. It stood strong and human-like, as tall as ten people with limbs like tree trunks. It moved like a Human, but it wasn't. It was Father Tree, the Great God of Justice and Ultimate Judge of the Souls of the Dead.

"You don't belong here," Father Tree said in the northern tongue. James tried to speak, but he no longer had a mouth. He no longer had a body. He was only a little wisp of a soul. "You've come too far. You do not belong here. This is a place for the dead. You should never have come." Father Tree moved towards James with long, heavy strides. James tried to run but found he could not move. Father Tree sniffed the air around James. "Oh. You are a seer. It's a bad time for gods and half-gods alike right now, I'll tell ya. Nevertheless, you must face the Pantheon just the same. Any and all who make it this far, must, at least, face the Pantheon. It's only right that we listen to you and cast fair judgment."

Father Tree hummed a song, and the sky opened up behind him to reveal a great golden plain. James saw a great fire burning down in the plain, spewing black smoke and shedding light into the dark sky. The dead souls were swarming around it, like bees who had just lost their hive. He followed Father Tree on more golden, grassy mud.

"Wait here." Father Tree vanished, and James stood alone.

There was purplish-black godrock thrusting up from the ground at sharp angles. Like thousands of giant *Essikahs*. The great fire was burning just beyond him, but he could still feel the heat coming off of it. And the dead souls swarmed him, gathered around, and clung to him. *"Helphelphelphelphelphelphelp."*

"I'm trying!" James tried to yell, but he had no body.

Then Father Tree, the Great God of Justice, was beside him again, and he wasn't alone this time, either. A beautiful Swan, a wise old Owl, a shady Crow, and two singing Bluebirds flew alongside. A smiling Hare, surrounded by her babies, and a glorious Stag walked behind. *The Old*

Gods... James was in awe. The Maw God wasn't with them, and he was thankful for that.

"What is it?" said the Swan.

The Crow shook its head. "It looks like a living soul."

"That is a living soul, dumb fuck," sneered the Owl. The Crow looked offended.

"How did it get down here?" The Hare nibbled on a corn cob.

"The same way Bazal slipped his numen," said the Owl.

Bazal... James had an overwhelming urge to hold *Essikah* in his hands.

"There are too many holes. Too many problems," the Stag puffed out his chest and raised its chin. "A fight is brewing."

"Too many old songs are being remembered," sang Ayla, the Bluebird.

Nox, her twin, had a stick in his mouth. "And too many songs forgotten." He placed the stick carefully in the nest he already had underway.

"Which is worse?" said the Hare, downing the last nub of the corn cob.

Adeqor spoke of old songs and Bazal. What is really happening here?

"Enough," Father Tree bellowed. "The Gateway of Rebirth has been closed. This one is the blood of the old Druid seers. The half-gods that walk betwixt worlds. He can open the Gateway if we show him how."

"The Gateway opening does not rid the world of these dark words rising," said the Crow. "We will all die if the Words spread again." And the gods all glared at the black-feathered goddess.

"Why is it always *death* with you? It's depressing, you know?" said the Hare.

"I am the Goddess of death, and so it concerns me greatly," said the Crow.

"And who gave us these titles?" The Owl seemed tired of the others.

"Stop this!" said Father Tree. "We must convene and decide the fate of this soul that has wandered so far off its course. The Druid seers have come to us in the past. We have always guided them," said Father Tree. It turned to James. "We are the Pantheon of Undergods. Sorry for the poor welcome, but we're a bit shaken up right now. A wicked soul, the great wizard Bazal, who was confined here by the powers of the Ailaryan Order, has escaped his numen prison to the world above. We believe the great wizard has been spreading ancient magics, and we have been under attack from the Old Words ever since. These are echoes of a war fought four hundred-hundred years ago before the Starfall. We are all quite wretched about it."

"Are we going to hear what this soul has to say or what?" said the Stag.

I am no god.

"No, god you say? Hah." Father Tree raised a tree limb finger. "So you are not like the others, are you? No. Why did you come here?"

To guide the dead down and bring the elements back to the world above, James thought. And the great Father Tree stood silent for a moment, staring at James intently with ethereal eyes, sniffing about the air.

"Yes. You have the smell of death all over you. Their souls call out to you. Your blood is Druid blood, the walking half-gods, the ancient seers. It has been so long since they have sung this song. I think we shall help this one to power," said Father Tree.

"I say this here is a seer," said the Hare, holding an uneaten corn cob. James surveyed the area and wondered where it might have come from. "Help him See the Ways. Let the lands be bountiful again."

"I can't believe I agree with The Hare." The Owl rubbed its forehead with a wing. "But I remember the seers of old. Amongst the wisest who ever walked the land above. Help them to See the Ways once more, I say."

"Let him see the beauty of the Ways," purred the Swan. "Let him save the innocent."

"Grant him the strength to see the Ways," proclaimed the Stag. "And courage. The poor thing needs it."

"Let the dead build once more!" said the Bluebird Nox.

"It's rather dissonant with so many of them stuck down here," said the Bluebird Ayla.

"Do we have any other choice?" said the Crow.

"Only war," said the Stag.

"Nothing else has come to us," said The Owl.

"Then what are we waiting for?" said the Crow. Father Tree faced James slowly.

"As the god of justice, I have taken court with my pantheon. We have decided helping you to See the Ways is our best chance at living," he said.

That's good news. James thought. *I could hear you the whole time.*

"Right," said the Tree. "Well then. If you are to See, then you must look with more than your eyes. Inside to the demon that lives there. It is your soul that sees the Ways of the Otherworld. You must look inward to your true self. Find what you really are and embrace it." It gestured towards the immense fire. "All fire is born of a single flame. The fire burns here eternally. What you see above is just a little window into this world. But the windows are shut, and the spirits that rule the elements can no longer come to life to guide the wind, clouds, fire, or earth." Father Tree stood before James as grand an entity as anything he'd witnessed. The other gods behind it were just as grand, and together, they were truly awe-inspiring. "Spirits have lost their way. Dead souls linger. And we could no longer guard the Great One, Bazal, in his numen prison, and his soul escaped above through the stump of a felled nytewood. The outcome for us is uncertain. Our powers are waning as the belief in us dies. Soon Eralis and Karaat will rule these plains, as well as the vast many others they already patrol."

Can you make the dead listen to me? I need to lead them. I can save them.

"For them to hear you, you must look at them with your whole body. With all of your senses. You must feel them, smell them, touch them, and taste them. Then you can *really* hear them. Then the souls will hear *you*. You are closed off and only see things one way. Open yourself up to the world below. Try to see it for what it is. Let it flow through you. Let *them* flow through you. Use the Ways to let your mind slip down below and power your soul with strength from the Otherworld. Use the Ways to prod the souls of the dead, grab ahold of them with your mind, you'll find that they will *want* you to. The soul gets cold and lonely after so many years of wandering. That monster you feel inside of you is just the power of the Otherworld. Run to it. The dead that follow you are only seeking purpose.

Give them purpose. Bind them to your will and *use* them. Now that you have walked worlds, they will have no choice but to listen." Father Tree said, his magnificent voice fading. "May your poor soul rest easy when this is all done."

"You don't really think he can do it, do you?" said the Hare.

"We're doomed, aren't we?" cawed the Crow.

James watched the massive fire burn ferociously and slowly fade away into a damp darkness. His head was clearing. He closed his eyes...

...opened them again and only saw the roof of a cave. His head was thumping, eyes on fire from salty sweat, stomach full of acid, legs full of jagged rocks. He was floating on some kind of strange silver fluid and the mushrooms sprouting out of the walls were aglow with purple light. *What is this?* He couldn't move. There was something scurrying around him. Then he remembered where he was. *Oh, gods...*

"You've come back." The Hermit grabbed James's wrist with dirty, crooked fingers and pulled him closer. It peered into his eyes with its ghastly grey ones. It had a look of pure shock and amazement. "And with your wits still about you. You weren't supposed to come back. They never come back."

"Rhhgg," James croaked. *Fuck you!* His mouth was sawdust, and he couldn't feel his tongue.

"Don't be trying to say too much, pink man. You've been out for weeks and with no food, and only the little water that I had spit into your mouth. It will take you some time to come down from a trip like that." The Hermit twitched as it spoke. "The mortal mind was not meant to make such a journey. You cannot convene with the gods and come back the same as you were. You must rest now."

"Rhhgh," James said. *No!* He felt weary. He closed his eyes. "Rhhgh," he croaked one last desperate time. *Maggie...*

"You can stay here. Yes. You can stay and be my pet. It will be better if you stay." The Hermit chittered and scurried off into the darkness. James closed his eyes and took a deep breath. *What did I just see? The gods?* He opened his eyes again and tried to stand. His legs were weak, and he was out of breath. He failed three times before he could get himself sitting up. Rocked back and forth like an unsteady canoe in the pool of quicksilver but managed to get out and fall to his knees.

"Fuck," he muttered. After some time, he was able to pull himself up and lean against a rock. After some more time, he walked. He wasn't sure where. *Out. Maggie.* And then the Hermit was in front of him with a length of rope. Its crooked grin turned into a vicious scowl.

"Sssskl'rhosss!" it hissed and lunged at him. The fairy sunk its yellow teeth deep into James's neck and shoulder.

James screamed. Nails as sharp as steel sunk into his torso. The thing was like a parasite, trying to crawl under his skin. James screamed again, and the dead flooded the cave. James took them in his lungs as the Hermit mauled him. *Fuck this fucking hermit.* New skin grew back where the Hermit tore old skin away. The Hermit had been with James most nights since he'd escaped the first time. Haunting him, laughing at him. He'd had enough. He was going to end it. James pummelled the Hermit on the back of the head. It still stuck to him like a leech, digging its bony fingers into James like dull hooks. Through the madness of the grapple, James saw fear in it. A little curl of its rainbow smoke hair hung in front of its haunted grey eyes. It almost looked Human. With one last heave, James sent it sliding across the cold stone. A knife came loose from its tattered waistline.

"Skkahzzanz!" it scowled, glancing quickly at the knife on the mossy ground between them. It was *his* knife. *Maggie's knife.* James dove and reached for it. Clutched the hilt with all his strength like the knife itself was Maggie's life. James jumped up and felt wobbly. The Hermit scurried back. James held the knife out, walking towards it on shaky legs. The dead gathered around him. James's head was a mess of clouds.

"It's so very lonely down here. I only have my pets to love. I just need a new pet. Something special, like you." The Hermit's eyes glowed with hope. It held its hands together, begging. "You wouldn't fault an old fairy for that, would you? You wouldn't harm me after I shared my secrets with you? I taught you how to eat life from death. I sent you to the Gods. I can *help* you. You see?" The Hermit walked closer, smiling. "See?" It flashed yellow fangs and lunged at him with the look of killing in its pale eyes. Like it knew it was over.

James took one step forward and wedged the engagement knife into the Hermit's skull. It screamed in agony as James twisted the knife around. The fairy beast cried out in bloody pain. Its eyes were bulged and bloodshot. The cave flickered wildly as the earth magics pulsated through the flora. James could feel a new energy inside of him, one that wasn't there before. The dead souls swirled around him, *through* him, and he twisted the knife again. The Hermit's earth magics faded, and the cave went black. James removed the blade and let the Hermit's pale body drop to the ground. He had always hated that thing, and now he knew all its secrets. He tucked Maggie's knife away in his waistline and followed the dead as they led him out of the Hermit's hole.

RISING UP

THE LARGE STONE HEAD stared at James with open, human-like eyes glowing a pale yellow in the cave's darkness. He had awoken something in these hills by killing the Hermit. An old curse had been severed. The dead souls led him back up through the water and into the small cave in which he entered. The woman and the boy screamed when James popped his head above water, gasping for air. She had blood stains around her mouth and looked even more haggard than he'd last seen her. James pulled himself up and went to the gibbet. He kicked at the locks that bound the cage closed. The woman screamed every time his foot hit. She seemed to hide something behind her with her body.

"I'm trying to help," James complained. He kicked the lock a few more times until his foot almost tore through his boot. He tried picking it with his knife, but it was no use; it was an old Lovasi lock with too many different wheels to turn. James shook the bars. Kicked the lock again. He was doing nothing to loosen it. The boy was talking loudly in his rune tongue, and the woman tried to calm him down. He seemed to be afraid of James. Then, James noticed bones, still covered in bits of flesh, behind the woman in the gibbet. A human head and torso were visible, unmistakable. The boy looked up at him, dirty face with a mess of brown hair and brown eyes, blood stains around his mouth and all over his hands. The boy looked terrified. James tried to smile. He didn't quite know what he had contorted his face into instead, but the boy cried.

"I'm trying," James said solemnly. "I'm trying."

The woman screamed at him desperately. It seemed to James she had been screaming at him in one long note since he'd first brought the scout in. *The scout...*

"Where is the scout? The one I brought down as payment?" James asked. The woman didn't understand him. Blood covered the woman's hands, too. *They ate him...* James pointed behind her at the bones. "The scout! Where is the scout?"

She only screamed louder now. She grabbed the bars with her blood-stained hands and shook them. She was half mad. *They bloody ate him...* James kicked at the lock a few more times. It was really no use.

"I'm sorry," James said, feeling his heart on fire. He truly was a monster. "I'm sorry," James said again and turned around towards the fresh air. He heard them screaming as he left. *I'm sorry... I'm so sorry... you're a goddamned beast of a thing...* James turned himself numb and kept going. For his country. For the whole damned world. *For Maggie...*

He followed the tunnel to where it ended, but there was no way up.

The hole had sealed over somehow. James didn't waste too much time before he just started digging. Clawing at black sod, swallowing the earth that fell on top of him to choke out another breath. Digging, digging, with cracked and bleeding hands, broken fingernails, and dirt blinded eyes. Towards the surface, fresh air, and the life he'd left behind. *Towards Maggie.* Up, through the roots and the rocks and the plot of land that held them all together. He'd come all the way from the Otherworld. He'd seen the One Fire and learned the secrets of the world. If he had to dig his way back up into it, so be it. He'd dig himself back to Maggie. To Wulfee. To pull the Hallow out of the hole it had been dying in.

Finally, his hand broke free of the earth. He gripped what felt like a root and pulled himself through the ground. First his torso, then his legs. It wasn't until he had completely pulled himself out that he realized the root he was holding onto was the bare leg of a dead Giy'er. There were dozens of cold, dead Giy'er fallen like felled trees. Bloody green hooded corpses littered amongst them. James studied the scene in awe and kept going.

It wasn't far down the trail before James could see Foulds from the hills above. The village had crumbled down. But on the wending path leading from the hills, he saw an unmistakable sight. The rag-clad wizard and his glowing dark skin radiated against the dull hovels. Adeqor stood, as if he was waiting for him, and drank from his wineskin.

His face lit up when he saw James coming.

"Mineera!" shouted Adeqor. "Oh, you're going to want to bring your ink and parchment, dear. Culdaine is back." The wizard took a long swig, tucked away his wineskin, and walked towards him, smiling. "Look at you! By the gods, look at you. You're filthy! How'd you get yourself out of that hole, boy? Oh my, nevermind, don't tell me yet." He cocked his neck around like an owl. "Mineera!"

"There are people down there. I need to go back for the boy. There is a small boy."

"What?" Adeqor said. "James, there is no going back. Not now."

James turned around and saw the hole he came out of had grown over with soil. He walked around the hill, looking for the mucous he'd peeled back weeks ago. But there was only dead grass and sticks and rocks and trees.

"There were people down there!" James shouted. Adeqor only stared. James felt his stomach twisting and his heart thumping. "A small boy!" James pointed towards the trees. Adeqor only blinked. *You can't save anyone. Not even when you try...* His mind turned to Maggie. *You can still save her, though... you can. She's in the hills with Haro.* James's blood felt like it might burn through his veins. "I need to find Maggie." He would go to

Foulds and get *Essikah*, then back into the Hills to get Maggie out of the hands of that Ranger.

The Lovasi woman came around the bend of the path. The once clean scholar was now covered in dirt and what looked like dried splashes of blood. She was holding a mess of parchment papers, flipping through them as she approached.

"He rose up out of the ground like some kind of undead wight or something," the wizard said with dramatic flair and followed James. *Haro... that god damned Ranger. I should have killed him. I should have killed him.*

Adeqor droned on behind him. "Come from the Otherworld below, through the flesh of our earth and back into the land of the living to save us from death. Now if that's not some kind of tablet-of-the-gods type prophecy shite, I dunno what is. The half-god king reborn, straight out of the bloody ground. So much drama. Such an allegory. What a story this is shaping up to be! Are you writing this?"

"Yes, with improved prose, I might add."

"What?"

"Improved pr—"

"Nevermind. I'm good and hammered drunk and don't care. That reminds me." Adeqor came running up beside James. "There are people here you may be happy to see."

James only stared at him.

"The one you've been searching for," Adeqor smiled.

"Who?" *Maggie?*

"Come."

"Tell me." *Tell me it's Maggie.*

Adeqor tsked. "Follow."

James followed Adeqor and Mineera down the path to the small village of Foulds. A dozen or more people were moving about. James recognized a few of them. Itchy, the bard, and Tam, the road smith. Eridan, the son of Derudin, sat on an overturned trough with his elbows on his knees and his head hanging. Dried dirt and mud covered his pants and spotted the rest of his body. He seemed to be brooding over something; Padraig, the Small, was rocking back and forth in his big boots and didn't acknowledge James at all. Berra Coldblood and Logan Too Tall were sharing a skin of something that smelled like horse piss, and their faces twisted into something that might have been a smile as James walked by, and a dozen more of Derudin's Blood Company and other stragglers clung to the broken hovels like fleas. He didn't see Derudin. *Where is Maggie?*

Roofs had crumbled; roads had rutted like trenches. There was an empty, fireless pit in the centre of the village. A well smelled sour from the dead bodies bobbing about in it. A mill with no wheel and half a roof brooded over the little hamlet. There was a wagon, a few mules, and a dozen or more horses hitched up and trying to graze amongst the brown grass and dried mud. *Essikah* was laid out on a wagon. It looked not at all like a magical sword forged of godrock from the Otherworld but an abandoned piece of steel.

Then, impaled on a twisted edge of the old mill wheel, James saw black clots of dried blood hanging from Derudin's head. The rest of him was hanging by his feet, swinging from the rafters of the collapsed mill. Derudin Deadmaker was butchered and put on display. Adeqor clapped James on the back.

"Eurick brought the whole lot of the Blood Company that had survived along with him. Once Derudin caught word that his precious Culdaine had left, he had to follow. He had it in his mind to see the Mother. Be a part of some song. Thought he could get glory out of all of this. Well, there are no songs about fucking around with a wizard." Adeqor spat the words. "He took my hands, so I took his head. You'll find the Blood Company answering to me, now." Adeqor merrily jaunted onwards. *You need to stop this fucker somehow...*

James noticed he was standing there with his jaw open and saw Eurick staring at him in disbelief.

"By the gods! You're back!" he cried out. James hadn't had someone care for him in far too long. The transporter ran over, and James gave him a big hug. "You legendary sum a bitch, you. Come here, man!" he said and pulled James in again. James couldn't help but smile despite the headless man hanging.

Mineera smiled widely, apparently immune to violence by this point. She wrote on her pieces of parchment as Adeqor dictated James's rising out of the ground as if he were there, accompanied with over-exaggerated gestures.

Itchy strummed a song James had never heard before.

"This one's for you, James. *The God King Rises,* it's called. Give it a season and all the maids and wenches will sing it from the Fells to Esher. If we make it out of this war alive, that is."

James couldn't help but smile. The bard had gotten a bit better—and found a new harp somewhere.

Eurick started stumbling over his words.

"There's... I have... We've found—"

Then, James saw a Feldarran warrior standing outside of one of the tents. His head was hanging, so James couldn't really make out his face. His hair was cut short in choppy patches that wasn't at all the noble head of braids James remembered. But he knew that old leathery body that looked like someone had carved it out of stone. Even in his sunfell years, that warrior was ripe with life. *Pike?* It could only be him.

"For the gods," Eurick said. "The folk that say they know you. It's *your* Maggie. She's here."

Maggie?

"What?"

"But she's not well, man," said Eurick.

Maggie? He said Maggie.

"What?" James choked out.

"There." Eurick gestured towards the tent that Pike stood in front of. *Maggie?* It couldn't be true.

"Pike?" James said. The old warrior looked up with big, black bags under his reddened eyes, cheeks, and forehead, wrinkled like worn leather.

"James? Boy, you look like shite." Pike cracked a faint smile and pulled him in for a hug, then held him by the shoulders. "Gods know you've been through as much or more than we have since late winter, eh? Come here." He pulled him in again. James looked into the tent but couldn't see anything from where he stood. His stomach fluttered. "She's sleeping now, been sleeping for most of the two days since we've been here. She's taken a turn for the worse since we left the Hills. Might do her well to know you're here, though."

James ran into the tent. His head was rushing, heart pumping like it might burst. Pike had covered her in a woolen blanket. Her feet were sticking out from the bottom, still with the bracelet she'd woven out of hemp grass around her ankle. His eyes danced along to her face.

"Gods!" He fell to his knees by her side. "My love." James found her hand under the blanket. Her eyes were gently closed, and her mouth hung open slightly. He stared at her thin pink lips, soft, white skin sparsely covered with freckles, and round cheeks he remembered so fondly in his dreams. She was here, right in front of him. Her brown hair was a mess, tied up in a rat's nest on top of her head. *She would hate that,* James thought, but left it be anyway. *It can't be true.* Her breaths were slow, and there was a soft gurgling sound in her chest with each one. He noticed the deep scars on her face, felt them with his dirty finger tips. Tears were still streaming down his face. *It can't be true. Maggie. I can't have come all this way to lose you.*

Pike came in the tent with his hands behind his back.

"Is she in pain?" James said. He wasn't as calm as he'd wished he was.

"I'm afraid to say she is." Pike reached for his shield leaning against the tent wall. "Her wounds are healed, but she is still dying. She says it's because the world is dying...the magics in her blood need the elements, James. And it seems the nytewoods give her strength, but there aren't any here." He looked like he was about to say more but stopped. *They have been through Hell to get here.*

"Where's Wulfee?" said James. Pike shook his head and looked to fight back tears.

"She's still in the Hills with the Rangers. They... they captured her and Gen. Giy'er that were displaced by the Banshee, the Wolf, or both attacked us in the night, and we got separated."

James clenched his fists.

Ellorin...

Calen Alder had haunted him most of his life. From the day he burned James's village and killed James's first friends, to the day he butchered his mother and father, to the day he sent the Banshee down from the mountains. Alder had made James suffer, and James took that suffering and lived with it. It was the fuel that drove him to do the horrible things he had to do to survive. James told himself that Calen Alder couldn't hurt him. No matter how hard Alder hunted him down, he couldn't break him. James Culdaine would break, cut down, and kill anything or anyone to hide from himself.

But seeing the person he cared about more than anything else suffering sent James to a dark place. The place that once he fell into, he didn't know where he'd end up surfacing. James knew it was time to face what he'd spent his life avoiding. He was born a monster. A monster so powerful that folk have tried to wield him like a weapon. His dad knew what he was, and so did Wulfee. That was why they kept people like him and Maggie around. Maggie had told him he didn't have to be the monster he believed he was. He could see now that she was right. That he didn't need to carry that around with him. He didn't need to be a monster. Not then...

But times were dark, and the dark was where monsters lived.

He was going to tear the head off Ellorin. Tear her to shreds and eat her soul to have her out of his way. To weaken King Alder. Then march to the Mountains of the Mother and use *Essikah* to open the Gateway. He would open the way for the dead and the fire. He would bring it all back and save her. Save them all. Make his parents' deaths mean something.

I can make it all right, Maggie. Just hold on.

Maggie took a strained breath, and the gurgling sound echoed in her chest. James brushed her cheek. Kissed her forehead and wiped away his tears that had fallen on her. *I will save you. Even if it's the only thing I'm able to do, I will save you. We will look into each other's eyes again and feel each other's hearts. I will fix it. Everything. I'm through with running, Maggie. It's time to face the truth. I'm a weapon. And I will save you.*

"Is he in there?" The wizard was outside of the tent.

"Aye," said Eurick, and the wizard came in.

"Culdaine! Well, this should do wonders for your morale, eh?" he said.

"Where is Ellorin?" James stood up.

Adeqor said, "She's, well, probably close. It's been a tough week for Mal Hallow. Dawning fell in a matter of hours. A ruler of the Glenn sits in Derudin's hall while Derudin has gone and lost his head." Adeqor sat down in a wicker chair and crossed a dirty foot on his knee. "Ellorin has joined up with the Hammer of the Glenn, Richard Brynmor. It's taken them a few weeks to travel through the Hills and garrison on this side of the river, but they're nearly there now. I was worried you wouldn't come back up, and we'd have to leave without you. They could be in Foulds any day now. There are two thousand on foot and seven hundred on horse. And not folk with boiled leather and swords. These folk are armoured in steel and armed with lances like the knights of the Hesterlands. The Hammer breeds monsters in those valleys of the Glenn. Some say his horses are carnivores that eat the fallen, dead or alive... Brinley stood no chance. Ellorin and the Hawka hordes continue to ride ahead of Lord Richard. Anyone who falls behind our host is being swallowed up, literally. If they reach Kallahorn before us, we'll never get you into those mountains to open the Gateway."

"So Brinley's host, gone?" James asked. "Just like that?" He remembered that the lord had said he would fight to the death rather than run.

"Retreated," Adeqor said. "Bastard is too stubborn to die, turns out. The lot of them have fallen back to the Lovasi bridge at Rosen. Lady Ruwen has dropped the eagle flag and flies her family's old black bear on icy blue now. The Hawka attacks had sent her son and daughter up to the cloud halls, and she blamed the Ayelish. The remaining Hallow rulers plan to join them and set up a last defence there," he said, shaking his head. "It would be a tragedy to see Pool fall. Truly. Up there amongst the greatest of tragedies, really, alongside the day Lindis burned. The world tree is a genuine wonder of this world.

"We've got but one chance left. We turn and face Ellorin, or we run. Like I said, they will be in Foulds any day, and if we run, they will surely catch us."

"I'm done running," said James. "She'll be marauding ahead of the army. So I'll stand and wait for her. I'm ready."

Adeqor grinned.

"I thought you might be. When the moon turns, we go."

James put his fist to his chin and nodded. Adeqor didn't nod back and rather just left the tent. The wizard wasn't much into traditions, James had learned.

James stayed by the bedside for a time longer.

"I have to leave, James," Pike said. His voice was tired and gravelly. "I need to go after Wulfee. I need to know if she lived or died. She would do the same for me. I can't leave her. Maggie is in good hands with you now. But I have to leave. I'm sorry. If Wulfee is still alive, I need to find her. I need to find Gen." The two stood up, and the old warrior pulled James in for a hug, which he gladly accepted.

"Find her and bring her back," James said. "Tell her I'm okay. Tell her *we're* okay. Give the big Giy'er a hug for me."

Eurick stayed in the tent with James and in no time, fell asleep. James accepted a change of clothes from Derudin's squire, who had come in with new trousers and a shirt, but he wouldn't accept the pair of new boots. He needed the ones he had if he was going to get through this. None of that mattered, though—he'd fight Ellorin bare arsed for all he cared.

Day had turned to night as he waited for Maggie to wake. To hug her and kiss her, and look into her eyes. She came in and out of consciousness.

He sat leaning his elbows on his knees and listening to the chirrups of the night crickets and the buzz of burn bugs when Maggie stirred.

"Mrrrmh," she said. "Nytewood." James sat up in a hurry, rushed to her bedside.

"Maggie, baby. It's me. It's James. There are no nytewoods in Foulds, only a stump."

She opened her eyes. Saw him and smiled. James smiled back and buried his head into her neck, holding her close.

"There is life in them," she groaned.

"I will take you to a nytewood. I just have to do one thing first. Then I will help you," James said. And he felt like he was talking to Maggie *and* the dead when he said it.

I'll make this all go away. I can stop it.

"My gods, Maggie, I never thought I'd see you again. I'm so sorry I left," he said, kissing her over and over.

"I dreamed of you." She kissed him back. "We were in that house by the lake. You remember the one?"

"Of course."

"We can meet there in death."

"We're meeting now. While we still live, Mag, look at me." He kissed her again. "I'm going to save you." He slid into the tiny cot beside her. And she shivered. James held her close, and the shivers turned to convulsions.

"Help! I need help!" he shouted. Eurick jumped up.

"There is no help to be had, man," said Eurick. "The world is killing her. Life is draining from her soul like water in a holey bucket."

Maggie cried, writhing on the cot beside him. He held her, but she shrugged him off.

"I'm here, Maggie. I'm here. I came back." He fell to his knees beside the bed and cried.

"Help me," she moaned, and James saw the Maggie that he remembered deep inside of her lost-looking eyes. One green and one blue. *One for the sea and one for the earth, she always said.*

"I don't know, but I will fix it. I will fix this, Maggie," he said. And she gripped his hand so tight his fingers turned red and numb. *I will kill the entire world if it meant you'd live.*

And after a long many hours under the hot summer moon, she finally calmed and fell back into her dreams. She almost resembled a corpse, her skin ghost blue. James sat brooding in his anger, thinking of his failures and how he would make up for every one of them. *His* time had come.

He waited for the high moon that would summon Adeqor. When the wizard came in, he smelled of cider. His pointed beard seemed sharper than usual. His dark skin glowed a faint silvery blue. He only nodded, and James knew what that meant. The wizard had found her. *Or the other way around.*

"Eurick," James said. The transporter's eyes flicked open, and he jumped up.

"Yes—" he cleared his throat, "—yes, what is it?"

"Get me my sword, would you?" said James. The raven grinned widely. "Of course."

WELCOME

WULFEE WOKE UP UNDER a bearskin and had to piss like a jackass. She hadn't slept too easy knowing that every minute she was stagnant, Sweyne and his host drew closer. She cracked her neck and cursed Father Tree. Over the rolling dead grass of the Hallow valley, hoary, old willows erected like big, shaggy headed mushrooms. *In seven days, I will be in Pool,* she told herself. The thought felt wrong somehow, but she revelled in it all the same. *This might be one of your last few times waking up, old braud. May as well enjoy it.* The morning dew was heavy, soaking the toes of her boots as she walked. She knelt to take a piss.

When a ruckus erupted in the camp, she quickly finished up and ran to see a dozen Rangers beating someone.

"What's going on here?" Wulfee said.

"The fuck does it matter to you?" said one Ranger. She tried to get a closer look, but the Ranger stopped her. They continued to beat the man, and Wulfee could hear him pleading for mercy.

Wulfee said, "He's begging, for the gods' sake, can we at least remain peaceful? If it's an enemy scout, we can question him."

Coal came up behind her.

"What do we have here?"

Finally, the circle widened, and one Ranger grabbed the bloody man on the ground by the collar to hoist him up. Wulfee felt a pang of guilt stab her in the gut when she saw his bloody, wrinkled face.

"Caught this one following us. He came back," said one Ranger. "Only the Maw knows why." It was Pike, with puffy bruised eyes and fresh blood dripping from his nose and mouth. He croaked something incoherent. Then the Ranger let him drop to the ground.

"By the gods, help the man!" Wulfee rushed in and pushed them aside. She grabbed Pike by the arms and helped him to his knees. He looked up at her and smiled.

"You live, Wulfee. How is it you always live surrounded by so much death?" he said.

She smiled back.

"I'm a stubborn old cunt, you know that." One Ranger spit on the ground in front of where she knelt.

"Why are we following this wild woman?" the Ranger said. "To get to Pool? Why would we want to go somewhere where we have never been welcomed?" He pointed a thick finger at her. "She's working with this spy. They mean to lead us into a trap as revenge for keeping them imprisoned in the barrow!" The Rangers started murmuring in agreement, but Wulfee had enough. She reached for her axe. Pike glared at her.

"It's not our time, Wulfee. You've come this far. Calm."

Coal stood up on a rock and boomed his voice.

"This is a war we're in the middle of. Anyone who wants to leave can leave. We've all seen what the Wolf is doing to people. If you want to take the heads off the whole kingdom, well, that's your choice. I choose to stand for the old way, as the Rangers of old once did when the Lovasi invaded. They kept the Mal blood alive, the very blood that ran through the first of our fellowship. The blood of E'daru. I choose to do the same. We've all heard the stories from our Cycle of Dain, of when the gods of Old Yehven and the Abori killed the Mother of Nature with the Starfall."

"The Reaper," someone called out.

"Aye. The bloody Reaper. Well, it's back. I know you've all seen the clouds in the north. And everyone is looking for someone to blame. There is something in our blood that scares these Ayelish. They'd see the Old Gods die, and they mean to be the ones to kill them. They believe us to be heathens, talking to false gods. The Ayelish blame *us* for the fires burning out. They don't like that we talk to the animals. They think of wargs as monsters. We live the old way. That's what Wulfee fights for, and without her, we will not be welcomed at Pool. But with her, we can unite with the clans of Feldarra. I'd rather be on their side than the side of this brigand Wolf."

"I choose to live!" shouted Leatherback. "We're Rangers, not bloody mercenaries. This is folly and a damned poor way to spend our last days."

"It doesn't have to be our last days. I've heard stories of Pool, as I'm sure the rest of you have. It's an ancient place of magics. A place where gods are born," said Coal. "Wulfee has told me much about its terrain. An island in the middle of a lake. Easily defended."

"The gods are dead. Can't you see this world is dying with them? What is left to fight for?" said Jerrick.

"Mrrghh!" mumbled Stackhand with half a tongue, and Crowseye agreed with him.

"Not only do the gods live, they walk amongst us," choked Pike, looking up at Wulfee. "James lives, Wulfee. He rose up from the Otherworld."

Wulfee smiled. *The gods... James...* She had known of his abilities for a long time. And they terrified her. *What sorcery...*

Coal walked over to Pike and helped him up. "What are you talking about, old man?"

"The Druid seers. The half-gods that walk betwixt worlds. From the Cycle of Dain." Pike stood tall despite the obvious pain it caused him.

"Hendurinn reborn. I've seen him with my own eyes. He had fire in his eyes and a storm at his back. Born again from the Otherworld. He carries the greatsword *Essikah*. He is journeying to the Mountains of the Mother with a Warlock from Old Yehven and a transporter of the Raven's Guild. This man will breathe life back into the lungs of the world. He will bring back the fire." Pike spit blood and wiped his mouth with the back of his sleeve. The Rangers were talking amongst themselves again. Wulfee caught echoes of their conversation, and it seemed like half of them wanted to take their chances surviving the war by hiding out in the deep arbors rather than fighting.

She said, "He wears no armour to battle because the souls of the dead keep him alive." Wulfee retold the story of the half-god, Hendurinn, from the Cycle of Dain from memory. "But if that bastard Wolf gets to the Lovasi bridge at Rosen before he does, the seer may not make it past the Fell River. We all have a part to play in this. We just need to believe, keep hope alive. The bards and poets will sing the tales of the Rangers who stopped an army for generations."

The Rangers lingered for a couple of hours. A couple of fist fights needed to be resolved, and Wulfee cheered with the lot of them. She was careful not to rush, despite the overwhelming feeling of wanting to. Ultimately, three bands left to go their separate ways, claiming that Rangers had never fought in wars directly, and they didn't want to start now. The remaining six bands, still nearly two hundred greenhoods, rode behind Wulfee, Coal, a bruised up Pike, and Gen.

"We're behind you, old kihl'dor. Just don't lead us into a bunch of shite, eh?" said Coal. Wulfee felt a pang of guilt in her stomach but ignored it.

"Of course not," she said. *It will be fine. Odhran will welcome you with open arms. People change.* She was so close.

W ULFEE HAD LED THEM right into a bunch of shite.

That fucker is right behind us.

Over the flat valley behind her, she saw the banners waving. The black wolf of Sweyne and the crimson eagle of Ayeland. *All these years of running him down, and now he's turned it around on me.*

"How are they keeping up?" said Jerrick. "We're riding our horses to their limits."

"And so are they. These are novice outriders," said Wulfee. *He's rushing. That's not like Sweyne.* Sweyne was the most patient bastard she'd ever met. He wouldn't run his army ragged before the fighting began, and he wouldn't have ordered a scouting party to run down wayward parties that were no threat. *The Sweyne I know would have kept the entire force together like an enormous fist. Now he's poking around the front lines with his pinky finger, even when he knows the numbers are on his side... but people change, don't they?*

"Fuck!"

"We'll give the horses another twenty minutes, and we'll be off again," said Coal. "I don't know how long we can keep this up."

Wulfee felt like a damned fool for thinking that Sweyne would march his entire host to Oster to sack a single village. *Of course, he'd send some of them straight to Rosen to see what he was dealing with at the bridge. Of course he would...* But she wasn't expecting them to run this far out and leave the wagons and supply carts behind. Wulfee had been keeping an eye out for the dust of wagons but saw nothing. *Tricked again, Wulf...* This was land she knew well. Mal Hallow. The mountains of the Fells stood staunch, beautiful, and unyielding in the dark distance. She was close now. So close.

"We'll reach Pool by sunfell tomorrow," she said. "We'll make our stand. Odhran will be there with the force of the mountains, and I'm going to smash Sweyne's head off the rocks."

"Grim," said Coal. "I can only pray that you won't be talking about me with the same lust one day."

"Don't get my son murdered, and you'll be just fine," said Wulfee.

Coal smiled unconvincingly. "When we reach Pool, I'm assuming you'll be well received? Rangers are not welcome in Pool, but surely you knew that."

Pike gave her that look that made her feel broken, like a pile of smashed apples. She knew Rangers weren't welcomed—and Hell, she wasn't welcomed herself. She reckoned that she'd deal with that part when the time came. Getting there was such a feat that she hadn't thought about the rest. There was still Odhran to deal with. The last time she had seen him, she was removing him and his people from their home at axe point and sending them off to the Fell Mountains. She hacked the man's arm off... She never imagined that he'd end up ruling over the clan members who'd left her. That he'd unite the clans and turn them against her. Wulfee had spent years running down pretenders of the tree and trying to break up Odhran's muster. *But you failed, didn't you? And the kihl'dor you once thought small has become a hundred times your size. And now what? How are you going to clean this one up?*

Wulfee grinned, "They will welcome us with a grand feast and song, and dance. Let's just get there before this lot, eh?" She remembered that damned cage Sweyne's army was dragging and shivered. *You'll be dealing with that sooner or later, too, Wulf. And here you are playing at kihl'dor again. Haven't you learned that it's time to run?* She knew that the wiser choice would be to dip off into the arbor and disappear. Maybe catch a merchant's vessel across the Old Sea to Edura and work out the rest of her days on the docks, sweating out in the heat of New Lovas. *Pfft.* She knew that would never happen. *You can't run from who you are. You can't run from Wulfee. You can't change, not really.*

When evening came, she sat alone beneath the drooping whip-branches of a willow. A wolf howled somewhere on the edge of the arbor that surrounded Pool, then the rest of the pack picked up its call. Wulfee remembered the bitch that followed her up the White. Thought of how vicious that big grey must have been. *You can be that vicious, too. You know you can.* She dug a small hole with her fingers and poured some water from her skin. In the moonlight, Wulfee saw her underself staring back.

"Don't let it all be for naught," she said. "For the gods, let Odhran forgive. And if he can't, then let me come out of it all with my life. Give me a chance to face Sweyne."

Her underself stared back at her sagely.

"If I can't have none of it... let my Braden live. Let him be happy somewhere. Let little Sweyne have a good, long life. Let him be all the beautiful things his dad was." She nodded. Her underself nodded back. She heard footsteps and peered into the night to see Pike. He was looking older and more beat down than ever, and it sent a shiver tracing up her spine.

"Shouldn't you be sharpening your blade?" she said with a grin.

"Plenty sharp already," he said, but it seemed like he couldn't quite muster the same level of grin that Wulfee had. He sat down beside her and moaned as he did, like it was a great effort. His joints all fired off loud cracks as he bent, like knots in burning wood.

"I never thanked you for coming back to look for me," she said.

"I never thanked you for getting my ass beat again." He managed a bit more of a grin that time, but it faded fast. "You know Odhran'll kill us all, right?" Pike's face was dead straight.

"I don't know if he will," said Wulfee. "It's been a long while, people change."

"They change, but they don't forgive," said Pike. "You're proof of that yourself."

"What other choice do we have?" said Wulfee. Pike looked up at the stars, as he often did, with a look of remorse. Wulfee reckoned he was mourning the fact he'd never fly up there with the moon.

"Suppose we're all out of choices," he said. "Unless we run."

Wulfee disagreed.

"I can't run, Pike. It ain't in me. I would sooner chance death with a friend."

Pike finally managed a full grin.

"And a fine death it will be," he said. Then they heard Gen's big footsteps.

"Wulfee?" said Gen softly.

"We're here, Gen."

"The Rangers are talking about being killed at Pool." He plopped his big arse down beside them with a thump. "We won't let that happen, though, right? The other karls will be there, and we'll stop them."

"No. We won't let it happen, Gen," Wulfee said, wishing she believed it more. Gen clenched his fists and punched the air a few times.

"I'm feeling a lot better now. I can help." Gen was swinging his fists in wide arcs and making *squishing* sounds. His wound had healed so fast that Wulfee never removed the stitching. The thread was still in his skin on either side of the big, pink scar on his thigh. Gen saw her looking and covered it with his hand. "I picked the scab," he said. "I know Maggie said you're not supposed to, but I did." Wulfee nearly cried at the thought of Maggie. *Will I ever see her again? Gods, let her live through all of this. Let her and James be happy.* She knew she should tell Gen to run off. Tell him to get as far away from all this as possible. She was taking long chances, and failure meant death. This was no place for a heart like his. Once upon a time, she believed she could turn Gen into a weapon. Just like she thought about James and Maggie. *But they're not weapons, they are your children. You need to let them go... let them have their own lives, not chasing after yours.*

Gen had a big heart and a curious mind, like any Human child, and it made Wulfee blind to the truth all of these years. *He's not a child, he is a young Giy'er that belongs with his own. Not with you.* Gen ran off chasing a fat, grey cat that had followed them from Foulds. Wulfee never understood how the cats always stayed fat in Mal Hallow.

"I've always known Tess won't recognize me when I see her again," Pike croaked, seemingly out of nowhere. "Gods, I won't even recognize her. I want you to know that I knew that. That memory of her, my little baby girl, was the only thing that kept me alive. Imagining her all grown up, thinking about how much time slipped away while I was off killing. I couldn't do it."

The old warrior let a tear hit the ground. When more followed, Wulfee put her arm around him, and she couldn't stop her own tears. "When we get to Pool tomorrow, if things don't go our way, I need you to know I won't be leaving with you. This is my last go."

Wulfee was surprised, but she knew she couldn't keep dragging him through the north.

"Where will you go?" she said, not able to imagine him doing anything but fighting.

"Mountains. Live out my days in peace. I reckon if this battle doesn't get me, it just wasn't in the winds for me to die by my enemy's sword. Might have to face down that ugly sum a bitch called Father Time for my last battle." Wulfee laughed at the image of Pike living in a mud hut with fish drying on a rack, covered in furs and hemp weave. "You've been the best kihl'dor I've ever followed, Wulfee. The bravest, fiercest, and wisest person ever to lead. You weren't like them other bastards who wanted glory and fame. You just wanted to live in peace with your countryfolk. Ah, I guess what I'm trying to say is that I would have been for the better if I'd found you sooner in my haggard, old life."

Wulfee choked back her tears. If she spoke, it would be discernible sobs. Instead, she grabbed his hand in both of hers. She looked out to the dark valley and the ominous black horizon where Pool hid and wondered how she would survive in this world alone. *Tomorrow. So close.*

THE BANSHEE

W HEN THE GHOSTS OF the dead rose from the cold ground and walked out of the boney arbor in a ghostly assembly, James realized that death had come to serve him. A dark feeling he'd gone too far simmered in his chest.

"Call to them," said Adeqor. "They should hear you now. They'll smell the Otherworld on you." James felt cold run through him as the rows of dead folk marched, dressed in ancient garb of fur, leather, and bronze. Adorned in rubies and jewels and gold. All held old Daggland steel in their hands. These were the kings and queens of the old Mal, the warriors of Daggland, and all the wandering souls cursed never to rest easy, and their vengeance was palpable.

"To me," James said softly as he prodded their souls with his mind, and the dead listened. They swarmed around him like carrion to a corpse. *Essikah* had turned to black ice in his hands, runes glowing an awful glow as if some old magics were being conjured from within the folds of metal. He grabbed the souls around him and forced them through his hands into the blade. *Essikah* glistened with their lingering lives and felt as light as air.

"Do you feel different?" asked Adeqor. He *did*. Where before there were only the cold shapes of the dead, now he could sense their energy. He could even reach inside of them and move that energy where he chose. He walked with Adeqor through the arbor at the base of the Hallow Hills and guided his dead folk with him. Their smokey bodies still held the features they once had in life, including the wounds that might have killed them.

"A hundred-hundred souls drifting," the wizard said wistfully, "lost in this world, waiting for rest. Consciousness without a body to hold it."

"But how?" said James, feeling the weight of each soul being dragged behind him as he moved. The burden of each of their woes stacked up like bones after a battle.

"The Mal Druids of old preserved the soul outside of the body. They taught the practice to the Daggland rulers who settled here. For centuries, they used runes and blood magics to live forever as ghosts. They broke their bond with nature's way by trapping their soul here. They are the past-living. The ones that you see sitting around. They are lost and scattered after so many hundreds of years. But they have gathered now. For you."

"To fight?"

"To haunt."

James walked back in the direction that he'd been running from for the past few months. He could feel the power of the Otherworld below him, pulsing through him with each step. And the dead felt it, too. Marching behind him and humming their song—the chant of the dead. A hundred-hundred dead voices bellowed out a memory of song from long ago. He led them through barren fields and past empty storehouses. Abandoned mills and farmsteads. Past corpses swinging from tree limbs and bones ravaged by dogs. All were dead, dying, or gone somewhere better. He remembered the green winter roses of Ockam, still blooming long after winter had gone, and the primrose and tulips, wisps of etta, and bright pink peonies and honey. The smell of them all merged with the smokey cook fires and whatever delicious aroma wafted off of them. Spring in Dawning was alive in his mind. Now it was black and grey and brown and pale green. The colours of rot and decay, but things wouldn't even rot, because that, too, required life. And so the smell of death sat stagnant in the windless sky, and James almost believed the earth was too far gone already.

I will bring it back for you, Mag. I will save you.

He marched alone in the dark. He didn't need to sleep. Not tonight. The Otherworld gave him all the strength he needed. He marched until the sun slowly rose and filled the world with an amber half-light.

In the distance, the horde swayed beneath the red sun of dawn. They were feasting on some big, dead thing. A Giy'er perhaps—James couldn't tell. But they must have smelled James. They came towards him like hungry carnivores that had marked their prey, and the ground rumbled. James saw their yellow eyes growing larger and the sinews in their necks bulging. The smell of blood and urine burned the back of his throat. Hundreds of them. Thousands, maybe. He pulled the souls close and gathered strength. Felt the power of the dead surging through him. Their lingering lives flowing through his veins like blood. Watched as the Hawka drew closer, steely teeth dripping with saliva. Saw the dirt and twigs in their black, matted fur. Battle horns went off behind them. *The Glennish?* James recognized Brynmor's warhorn. It sickened James to think of Brynmor in the company of the Hawka. Sleeping and dining beside those beasts. *Now you'll die with them, too.*

And James waited. Alone and armourless. The ground shook from their claws ripping into the earth. Sniffing and snorting primal grunts. And when they were close enough that he could almost smash one with his axe, he let the energy go. The cold smokey bodies of ancient warriors rose up from the earth beneath the Hawka, and the mutts howled. They squealed and scattered with terror, leaping into the air, breaking free from Ellorin's hold. *Mutts can't handle the dead.* Seemed it was more than a little true. They split into a thousand single beings, disappearing in a delirium of madness. Screeching macabre notes in their crooked tongue as they fled. James's body shook as the dead moved with him. Their old lives pumped in and out of him as he commanded their souls. Their swords could do no harm to the living, but their souls were full of hate, and the mutts couldn't handle it. The ghosts conjured a fear deep inside of the Hawka, as primal as their instinct to feed. They writhed like salted leeches on the ground, screeching as the dead took over their mind and soul, and stole their bodies.

James slowly moved forward and watched the terror unfold. The dead souls chanted a drumming beat in a sombre tone as they filled the world with their vengeance. James showed his victims no mercy. He would chase them to the ends of the world if it meant avenging Maggie. He would inflict all the pain she felt and more on anyone who stood in his way. The cold smoke army would savor every mile of running the Hawka down. Off in the distance, James could hear the sounds of the Lord of the Glenn's army being torn apart by the wild Hawka charging back towards them in retreat. Without Ellorin's control over the Hawka's minds, they were no different from beasts. Wild Hawka held no alliances. And James felt no sympathy. He would put an end to this.

James moved through the battlefield towards Ellorin. He gripped *Essikah* as it filled with magics, and the runes on the greatsword lit up. His forearms trembled with adrenaline. He had failed his parents, his partner, and his country, and now he would make it right.

Ellorin dropped her black feathered robe to the ground and unsheathed a long, skinny sword. The polished silver glistened a warm red when it caught the sun. It was engraved with the symbol of the Ailaryan Order, the burning comet. She was taller than any Human James had seen and had skin so pale and wet that it seemed to eat the shadows. She shimmered as she moved in long, crooked strides like an insect crawling over the gnarls of a thousand-year old oak.

"I had a chance to give this up, you know?" Ellorin spoke calmly. "The birds told me you'd made a pass under to the Otherworld. They told me to run, but I stayed. I thought, what could this boy possibly learn to threaten *me?*" Her voice was like a smooth breeze. She looked him up and down with the confidence of a goddess. "But you're not a boy anymore, are you?"

James stared at her, gripping *Essikah*; its golden-blue light danced in the runes.

"Not so much," James said as he kept walking towards her.

"You're stronger than I thought," she said. "I've taken too long to hunt you. It was my hope that the Words would regain their proper strength by now, just as the mere trickle of a dying river will swell again when the world is reborn in the Rise of New Spring."

Ellorin let forth a bat-like squeal and burst forward with an avian quickness that reminded James of his first encounter with Eurick. He lifted *Essikah* just in time to catch the point of her sword. James turned to face her and caught another thrust on the flat end of *Essikah*. Golden sparks erupted from the blade. James swung once, twice, but Ellorin was far too fast. A breeze brushed his face as Ellorin's blade nearly sliced his lips. He dodged another that almost caught his gut. He swiped low for her legs, but she hopped over the sweep and nearly took James's head off. He fell back and tried to gain space to think, but she was on him in an instant.

The dead were with him, but to Ellorin, they were nothing. Another parry and another step back, and then he felt Ellorin's sword pierce his torso. He raised his sword to swing, but she had already removed her blade and stepped back. She had a twisted smile on her pale face as she watched him. *She has you. You can't beat her with this sword. She knows she has you.* He held a hand over his bloody wound, inhaled the life from a soul, and felt the hole close over. Ellorin continued to attack him with increasing intensity. His mind was blurry from the souls coursing through him, healing him. His insides were frozen. Arms throbbing—muscles ready to give out and drop the sword.

"You're no god," she said. "You're a disappointment." It was all he could do to match her strikes, let alone find her weakness. "Lay down that sword and die with some honour!" She swung for his neck. James sensed her desperation to kill him. "Let the people of the next world have peace. You don't understand the power that's unleashing on this world."

"You and Calen Alder are a plague," James shouted.

"Calen Alder is a hero. He sacrificed his whole life to fight for the Ailaryan Order and to stop the spread of this vile plague of black magics. If there were more folk like Alder in this world, maybe it wouldn't be so far gone." Ellorin circled James, and he felt like whenever she decided to move, it was going to hurt.

"Folk are saying that you *carved* him." James took a swing and missed.

"The Blood Words carve themselves if the soul they graft onto is strong enough. I merely said a few Words. Karaat did the rest."

"You two have gone mad. What is the point in all of this?"

"Because the Ailaryan Order has stopped the spread of these dark Words through many epochs, and I mean to uphold that tradition. If the songs of Yehven seep into the Otherworld, the whole workings of our world could be damaged or altered in irreversible ways. The Words would kill the world, and it could never be reborn." Ellorin moved in slow, unpredictable movements. "But the Gateway offers a failsafe. The Ailaryan Order can just kill off most of humanity and help the survivors rebuild. Just like we did with Lovas after the Starfall. So we can't let you open it, Culdaine."

Ellorin swooped in with another strike, but James blocked it easily on *Essikah's* wide blade. James struggled to parry her every move and soon realized he would not beat her with *Essikah*. He dropped the greatsword and instead grabbed hold of the souls around him. He remembered what he had learned in the Otherworld. *Hearing is not the only way to listen. Look inside of yourself, and face what you find there.* He listened to the earth, and he felt the power of it somewhere deep down below the soil and rock. He pulled on that energy and let it flow through him.

Ellorin jumped in front of James. Under the moonlight, her eyes were like the pool of quicksilver. "Adeqor, Bazal. These are Warlocks that were stripped of power and are very dangerous and extremely unpredictable. Neither of them works for us anymore. The Ailaryan Order has to stop them or nobody else will be able to. This is the only way." Ellorin quickly thrust a feint high and then stabbed James low. This time, he felt the blade scrape against his ribs. "If you fight with them, you must die with them."

James pulled her closer to him. The blade went deeper, piercing bloody sacks of organs inside of him. He felt the blood running warm, pooling at his waistline, then slowly trickling down his leg. He had gone mad with battle fever, and all he could do was laugh because he had her now. She twisted the blade, tearing apart his insides, but he giggled through the agonizing pain.

He gripped her by the head, one bloody palm on each ear, and squeezed with the mind to make her head burst in his hands. Her cold eyes had turned fearful and unsure. He sensed that, and stared into her, *through* her, prodding her mind with his magics until he found the little wisp inside of her. Loud cracks beneath James's palms as her skull fractured. And Ellorin sunk her sword deeper. James only laughed. He had her soul in his grips. The little wisp inside everyone that held so much life and love, and hardship. The wisp that turned a sack of flesh and blood into something beautiful. He gripped it, tugged on it, and felt something tearing loose beneath it. Ellorin screamed in agony.

"What the fuck are you doing!" she screamed, not so much a question as a realization. It felt so good—*oh so good*—he found himself filled with relief.

"Ending you," said James, and he tore the soul free of her chest and swallowed it. Ellorin's lifeless body thumped to the floor in a pile of flesh and limb. James could feel her life inside of him. A hundred-hundred emotions, pent up anger and hate, her hurts and her joys. Everything she had loved and reviled. Everything she had ever known flooded his mind and body. Physical sensations and emotional hardship. He fell to his knees, sobbing relentlessly, letting her memories flow through him. *You have to get it all out after you take it,* the Hermit had told him. He pounded the ground and cursed the red skies. His stomach, his throat, his eyes were burning cold. He let the dead heal him. And Ellorin's soul took hold of his mind.

He could see glimpses of Calen Alder, his skin freshly carved with Words, on the throne at Kallahorn. He saw Alder crucify Lord Baleth onto a twisted nytewood. He saw Ellorin wandering the arbor to bind the

Hawka with her silver mind thread. Then, in a flash, he saw a dark-skinned man on his knees begging. *Adeqor?* A woman with a crown of honeysuckles resting on her matted brown hair stood before him as earth magics danced around her.

"You've gone too far this time, Adee, too far. It's over," she said, rolling her runes. She smiled at whatever the runes showed her. Then she sang a strange sounding spell to remove something from the wizard's head. *"You'll never speak the Words of Karaat again."*

The wizard was laughing. *"Don't you ever tell me it's over. I'll be back for you. I don't care if the Order calls you the Mother of Nature. I wouldn't care if you were Father fucking Sky. I'll be back for you, and I'll have what's mine."*

Slowly, the memories flickered then faded from his mind. The last remnants of a soul devoured. Ellorin would never rest easy.

In the distance, screams echoed from Brynmor's camp. The song of a horror James had already heard once from Wulfee's camp. The lord of the Glenn was having a hell of a time with the displaced Hawka. He hoped that would give him the time needed to get to Kallahorn. Behind him, the Mountains of the Mother stood staunch and undeniable on the reddened horizon. There was only one thing left to do now. *Then it will all be over.* He wondered what kind of army Alder had inside of those massive walls and how they could breach Kallahorn's gate with whatever folk the Hallow had left. James had marched on those massive gates at Kallahorn once before and watched oceans of folk who wanted to kill him pour out like a broken dam. That sea of killing swept James up, and he had barely made it out alive. He wished he'd never have to go back to that place. But times were dark, and the gods weren't hearing folks' wishes. *There is no escaping Hell when it swallows you up.* All he could do was hope to make it out the other side. But he didn't have to pray to the gods for hope anymore. He'd provided his own.

THE FELL RIVER

"WE'VE GOT TO GO, *now!*" Coal shouted. "They're right on top of us."

Under the light of the rising sun, dust clouds rose, and the ground rumbled.

Wulfee quickly scrambled to pack up and rode the hardest she had in her entire life. Twenty hard miles to Pool and all this would be over. *One way or another, right, Wulf?* Looking back, she reckoned there were more than a hundred following them. Armoured and horsed.

Coal shouted, "We have no heavy armour and would stand no chance on open ground against this lot. We use the hills and the arbors to wage our wars. These highland garrons are no match for their palfreys."

"We may need to make sacrifices to get there before we're caught," said Wulfee.

"We could turn and fight," said Coal.

"Aye," said Pike.

"If we face them in open land, they will slaughter us," said Wulfee. "We need to make it to the river and swim across. They won't abandon their horses to chase us. If they do, we're even again. On foot."

"If they get too close before we reach the river, we turn and fight," said Coal. "None of us are going to die running."

The sun beat down on Wulfee's back and cooked her neck as the thousand-foot nytewoods of Pool appeared closer and closer. Bigger than anything ever made by Humankind. Not even the great Lovasi Empire could match them. The golden flowers were fully in bloom despite the droughts, and they lit up the sky with twinkling reflections of the sun's light—and the nihr'el rose above them all. Soon she could see the Fell River and the Mountains of the Mother beyond the nytewoods. *I'm going to bloody make it,* she thought.

And then the first horse collapsed. The horse threw the rider off its back when it went down and the Ranger landed on his head. Wulfee reckoned he wasn't ever gonna get up. Not long after that, another one went down. And then two at the same time. Other Rangers were stopping to help the fallen. And Wulfee knew this battle was lost.

"We have to turn and fight. I won't kill this horse." Coal reared up. His eyes rolled into the back of his head, and for a moment, Wulfee saw Coal's eyes looking at her through the horse's head. Coal blinked, and he was back. Some of the Rangers were still riding on while others slowed down to turn around. It was a mess of confusion.

"If we can just make it across the river—" Wulfee tried to lead again, but it was too late—no one was listening to her now. The Rangers were dismounting and notching arrows. Pike rode up next to her.

"To the river, Wulf," he screamed. "Come on." Dozens of greenhoods still rode on with them. Gen ran beside Wulfee and never got further than a couple of feet away. Wulfee's horse groaned grumpily and nearly threw her off its back when she tried to cross the river. She couldn't believe the mighty Fell River was only two-thirds its usual size, and still, it was massive. At Rosen, it took a hundred feet of Lovasi magic to bridge over the river with stones, and here she was—planning to have a swim. She was going to have a hell of a time with it.

"Jump in!" she hollered.

"Wulfee, I can't swim!" Gen shouted back to her. Her heart stopped. *How did you forget?* Two more horses collapsed before they reached the river. The brigade was close enough that Wulfee felt the ground shaking from their horses.

"You have to try, Gen. You have to try, please," she said. *How could you forget the lad is terrified of water? It's in their blood... how did you forget?*

"I can't! Wulfee, I can't. I could never. Please don't make me, Wulfee. I can fight. Just like a good karl does. I will fight to protect our lands," Gen pleaded. There was a terror in the lad's eyes that made her feel sick.

"You can't be a karl unless you cross this river, Gen. Pool is right there. We have to get to Pool! It's the only way." She pointed to the trees sticking up in the distance, black and golden. "The nihr'el, the well of seers. We're so close." Gen looked at the water, then back at the Wolf's brigade thumping towards them. *Gods, he's more scared of the water than the steel.* Wulfee could see it in his eyes.

"We can beat them, Wulfee. We can win. We always win," said Gen, clenching his fists. "The Old Gods will make sure that we win. We are Feldarra."

Wulfee looked at his cut up hands, his scarred thigh and calf. His wispy blonde hair and orange eyes.

"The Old Gods died when the world died, Gen. We can't win. Not here," said Wulfee. She looked back at the brigade and saw a tall man in gleaming Daggland steel armour, mounted on a black destrier. He had ridden to the front, looking glorious and dangerous. Her breath left her. He was wearing a bone wolf helm. *The* wolf helm. *He's here. He's fucking here to kill you.* The Wolf held a long, double-sided waraxe, its shaft painted bright red. They would be on top of them in a minute. Wulfee searched the ground in a panic. She found a muddy piece of grey driftwood on the riverbank and picked it up. She washed it off in the water as carefully as if it was her child. She held it up to the top of Gen's head and unsheathed her axe. "On your knees, Gen," she said.

"What are you doing? Wulfeeee?" Gen whined, sobbing. She was acting outright mad, and it probably scared the lad.

"I'm making you a karl. Fuck the world tree. Fuck it. If this is where we die, you die a karl, Gen. I won't have it any other way." She felt her sanity slipping. She couldn't save her sons, James, or Maggie. She stripped Pike of all of his honour when those grey strands hit the ground. And now she'd led another one she loved to their death. She'd gone and ruined this poor lad's life. Given him false hope and let him believe it. She stole him away from his family and gave him nothing. She only took. Used him to win battles. To feel better about herself. She was sick of breaking promises and not giving the people she loved what they deserved from her. This promise she'd keep. "Because you fucking deserve it, Gen. You're as good as any fucking karl I've ever had."

Tears slipped off her cheeks as she spoke, and a madness raged in her belly as she watched the cursed wolf helm come closer.

"They're coming, Wulfee. I'm scared," said Gen as he knelt. Wulfee held the piece of driftwood over his head. It wasn't nytewood, and wasn't even living, but she was sick of the gods and their damned particulars.

"Gen of Wick, do you swear to fight and protect this land with your life?" she said, sobbing. Gen looked at her, bawling. "Do you?" she shouted. *He's terrified, Wulf. Calm yourself.*

"Yes, Wulfee, I—"

"Do you swear to stand tall in the face of death and never turn your back on your enemies?"

"I swear!" he yelled. The ground thumped louder than drums.

"Do you swear to fight until the very end?" Wulfee shouted.

"Wulfee, they're coming, I—"

"Do you swear, Gen! For fuck's sake, do you swear?"

"I swear! I swear! I swear!" Gen screamed back. Wulfee could smell the horses, the sour sweat of the armour laden folk riding them. The cursed wolf helm bobbed, and the black wolf flag waved overhead. The waraxe in the wolf's hands drank the sunlight with its thirsty red iron mouth.

Wulfee tapped her axe on both of Gen's shoulders. The Giy'er was completely calm in that moment. Like he was trying to make it last forever.

"Now stand a karl of the Fells, an axe to a kihl'dor of Feldarra and a shield to Mal Hallow."

Pike drummed his shield. Tears fell down the old warrior's cheeks. And Gen stood as proud as Wulfee had ever seen any living thing. Pike drummed louder, and Gen stood prouder. The Giy'er looked at Pike with the sort of admiration that an apprentice might look at his master with. A look that said "I'm one of you now." And Pike gave him a nod that said. "Aye, lad, welcome." The Rangers who followed Wulfee this far had all dove into the river rather than fight to their deaths. *This is where you die. With the only folks that still love you. This will do.* She found a strange calmness falling over her. She was ready to die. Pike drummed until the enemy was so close that he had no choice but to pull his axe and get himself ready. Wulfee gripped hers and looked at the wolf helm bobbing. She imagined Sweyne's smug face beneath it, all the horrors and delights, pleasures and pain that she'd seen plastered all over it. Gen took another look back at her, at Pike, and smiled. His tears were drying, and the fear seemed to have faded.

"I just want to make you proud, Wulfee. For saving me and making me a karl. You always made me happy. I don't want to be afraid anymore. I don't want you to worry about me anymore," he said, running at her so quickly she had no time to react. He thrust his big palm into her chest and sent her flying into the river. Took the breath out of her. Pike and a few of the Rangers *kerplunked* in behind her before Wulfee heard Gen roar.

"For the Fells!" Gen shouted as the Wolf's brigade charged forward. Wulfee bobbed up and down in the current as it swept her away.

"Gen!" she shouted as water filled her mouth. She choked on the water, clawing at it trying to get back to Gen. Finally, her lungs allowed her a big gulp of air.

"Just get in, Gen. Try!" she screamed, drifting ever further away. "You have to try! I command you to get in! G—" Wulfee choked on water and went under. The droning silence of being underwater enraged her—she had little control over it. She felt her axe slip out of her wet fingers as she fought her way back to the surface. She had a cramp in her side that felt like it was tearing her open. Her lungs were caught in her throat, and she could hardly breathe.

When she broke the surface, the sounds of steel on steel rang out in harmony with screams and moans as the Wolf's brigade smashed into Coal and the Rangers who had turned to fight with him. *You're no kihl'dor... this is what happens every time you play at it. Your clan gets fed to the birds.* She bobbed up and down as she tried to stay afloat. She saw horses riding toward them on the opposite shore as well. More and more of them poured over the horizon, and Wulfee knew at once it was Odhran who'd come. He must have been expecting some sort of attack. The current carried her to the opposite shore from Gen. She swam one stroke at a time and then another, then another until she dug her bruised hands into the dirt and pulled herself up onto the shore. Pike was a couple hundred feet downriver and the other Rangers were all landing at different spots. Two women from Odhran's clan were firing arrows across the river from horseback. A greenhood crossing the river took an arrow to the shoulder but continued to swim. Wulfee looked back. Coal was dead. His Rangers were dead. They were gone.

And Wulfee saw Gen, alone.

She heard him screaming in a mad rage as soldiers smashed into him on horseback and bounced right off. *The rage of a karl...* He stood tall and swung his fists in wide, sweeping arcs that bludgeoned any rider who came near him. The wolf's soldiers were forced to dismount and aimed at Gen with spears and shortswords that barely phased the lad. His fists crushed skulls and bodies, splattering blood with every swing. Then, Wulfee heard something terrifying. She looked up for a moment because she thought maybe a star was falling, but she realized it was only Gen screaming. *He's gone bloody mad with the rage of a wild Giy'er...*

"We've got to go back, Pike," Wulfee said, not knowing how. Odhran was approaching from one side, the Wolf on the other. "We've got to go back for him."

"We can't go back, Wulfee." said Pike, dripping wet and panting. She looked back at Gen, the Wolf's brigade closing in around him.

He can't fight all of them...

"He made a choice, Wulf, one that meant something to him. To show us he's not afraid. He wanted us to see that he forgives us." Pike rested his hand on Wulfee's forearm.

I'm so sorry Gen. She watched as the Wolf dismounted and approached Gen with his waraxe drawn. She watched as the mass of fighters finally surrounded and overwhelmed Gen, and brought him down to the ground. He screamed like something she didn't recognize any longer. He thrashed and writhed and killed folk even from the ground. She turned away, and Pike caught her glance.

"Hey," he said. "Look at me. Don't watch, Wulf." But she had to look back and watch as they held Gen down. The Giy'er thrashed his head and killed a few more of them with his skull. She watched as the soldiers pushed his face flat into the dirt, and the Wolf walked closer with his axe.

"NO! Sweyne, you fucking prick! Fight me! Fight me instead, you fucking—"

The Wolf stood over Gen for a long while, and for a moment Wulfee thought he was going to set him free. Then Gen writhed again and sent more of the soldiers flying. He killed two more with his fists before the Wolf swung his axe into Gen's stomach and stopped him from writhing. More men held him down. Dozens and dozens of them piled on, and even so, some of them were flung off.

"THE FELLS!" Gen screamed, and for a moment the voice of Gen the karl was so grand it drowned out the Fell River and seemed to hold time by the throat so that it wouldn't move.

The Wolf sunk his axe blade deep into Gen's neck. He hacked and hacked at it and red chunks of the Giy'er flew with every backswing. When the Wolf finally cut it off, he bent over and picked Gen's head up by his wispy hair and held it up to the sky—

She turned away and wretched up a small mouthful of yellow bile. "I'll fucking kill you! I'll fucking kill—" She was slobbering. Pike holding her was the only thing keeping her from completely keeling over. An arrow landed in the ground right in front of her and wagged like a dog's tail.

"Fuck you!" she screamed, curling into a ball. "I can't... Pike... I—"

"You can." He pulled her along as they, and the few Rangers who made it across the river moved towards Odhran's clan. They were their only hope of survival now.

The Last Blood of the Mal

JAMES WALKED BACK THROUGH his dying country and felt the weight of its death gone from his shoulders. He should have felt something, maybe pride in what he'd done. *So why do you feel less than human?* A cold ran through him. His family had died because he had never come this far in facing the demon. Now that he had, it scared him, but he needed to make their deaths worth something.

It was a wet and foggy morning in the Rise of autumn, and the cold dew teasing the grass with frost said summer was really over. There would be no harvest come the Fell of autumn, and then another battle would begin. Mal Hallow needed a ruler to guide them if they were to see it through this winter. James knew that, and still, all he could bring himself to care about was Maggie.

He could see the great hundred-foot Lovasi bridge of Rosen poking through the smokey fog. The flags of the remaining lords of the Hallow hoisted high above, wrinkled and hanging sadly. Not a red eagle amongst them. He knew these colours from his boyhood. Brinley Scareye of Dawning and his black crow on yellow, Claydon Coldfoot of Tusk and his grey mammoth on green. Ruwen the Strong of Rosen and her black bear on blue. Eridan, son of Derudin, and the remaining Blooded Folk had hoisted Derudin's flag—the bloody hand on white. Standing tall above the rest was the brown bull moose on yellow. Bren Culdaine's flag, carried on from the ancient bloodline of the Mal King Dain. Raised in honour of James and the house of Culdaine.

These five families, the last blood of the Mal, were together for the first time since their clans surrendered to King Alder ten years ago. If they lost this bridge, their lands would be lost to Ayeland forever. Just as James's dad had feared. James knew that, and still, all he could bring himself to care about was Maggie.

As James neared the camp, he could feel the memories left to him by Ellorin rolling around in his mind and the wizard begging to some earth witch who scorned him. He remembered Itchy the bard telling him the wizard wasn't what he seemed. He thought about what he'd just done. *You raised the dead and used them. Got into whatever was left of their souls and guided them. You don't need that wizard anymore.* The dead souls walked with him like a moving sky full of clouds. He felt cold, and it felt *good.* It was coming from *below*—the Otherworld.

The village of Rosen sat on the north side of the bridge, but a smaller hamlet sat on the south side, where James could see Adeqor mingling with the other lords. Mineera scribbled on her parchment as she listened to them. Dozens of Hallow Knights in their hard leather and iron guarded the wagons full of food that Brinley had salvaged from Dawning. It was all they had left for the entire muster of soldiers and smallfolk. James passed by dozens of folk whispering *reaper* and pointing at him.

"I knew he'd be victorious," Adeqor shouted at Mineera. "I was there and saw him raise the dead souls with my own eyes." He pointed at her parchment. "Write this down. *Ahem.* It was centuries in the making, the return of the king. Wait. No. Don't use that."

Eurick ran out to greet him.

"By the gods, man. You're still here." He pulled him in with a big grin. James even hugged him back. Adeqor didn't move but glared at James with an all-knowing grin that made him shiver.

"Where is Maggie?" James said.

"She's been asking about you," Eurick said. "She's by the banks on the north side of the river, below that old dead nytewood. Wasn't dead when we got here, though... folk are saying things."

"What things?" James said, clenching his jaw and fists.

"Just go see her, man."

James rushed towards the bridge, ignoring the plaudits from the mustered lords and knights. Ignoring the hunger pains in his stomach, the knots in his back and legs. Eurick followed him. The Lovasi did not design the Rosen bridge to keep intruders out, like they did the bridges at Tusk. The Rosen bridge was wide enough to fit twenty folk abreast. *How the fuck can anyone defend this?*

James put his hand to his belt and felt the engagement knife still there—its kraken claw handle and opal ice stone.

"Don't waste anymore time with that, eh?" Eurick said as he touched his own engagement knife. "If you mean to give it to her, give it to her. Every minute, the both of you grow closer to death. For matters of the heart, every minute counts, man. Every second, really. You can't tell what tomorrow's going to bring. All we have is now, this present moment. Nothing else is promised to us. Nothing else is certain."

I will. I will give it to her now. Gods know we might both be dead by winter if I can't bring the fires back.

"Will you ever try to find Eronel?" said James.

Eurick shook his head.

"I swore an oath. My life is for the Guild. I couldn't run but for a week before they found us. He's long gone, man. The Guild would have killed him if I didn't leave. They'll kill him if I go back. And the torture they put me through... what I went through when I got back. I never want to go through that again. The only thing that got me through was knowing that

Eronel lived. That he wasn't suffering for our love like I was." He wiped his eyes with the back of his big hand. "You can't hide from the ravens, man. They will find anyone, anywhere. That is our reputation."

James put his hand on Eurick's shoulder. He knew what it was like to love someone like that and what it was like to lose them. James would make damn sure he never lost Maggie again. He pulled out the engagement knife to look at it one last time before he gave it to her.

"We'll get through this, man." Eurick smiled. "We'll get through it, and you two will live happily."

James had an idea. "After this job, you could leave. You could find a way. I'll tell them you died."

"They would search for my body."

"We could say the wizard melted you into that bog mire shite." James smiled.

Eurick returned the smile and looked up to the sky. "Maybe there's a way. Just maybe."

There were many hundreds of stragglers and followers crammed around the large village of Rosen. Scabby, dirt laden folk from all over the Hallow overflowed the narrow dirt roads. The Fells folk had lined the riverbanks, staring into the water and praying to their undergods. James realized that this was it. *This* was the last of his people. Hundreds of generations were on the verge of extinction. The dirty canvas tents of the Fells folk sprouted up in clusters around the village like mushrooms after a rain.

It was clear which tent was for the wizard, though. Nearly twice the height and thrice the width of any other. It sat beneath the thick, empty branches of a chunky old nytewood along with hundreds of souls of the dead. The Mal folk had apparently abandoned that tree to pray to a living one. The golden petals from the nyteflowers were falling like snow all around them.

James rushed in to find Maggie sitting on the edge of a cot, wrapped in a blanket. A woman knelt in front of her, holding her hands. There were dozens more in the tent on other cots, and they all looked over when James walked in.

"Maggie?" said James. She looked then, snapped out of a trance, and smiled widely. She jumped up and hugged him tight.

"You wouldn't believe what happened to me," she said. James looked her up and down. Her skin was bright with life, and her eyes were full of their usual mirth. He ran his calloused hands along her smooth arms.

"You look strong."

Maggie leaned in close and put her lips close to his ear. *Peonies and honey...*

"I took the life out of that nytewood. I just felt it, sitting right there, and I took it." She smiled. "I'm going to die, James. Without the spirits, I'm going to die."

James hated how sure she sounded. "I'm going to bring them back, Maggie. I'm going to save you."

"It could kill you in the end."

"Then I will die for you."

Maggie held his hands. For a moment, they were lost in each other's eyes. *The Swan blessed you with every ounce of beauty in the living world.* "It's written in the stars that we die together. I have to go with you."

James felt like he should tell her no, that they both didn't need to risk death. But he couldn't bear the thought of being without her again. "Of course." James kissed her. "I need you with me."

"Sometimes I can't believe I actually found you," said Maggie. "Stay here with me, will you?" Her words faded into mumbles. "Just for a while, before we go?"

James sat by her and stroked her hair gently.

It's not all as it seems... the wizard isn't telling you the truth... Itchy's words and Ellorin's memories haunted him as he sat in silence. He looked at Maggie. She had drifted into sleep. *Gods, she is beautiful.* His heart had never been so vulnerable to breaking.

The tent flap opened up, and Adeqor ducked in. His skin gave a faint glow to the dark interior.

"Oh, great seer, king of the Hallow, the world walking half-god Druid, your company has been requested at the round table with the other rulers. Such is the duty of a king, your grace."

I'll give her the knife after, he thought. He wanted nothing more than to stay by her side, but he had made his choice to save her. He couldn't do it in that tent. James picked up his great sword—as heavy as a fat sack of barley—and followed the wizard.

T HE RULERS HAD ASSEMBLED beneath the bare limbs of a gnarled oak tree. James thought they looked ragged at best. Brinley knelt over the large map spread out over a round table of worn chestnut, moving his stones around as a scout heralded him with her findings. He scratched at his scarred eye and cleared his throat.

"The Wolf and the full force of his army are marching to the bridge as we speak. They will be here by daybreak. In the south, the Ayelish have crossed the White River and occupy everything east and west of Ockam. They will move on Dawning shortly to clean up the mess Brynmor left behind. And Calen Alder has fortified Kallahorn with his host of two hundred. Some scouts say he has a thousand folk behind those walls, but the likelihood is low. He marched last fall with two hundred, and no one has seen anyone come or go. They have been there since the Rise of spring, so they are probably very short on supplies by now." Brinley rubbed his hands together. "The worst fear we should have of Alder at this point is whatever those Blood Words did to him, not the small force he has with hi m."

The scout crossed her arms. "The Wolf will surely look to resupply and fortify Kallahorn. We may just starve them out if we can hold the bridge."

Brinley slammed his fist down on the map.

"Fuck!" To his daughters, he asked, "Can we hope to hold the Wolf here?"

"No," said Aione. "Not without the clans of Pool. The Wolf has the biggest army I've ever seen. Brigands, mercenaries, trained warriors, clansfolk, refugees, and smallfolk from all across Ardura. Desperate folk who were promised titles, land, and glory if they win."

"The clans of Pool declined to help," added Ruwen.

Claydon said, "We could still make it to the north coast if we take the Dagg Pass through the mountains. Perhaps get a ship there and sail to Daggland."

"Fuck!" said Brinley. "We can't abandon it all now. We have to delay them long enough for the seer to make it to the Mountains of the Mother. We must at least do that. I have to *believe* in something right now. With fire, we can rebuild. We can bloody well live again!"

"With fire, things burn!" Claydon swiped the stones that represented themselves off the map. His thick beard stuck on his chin like a blonde mountain. "We need to leave these lands to the Ayelish and head north! We can rebuild there, in peace."

Ruwen thumped a fist on her shield. "I'll die before I leave these lands!"

An argument broke out amongst them.

Adeqor jumped up on the round table. His dirty bare feet smeared the map with loam and loose pebbles. And everyone was silent.

"The only thing that matters now is getting Culdaine to the Mother alive. You must realize by now that if you don't die here, defending this bridge, then you will all die come winter." Adeqor took a long swig from his wineskin. James imagined him drowning in it and dying. "Soon you'll be bones. A mere name in a song, at most. Even that is just a sound in the mouth of a drunken singer. The animals have no name for you and neither do the gods. The life of a human is stale, trivial, and ultimately meaningless. You have but one purpose, and that is to do something worth being remembered for. Each of you is a part of the greatest story that will ever be told. The rising of the old blood of half-gods, the seer of the souls, the last blood of the ancient Mal Druids, and the rightful King of Mal Hallow. He led you to this very bridge. He stood alone before the Hammer of the Glenn's army and a horde of Hawka, the likes of which had never been seen before, and defeated the Banshee of death. A Warlock of the Ailaryan Order! And every one who stood with her, single-handedly." Adeqor tossed the empty wineskin. "Now you must make a stand! Revel in the pure heroism of it. Realize that history has caught you in its blood wet fingers, and you cannot swim out of it no matter how hard you try to avoid it." Adeqor pointed at Mineera. "Are you writing this down?" The scholar nodded and pulled another piece of parchment out of her pack. He turned his attention back to the assembly of great people. "When that brigand Wolf tries to ride across this bridge, we'll give him one hell of a fight!" Adeqor thrust his arm into the air. Ruwen let out a loud, drunken roar, and the rest couldn't hold back either. Even Claydon seemed to have changed his tone. James knew Adeqor would be nowhere to be found when the fighting started, but he was quick to scream with the lot of them. It felt good to let it out. They were the rulers of the Hallow. The old blood of the Mal. They just needed some good words to rile them up.

I T WAS THE SAME crescent moon from the night the Hawka came. He and Maggie had sat beneath the moon smoking chuff and watching the golden stars dance on the black night.

Even though the moon was the same, everything else had changed. After the meeting with the other rulers, James wondered why he was even here. The rulers only saw James as the way to bring back the fires. *That's because that is all you are... not a king but a weapon.* As he found his way back inside Maggie's tent, he kept thinking about the way Adeqor riled everyone up. Did James *envy* Adeqor?

The tent inside was honey and peonies, pink and golden in his mind—and James wished he had never left at all. Maggie's chest rose and fell in slow breaths as she slept. *Is she dreaming about you?* Deep scars ran down her cheek and onto her neck. More on her chest and torso. Something had brutalized her. James lightly traced her scars. *Ai'mair darra, baby, forever. No matter how deep your scars are.* He had avenged her. Left the Banshee to be eaten by the wild. *Do you feel better yet?* It horrified him to know that he didn't.

Maggie stirred, opening her eyes. She reached out and grabbed James's hand.

"You wouldn't believe what I saw in my dreams." Maggie sat up.

"It couldn't be more mad than what I've seen in the waking world.." James held her tight and stared into her eyes. *One green and one blue...*

"I don't really want to talk about it." Maggie kissed him.

"Me, neither." James reached down to his belt and pulled out the knife. She looked at it, up at James, then back at the knife. Then took it and admired it.

He said, "I love you more than anything. It even feels like I love you more than myself sometimes... and you know, it's just really—" She put her finger to his lips and smiled until it looked to strain her scar tissue.

"You're not much for words, my love," she said. "Of course. Let us heartbound."

"On the morrow?"

"When it's over," she said. Looked at *Essikah* sticking up over his shoulder. "The world needs you now. I can't be selfish and keep you to myself."

"I'm going to make you better. I'm going to fix this," said James.

"I know. And if this is the end of our story, then at least it ends with us together again," she said.

"All the worst things in my life have happened away from you." James climbed into Maggie's bed and wrapped his arms around her—breathed in her smell. "I'm not letting go of you this time."

"I dreamed we had laid out beneath the stars and watched them fall on everyone but us," Maggie said as her eyes fluttered shut. "I dreamt I didn't have to hold it all in anymore. I took whatever life was there. All of it. From everywhere."

He lay with her in silence for a time. Listening to her breath as she drifted into sleep and feeling her warmth. He tried to forget about Ellorin. About the Hermit. About Calen Alder. But trying to forget just made him think about them more.

"Tell me more of your dreams," he said. But she was already asleep.

One Last Moon

CROWSEYE TOOK AN ARROW to the back of his head and fell dead hard. Wulfee counted only six Rangers with her now, plus Pike. Odhran's riders were dressed in furs and bone, brass and iron. *Feldarran Clansfolk*, with Odhran Ironfist in front. He wore a thick coat of white grizzly fur, and his long iron-blade arm glistened in the sun. As they got closer, Wulfee could see Odhran's crown of bones atop his head. He wore a gold-dipped skull on a steel chain around his neck. He jumped off his white horse and sliced the air with his blade arm. It was four feet of cold iron, screwed right into the bone of his elbow in place of the residual limb that was otherwise there, and sharp as all hell. *The injury you gave him, Wulf. Don't forget that part.* Wulfee looked around and saw many folk she knew. Golla Grace, the She-Wolf of Urum. Tennit Boneshaker, kihl'dor of the Bone-Eater clan. Tilly One-Eye and Killer Jobe, the bastard son and daughter of the former kihl'dor Collen of the Rock, and Six-Toe Dillon of the half-breeds, a clan that mated with the El'vie and produced children with webbed feet who, Wulfee had heard, ate trout eggs instead of mother's milk. All folk who she'd fought and bled with, drank with until their bloody ears felt like they'd fallen off. Odhran walked towards them and smiled when he recognized Wulfee.

Gen... you were so close... We were so close. The gods... so much for the fucking gods... so young, like my son... my son...

"The fuck are you doing here, Wulfee? Almost didn't recognize you without all that hair," said Odhran, looking away at the folk crossing the river. Then his eyes caught Pike. "And this one," he whispered to himself. "Look who's back, Tess. The man who murdered your mom." A woman stepped forth, two dozen braids in her matted brown hair. Wulfee was stunned by her ice-blue eyes that looked like the same ones in Pike's head. The woman looked Pike up and down with those eyes, took his measure, and didn't seem to like what she saw.

Pike shouted, "There is a bloody army coming! Can't you see? We must get a force to Rosen!"

Odhran Ironfist showed no fear in his hard face. Instead, he said, ignoring Pike, "We'll bring these two back with us in chains."

"Let's just kill him right here," said Tess, and Odhran laughed.

"Why not?" He took out a shining iron dirk and tossed it to Tess. The first of the Wolf's brigade had made it to the riverbank but jumped back in when they saw Odhran's host.

Wulfee could hardly breathe. *How could you let Gen die? You're worthless. Less than nothing. Why do you destroy everything good? Why are you such a failure?*

"I challenge you to combat," said Pike. And the whole host seemed to hold their breath for a moment. A kihl'dor couldn't refuse combat and still call themselves kihl'dor. "Let me fight for my life. Let me prove my innocence." He smiled at Tess. "I'm a lot of things, Tess, but I'm not the monster you think I am. What I did, I did because I love you."

Odhran scoffed.

"What makes you think you've earned any kind of clean death? You're a wife-killer, and a child-abandoner."

"I'm only guilty of loving my wife and my daughter so much I'd do unspeakable things to save them," said Pike.

"And what did that get you? A dead wife," said Tess.

"Aye. But it gave me a living daughter, too," said Pike. Tess squinted her eyes at him and said no more.

Odhran smiled and said, "Right then. I'll kill the old fella this evening in combat, and then we'll hang Wulfee from the branches of the nihr'el she spurned all those years ago when she broke her oaths. Should be a good little show. Just what we need to lift our spirits in these dark times. I don't want these skincrawlers hanging about, though. Kill them, and let's be off."

Wulfee felt her heart sink, then an elbow to her temple knocked her to the ground. She heard fighting, war cries, and it was over, just like that. The Rangers who had followed her hoping for salvation lay dead in the dirt, their warm blood pooling beneath her.

WULFEE FELL INTO A waking dream in which she was carried off on the back of Odhran's horse and dropped like a corpse on the rocky shores of the Lake of Pool. Odhran's clan hitched the horses at the edge of the arbor. When they rowed a small boat across glistening waters of emerald green to an island infested with towering trees of black with sprawling canopies of gold, she thought she may wake up at any moment. And when she saw the El'vie—pale, slimy beasts that lived in the shallows of the well of seers—flexing their gills and writhing their muscles, she knew they were close to Pool. When she saw the faces of gods carved into the rocks, she knew that she'd finally made it.

This is no dream. Just as you're no kihl'dor. This is Pool, and you're alive. Now do what you came to do. Don't make it all for naught. She closed her eyes, thought of Gen and cried, but the tears seemed to be drained out of her. Then she thought of Sweyne and brooded in the fury he conjured in her.

She snapped out of it when the small boat nudged up against a small dock. Odhran howled and hundreds of folk howled back from the shore as they came down to meet their kihl'dor.

"I've brought a gift for you all from the mainland! Vengeance!" Odhran screamed, and hundreds upon hundreds of haggard and hungry looking folk howled back. They made their way up from the shore towards the nihr'el along a path that wound through rocky crags and groves of nyte-wood.

The first sign of Odhran's madness were the skulls mounted on spikes, lining the lakefront and roads, hanging from the branches of nytewoods. Hundreds more piled up beneath the world tree. Wulfee walked towards the great nihr'el, the sacred world tree, and tried not to be sick. She let it draw her in, let it touch her soul. It was far more beautiful than she remembered. Wulfee traced her hand down the rigid lines of the oily black bark and put her palm flat on the gnarled face carved into it. It was wise, aged, and all too Human. She felt the energy flowing through the trunk, heard the spirits in there dying. Felt the roots writhing in the earth below her. She stared up into the golden canopy from below and couldn't see an end to it. It went up and up until it simply disappeared from sight. A hundred thick branches sprouting a thousand smaller ones grew out and out and blossomed into nyteflowers. And a smell, equal parts pleasant and acrid of honey and corpses, wafted from the enveloped pocket between branch and flower. It was the sacred nihr'el. The first life that was ever born into the world; the tree that birthed the first Humans. And now it was defaced by treachery and infested with crows. Cold, dead bodies still hung by tendrils of torn flesh from their nooses, being picked and torn at by hundreds of black beaks. More corpses sat in gibbets, hanging off the branches like macabre lanterns that radiated darkness in place of light. Odhran had piled skulls up at the base of the nihr'el like stacks of firewood.

Wulfee dropped to her knees in the soft dirt and tucked her chin into her chest. She was overcome by the majesty of the nihr'el. *Nihr'el nur amo ruso. God of gods, I pray to rest easy when it's over. Oh, gods please hear me.* Odhran kicked her in the ribs.

"Get up, you," he sneered. "Your time to pray is long gone."

"What is all this?" Wulfee gasped.

"Can't trust anybody nowadays," said Odhran. "Clans come down from the mountains pretending to be friends. Tried to kill us while we slept. It's the birds for them." But Wulfee saw more than mountain clansmen. She saw the tattered flag of Lady Ruwen of Rosen. She saw the black-winged cloak of a transporter from the Raven's Guild. The sash of a merchant. She saw the red, wool coat of an Ayelishman and the brown wool coat of a Glennishman. Odhran was killing anyone who came here. Anyone at all.

Wulfee didn't even realize she was sobbing again. "You won't be able to stop the Wolf by killing all who come here to fight. If you cared at all to save this place, you'd unite all of the Fells and defend the bridge at Rosen. Have you gone mad? These are our people."

"Mad? No, not mad," said Odhran.

"Well..." said Tess, "Maybe a little. But ain't we all gone a little mad since the fires went out?"

Odhran said, "Our people live in Pool. We stay in Pool. All others are enemies. You trust too much, Wulfee. Too much hope in you. No worry, though. We'll kill it out of you soon enough."

They plodded along to Odhran's hamlet. The mud brick and sod-roofed hovels built in neat lines looked outlandish amongst the goldenrods and chicories, the buckthorns and brambles. The towering nytewoods were beautifully in bloom, but the pale brown and yellow dried mud and dead sod drowned all the colours from the land. *This island was never meant to be settled.* Her dad had always told her. It was a godly place of pure, untouched magics.

Wulfee felt sick. *You caused this defamation when you cut Odhran's arm off. You did this, you haggard old bitch.* Raw meat hung on racks and flies buzzed about loudly. Children ran naked through the pathways, and gaunt, old folk sat out in front of their homes and stared suspiciously at Wulfee and Pike. At the centre of the hamlet, a black mark was burned into the dirt where raging fires once blazed. Pike looked around without saying a word. His face was firm and unyielding. Wulfee had seen the old warrior face death like no other. He could stare the fucker down and chase it off, time after time. Death hadn't caught him yet. No doubt he believed he would win this fight. But Wulfee wasn't so sure. Odhran threw off his albino furs and jumped into the circle to the applause of the clansfolk.

"Tonight's the night, old man. Your last moon." Odhran pranced about the circle like he was battling an invisible enemy. "And tonight's *our* night! The gods walk amongst us, and the world is dying. Now we must show them we see them. Tonight we make a sacrifice and earn our place in the new world." He pulled out his axe and howled. "Bah-Roooooo!" The clansfolk answered the call, cheering out in a drunken frenzy. They were all passing around skins of shine and hooting and whistling.

"All right, you. Let's go," said Tess. She prodded Wulfee with a long, rusted dirk, leading her to a large stake in the ground. Tess tied Wulfee's hands and feet to the stake, and then did the same to Pike. The old warrior did as he was told and watched on with despair in his eyes as his daughter bound him as a prisoner. All around, the stone faces of the gods watched on from the rocks. They were in the shade of the nihr'el, where magics were born. She could feel the old energy lingering. It was the same thing that she felt around Maggie. Some power of the spirits.

"You need to know what really happened, Tess." Pike pleaded. "My side. Not whatever you've been told. At least give an old man that one last shred of decency. Hear my side of it."

Tess laughed dryly.

"I don't care what you think really happened. I've heard enough sides of the same story to know that you're a bloody coward."

"Aye. I'm a coward and a killer. Always had done. But I never hurt your mother. I left you two behind in the dead of night because I knew you'd be better off with your uncle. I hoped for something better for the two of you than what I could give you. It was a piss poor decision, and I was a piss poor kinda man back then. But your mother always thought otherwise. She woke up, saw that I was gone, and came after me. I told her I was no good and would just let you two down. She carried on, and the two of us made too much noise. Next thing I knew, she had an arrow in her neck from the out watch. They thought us to be intruders." Pike looked around. "It was two of you that did it!" He shouted over Tess's shoulder at Odhran. "Two of your own clan! Thank the Swan I got away without being shot down myself—at least She knew my innocence. But as I ran through the arbor, another guard found me. He said he saw me kill that woman back there. *That woman* was my wife! I screamed at him. When he came at me with his axe drawn, I killed him dead in a frenzy of rage and grief. There was no way to go back without being killed myself, so I ran. I bloody ran. I couldn't bear the thought of dying a dishonourable death and you seeing it happen. I'm a bloody coward. I should have been there for you, Tess. I'm a bloody failure, but I didn't kill her. I never meant to hurt you."

"Why didn't you bury her?" Tess asked. "We found her torn apart by wolves. Half eaten by the crows. We blamed you for both of those deaths. But if you loved her so much, why didn't you bury her?" Wulfee saw tears forming in her eyes and knew that Pike had reached her.

"I would have been shot! You don't think I wanted to go back to her?" Pike said. "Besides, she deserved a ceremony. It needed to be you and her brother that put her down. It needed to be proper. It needed to be more than what I could give her. I was—am nothing."

"There was nothing proper about it," Tess spat.

"I'm sorry, Tess. So sorry," said Pike. Tess walked away. Wulfee wondered what the god-faced stones thought of it all. Pike looked torn apart, tears falling down his wrinkled face.

"At least she knows your side now," said Wulfee. She tried not to think about how Pike beating Odhran in combat was probably her only chance at surviving the hanging.

"Aye," he said.

"You're the toughest man I know, Pike." She patted him on the shoulder and wasn't sure if it was to make *him* feel better or herself.

"My best days are gone, Wulf. But I still have more left in me. I can get her back, in time. I just need to win some time." Pike laughed. "I've been waiting all these years for a chance at a good death. Now it's right in front of me, and all I can think of is life."

THE SUNFELL WAS NOTHING unusual. Wulfee imagined her last time staring into the pink, orange, and red would be some kind of romantic ode to the Crow, the goddess of death. But dying made her stomach turn and her mind stir. *Sweyne could be here by sunfell tomorrow if they breach Rosen. And then what? Is this lot going to hold them off?* She examined Pike and saw a stone-faced killer at the end of his time. He was stoic. Cold. He hummed the death song to himself as if in meditation. *He's never been afraid of death.* And he certainly didn't seem scared now. Wulfee wished she had prayed more to her underself when she had the chance. Then her mind drifted to Gen. And from there it found Sweyne, in that cursed wolf helm with that god damned waraxe. *And that bastard is going to outlive you. He'll show up here to cut down the world tree, see your body swinging from the branches, and laugh. He'll laugh his arse off. And you'll die a bloody fool. Just as you lived. Kihl'dor Wulfee, a bloody fool of a cunt.*

Tilly One-Eye and Golla Grace came for Pike at the high-moon. Pike saw them coming and looked at Wulfee. Put his fist to his chin and gave her a nod. She returned it. The gods knew they could both use some luck right now.

"Alright, it's time to go now, fella," said Golla.

"Let's go, old man," said Tilly, untying both of them. "You're coming too, old red. Odhran wants you to watch this'un die." *Old red? Really?...*

"That old man used to be quite a warrior." Golla chuckled. "Looks pretty funny without all his hair, but it used to be full of braids. I remember that much."

Tilly crooked her one eye at Golla and spat.

"The fuck I care about some old, grey beard who kihl'dor Odhran is about to slice up?"

"That's what I'm saying, you dumb drunk, is that grey bearded bastard might not get sliced up so easily. Head used to be full of braids is what I'm saying, and I remember seeing this fucker do some work to some bloke up in the mountains back not to long ago." Golla grabbed Pike by the back of the neck to lead him along. "What happened to you anyway, old chump? Why'd you go and cut off all that hair? Did a fuck of a job at it, if you ask me. It's all in patches and what not?"

Pike shrugged.

"Not much for talking, eh? Well, I get that," said Golla.

"You don't get none o' that. You couldn't shut up even if you had a knife down your throat," said Tilly. And the two women continued to argue as they walked to the hamlet. Wulfee could hear the drunken revelry as they approached. There were a thousand or more people there. Wulfee couldn't believe how much Odhran had mustered. Men and women of all ages crowded into the centre area surrounding the firepit. They sharpened spears, axes, arrows, and carried buckets of water. They stitched and mended, sowed and repaired, ground and hammered. Wulfee couldn't believe what she was seeing: Odhran's hamlet had become a proper town. A living thing with a pulse. *This is the biggest clan to exist in these parts. You thought you could fight this?* Great, big destriers, wearing heavy leather barding, grazed in the grassy patches between nytewoods and neighed loudly. A dozen lines of mud that used to be streams of crystal clear water stretched out in every direction from the well of seers in the middle. The stone faces of gods watched over all with harsh judgement. Pool and its magics seemed most alive under the stars. Slimy, white, human-like fish called El'vie, which meant merrmonster in the old rune tongue, dwelled in the shallows of the well. They lived indifferently to the Humans while they bathed their silvery skin in the moonlight. The town had become one with the island.

Odhran was waiting. There were already a hundred or more crowded around the circle. The kihl'dor of Pool stood in the centre, shirtless. Long, black hair rested on his shoulders. His iron arm reflected the big silver eye of the moon. The crowd cleared to allow Pike in. He walked forward without ever looking back at Wulfee. *What more is there to say?*

Odhran pointed to Pike's axe and stuck his blade down in the earth.

"Your weapon."

"Not the one I choose to use." Pike crossed his arms.

Odhran grinned, swinging his iron arm.

"You have a reputation with the axe, old man. What? Do you *want* to get killed? You really are a coward, aren't you?"

Pike shook his head.

"You have a reputation for killing folk who fight with axes. I'm done asking for death. I want my shield."

"That clunky wooden thing? Is this a joke, old man? Times have been dark since the fires went out. We want a bloody show of it."

"It's no joke," he said. "Who has my shield?" Nobody moved. Pike stared at the kihl'dor, unwavering. Wulfee grinned at the sight of that chiseled face. Odhran looked at Pike with a suspicious glare. Then let his malicious grin takeover.

"You heard the old karl. Who took his shield?" Odhran said.

"It's here." A grizzled man with a gravelly voice came forward and offered it up. Odhran took it and threw the shield in front of Pike. The old warrior picked it up. Wulfee knew what that shield meant to Pike. A hundred different axes and arrows had notched and chipped the gnarled old thing over generations. Faded green paint still clung to it in places like clusters of mould. But the rooted nihr'el, the symbol of the Feldarra, carved into the shield generations ago by Pike's ancestors was what meant most to him. He held the shield high above his head, and Wulfee knew he was saluting the gods. *But was it the Crow or the Stag...*

Wulfee forced herself to the front and saw Tess standing close by. Odhran took off his crown of bones and his chain of a golden skull.

"Keep em' warm, sweet girl," Odhran said, placing them in front of Tess. "I'm going to avenge your mother."

He turned around and lunged at Pike. Pike was far enough that he got out of the way with ease. He looked up one last time, and Wulfee caught his eyes and nodded. The old warrior was the closest thing she'd had to a friend since she was a little girl named Etta, who was allowed to have friends, and Wulfee wasn't ready to let him go. He looked down just in time to dodge another of Odhran's lunges. And then the kihl'dor was backing him down, swinging his iron arm wildly. Pike caught each blow on his shield, chips of wood splintering off under each one. Odhran sliced right, then left, then straight, forcing Pike to run away into empty space. But he couldn't.

"Make a bloody show of it, old man!" screamed Odhran madly. Slicing. Hacking. A hollow thud of iron on wood that Wulfee felt in her chest from twenty feet away. "I remember when you had braids in that hair," Odhran barked. "When you actually meant something to the world."

Pike dodged another blow and got to the side of Odhran. He swung his shield weakly and missed, leaving himself wide open. Odhran sliced at Pike's ribs, and when Pike deflected the blow with the edge of his shield, the iron arm sliced Pike's leg instead. Pike let out a scream. Wulfee tried to run into the circle, but many arms pulled her back. She could only watch.

Odhran raised his arm to swing at Pike's neck. Pike thrust his shield at Odhran's open gut and knocked the kihl'dor back. Now Pike was walking Odhran down. The kihl'dor swung his iron arm madly, and each one was met with the hollow thud of Pike's shield. Pike took another step forward, and another. Smacking. Thudding. Another step, and another. Odhran swung and swung and never seemed to tire. Thick muscles writhed in his working shoulder. Sinews bulged like ropes in his neck. Spittle hung from his mouth and chin as he screamed in primal rage.

"This is for my sister. You fuck! This is for Alissa!" Odhran howled, and many of the clan howled back. Wulfee felt the hair on the back of her neck rise from the intensity of it. *This lot all together is as strong as a waterfall.*

"Fucking kill him!" Tess screamed, and Wulfee couldn't really tell who she meant it for. Pike was looking old and frail. His shield was dropping lower and lower. But he stayed on the offensive.

"I didn't kill her!" Pike screamed, but it was lost in the crowd's din. "The gods know it!" He swung his shield side to side, hoping to catch Odhran with a bludgeon. But the kihl'dor dodged, moved around, and showed the difference that ten years made in a person's knees. Pike took a blow to the shield that stumbled him back. From there, Odhran leaped in the air and kicked him with both feet. Pike fell onto his back and gasped like he was struggling to breathe. Odhran jumped up in a hurry and charged to finish Pike with a downward slash of his iron arm. Pike got his shield up in time, and Odhran's blade arm pierced it with a splintering crash. Odhran tried to wretch it free but found it wedged in the thick and gnarled wood. Then Pike used his free hand and flattened the kihl'dor's nose with his old fist. Odhran stumbled back. Blood dripped down the kihl'dor's face. His arm drooped, weighed down by the shield he'd brought with him as he stumbled. It gave Pike enough time to stand up again. He went at Odhran with his fists now, landing another blow to his head. Odhran swung his blade arm, but with the weight of the shield, it was slow and weak. Pike moved around him easily and threw his fist at Odhran's exposed gut. The great kihl'dor winced as he panted loudly. The crowd was growing silent.

"Gah-fuck," he said. And Pike hit him again and again. Odhran shook his arm madly to get the shield unstuck. Pike kicked him in the shin.

"Fuck you!" shouted Odhran.

This bastard is going to pull it out. He's going to win. Wulfee had seen the old warrior pull some long chances out of his arse before, but this... this was a gift from the gods. Finally, Odhran used his foot to prop the shield and yanked his blade arm out. He kicked Pike's shield aside. He was wheezing heavily.

"Come get your due. You know what you did. I know you fucking know it," Odhran growled.

Pike backed away from Odhran's iron arm.

"I didn't kill her. It was your own guards." Pike easily dodged another slice. "It's your own fault!" Pike seemed somehow nimbler now than he did at the beginning. Like he'd shaken out some of the old dust in those bones.

"And why'd you leave her and your child in the first place? What kind of man leaves his family like that, eh?" said Odhran, slicing. Pike spat, dodging.

"I left because I'm a bloody killer. Always had done. I ain't no father or husband. They were better off without me."

"You got it wrong, old man. You got it all wrong. Alissa loved you. And you left her. And you left Tess, and if you didn't leave, there never would have been anyone chasing you," said Odhran, swinging. Missing. "Alissa never would have been on the road in the first place. Don't you see, you fuck. You killed her whether or not you had loosed the arrow. And worse yet, you're a bloody coward. Running from your responsibilities and making up excuses." Odhran sliced again. This time, he put all he had into it and let his momentum carry him through. Pike jumped out of the way and landed hard on the dirt. He rolled towards his shield as Odhran charged at him, blade first. Pike picked up his shield by the edge and threw it like a disc into Odhran's shins. It made a loud crack as the wood hit the bone, and Odhran fell to the ground. Pike jumped onto Odhran's back and with his knee on Odhran's blade arm, he forced Odhran's head into the dirt. The old warrior seemed to pull strength from twenty years ago. He bashed Odhran Ironfist's bleeding face into the dirt, over and over.

"I didn't"—*smash*—"fucking"—*crunch*—"kill her." *Smash, smash.*

Odhran wasn't moving when Pike crawled off him. The old warrior walked to his shield and picked it up. He surveyed the crowd. His gaze lingered on Tess, but she only looked away. He stepped over Odhran and smashed his skull open with the edge of his shield. One, two, three times. Blood and brain splattered. Four, five, six times. Squelch, squelch, squelch. He halted, as if snapping out of some kind of maddened trance.

"You let us go!" he screamed. Almost slurred it, spittle flying out of the corners of his mouth. "If you won't fight for your country at Rosen, if you won't uphold your oaths as Feldarra to protect these lands, you at least let us go."

There was only silence. It seemed that none of the clan knew what to think. Wulfee saw a battle drunken monster, covered in blood, and screaming nonsense. *My saviour, again.*

"We're going," he declared one last time. "Come on, Wulfee. We're leaving this place." He walked towards her, and the circle closed in. The clansfolk weren't quite ready to let the man who just killed their kihl'dor walk away. Weapons appeared, shouts of "kill him!" and "tear his head off!" came from the crowd.

"Let them go," said a powerful voice. And everyone beheld her. "He claimed victory. His prize is freedom. Let them go." It was Tess. "Take a boat and leave the island." A clearing formed as the crowd parted. And Pike, still bleeding from his leg and walking with a limp, led them out of the village back towards the world tree.

Wulfee thought, as she looked at Pool draped in pale, silver light, that this was one hell of a last moon for Odhran Ironfist.

More than Death

A DEQOR WAS ALREADY DRUNK by sunrise, screaming at Itchy to play a song. When James and Maggie came out of their tent, he was smiling at them.

"Still haven't found a decent pair of boots, eh, man? Hahaha. Oh, man." He wiped his eye. Looked at Maggie. "It's beautiful, you know, all of this love. All of this magic. It's almost like the days of old. You know, just without light at night and any decent food."

"I don't want to waste any more time here," James said. Itchy started plucking away and singing *Burnt Bread for Breakfast* at Adeqor's request.

"That's the wisest thing I've heard come out of that mouth of yours, seer. The Mother awaits!" Adeqor said.

There were two nytewoods in Rosen. A weeping, hollowed one Maggie had stolen the life from and a big old chunky one in full bloom. The survivors were all gathered beneath the living one. Some were praying, others sulking. Most folk James talked to weren't sure if they'd see another sunrise. Maggie walked towards the tree, and James followed her.

"We have no time to waste, Mag. We must be on our way to get as far ahead of this army as we can," said James.

"Surely we have time for one last prayer," she said. So they prayed together beneath the nytewood. James prayed to the Stag for strength and courage to make it to the end and to the Owl for the foresight to sense when he was making the wrong move. It felt good to pray again. James could see the memories of Ellorin stirring in his thoughts. He could hear the screams of her victims, smell the blood of their flesh in the same way she smelled it—sweet and savoury. He remembered what Father Tree had told him. That the dark words were staining the earth and seeping into the Otherworld. If the stain got any worse, the world would be lost forever. He looked at Maggie, the life drying up in her like the water from the rivers. He looked at the runes carved into *Essikah,* and wondered again about what they might mean. *How is this going to end for you?* Dark clouds rolled in over their heads and threatened a storm that couldn't come. A chill rolled off them that bit into James like teeth. He had no idea what awaited him at the Mother's shrine. He could only hope now that he had what it took to finish.

Eurick was already waiting for them by the road, leaving Rosen. He had fallen a long way from the first time James had seen him in the cave. He'd had many saddlebags full of supplies, two horses, and a few less scars then. Now his winged raven's cloak was tattered, he was bandaged up and bruised but just as ready as he ever was to do his job. The remaining Blooded Folk were gathered there with him. Itchy and Padraig. Mineera, Tam, the road smith, and Logan TooTall. Berra and Karillin. Eridan, son of Derudin, led them proudly and obeyed every word Adeqor said. James couldn't blame hi m.

They looked withered to the bone and long overdue for some rest and a bath. They all blankly stared at James, asking for answers, equally terrified and confused. Probably thinking the same thing he was. *How the fuck are we going to get out of this one alive?*

"One last road to walk down, man," said Eurick.

"And one hell of a road it is," said James. He looked at Maggie and couldn't help but imagine a life where they weren't dragged into all of this. "Still don't know if it's the right one. Guess we'll find out."

"You can't know if it's the right way until you get to the end," said Eurick. "It's one of life's old tricks. The wrong path has a way of making a person feel comfortable until it falls out from under you. Sometimes the right way can drag you through mud and shit for a hundred miles before you pop out somewhere warm and smelling pretty. I've seen it go many ways. Not one journey like the other. Some of us have a longer, harder journey than others."

"And what about you?" James asked. He had wondered more than once what the raven was getting out of any of this.

"I don't know yet." Eurick shrugged. "I guess I've been on the same road so long there ain't no point in going back. May as well see what's at the end. Find out if I come out smelling like roses or just die in a pile of shite."

"What's at the end of this one, you figure?" James figured it was more than likely that the only thing waiting for him at the end of this was a painful death.

"Can't say. Maybe that's why it's so hard. Why it scares me so. Every path I've been down, I knew the destination. Even when I found Eronel, I knew it would end. Now I don't know what we're going to see in those mountains. I don't know, and it scares me something fierce."

"Nothing to fear, gentlemen," Adeqor said. "Nothing at all. With the great sword *Essikah* and the great seer, nothing can go wrong. I've seen this play out before. It's woven into time like a crest on stone. The spirits will live again on this plain, and the people will have a new god to worship. A god that is *worthy* of the title and has worked tirelessly for generations to attain it. Whatever fallout occurs in the meantime is purely consequential to a much larger plan. The old world of Yehven still lives in the veins of this world, and it needs to be squeezed out. The memory of their song needs to be forgotten. The Ailaryan Order needs to be ended, for good."

A few of the crew scoffed at that, but after seeing what happened to Derudin, not a person said a thing about it. There were just some things that were simply too big to comprehend. Sometimes it was just easier for James to look at what was right in front of him. *It's too late to turn away. This is all there is now. This is either the end or just another story.* A person couldn't question nature, and they couldn't question love. Both were just as unpredictable as the other. James grabbed Maggie's hand as they walked. In that moment, his love for her was the only thing holding him together. The folk around him geared up for war, suspended in what could very well be the last moments of their lives. James remembered that feeling all too well. Wondering when the enemy will come and how many. Wondering if he'd make it through the night. Or the next night. He looked at the folk securing the watchtowers with slats of wood across the doorways, locking the archers inside. At the others, who were digging wooden spikes into the ground for defence against the charge. They were sharpened to a point and banded with cooper hoops to avoid splintering. If these folk couldn't hold off the Wolf long enough for James to get past Kallahorn and out to the mountains of the Mother—James didn't want to think about that.

"Hey," said Maggie. "Don't worry so much." She squeezed his hand tighter. The dead marched solemnly behind them.

"There is just so much death. I'm so fucked up, Maggie, I've killed so many people." James rubbed his forehead—his head was thumping like battle drums. Ellorin's memories pecked at his brain like a mad crow. *The dark words are staining the world. If they seep into the Otherworld, it will be lost forever.*

"There is more to you than death, James. I've seen it. I've felt your heart and know it's true. I dreamed that everyone across the entire world bowed to you. That they were all afraid of you. I dreamed of fire and rain. I tasted the salt of the sea on the winds, and I saw flowers and barley, and brambleberries. And I saw you, the Hallow King, leading your people back into their homelands when this is all over," said Maggie. She kissed him. "I saw *us,* James. I saw a child." He pulled her in close and held her tight. The thought of a child made James's head quiet. He had dreamt of a baby girl who looked at him with eyes like Maggie's, and he figured that was the best dream he'd ever had. James ran his hands up Maggie's ribs, protruding like tree limbs. She was so frail now he was worried he'd break her if he squeezed too hard. *You're so cold, Mag.*

They had gathered what little supplies they could, passed around a skin of shine to get the muscles loosened up a bit, and started out from the bridge. They were just ten miles out of Rosen when two stragglers appeared. The old man had a bad limp. The other was a woman who appeared especially wan.

"Help!" she yelled, and James ran out to them. When he got closer and saw her red hair and her face, he stopped in his tracks. *Is that?* He held his hand up to his forehead to block the sun and studied her face further.

"Wulfee?"

THE KIHL'DOR

"**J**AMES?"

Wulfee wasn't sure if she'd completely lost her mind or if she was actually seeing James, and was that... "Maggie?"

"By the gods..." Pike muttered.

"We need help!" she screamed. Pike had gone pale as snow. Black, crusty blood soaked his cut leg. Wulfee had tied the ripped fabric of his pant leg below a large wound and stuffed it with mud. James ran towards her, and as he neared, Wulfee fell to her knees. Her body seized by all the emotion she'd pent up over the last twenty years. Seeing James and Maggie alive brought it all back. At least *they* had lived. She couldn't save anyone in her life, but *they* lived. James knelt and grabbed her by the shoulders.

"Wulfee. I can't believe—" James hugged her with all the strength she remembered him having.

"By the gods, it's really you, boy. You're alive," she said. "And Maggie." She cried ugly tears. She could hardly catch her breath between sobs. The memory of Gen being killed came back and stabbed at her like a knife. The wolf's mask sat in the blackness of her mind like a boulder that would never move. James was crying with her now. He wasn't the same person since she'd last seen him. She could feel something had changed in him. Wulfee just stared at him for a moment. It was the same young man she found in the arbor, only now he wasn't scared and not as young. *He's strong like... like you...*

"I got shit faced with a wizard, Wulf," James said proudly, tears falling down his bearded cheeks. Wulfee burst out laughing. Maybe he wasn't so different after all. He couldn't stop staring at her, like he knew something had broken inside her, and he could feel it.

James threw one of Pike's arms over his shoulder to hold him up. Wulfee took the other.

"Wait. Where is Gen?" Maggie asked. Wulfee burst out sobbing and hunched over. Maggie broke down in tears as well. Wulfee was barely holding onto whatever bit of herself she had left, and it must have been obvious now. She stood tall and then said, "We should get to the bridge. The Wolf is coming."

"We don't have the time to go back, Culdaine." Adeqor crossed his arms. "You know this. Not even the dead can save you if we get caught between the Wolf and Kallahorn. We go now or not at all."

Maggie looked at James, and Wulfee felt the pain seeping out of her.

"We have to go, Mag. I don't know how much longer you have left. This is our only chance," James said.

James looked at Wulfee, but she already knew what he was going to say.

"I can't go back, Wulfee. The Mother of Nature needs me. Reckon it's about time I stuck to something instead of turning to run," said James. Wulfee smiled. Looked at Maggie, then back at him. She wiped her raw red eyes. *These are your children. Don't fail them.*

"Sticking ain't always the way. Not if you're stuck on the wrong thing. See what it got me?" said Wulfee, holding out her hands. "Nothing. Reckon if you wanna stick, you two should take off somewhere when this is all over. Start a family. Stick for each other, and don't make the same bad choices I did," she said. James and Maggie smiled. "You did good, kid. You rose above your own demons so you could face everyone else's. More than I could say I've ever done for myself. The both of you are better than I could ever dream to be. I've given you everything I can. There are things in my life I can't change. But finding the two of you showed me a light I hadn't seen in far too long." She hung her head in thought for a moment, then said: "Just do me one last favour?"

"Of course." James leaned in. "What is it?"

"Don't turn out like me, eh? Don't ever turn your back on love," she said, and with that, she turned her back and helped Pike stand. The two of them limped towards Rosen and Wulfee knew that whatever happened, if James and Maggie were together, they'd be alright.

PIKE'S WOUND STUNK WHEN Lady Ruwen's wise one dug out the blood-clotted mud. Few come back from a rotting wound like that. Wulfee knew it better than most.

"Looks like the bastard got me after all, Wulf. At least he isn't alive to see me go," said Pike. "Fuck!" he gasped as the wise one stuck her finger into the wound.

"You won't be going anywhere yet, old man." The wise one fingered around in the wound a bit more. "This is nigh but a flesh wound, nothing the ander and a poultice can't fix."

"Why is he still rotting when the earth won't?" Wulfee staked the wise one with her gaze.

"Because bad blood and decay are two different things. And the earth is made of more solid stuff than we." The wise one prodded Pike deeper.

"Fuck!" shouted Pike. Wulfee held his arms down. She couldn't understand what sorcery had stained the world or how it worked. "I don't want any ander. I've seen what it does to a person."

"You've seen what it does to a person when abused," the wise one scoffed. "In the Hesterlands, we grow ander in our gardens for its beauty and for quick access to fresh leaves."

"Just hold on for a few more hours, Pike, and you can die with the rest of us," said Wulfee. She kept peeking out of the tent at the people rushing by. The wise one spread the velvety blue paste on Pike's wound. The old warrior sighed in relief.

"Fuck, Wulf. Easy for you to say," he said. Just then, a tall, thick bearded man with a black scar on his eye stuck his big head into the tent.

"Wulfee?" he said.

"Aye." Wulfee's face was stiff. The man ducked his head and walked in, clad in steel armour with a crow etched into the chest plate.

"I'm Lord Brinley of Dawning. My herald has advised me you were a kihl'dor of the Fells once," he said. "Is this the truth of it?"

"Aye," Wulfee spat.

"That's great news. Great news indeed. We find ourselves in a shit position. None of us will see tomorrow without a bit o' help from the gods. We only have one bit of hope left."

"My hope is gone," Wulfee said. "What is it you've come to me for?"

"We want to send you to Pool to seek the help of the clans of Odhran Ironfist," said Brinley. "They're held up there and—" Wulfee started laughing loudly. Brinley looked disagreeable.

"We've just come from Pool. It was the clans that did *this* to us." She laughed louder. Pike laughed, too, and blood filled the gaps in his teeth. "They're not coming. This is it. This is the end of the Hallow. These are the last prayers for the Old Gods."

"As long as I'm breathing, the Hallow has a chance!" Brinley shouted proudly. And Wulfee felt that the mad bastard actually thought it to be true. She used to have a shite load of blind courage, just the same. But it had all been drained out of her over the years. Like blood from an open wound, she bled herself dry of it. Braden might never know she'd left him all those years ago for love and not the opposite, and her heart throbbed a sharp pain at that thought. All she had left now was the cold and bitter hate for one person. The Wolf. She was going to kill him or die in the pursuit of it, and that was all there was left for her. *No, there is little Sweyne. There is still little Sweyne...*

Wulfee stood taller, prouder. This was her last stand. *This is it.* She finally felt at peace knowing it was going to be over, one way or another. "The kihl'dor Odhran is dead, by my friend here's hand. The mustered clans will fall into a battle for leadership that will end in bloodshed amongst them. Whatever hope there was of bringing them here died with Odhran. We tried to talk with them, and they slaughtered everyone I brought with me. They would have killed both of us too if it wasn't for Pike. They have gone mad beyond reason since the fires went out."

"We can all go there to beg. Surely they can't resist," said Brinley. "The Wolf would have to cross the lake and—"

"They killed all who tried. There were skulls stacked up in crude hills of bone. They slaughtered everyone who came to them for help," Wulfee shouted. She didn't care if this man was a lord or a bard. "I fought against the Wolf's army at Tusk. Their leader fathered my children. Any chance we have to beat him lies with me now."

"So what then?" said Brinley. Wulfee gestured to herself. Ripped and dirty clothing hanging off her sore and haggard body.

"If I knew how to beat him, I would have by now," she said. "But I'm not going to die sitting down like no dog."

Pike sat up and groaned as he got himself to his feet.

"The fighters need shields. All of them." Brinley looked at him sideways, then down at Pike's bloody shield.

"Shields? We don't have enough for half," Brinley said.

"Well, let's make some," Wulfee said. "Take the wood off buildings, the bottom of wagons. Anything. Get every fighter at that bridge a shield."

Brinley nodded in agreement and left the tent. When Pike had been bandaged, he and Wulfee left, too.

As they walked through the dirt roads of Rosen, Wulfee found them barren. Every living person was at the bridge or around it in one of the towers or fortifications. Wulfee saw a child who must have only been five throwing a spear into a target. Men and women, old and young, were preparing to give their life for the land they live on. Some were crying, some were praying, many were cursing, but they were all there for the same cause—they had no other. This was the last stand of Mal Hallow. Wulfee watched as people started pulling boards off hovels. Floorboards, roof boards, siding, or fence boards, it didn't matter. The carpenters cut and hammered them together in small squares, and Wulfee had them nail a curved piece into the back for a handle. Then she helped hand them out. Wulfee and the carpenters instructed other folk, and soon they were producing shields at a fast enough rate to arm the lot of them. There were less than a thousand here, and a haggard bunch at that, but they obeyed Wulfee's word. *Okay, old kihl'dor, what can you pull out of your arse this time?*

"Every person gets one," Wulfee shouted at folk as they passed. "They have enough magics in their bows to kill us from five hundred feet. When the Wolf fires, we hide behind these shields. All night if we have to." To Brinley, she said, "We have to *make* him attack us."

"I saw their bows at Tusk," said Claydon. Wulfee heard that voice and lit up with raw emotion.

"Aye, and I saw *you*. You abandoned your folk and locked them all in the castle. Your own guards were killing us," Wulfee said.

"I did no such thing!" Claydon yelled. "We mounted a defence, and we lost. I tried to defend the Hallow at the crossing!"

"Your guards wouldn't let us leave. They started a riot."

"It was by no words of mine. When I left, I only told them to hold the castle, not stop anyone from leaving."

"So you're admitting you left."

"I retreated strategically to avoid having my family killed."

That pissed Wulfee off. "You're a goddamned coward cunt of a fuck!" She charged at him.

Pike held her back. "Calm, Wulf!"

"Enough!" boomed Brinley. "We're all here now. And we've all made mistakes. And besides, we're counting on you, kihl'dor, to lead this defence. We need to focus on that."

Claydon looked at Wulfee, gave her the old northern sign for luck. Wulfee returned it.

"Aye," she said. Didn't change what she thought about Claydon, though.

"Aye," said Claydon, and Wulfee figured it probably didn't change what he thought about her, either.

Lady Ruwen and Claydon Coldfoot gathered at the round table with their cohorts, studying Brinley's map.

"Scouts have his front line at six hundred feet out from the bridge. They could attack anytime now and be on us in minutes," said Claydon. "They're just waiting for their moment."

Wulfee leaned in and pointed at the map. "He will send the archers first. They may fire arrows at us for days before he sends in his bulk." *And don't forget about the cage, Wulf. You didn't forget about the monster, did you?* "Sweyne is as patient as a hillcat. He'll see how far he can push us into madness before he smashes us to pieces."

Brinley scratched at his scar. "What matters is we keep them from crossing that bridge for as long as we can. Just give the seer a chance to work his magics at the Mountains of the Mother. If this army gets past this bridge, there is nowhere for James to hide. They'll swamp the seer, and we'll all be doomed." He pounded the crow on his steel chest plate. "We wasted so much time fighting each other that I never stopped to think about how fragile our kingdom was. How weak our morals had become. I never imagined my very identity would be threatened."

"If we die here at this bridge, we die as folk of the Hallow," said Ruwen, pounding the bear on *her* chest plate. Claydon did the same on his mammoth. With no symbols to touch for luck, Wulfee spat into the dirt.

The four of them walked to the bridge and inspected the spikes in the ground. They were sturdy enough, sharp enough.

Wulfee kicked one. "Have the folk dig these out and lower them. Cover them in dirt. Let the horses charge us, and at the last moment we will raise them into the chests of the steeds. We can take out the whole front line in an instant and halt the rest."

"You would have our soldiers stand in front of the bridge?" said Claydon. "And who do you think is mad enough to agree to lead this?"

"I will lead them myself. But we must hurry." She loved the look of feebleness that fell over Claydon as he realized she was serious. *A kihl'dor does not fear death, lord cunt. Welcome to the Fells.*

Claydon ordered them to follow Wulfee's plan, and they frantically dug out the spikes.

Wulfee looked up to the blue sky. The sun was setting fast. It was betwixt night and day, a time when the world was alive with magics that most were blind to see. A time when the wolves ruled the wild.

Armed folk ready to kill filled the watchtowers that shouldered both sides of the bridge. The tower doors were barricaded off and locked so the people could rain arrows on those trying to break down the door.

"How many do we have?" Wulfee asked.

"Eight hundred. Or close to it," said Brinley. "Less if you exclude the children." Wulfee closed her eyes and took a deep breath.

"The Wolf has well over five thousand folk marching behind him," said Claydon. "This is going to take one hell of a fight." He turned and sighed, sounding unhopeful.

Five thousand is more than all the people living in the Fells.

At her place on the bridge, Wulfee saw Pike limping with one crutch and making his way through the throng of soldiers to get closer to the front.

When he was close enough she said, "You still have time to get out of here, old man. Head off to the mountains like you talked about."

"I can't go, Wulfee. You know I can't leave your side when there's a fight to be had." He smiled. "I was always meant to die here. Defending this land against invaders. It's in my blood to do so. The same as yours. Folk of the Fells. The Oaths of Feldarra."

He stuck his fist under his chin and nodded.

"The wise one dressed your wounds with ander again?" said Wulfee after she returned the old northern sign for luck. A poultice was wrapped around Pike's leg with neat precision, and it smelled of the blue paste.

"I needed to be out here for this," said Pike. "Front lines."

He gave a half smile that wrinkled his whole face, and Wulfee saw some kind of sick joy in his eyes, like a hungry man coming to dinner and his feast was death.

Wulfee looked out to the field as the setting sun stained the sky blood red and violet, and saw the first of the Wolf's soldiers break the front line. A hundred horses came plummeting through the valley and a hundred more behind them.

"Those don't look like archers," said Claydon.

He's rushing in... It wasn't like Sweyne, and she didn't like it.

"I'm going to the front lines to lead the folk with the spikes," said Wulfee.

"And I'm with her," said Pike. They crossed the bridge, bringing folk with them to the front. Wulfee and the soldiers were packed tightly on the bridge, twenty folk abreast and armed with spears and shields. Layer upon layer in phalanx formation—like Emmer led the Feldarran warriors of old. When the person in front fell, the person behind lowered their spear.

The ground was shaking beneath Wulfee's feet now. They were seconds away from the impact. Down the line, a hundred spikes were ready at the soldiers' feet to raise up at her command. She held her new axe in one hand, gripped a piece of the door to someone's house in the other, and took a deep breath. She looked down at the spike below her and imagined that

Gen would have probably held two of them, one in each arm. *I'm so sorry. I'm so sorry, but if I could go back, I would still have taken you, Gen. Because you changed me. You made me realize what life could be without a grudge, without regret. You showed me true innocence, and I wouldn't trade it. I'm so sorry, Gen. And Braden, I hope you know your mommy loves you, always had. If I could go back, I wouldn't have left you. I hope you know that, somewhere in your heart. I would never have left you if I had another chance. I would trade everything to go back to that day.*

"It will be an honour to die by your side, Wulfee," said Pike.

"Let's face that old cunt called death one last time, eh?" said Wulfee. *It's always one last time.* The horse riders were howling, chanting a war cry, waving their black wolf banners and the red eagle. The ground shook harder as they closed in. All the folk who lined up to take the blow looked at Wulfee with wide, expectant eyes. They were waiting for her word to rise. Waiting on her word to take what could be their final breaths. They got closer, and she grit her teeth. Too early and they would rear up and surround them. Too late and they would be trampled. She heard the hooves rolling like thunder, the howls, and the chants of the riders. Rumbling, roaring, waiting. Waiting. The smell of the Wolf's army was on her now. Waiting. The folk all looked at her nervously. Now? When? They were asking anxiously with their eyes. She looked out and could see the sweat on the brow of the woman leading the charge. Could see the wrinkles in her skin. Saw her smile as she raised her lance and readied herself for what she thought would be a clean kill.

Wait for it...

Wait for it...

"Now!" Wulfee screamed, and they dropped their weapons and rose with the spikes. Held them firmly in place as they pierced the chests of a hundred horses. The riders were flung off and skewered into the rows of spear folk behind. Wulfee impaled a big white destrier, and the impact sent her onto her back. Horses squealed. Flesh smacked on flesh. Slammed, panicked. Kicked, rolled. Folk died on top of her, below her. Steel squelched into flesh. And Wulfee got up, finding an axe just in time to chop down another enemy. Pike was fighting without ever moving from the spot he stood. All around, the horses scattered. Folk screamed, killed, died. Confused, they just pressed and pressed. Many had dismounted, and Wulfee lost her axe in the gut of some bastard who tried to chop her down. She was trying to get back to the bridge but couldn't tell which direction she was going in. Horses galloped all around her, squealing. And the screams. *So many screams. Who?* Folk muddied the dirt red, and her feet were soaking in it. *Wolf. Where?* Then she heard the snap crack of a thousand bow strings and ran.

"Shields! Pick up your shields!" she shouted, but wasn't sure if anyone heard her. Couldn't even find her own damn shield. She knelt to pick a stray one off the ground, and then saw a rider coming right for her, steel sword raised and about to drop on her head. She ducked and tried to jump out of the way, but instead, collided with the breast of the horse. Her head was turning when she landed hard on her head—*fuck*. She thought she might be dying. Tried to stand and found she couldn't tell which way was up. Arrows rained down all around her as she raised her shield with shaky arms. One thud marked the first arrow, and two more came soon after. She heard another snap of the bowstrings. *They're firing on their own damn people.* She lowered the shield to see another wayward horse coming and dove out of the way before it trampled her. Wulfee found herself tumbling down a steep riverbank. Her body was being torn up and bruised by rocks, and dust clawed her dry throat. Soon the water bit her, and she sank like a stone. Her arms wouldn't move. She finally felt at rest. Soon she couldn't breathe and was sure that she was drowning.

MEMORIES OF THE DEAD

THE DEAD VALLEY WAS a barren, rocky place. Full of bones and ashes, forgotten souls and lost time. James felt no warmth there, and the black clouds overhead seemed to have eaten the light out of day. He prayed to the gods that his kin could hold the bridge long enough for him to cross this forsaken place. The castle stretched out before him. Its silhouette dominated the landscape and demanded attention from anywhere in the valley. The wonderfully ugly, the beautifully monstrous Kallahorn. The castle was like a cold shadow James could never quite escape. Every time he thought he was leaving the place behind, he got called back to it. Maybe his destiny was somewhere behind the castle in those mountains.

James's dad was obsessed with Kallahorn. He claimed that the power of the gods was hidden somewhere below that dark stone. The Lovasi were obsessed with it, too. Kelson the Conqueror, found the black walls already erected when he'd arrived in the north. Its walls were made from a black stone that looked like hardened nytewood stumps made with magics that even the Lovasi couldn't understand. Kallahorn was Ardura's biggest mystery. Why it was there and who built it were answers lost to time. The

Conqueror spent more time there than anywhere else in Ardura and built many more structures on top or into what was already there. Three dozen turret towers interspersed along thick, curtain walls of greasy black stone circled the castle. A twenty-foot wide trench surrounded the walls. It was three times as deep as it was wide, and the castellans over the years had filled the bottom with jagged scrap metal and wooden spikes and countless bones. The northernmost wall was built directly into the mountain face, and a great forge once burned beneath the rock there. James's dad had told him that the forge had burned for thrice times three thousand years without ever going out. The towering barbican housed three portcullis gates forged of Daggland steel. The keep was a castle in its own right, cornered by four drum towers and surrounded by a moat; a second set of curtain walls were lined with turret towers. It stood half as tall as the living nytewood that grew in the courtyard. Its leaves would fall all around, beautifully golden against the black stone.

"It's a long way around, man. But it'll get us to the Mother's shrine without having to go through the castle." Eurick glanced at the ridge and ran his dirty finger through the air, tracing the mountainside. "I've heard that it's been done before. Surely I can find the way, even with these raggedy maps."

James saw Maggie was losing strength again. She was holding onto her reins with a rugged determination, sweat dripping from her face, dark bags under her eyes.

"We're going to make it, Mag. Hold on for me." James was starting to feel desperate, and he hated it.

"Don't worry about me. I'll be here with you." Maggie gave a thumbs up and nearly fell off her horse. James slowed his steed to a trot so he could be close to Maggie as they rode. They listened to Itchy sing as they followed Eurick into the mountainside. Mineera watched them and wrote on her parchment. *Is she listening to us talk?* James had felt strangely threatened by Mineera and didn't understand why.

"What are you doing that for?" asked James. He'd meant to ask her a dozen times over the course of their journey. Mineera gave him a cheeky grin.

"I'm inspired by you, James," she said simply.

"Inspired?"

Mineera tucked her papers away into her sack.

"The people of New Lovas, Neira, Ni'an, and all the other countries of the east dream of what exotic things lie to the west, beyond the Old Sea. Some of the wealthier folk have sailed to the Hesterlands and Esher. Some have even made it as far as Ayeland, following old Lovasi roads or sailing the Roaring Sea to Harbourtown. But most will never set foot in these lands, yet they long for the stories they hold. You see, it was common knowledge that wild barbarians, savage as they are dirty, live in the northlands of Ardura you call Mal Hallow and the Fells. I voyaged here to record the tales of such people. But you folk aren't the savage, wild people I expected. Though dirty, you have hearts just the same as the folk in the east. Full of love and hate. Hardship and well-being. It's quite beautiful, really." She held a finger up to James's face and wrote something down. "I used to believe I had it all figured out. I spent my whole life learning to read and write, and I dreamed of writing my account of the history of the world one day, just like the great Audacio. Making a name for myself as one of the eminent scholars of Lovas. But there is so much more to life that I haven't experienced. I haven't loved, I've barely lived. *This* is really something. I had never been hungry before, truly hungry. And amid my suffering, cursing the pains in my stomach, I realized that *this* is what it means to be alive. To *really* feel something. I don't even know if I'll see tomorrow, and it makes today so much more special."

James still didn't really understand what it meant that he inspired her, but seeing the peace on her face made him feel like it must not be that bad of a feeling. He was grateful to provide it for her.

They rode for hours through the dead valley, and James got a whole new understanding of why it had its name. The dead weren't resting easy, and they gathered here in troves. James remembered Gran's tales from the Cycle. The Mal had used their blood magics on entire battlefields, trapping every soul who died. Hundreds of hundreds, maybe thousands of thousands, of lost souls were forced to relive their last actions over and over. Cold Daggland warriors and rugged Mal were maimed, sliced up, and bludgeoned into disfigurement. The dead were all ready to go home, and James was ready to send them down.

As they approached the castle from the far side of the valley, James noticed Ellorin's thoughts stirring in his mind again. *The dead just don't stay dead. Not for you.* He could hear the Banshee having a conversation with King Alder as if she were right in front of him.

"Adeqor got to Lord Baleth somehow. He used him to spread these words like a plague. He used him to free Bazal. He's left us no choice but to awaken the Mother to close the Gateway," said Calen Alder.

James could see him in his mind's eye as clearly as he could recall his own dad's face. And Ellorin was there with him.

"That's exactly what Adeqor wants us to do," Ellorin said.

"The world will die if we don't."

"If we close the Gateway, he will come. He will look for the World Walker, too. He has more than likely already found him, long before he freed Bazal. You should have never lost track of Culdaine. You should have come to me as soon as you saw what he was. Adeqor has been planning this. Probably since Lindis."

"Lindis burned over four hundred years ago."

"I don't need reminding of Lindis from the likes of you."

Ellorin's rage was burning inside of James.

"How would we fight him?" Alder asked. "How would we interrupt such a plan?"

"The songs of Old Yehven."

"Don't be foolish, Ellorin, I need you if I have any hope in this," Alder said. "The songs will consume you."

"I will be consumed one way or another. If the Words elevate to the point of another Starfall, none of it will matter. I can gather the Hawka from the arbors. I can weave their minds to my control with a silver thread of song. The Words are strong enough for that, at least. I can use them to track the World Walker and kill him before any of this even starts. Make sure he will play no part in it. I'll take out every settlement in the north if I have to. If that's what it takes. If Culdaine comes to realize his power..."

"He won't," Alder barked. *"We'll make sure of it. It's Adeqor gaining his power back that we have to worry about right now. I know it was him that freed Bazal. And we know it was Bazal who taught Baleth the Words because Adeqor can't. If we find Bazal, he can help us..."*

James shook his head. *What the fuck is going on?* He rubbed his temples—his head was throbbing suddenly. Ellorin's memories were latching onto his mind, taking root and growing into his own.

"Bazal is a traitor to the Ailaryan Order. We don't work with traitors," Ellorin said sharply. *"Our only hope to save this world and to build a new one is to keep the Mother alive long enough for the Words to die. It could take decades, centuries. But eventually Humans will die without the elements, and there will be no one left to worship Karaat. His power will fade to nothing and so will His Words. Whoever lives will be stripped of all civilization, culture, and humanity. Their minds will be clay for moulding. If someone, somewhere, is using the Words, finding them will be easy amongst the squalor. So long as the Mother lives, her spell on Adeqor will hold."*

"As long as Adeqor can't speak the Words, we have a chance. If I have to stay here and guard the shrine myself, then so be it. I will fight to protect the New World."

"You couldn't fight, unless..." Ellorin stopped mid sentence as if she realized what Alder was thinking of doing. Alder looked at her and smiled. Ellorin glared back at him. *"You wouldn't."*

"I have to," Alder said painfully.

"Your family. Your children..."

Ellorin's pain pierced James's chest.

"...My children will make heirs to a great new world. If I can save it for them. Surely, the Ailaryan Order will see that they live as payment for my part in this."

"Of course, your children are under our protection. But the power that the Blood Words give you will kill you in the end. Even if you succeed, you can never see them again."

"I know the legend of Blood Words. Like you said, we will all be consumed, anyway."

"You can't carve them into your own skin... you'll need—"

"You."

"I gave up on blood magics when I left the Ailaryan Order."

Ellorin's heart was throbbing though James's. An old thrill had coursed through her veins that flowed through James now. Her thoughts danced freely in James's mind without restraint.

If I could sing the songs of Yehven again, why not use blood magics, too? Why shouldn't I?

Alder said, "The Ailaryan Order must return, and you're its harbinger. I know this will be difficult for you. But with the Blood Words, the seer can't use his magics."

"I'll do it. It's time to bring the New World. I will carve you into a god. I will summon Karaat once more."

The memories were all mixed before, an incoherent mess, but they were coming to him clearly now.

"Are you okay?" said Maggie. James only saw her mouth move.

"Fine," he said, a chill rolling down his spine. He looked at Adeqor and didn't quite know why. He was walking with Eurick at the front of the pack. Barefoot and filthy. Wearing the same torn rags that James found him in. *Or did he find you?* He thought back to that first night with Eurick. *To be that far into the mountains, he must have left long before the Hawka came... he didn't come to rescue you. He came to take you to the wizard out of bound duty. This has all been a careful plan...* The aura around Adeqor was undeniable. He had something in him far more powerful than a soul. It was like the power of the whole world and all the stars were inside of his heart, and he could let it go at any moment. James had been told time after time that the wizard was not to be trusted, yet he had listened to every word the old Warlock had said to him. Adeqor turned around right then and gave James a knowing grin. Like he knew James didn't trust him but knew he wouldn't do a thing about it. Eurick turned around also, a strained look on his face, like Adeqor was making him anxious as well.

Eurick held out his map. "Still a few miles till we reach the pass. We'll have to go on foot from there. Pray to the gods that those folk can hold the bridge for us for the night. We're just sitting crows out here. Nowhere to hide." All of their hopes lay in Eurick, getting them there undetected. They wouldn't win any battles, not now.

"We'll set up camp here," said Eridan. "No point in us going any further. We'll be here when you return." James gave the sign for luck—he was hardly paying mind—and kept riding with Maggie by his side. With muffled sounds of goodbyes behind him, James looked up at the wizard and the transporter leading the way. *You've been following them the whole way. You didn't question much of anything... You never even asked*—Maggie rode up beside him.

"What's wrong?" she said.

"Nothing."

"It's the wizard," Maggie said. "He's bothering you. I can see it in the way you watch him."

"He's false," said James. "I don't know what he really wants."

"In every dream, he was leading you here. He's important, somehow."

"Maybe he's got something to do with the dreams we have. To drive our motivations," said James. Terror glossed Maggie's eyes, like perhaps she already had that thought herself.

James glared at Adeqor. *Confront him. Now.*

"I need to talk to him."

"Be careful," Maggie sighed. "James, look at me. I'm serious. He's dangerous."

James was drowning in her eyes. "I just need to talk to him." It took all his will to look away. He snapped the reins, and his horse sped up towards Adeqor.

The wizard and Eurick were arguing about something when James rode up. Adeqor glanced over his shoulder at him.

"Ah, finally come to lead like a proper king rather than muck around in the back, eh?"

"What's your plan, wizard?" James said.

Adeqor looked surprised, then he grinned widely.

"My plan?"

"You've told me as little as you could this whole time. You've given me this sword, and you've dragged me all of this way. But I can handle it from here. If everything is as you say, then we don't need you here anymore." Adeqor stopped his horse. Turned around slowly.

"Don't need me, eh?" he said coldly.

"If everything is as you say. If I can open the Gateway with the great sword *Essikah* and save the Mother of Nature, then we don't need you anymore," said James. "You've done your job. You can go back to your arbor and celebrate, alone, with all the shine you can drink. Eurick will take me the rest of the way."

Eurick gulped.

Adeqor smiled. He seemed woefully sober.

"You're getting braver, young seer. You couldn't even confront your own lies to yourself when I first found you, let alone confront the lies of another. Seems as if you really are growing into that cute little role of a hero. Too bad we will write the history from *my* point of view." James balled his hands into fists. "If I told you what's really going on, you would crumble. You're so weak you can't even control your own mind. Always doubting yourself, fearing the things set out before you. If you knew what I really was, you would turn and run. Like you always do."

"I'll show you what weak looks like, wizard." James pulled out *Essikah*. It had become as light as a bone as he filled it with dead souls. He pulled energies from below and filled himself with strength. "We don't want your help anymore. We will go on from here without you." The dead filled him with adrenaline. "This is my task and mine alone. Either you tell me the truth of it all, tell me what's in all of this for you, or we fight to the death. I know you don't want me dead or you wouldn't have gone through all of this trouble to get me here."

A twisted and vile laugh of satisfaction came from Adeqor's throat. He waved his arms in the air like he was trying to conjure some magics.

"We were so close," he said. "Why do you Humans feel so compelled to have your feelings validated in the utmost crucial of circumstances? We have death all around us, and you'd risk the small sphere of safety you've found for yourself and your loved ones?" Adeqor tilted his head at Maggie, and it made James's stomach turn. The wizard fell silent as he glared at Maggie, at Eurick, back to James. Finally, up to the black clouds above, then sighed. "Honestly, I thought you would have figured it out on your own by now. Especially after defeating the Banshee. She had many nasty secrets inside of that head of hers. She's been a thorn in my side for far too long now, that one. But alas, you have caught me. It was I who freed Bazal from his prison. I knew he would start spreading his magics. Then it was just a matter of time before Ellorin awakened the Mother. It was a perfect plan, really. Foolproof. But you could not do this without me, seer. Don't think for a second you'd be anywhere near this place if it wasn't for me."

James pressed his horse forward, *Essikah* drawn, threatening Adeqor enough to make him move his horse away. James's head was spinning with broken memories.

"Tell me the truth, wizard! What do you want?" he screamed, spittle flying from his mouth. Memories of the dead pecked at the inside of his head. Hundreds of thoughts, last words, love and hate, and anger and joy flooded him. The minds of every dead soul left behind in this cruel world converging into him, powering him up. He was feeding off it. Off of their pain and their strength.

"Only I can open the door to the Mother's shrine. It is hidden under a veil of magics that *I* created and sealed behind a door. You couldn't even open the door if I wasn't holding your hand." Adeqor chuckled and took a drink. "But you are not Human, oh no. Far greater, but still infantile in your understanding. You are a World Walker reborn, James. There is a reason you have never felt right, why you've always been uncomfortable. You were born for one purpose. To bring death. To stop new life crowding in to take the place of old. Like Hendurinn."

James swung *Essikah*, but he missed badly. He couldn't fight for shite from horseback. His mind was flooded, tripping over itself in thought. He nearly fell off his horse.

"Hendurinn was a hero."

"No," Adeqor said, "In the end, he really wasn't."

James felt depleted.

"Why are you doing this to me?" James asked. Dark clouds covered the sun like Ellorin's memories taking over James's own. Every breath was strained, and his heart was threatening to burst. *How can you save the world when you can't even save yourself?*

Adeqor put his ice-cold hand on James's back.

"You're a half-god, Culdaine. The World Walker. You're meant to bring life through death. I need you to kill the Mother of Nature so I can *live* again."

SCARS

WULFEE SWALLOWED MORE WATER. More arrows splashed down around her, and she reckoned she was pulling all kinds of luck out of her arse right now. The thick water was pulling her down, sucking at her boots and tugging on her clothes. Wulfee kicked and swam until she finally felt the mud beneath her. As she clawed herself up out of the water, Wulfee saw the shadows of arrows move towards her. Then the sharp sting of one piercing through her hand. She watched the shaft wobble back and forth for a moment before the pain hit her hard and fierce.

"Fuck!" she screamed, wrenching her hand with the arrow out of the mud and climbed up the steep riverbank towards the closest chunk of people. "Shield!" she yelled. But nobody was listening. *At least we're still fighting*. And when the arrows came again, she hid beneath someone else's shield. The person beside her took an arrow through the neck and collapsed. Wulfee moved forward and took the shield of a dead woman. She could hear the snap of a thousand bow strings above the din. And she ducked beneath her shield again. Two arrows thumped into it. She stood up and pulled the arrow out of her hand and didn't realize she had started screaming—not in pain but in battle-drunken madness. Now she was bleeding badly. She ripped the dead woman's shirt and wrapped her wound. *Sweyne...*

Wulfee examined the battlefield.

The fight was still in front of the bridge, not on it yet. A mess of dead bodies, horses, carcasses, splintered wood, and arrow shafts blocked the way. The Wolf's soldiers were working to clear it. Archers rained arrows down on them from the bridge's watchtowers. Pike was still fighting on the front line. Wulfee ran towards the bridge again and fell in behind the battle cries of Claydon Coldfoot and his two sons, Aron and Macts.

Then she saw the thick, black bars of the cage, the long ropes dragging it, and the rotten thing inside.

"We have to get the spikes back up," she called to Claydon through the din.

"Out front? There is no bloody way. It's flooded with bodies now. There is no way," said Claydon.

Wulfee shook her head.

"We have to try. The drayke will run us over and ground us all into the dust."

Claydon scoped the field, mouth hanging open. He saw the black cage and looked back at her.

"Well, fuck."

"Pike is still out there. If we can get to him, we can form another line. We can use the bodies as a shield and get the spikes set up behind them," said Wulfee. Claydon and his sons hurried towards the front without another word.

Wulfee watched as waves of the Wolf's soldiers poured in on foot between showers of arrows. They smashed into the front lines of spears and struggled to get far.

"Hold!" Wulfee shouted as she made her way towards the frontline.

The Wolf's soldiers could only make ground when the arrows fell. But the arrows continued to fall. The brigade kept pushing, and Wulfee kept shouting.

"Hold!" As if the folk holding didn't already know that was their job.

When she got to the front, she saw Pike fighting with a small group. Circled by dead horses so that the enemy couldn't quite surround them. They weren't the target, anyway. The bridge was, and the folk on the front lines were slowly being slaughtered. *By the gods…*

"Pike!" she screamed, but he couldn't hear her through the din. "Pike!" she screamed again, and the old warrior looked up this time. "The drayke, Pike. It's coming. We need to raise the spikes again." He just nodded and yelled at the folk who were fighting with him.

"Aron!" Claydon screamed. "We need those spikes raised. Take twenty folks with you and go!" Aron nodded and went to it. More arrows fell, and Wulfee took two shafts in her shield. Closer and closer, the cage came. It rolled forward behind waves of chain-clad fighters. She knew that Sweyne would have convinced every one of them to give their life to take this bridge.

"Most of the spikes are splintered!" Aron shouted.

"Use the splintered ends!" Claydon shouted back. And wave after wave of soldiers came at them, and wave after wave fell against the spears of the Hallow folk. Wulfee wouldn't be driven back. She resisted each thrust in turn. Took each blow on her shield and held her ground. She picked up a spear and joined in the offensive. Kill after kill, Wulfee held her spot. And with every step, the drayke came closer. *And can we hold the line then?* She reckoned not. Wulfee could hear the thing squealing now. Smelled its burning, rusty stench in the stale air. The field was full of the enemy. It was really just a matter of how long Wulfee and the Hallow army could hold them. And if they could stop the drayke, Wulfee might see out the night. *You couldn't save your son, and you couldn't save Gen, but you can save James and Maggie, and maybe the whole damn world if you just hold out the night.* She was bleeding from an open hole in her hand that would surely need ander, but she found a spear and joined the line for what she reckoned might be her last go.

The thumping of steel on wood. The squelching of steel in flesh. The cracked and torn voices of the suffering, begging for help Wulfee couldn't give. Over and over, until her arm was numb with the pain of burning muscle, and then still, she carried on. Folk beside her were covered in sweat and blood. Sinews popped out like ropes on Pike's neck as he fought. Wulfee was sure he was possessed by the Stag Himself.

And then the drayke squealed like some kind of rabid bat. Wulfee peered around, and by the way everyone was looking back at her, she could tell they all thought the same thing.

They had uncaged the beast.

"Ready the spikes!" she called out, but couldn't see any of the folk who had gone out to raise them. Claydon was nowhere in sight, either. It was only her and Pike, and a hundred other folk sentenced to death. The man next to her looked tired and sore, like he wanted to give up.

"It's not our time, yet," Wulfee said, and the man seemed to light up. The moon hadn't even reached midnight yet, and she reckoned that the sun was still a long way off.

"Clear!" she heard shouts from the enemy. "Clear!"

"The spikes!" Wulfee shouted the moment she knew the drayke was coming. But there was no one to hear her. They had been pushed back onto the bridge now. And each wave of arrows was taking out more and more of them. The Wolf's soldiers were whittling Wulfee's down like a twig.

"Ahhh!" the Wolf's men screamed horribly. Many of them flew ten feet into the air, others melted like candles into piles of flaming mush. Then she saw the beast, standing on four legs thrice the height of a horse and covered in black scales. It had crooked bat-like ears that were ripped up and horribly twisted.

"Don't look it in the eyes!" people were shouting. "Its eyes! Its eyes! Don't look at its eyes!"

Folks all around were melting into charred piles of steaming mush. Ayelish and Mal. *The drayke knows no difference.* Wulfee gripped a spear as she indulged a wild thought.

"Jump, Pike!" she said, flinging herself into the dying river again just as the drayke trampled through the front line and annihilated the people she was standing with.

Wulfee heard another splash before she surfaced and knew that Pike had followed her. She surfaced to the sound of a horrible squealing. The river slowly carried her away, and she watched from the water as the wingless dragon ran across the length of the bridge. It took dozens upon dozens of spears into its thick, scaly body as it tore soldiers open with dagger-like claws. The drayke ripped them apart with its gauntlet of teeth and turned them into puddles with its eyes. *What the fuck is this thing... Swenye must have pulled this from Hell.* She let the river carry her as Wulfee gawked at the beast. Its scales were oily black, slimy and rotten, infested with maggots. Its crimson eyes were burning, killing, destroying. It ran through the mass of Hallow folk and swatted them down like flies. Wulfee wondered if she'd be better off to just let the river carry her away. The folk below the bridge were trying to collapse the drayke with their pickaxes and had absolutely no luck. It was too strong, too sturdy, and they had clearly done nothing like it before. Soon, they all abandoned the cause and ran.

On the other side of the river, the Wolf's brigade cheered. That was enough to snap Wulfee out of her trance. *One more braid, old braud. One more...* Wulfee grabbed a hold of Pike, who was floating next to her, struggling to swim with his cut up leg. She dragged him to the shore, and they got to their feet. The folk of the Hallow refused to retreat. Brinley Scareye led them from the left. His daughters, the three Crows of Dawning, were by his side waving the black crow on gold above them, and their army was screaming behind them. Lady Ruwen led from the right, waving the black bear on blue she had stitched with the names of her dead children, each killed by an Ayelish soldier. She was screaming so fiercely Wulfee reckoned she was probably more deadly than any bear, and her whole crew was feeding off her energy. They would fight to their deaths; Wulfee could count on that much at least. The Wolf's army flooded the bridge, ran across behind the drayke, and the fight picked up on the other side. And then she saw him. The rotten, yellow wolf helm bobbing above all the rest. Blue and black wolf flag over his shoulder. He sat smugly on his horse, safe behind hundreds of armed fighters.

"You fucking bastard!" she screamed into the throng. Her veins were hot with bad blood. She ran towards him, but a fight erupted in front of her.

Brinley had the drayke surrounded and was pushing it back towards the bridge. Prodding it from every angle, but it ripped them all apart, slowly, one by one. Not one of them could pierce it deep enough to do any harm. Then the beast roared out like a thousand rabid bats burning in the hot sun. It swung its head around and melted Brinley's oldest daughter, Tilda. *By the gods...* Brinley screamed and fell to his knees. He battered the ground with a gauntleted fist and a madness took over him. Wulfee hadn't even realized her hand was covering her mouth. The Wolf's army flooded the bridge and started flowing across. *By the gods, Sweyne, what sorcery is this?*

It was all over. They had lost the bridge in hours, let alone holding out the night. *Another failure, Wulf. You've doomed James and Maggie. You couldn't save a goddamned thing!* Then the wolves howled. *Wolves?* She didn't remember wolves. Another pack picked up the call, and she reckoned there must have been a thousand of them. They howled and howled louder. And she heard them charging. Wulfee couldn't see a thing but bodies, mingling and killing, falling and dying. Eagles came from above and picked at the drayke. The drayke swatted and nipped at them easily but was distracted enough that Brinley threw his spear through one of its eyes. Wulfee felt a primal hate seeping out of the lord as he loosed the spear. It was contagious, and she gripped her own spear tighter. The drayke writhed and twisted, and that was enough for the wolves to get in close. They jumped and bit from every angle. Ruwen stuck her spear through its forehead. Somehow, the drayke still lived as it moved and wriggled and swatted the wolves down, melting folk with its good eye.

And then Wulfee saw the Rangers coming down from the hills in the south, out of the Wick Arbor. *Skincrawlers... they came in the bodies of beasts. They bloody came. Good gods, Wulf, its another fucking miracle.* Dozens of wild Giy'er ran in front of them, crushing the Wolf's soldiers like a rockslide of flesh. The Rangers rained arrows down on the Wolf from the sides, forcing the brigand lord to keep pushing towards the bridge or retreat. Bears, hillcats, great horned elk, and wolverines ran out of the arbor behind the Giy'er towards the throng of Ayelish from their rear.

Then, behind Wulfee, from the north, came a rolling thunder, and thousands of mounted clansfolk burst onto the horizon. Horns bellowed out, rabid screams echoed in unison, shaking the ground with the thunder of their coming. *The clans... by the gods...* The Wolf had lost control of his army and some retreated back towards the Rangers. Others kept on pushing north, and the clansfolk rolled in and slaughtered them. The Wolf's army was scattered. The battlefield was in complete chaos. The clansfolk came smashing into the front of the main bulk with the force of a hundred-hundred rocks. Tess was out in front leading them, as vicious as all Hell.

The drayke was still fighting off the wolves and eagles, two spears sticking out of its head. Wulfee gripped her spear and ran at the thing. It whipped its tree trunk of a tail and swiped its steel claws blindly. Wulfee rolled under its tail as it swung around to face her. She felt like it could turn her to ash at any second, but the drayke was swatting at eagles. She dove into the air and thrust her spear through its other eye—and screamed.

Hot, sticky sludge burned Wulfee's arm as her spear slid all the way into the beast's eye. She cradled her hand as she fell off the drayke, and her breath was smashed out of her by the ground. Red slime burned her flesh and oozed into the open wound from the arrow. Wulfee screamed wickedly.

She rubbed it on the ground, on her clothes, desperately trying to make the burning stop as it cauterized her flesh. When the drayke rolled over and hit the ground, Wulfee could have sworn thunder cracked above. She got up again. Folk were stabbing the drayke at every angle. But it got up and spun in a circle like a cat chasing its tail. *Just fucking die.* Then Tess stood in front of it, timing the spin, and with one swing of her battle axe, took off one of its legs. Struck right behind the knee where the drayke had no scales. It rolled over, and the Mal warriors and Rangers swarmed it, and they filled it with iron and steel. Sword and axe, spear and arrow. Brinley Scareye attacked it most viciously. As he struck the killing blow to the drayke's skull, Wulfee saw his steel eye shining in the moonlight. Pike was beside her still. Sweat dripped from his brow, and blood splattered on his face. It was the dark of night, but the moon was burning brightly. Wulfee could see the Wolf and his helm shining once more. He was crossing the bridge now. Came to join the fight to boost morale. *So proud he won't even turn and run. He was too sure of himself.* Wulfee looked at Pike. The old warrior put his fist under his chin and nodded.

"Go get him," he said. Wulfee picked up an axe, gripped it like she was wringing Sweyne's neck already, and moved through the throng to meet the Wolf.

Pike battered folk aside, clearing the way for her as she approached Sweyne. The Wolf was killing folk with his waraxe, making a show of it, howling and hooting. He hadn't acted at all like she thought he would. He had used none of the same tactics and had none of the same patience. This was a desperate version of the man she once loved. A low-down imitation of who he once was. He had caused her the greatest pains in her life. Chewed her up and spit her out time and time again. As the years went on, he killed every ounce of Etta left inside of her. All that was left was a hardened shell called Wulfee. Kihl'dor of the Feldarra. The shield of Mal Hallow. And all she had left was to kill Sweyne.

"Sweyne! You fucking bastard. Come and fight me," she yelled. "*I'll fucking take your head off like you did to Gen. I'll fucking leave you for the damn dogs... you fucking—*" She was muttering to herself like a madwoman.

He turned his head, yellowed wolf helm gleaming in the moonlight. All around Wulfee, folk slashed, cut, killed, and died. Bled and screamed, cried, begged, and prayed.

First, he walked towards her, then he ran. And she met his attack with a hard swing of her axe. The bastard moved aside, and she nearly slipped. *Easy now, Wulf. Slow it down.* Wulfee knew Pike was standing by. He'd step in if he had to. But this was *her* fight. She needed to take this bastard's life and let the gods see her do it. He came at her as calm as a wolf. He sliced the air with his axe a few times to let Wulfee see his blade, then he went on the offensive. And Wulfee countered his attacks with ease. He moved around her at varying speeds, trying to trip her up. His armour looked thick and hard, but he seemed to move in it with grace.

"Why have you done all of this, Sweyne? What madness has crept into you?" Wulfee cried. The Wolf didn't respond. And Wulfee almost thought she saw the wolf mask snarl at her and give a twisted smile. He swung his axe, and she moved aside. He came at her with all the confidence she remembered. His axe swings were precise and calculated the way she remembered.

"*The axe only went where he wanted it to go,*" Sweyne had once said when he taught her combat.

Wulfee countered every movement, every blow. She noticed his braids hanging out from under the wolf mask. They were dark black without a fleck of grey. And Wulfee felt sick. *Who is this?* She countered another swing. He moved like Sweyne in every way. The fluid wielding of his axe was unmistakable. But he was too skinny in the neck, and his beard was dark black, too. *Sweyne would be at least half grey by now. Who is this?* The Wolf seemed to have noticed her hesitation and rushed in with his waraxe, but Wulfee was too quick and jumped away. For a brief moment, the Wolf exposed his torso under the armpit, and without thinking, Wulfee swung her axe. It sank deep into the flesh there. Hot blood rolled down her hands. The Wolf dropped his weapon and stood frozen. She kicked the bastard in the chest, and he fell backwards. But something didn't feel right. He crawled backwards on his heels and elbows, leaving dark streaks of blood gleaming in the moonlight as Wulfee walked him down. He stopped moving. His breaths were wet and gurgly.

"Let the gods see I'm the one who killed you," Wulfee said, standing over him.

She took off the wolf helm.

Her heart skipped. And she lost her breath. The man staring back at her had a large scar on his cheek under his right eye. *The same scar as—*

What the fuck... no. no no no no no. The fuck, no. She dropped the mask and took a step back. The din of war rang out around her, thrumming in her ears, her chest. She couldn't breathe. Couldn't think. *No no no no no it can't be. It's not true. It can't be.* She studied the face of the man before her once more. He looked just like Sweyne did twenty years ago. *For the gods' sake no. Why? Why why why?* She leaned over, tears falling off her face. She held his neck once more.

Braden was gasping for breath. Still alive. *You can save him. Save him!* Her son looked at her with the terror of a little boy. His beautiful eyes said *help.*

"Why, whywhywhy, why," she blubbered through her sobs. She didn't know what to do. "Why why why?" His blood soaked her arm. He coughed, and blood gurgled out of his mouth. He was trying to speak. Wulfee leaned closer.

"Vengeance," he choked out. He started to make a move for his dagger. He was going to kill her. His eyes had turned to those of a madman. She saw a soul lost to darkness in his cold glare. "No no no. Please don't make me," she said. But he grabbed his dagger out of its sheath. *Let him kill you. Let it all be over with,* she thought as her son gripped the hilt, pulling out the knife with malice. *Or kill your own son and stop him from becoming Sweyne.* He tried to stab her, but his arm went limp as Wulfee swung her axe into the right side of his head.

She let out a curdling wail as her son's eyes glossed over with death. This was her baby boy. She sat down, rested his neck on her lap, letting the blood soak her fingers, hands, legs. And she didn't move as she felt the blood draining. Then his eyes went blank, and the blood stopped, and his skin was cold. This was her baby boy...

"Come, Wulfee. We're driving them back. Then we march to Kallahorn. The Rangers heard your good words, Wulf. They echoed down the hills. They're fighting for the old ways. They're fighting for you. It's not time to lie down yet, old kihl'dor," said Pike as he hauled her up. Wulfee broke free of his grasp, keeled over, and wailed. She was a puddle on the ground. She couldn't move. She just wanted to die.

"Don't *touch* me," she screeched, pushing him away. "He was my son, Pike. He was my baby boy, my baby boy." She pushed the locks of brown hair out of his eyes and kissed his forehead. Her tears smeared lines down his face as she closed his eyelids. The world was a cold blur. Her thoughts were dream-like. Memories of the wisp of etta—she had wanted so badly to pick them with her own sons.

"It's okay, Wulf," said Pike. "It's going to be okay." But she only moaned and rocked back and forth. She had lost her sense and her mind.

Pike rubbed her back as she wailed out in pain. She was completely empty. *More empty than the days my boys came forth squalling. More empty than that.* When she knew her womb was barren and that her sons weren't a part of her anymore. Now they were gone forever. *Forever.*

"We have to keep fighting, Wulfee. We can drive them back. We will win this battle if we keep fighting," said Pike.

"He's gone, Pike. He's gone. I killed him, and he ain't ever coming back."

"I know he's gone, Wulf, but you live. You must carry on."

"I can't. Pike, I can't."

"You must. I need you," he said. "We all need you."

Wulfee wasn't even listening. She could only feel her insides melting into nothing. Her heart had exploded. She was nothing.

"I can't."

The old warrior always told her she could do anything. He never let her give up before.

"Then go. To the mountains. Get away from it all," he said. "North and west. Remember? Somewhere safe." Wulfee nodded, and the old warrior nodded back. "Find peace, Wulf. In your heart."

"You're not coming," she said. Not a question, but a statement. She couldn't ask Pike for more. He'd already given her everything.

"My place is here with my daughter. Can't leave her again," he said. And Wulfee understood that more than anything. She knew that this was it. She was leaving her longest friend. She looked around. Death and more death. All of this, and she still hadn't found Sweyne. *What's it all for Wulfee? Just move on.* The corpse of her son laid out before her, cold and stagnant, soon to be picked apart by birds and dogs. *You should have let him kill you,* she thought, but knew in her heart she didn't believe that. Any bastard capable of what he did deserved to be cold and blue. As hard as that hurt, it was the truth. The wolf skull mask lay beside him. *I never even looked at what Braden put in that bag. I told him to fill it with what was most important to him. I never even looked at what that was...* Wulfee picked the mask up and let her tears soak it. *This...* Then she dropped it in the dirt and crushed it beneath her boot.

Pike nodded at her. "Good bye, Wulf." But she couldn't speak. She'd made a lot of bad choices and wasn't sure if this was just another one. Reckoned she'd find out the hard way. But she got up and walked away, and nobody tried to stop her. Just walked towards the mountains in the north and west. Away from the life she refused to chase any longer, away from the din of the fading battle. She walked with the rising sun at her back and knew that she was alone.

The Mother of Nature

"Y OU MUST WATCH EVERY step you take here," Eurick said. "These rocks could give out and you'd wind up at the bottom without your brains."

The sky was dark at midday. There was only silence amongst them. The sound of each step was the toll of a march that only ended in death. A stench of afterlife drenched James like a warm fog that pressed them low to the ground.

The trail was steep, covered with jagged rocks and thorny brambles. All growing off the life of the nytewoods that grew all around them. Eurick led them through one treacherous path after another. They had faced no resistance in getting this far. The only challenge was the road itself. James figured that meant the folk of the Hallow had held the bridge at Rosen. *Don't make the same bad choices I did, eh?* He remembered Wulfee's words fondly. He hoped to the Old Gods that she had lived. She had held the bridge for him, and now the Mother's shrine was in sight.

"This way," said Eurick. "Come on, now." The transporter walked to the edge of a steep cliff and treaded along the skinny rock ledge that connected to a trail on its other side.

James looked at Maggie and gulped. She smiled and said, "Go on then."

"I'm more worried about you."

"I'll be fine, now hurry on."

She might be mad. James smiled. He made the mistake of looking over the ledge. His big toe looked back at him through a big hole in his boot. He was scooting himself sideways with his back pressed flat to the rock and only a heel's worth of ground to work with. He held *Essikah* out in front of him. The heavy piece of godrock threatened to take him off balance when he mis-stepped.

"Watch your step there, man," said Eurick when James stumbled. He nearly shat himself more than once now.

"How much more of this, raven?" Adeqor asked.

"The shrine is at the top of this rock face," Eurick sang. James could see the black branches of nytewoods above, stretching far beyond sight. Their golden blossoms fluttered down the mountainside, shimmering in the soft light of the sunrise.

They rounded the cliff, climbed a steep incline at the back of it, and there it was—the Mother's shrine. Two nytewoods tangled together in a gnarled mess grew all the way to the clouds. An old face was carved into the trunks. Sage and wise it was, and in the mouth was a door of whitestone. Green, glowing runes arched around its frame, and the flaming comet of the Ailaryan Order was carved in the middle. *By the gods...* Maggie grabbed James's hand. He was entranced by the shrine, lost in its beauty peering up and up at the canopy. Maggie squeezed James's hand tighter, and he knew she was in the same kind of awe he was.

"This is it," said Eurick. "This is the shrine. The job is complete." He tilted his head up at the two trees. "It's the most beautiful thing I have ever seen. It connects every element of nature. The roots go down to the fiery core of the earth, and the trunks carry the tree into the misty, wet heavens above the clouds. Earth and fire. Air and water. It's beautiful. I've always wanted to see this shrine. Ever since I learned the road to get here, and I never came."

"You're here now." James patted him on the back.

"There are a hundred things I could have done but didn't because the job didn't take me there," said Eurick. He seemed to have a bit of a moment.

"Excellent work, transporter! Couldn't have done it with you." Adeqor clapped his hands. "I will send an eagle to the Guild with the rest of your payment as soon as all of this nonsense is over. Surely, you understand, I don't have the currency on my person. The Guild knows I'm good for it. We've been in good standing for the past few hundred years."

"Yeah, of course," said Eurick. He seemed upset and lingered, gazing at the shrine. Then, he sighed and walked away.

"So, just like that, you're leaving?" James held his arms out.

"Just like that, man."

"Who will take us back?" Maggie asked. Eurick looked saddened by that.

"He's a raven, Culdaine," Adeqor sneered. "He's done his job, and now he's leaving. That's what ravens do. They don't linger. This is part of the reason why they are so renowned. Nobody likes a guest who outstays their welcome. They do their job and get on with the next one."

"You don't have to go," said James.

"I do," said Eurick. He walked up to James and stuck his hand out. James knocked it aside and pulled him in for a hug. Eurick had saved his life the night the Hawka attacked, whether or not he meant to, and several times since. This man had become his friend. Eurick squeezed him back. He hugged Maggie as well and offered one to Adeqor, but the wizard refused.

"This thing you have to do, it's going to push you like nothing else has. Promise me you'll keep going, man. No matter what. I want to light a fire tomorrow and know that *you* did it," Eurick said. James remembered the first night he met Eurick and tried to fight him in the cave. The transporter had seen that Hawka skewered to the tree out front of his cave and still came in to help him. This was a man who ran from nothing, and he made James want to be the same.

"I promise," James said. "We'll meet each other again one day."

"Aye," said Eurick, then looked at Maggie.

"Take care of him, eh?"

Maggie put knuckles to her chin and nodded. Eurick returned the gesture, and just like that, he turned around and walked back the way he came.

"So what now, wizard?" said James.

"We open the Gateway, of course." Adeqor made a sweeping motion with his arms. He walked towards the twisted nytewoods with the carved whitestone door, then halted, as if there were a wall in front of him. "The veil," he said, so quiet James figured he was saying it to himself.

"Follow behind me."

Adeqor walked forward and disappeared into thin air.

James looked at Maggie, her brown hair messed into a bun on top of her head, black bags under her eyes. She needed him as much as he needed her. He took her hand, and they walked towards the Mother's shrine on the same path as the wizard and seemed to be enveloped by a different world. The cool, crisp air of the mountain turned hot and sour, like they had entered a small cave. The shrine was no longer beautiful. Golden blossoms turned into rotten brown pulp. The nytewoods resembled hundreds and hundreds of black boned skeletons that had been torn to pieces and put back together in the shape of two trees. James knew they had entered a new world—the Mother's world. The world that lived beneath the veil of beauty in nature: black soil filled with grubs and worms, and the bones of the dead were hidden beneath green grass and flowers. This was where nature was born. Below, in the dark. Only with time did it become sublime.

James's jaw dropped when he saw the horrid figure creeping out of the shadows. Bare-chested and wearing only trousers and a steel helm. He had bloody red runes carved into his flesh. Bulging muscles filled his skin like sacks that were close to bursting. His face was sunken in and pale beneath his steel helm. It looked like he had forgotten how to sleep. He was breathing heavily, dirty and haggard, like he'd turned feral from living outside too long. He held a two-handed greatsword with one hand. The blood red Daggland steel blade of the King of Ayeland with a spread-winged eagle on the hilt. James could never forget it. The sword that killed his family. It was King Calen Alder. Behind him, the purple-blue corpse of a man hung, nailed to the trees with thick nails through each limb. A dirty red eagle flag dangled beside him.

"The fuck is this?" James blurted to no one in particular. *Essikah* became so cold it burned James's hands.

"That was a veil," Alder coughed. His voice was gravelly, like his throat was choked with charcoal. "The Mother's earth magics keep this place hidden. This here is the late King Baleth." He pointed to the hanging man. "He is no king now. He won't even rot. Can you believe that? Haha!"

James saw Adeqor run off behind the trees somewhere. Alder took another step forward, and James could smell the sulphur spewing out of him.

"Oh!" James yelped. "The fuck happened to you?"

"Happened?" Alder looked offended. "Nothing *happened*. It is *happening*. Can't you see? The Words have given my soul to Karaat, so you can't take it from me with your magics. A piece of His twisted mind lives in me now. He walks in my skin and hawks venom with my tongue. The dead don't linger in Karaat's presence. They can't help you now. You won't get me like you did last time, Culdaine. I'm ready for you now."

The King of Ayeland raised his blade. The red gashes dripped blood and seeped black smoke. Alder came at James fast and swung his sword. The runes hissed as they spewed smokey sulphur.

"Last time? Are you fucked up mad? You killed everyone in my life and left me to die."

Alder looked at him, dumbfounded. He walked forward in a fighting stance, crouched low with his blade out.

"You don't remember that day at all, do you?" Alder said. He was truly in shock.

"You and your folk slaughtered us. You gutted my mom. Butchered my dad. Killed everyone I knew," said James. "You took everything from me and left me to die in the snow. Why did you leave me alive, anyway, just to hunt me afterwards?" The question had burned in him since it had happened. Alder shook his head and smiled condescendingly, unbelieving.

"You really don't remember..." he said, and laughed. James had had enough. He walked towards him with *Essikah*. It was ice in his hands and still heavy. James called on the dead, but they weren't coming to him. "You thought I had left you alive? For some special reason?" Alder continued. James stopped. "Haha! James, it's you who's gone fucked up mad. It was *you*, James. *You* killed them. All of them. Everyone. Your dad and mom, your kin, everyone who followed the Hallow north to Kallahorn, and most of the kings and queens themselves, and hundreds of my folk. We ran you down into the arbor, and when we finally caught up to you, we found everyone slaughtered. Strewn out in the pink slush. Only you stood before us, alone and unarmoured, with an axe in one hand. The dead possessed you, Culdaine. You screamed in some dead tongue, your hair stood tall. No one could kill you. A hundred of my folk claimed your wound closed up and pushed their steel right out of your flesh. You kept inhaling the air like some kind of madman. And you slaughtered us in your fury. I got away with my life, along with a few others, but it was only luck that got me away from whatever you became that day. You must have passed out in the snow somewhere when you had finished, forgetting all about it. Makes sense for the mind to erase something like that."

No. He's lying to you.

"That couldn't be," said James. He shook his head, remembering. Everything before he woke up in the snow was blurry. The battle was foggy. Maggie reached out to touch his arm, but he shook her off.

"Haha! I think you know it happened, deep down," said Alder. His muscles writhed below sacks of stretched out skin. "You were covered in blood, weren't you? Haha! Weren't you?"

You were. You were drenched in it. Your hands were cut up and bruised. You were so exhausted after you killed them you fell asleep in the snow. You... passed out... in the snow... after you killed your family. It was you.

"I almost feel bad for you. All this time and you didn't know. I thought you were some kind of evil bastard, but you were just possessed by the dead, weren't you?" Alder came towards him. He raised a bleeding hand and sliced the air with his blade. James met his glare. "I can't let you in that shrine, Culdaine."

"If you keep the Gateway closed, all of us will die," said James.

"You're fucking crazy," Maggie added.

"But the world will live on, free of the Words that brought the Starfall." Alder admired the Words on his skin. "My blood lives on through the cataclysm and makes my sacrifice worth it." He moved towards James with a mad look of rage on him. James gripped *Essikah*, waiting for it to lose its weight and become as light as bone, but it was a lump of heavy rock in his hands, and that was all. He felt no energy flowing through him. The dead were nowhere to be found in the presence of Karaat. Alder came at him. James caught his first swing with his lump of rock sword. The second and third, too. But Alder was fast and swinging like a man gone mad. Spittle flying from his mouth and a cocksure grin on his face. The runes on his skin dripped blood and hissed with black smoke as he moved. He walked him down and, with blow after blow, sent James moving back. James cowered below Alder, doing everything he could to meet Alder's blows with his awkward sword. James thought of dropping it. He looked at Maggie and knew she was inside of herself, feeling her magics.

James barely had enough time to turn around and dodge another blow from Alder. Then another swipe came, and James was on his heels. Alder was hulking with muscle that made each swing nearly knock James over. Moving back. *Running again...* It was all he could do to get out of the way. He had no souls to heal him now if Alder hit him. He rolled in the dirt and tried to slice at Alder's legs from the ground but missed horribly. When he got back up to his feet, he noticed Maggie was gone now, too. The air felt heavy, like life was being drawn from it. He moved sluggishly and noticed Alder did too. The lack of life sat heavy on James's shoulders.

"She left you, too. There's no love left for you in this world. Just die already," Alder said, and nearly took James's head off with a slicing swing that James only just got underneath of. Then James noticed the dust and debris on the ground dancing around his ankles. *Maggie.* He looked up at Alder and smiled. This was the person he had attached so much hate to. Brewed in so much anger over. He had held Alder responsible for the greatest trauma in his life. Anytime he woke from a nightmare, after seeing all of his friends and family strewn out in that red slushy snow, it was Alder he blamed for that pain.

"She hasn't left me," he said, moving out of the way of another swing. But he moved in exactly the way Alder had expected, and James felt the cold Daggland steel of Alder's sword bite into his rib bones and pierce his lung.

"Gaahhff," James puffed. He had lost all his breath. Fell over and put his hands to his torso. Blood poured out of him. He fell back on his arse and pushed himself away with his heels and elbows, trying to hold the wound shut with one hand. "Hey!" he shouted, blood coming out of his mouth, filling the cracks of his teeth. Each breath was wet with the gurgle of dying. But the dead weren't coming to him. Karaat's presence bled out of Alder's runes.

"You can't stop me," James gurgled. *Even if you can, you can't stop her...*

"I can stop you, and I will. This is what I was born for. To be the Hero of Ages. The world needs to be wiped clean of its old memories," Alder said. He was burning with power now. The Blood Words burst with crimson as he roared to the sky in praise of Karaat. He slowed his pace, let James bleed and crawl like a bug. "Humans have turned to complete shite by fighting over the ruins of a past civilization we could never live up to. We are stuck, making no progress, and killing more of each other by the year. The memories of Lovas and Yehven need to be erased, their songs forgotten. The Ailaryan Order must live on. Can't you see it's the only way? We are resilient creatures. Our ancestors will hide in caves underground and eat bugs, but some of us will survive. With the help of The Ailaryan Order, what few are left can rebuild from scratch. A New World. A better world. They have done it before, you know? We can be as grand as Lovas was. We can have peace in this world."

Eat bugs? The fuck is this guy saying? He could hardly breathe. Alder was becoming blurry. James's eyes were heavy. Everywhere was blood. He prayed to the Old Gods but only one answered him. *"You should never have prayed to me and turned your back, boy,"* The Maw God taunted him from below. *"This is what you get. A cold death. And you'll never rest easy."*

"I'd see the whole world die so she could live, even for just a little while longer. I'll open the Gateway and bring life back to the world. I'll deal with whatever comes of it," said James, looking past Alder to see Maggie appearing on the hills in front of the nytewoods. Alder must have felt her there, too. He turned to look at her. She was pulling her magics out of the air. Sticks and pebbles, dust and leaves were floating all around her, woven with a thread of blue smoke. The nytewoods and all the life they supplied withered. Birds fell out of the sky, squirrels fell from the trees along with the leaves. Life drained from everything around them as Maggie shouted something to the sky. James could feel her energy flowing. She was building it up, pulling it from the earth and the stars, and the mountain depths. She was pulling the very core of the earth, she had told him; she ate from all things alive. A mass of energy all flowed into her and wanted to come out.

Alder spun back around and grinned at James. He took his helm off to reveal a flaky bald scalp and a gaunt face beneath. All carved and bloody with runes. James thought Alder had defeated himself already. He opened his mouth and said, "Don't kill the Mother, Culdaine. Don't do it. I know you're better—" Maggie let go of her energy and turned Alder into smoking ash. It looked like a wave in the sea rolling through the sky, leaving all in its wake dead and grey, and when it crashed into Alder, it enveloped him in its force. James was thrown into the surrounding arbor, his ribs cracking on a tree trunk.

Maggie stood tall, with glowing energies moving wildly around her body. The stars and the moon were just becoming visible, pulsating as the sun set in the mountains. The dead souls emerged from the arbor and filled James. His wounds closed up, but he still lay lightheaded and in awe. He could only stare at her. He noticed the bodies of many dead birds and animals strewed out around him, and he couldn't quite register what had actually happened.

And then Maggie came to him.

"This is what we were meant for, James, this is where we win back what was taken. I've never felt so good. Kill the Mother and let us have the life we dreamed of. You know we're bigger than these bodies. I know you feel it too. We were meant to find each other, again and again, in this life and the next. It's in our blood, and it's right there in the stars, baby, look. We can be gods."

Faint stars glittered in the pink and purple sky. Maggie's words made him feel so powerful. *Our souls are connected.* He always knew it, but now he felt it. That was why he couldn't face himself when he was younger. *You were meant to find each other, in this life and the next, and the next. Always.* He couldn't face himself before because he only possessed half of his soul. Together, they were whole. Together, they had the power to kill worlds.

James looked at the whitestone door and saw runes glowing a crude green. Adeqor came out from behind the nytewoods.

"What a show! Maggie! What. A. Show!" The wizard waved his arms in the air in praise. "A mage of the old blood. They say you'll bring the end, you know?"

James swung *Essikah* at him, and Adeqor dodged it coolly.

"Reeelax," said the wizard. "We've come all this way. Do you really want to fight me? You don't know what you're about to face, seer. You're best to save that energy. To open the Gateway, you will have to kill the Mother Of Nature, and she won't just allow it. She will get inside of your head and make you fight *yourself* to get to her."

"Why are you here?" James blurted. He needed a reason not to kill this wizard dead right now. He felt Maggie's hand on his arm, warm and soft.

"Because my Words were stolen from me!" Adeqor barked, then composed himself again. "They still bounce around in my mind, each carrying the joyous memories of indulgence that they have brought me over my years. But when I get them on my tongue, they just slip away before I can say them. The Mother stole them from my mind almost four hundred years ago as punishment for the tragedy of Lindis. A *punishment*... as if it was *my* fault. We *all* wanted to wake the Creators... I was outcast and thrown in judgement by the Order that *I* created! Robbed of my dignity by all the gods of the pantheon. I'm a bloody Warlock. We're gods in our own right. We ruled Yehven once, long ago, you know, we ruled the *world* and they had NO right to betray me." Adeqor's eyes turned dark, his aura was cold. "That is why I broke Bazal out of his prison and started this. I knew Bazal wouldn't be able to resist using the Words once he rose up. I knew Ellorin wouldn't be able to resist her old vows of the Banshee and would wake the Mother. It's all in place now. So, go, open the Gateway, and let the Words grow again. Break the curse that the Mother has laid on me and kill her dead. We are all the better for it. Surely you see that now, James. The world is a rotting mess. We can restore it to glory with a little magics. You only need to kill the Mother of Nature. Easy."

James gripped *Essikah* and walked towards the wizard.

"Gentle now. Can't you see? You're better off with me and old Bazal running around and singing songs than letting the Ailaryan Order rise again to starve out the world. The rest of the Ailaryan Order are cowards, always were. They are afraid of the potential of the Words. They've spent all these years nullifying Karaat's power. They never broke the laws laid out in our books. Only *I* had the bones to attempt something greater. Something from the Book of Insa. So, go on seer. Save your Maggie. Make your parents' death worth something. That's what you care about, isn't it? That's what you're always droning on about in that thick head of yours."

James wanted nothing more than to kill the wizard right then. But Maggie touched his hand. He needed Adeqor to save Maggie. He would do whatever it took to save her. Even if it meant following this wizard.

"Open this door for us. I don't want to hear you talk anymore. All you bloody do is talk." James strangled *Essikah's* hilt.

"Magics seal this door." Adeqor moved his residual limbs all over the door as if he was feeling for something. He whispered something to himself, shook his head, and moved over to the left a few steps. "You need to understand, Culdaine, that the Ailaryan Order built this shrine as a prison for the Mother of Nature. More specifically, *I* built it. When we rebuilt the world after the Starfall, we knew there needed to be a limit to the magics we used. Only the Ailaryan Order had the privilege to use it and we followed specific guidelines on *how*. Seven laws as laid out in *The Book of New Order*. We built the shrine as a failsafe, a way to destroy the world if the Words spread out of hand. The Ailaryan Order would live and rebuild again. Another role of the runes." Adeqor laughed as the door glowed green. "When the Ailaryan Order cursed me, they used the Mother against me to keep what meant most to me in a prison. My Words live inside of her head. Sealed inside of this prison by a door that can only be opened by those Words. I can almost taste them; they're so close. I will eat the Mother's soul when you slay her and get my Words back. They are rightfully *mine!* The world will be as it was before Lindis fell. Maybe even as grand as it was before the Starfall. Maybe even that... It will be as it was, and I will be redeemed. The Ailaryan Order will have no choice but to bow down to me again. They believed the Mother would be safe here. What they don't know is that there is one word written into the heart of the magics that is stronger than every other. I wrote this song when I built the shrine, so that no matter what, I would always have complete control. I could override anything the Ailaryan Order did with a single Word. One that the Ailaryan Order didn't strip from my tongue because it's not Yehvenki."

Adeqor stretched out his arm and touched the door.

"Ai'mair," Adeqor commanded.

And the whitestone door lit up with magics.

Adeqor smiled. "I always found the runish tongue of the Mal to be so beautiful. It's a pity Lovas committed most of your folk to genocide so long ago and nearly destroyed the language."

"Ai'mair," James repeated, remembering his mom. "And what do you know about love?" he said to Adeqor. The wizard looked at him coldly.

"More than you could ever imagine..." he said, turning and walking into the shrine. James was so thrown off by hearing that phrase that Adeqor was gone and out of sight before James could even move.

Maggie looked at him and nodded, and together they entered the Mother's shrine through a thick, circular tunnel carved into the trunks of the nytewoods. Damp tendrils of root and moss hung above, stroking him as they moved through the tunnel. There was a rich smell of soil and decay as they stepped down writhing, black roots. Finally, they came to an open space. James could tell by the echoes of their footsteps that it was a wide cavern. It was pitch black but for a dim light in the middle. A pathway carved into the bedrock spiralled down towards a glowing, silver pond deep below. James thought he heard someone else's footsteps echoing behind them but wasn't sure, so he carried on.

On the way down, the runes on *Essikah* lit up green and purple and pink; Maggie watched it and smiled.

"It's the very best sword, isn't it?" said a voice from behind them. James turned around and saw Adeqor, his veins glowing blue with magics in the darkness. "I knew you'd get it here alright."

James had heard enough. He swung *Essikah* at the wizard, and Adeqor cooly dodged it. Then something seized James from the inside. He could feel something tugging on the inside of his chest, pulling out his soul. By no will of his own, he faced the wizard.

"Don't fuck with me, Culdaine," Adeqor said. James felt the hold on his soul release, and then Maggie gasped. Her face was strained. The wizard had her soul in his grasp now. "I'll kill her right now, you fucking imbecile. You turn around and do your goddamned job."

James's heart banged on his ribcage like a caged dog. He lost his breath somewhere down in his lungs.

"Let go of her," James begged, gripping *Essikah*. "Please, I'll do it. I'll kill the Mother."

"Walk," Adeqor said.

"I'm going down there to finish this because I have no other choice. But I want nothing to do with *you*. You leave us alone when this is over," said James. "I don't want to see you again. *Ever*."

Adeqor smiled.

"And you won't. I will be gone from these lands," he said. "Don't take this lightly, Culdaine. The Mother is a tortured deity, the soul of a god trapped in a disfigured, human-like body. Kill her the second you have a chance. Don't listen to a word she says."

James grit his teeth. His temples throbbed like a heartbeat. Maggie exhaled as Adeqor let go of her soul.

"Forget him, James. Whatever happens down there, you come back to me," said Maggie, and James kissed her hard.

"Of course."

The three of them descended.

The cramped, dark room with the silver pond was another veil, and behind it was another door.

"Ai'mair," James said. But nothing happened.

"Only a friend of the Ailaryan Order can enter." Adeqor touched the door gently. "Ai'mair," he whispered, and the door opened.

The silver pond was far bigger than it looked from above. It stretched, long and narrow, towards a disturbing red glow that spewed out of the void where the water disappeared.

"That is the true power of our world," said Adeqor, ogling the red glow. "This is where the Creators live. The powers that created the gods. There is incredible power in these mountains." The wizard breathed in the dank air and smiled.

Tangled roots and vines hung from crevices a hundred feet above; small growths of yellow mushrooms and green moss, and red spongy liverwort sprouted in patches along the cold rock surface. And butterflies, a hundred-hundred and more, fluttered upwards towards the cavernous environs of the shrine in a flurry of colours. To one side, the butterflies swarmed around a woman sitting upon a mess of roots and rock. She felt like a midsummer night. When she saw them approaching, she rose with the butterflies. They fluttered around her in a rainbow flurry. Roots and vines hung like ropes around her limbs and neck. They were the chains that the Ailaryan Order had bound her in. Her hair was like long, ragged strands of moss. Her eyes were burning chunks of amber with no pupil. She wore a crown of black roses upon her head. The thorns had dug so deep into her skull that blood trickled steadily down her face. The rest of her was bare, covered in fine green hairs and smeared with grime and filth. Her nipples were flower buds. And her finger and toenails were leaves. James could feel her energy pulling him in. It was the Mother of Nature. He reached for Maggie's hand as he approached, but he couldn't find it.

And at once the silver pond was gone, and the cavern turned into a dark, snow-covered arbor. James could hear battle cries, faint and far off. The sounds of an approaching army flared up: cracking sticks and rustling bushes, the thunderous droning of hooves on dirt. And it snowed, falling in chunky white flakes from the purple sky, between the black and bare branches of the arbor.

"Do you see this?" James said, but Maggie was gone. Adeqor was gone, too. He was alone but for the mossy woman in the distance and the approaching army. He wanted to turn and run, but he couldn't leave Maggie to die again. *Never again.* In seconds, the snow piled around his ankles and kept piling. "Hello?" he screamed, but it only echoed with the rumbling of approaching horses and the guttural screams of bloodthirsty folk forced into combat. The terror spread through his body and paralyzed him. And the snow kept falling. The crisp smell of it was like frozen wood. He couldn't move. He could only fall over and lay his head in the cold.

His body was getting colder. He shook, and his teeth chattered. His dad shouted at him. *"Come on, boy! We're all going to die if you don't bloody try! Now!"*

He could hear his mom crying. *"Please, James, talk to them. Call to the dead, James, please."*

"I will," he screamed. *I will save you.* But the snow was up over his head now. *You're going to die here, in the snow, like you should have back then.*

The sounds of the army closing in on him were closer, more intense. Alder and his army were going to kill James and his family. The souls were surging through him, taking him over. He was freezing. He had to get out of the snow or he was going to die. *"You have to try, James. Please try."* His mom was crying now. His dad grabbed James's shoulders and shook him.

"Now! Now! We're all going to die if you don't—"

"I can't!" screamed James. His mother smiled— a kind of sad and distant smile.

"I never told you about the day you were born, James. You're a miracle, you know that? You came out dead. Blue and cold, just a little corpse. But something breathed life into you, a miracle. There's death in you, James. Let it out. Help us." The army was visible now, through the trunks and branches. He could smell their horses as they ran them down. His mom smiled. *She had such a beautiful smile...* His dad put knuckles to his chin and nodded.

"I love you, son. I'm so sorry for what I've put you through. You have no idea how much it hurts me. It has broken me that this was our life together. I love you so much, James, and I'm so proud of you. But I had to do this for our country. For the world. *You have to become what you are. You have to."*

I don't want to...

And then the souls took over his mind. He surged with the power from below. He gripped his axe with malice. His dad's eyes went wide with horror. James had become a monster. The half-god seer of old, like the ancient Mal warrior, Hendurinn. James lost control. He killed everything that moved.

Now, in the present, he was alone again but for the Mother. Snow drifted down on them.

"Listen to me, child. You don't have to do this," the Mother said. Her voice was as smooth and cold as ice. "The Words of Karaat have the power to overcome a person, to take them over. They're addictive, and Adeqor is an addict. It was the Ailaryan Order that begged me to take the Words from his head because he had become so dangerous wielding them. No one felt safe holding his Words in their mind, and we couldn't kill him. He was much safer paralyzed than dead. It was the same way they begged me to banish Bazal's soul to the Otherworld. Adeqor was cursed and banished, an outcast to the fringes of the world. But he has never stopped trying to get back at the Ailaryan Order. He would have destroyed the entire world had we not stopped him. He broke every rule the seven sages laid out for us in *The Book of New Order*. I wove the spell to keep his tongue from ever saying them again myself. I have seen his evil with my own eyes. I know his true motives. He craves the power of the Creators. The power beyond bodies. He wants to be *one* of them. If you kill me, he will be free to sing his songs once more, and he will pursue his motives at the cost of everything else. He will kill the gods. He is no different from Bazal, another Warlock who lost control of his tongue and mind. Bazal was a traitor to the Ailaryan Order. He was so far gone he had to be stripped of his bodily existence for the world to remain safe from his hubris." She walked towards him, and it was silent now but for the sound of the Mother's bare feet breaking through the crust of the snow. "Turn around and go. You've avoided becoming *this* for so long now. You don't have to become this monster."

"I have to do it. I have to make their deaths worth something. I can't let anyone else die because I was a coward. I can't," James said. Tears fell from his eyes. *Make it right, James. Make it right.*

The Mother's eyelashes had turned to ice and curled into flakes of snow. She seemed to blush in the winter storm as blood had turned to red ice on her cheeks. Glowing chunks of amber with no pupil leered at James, shaking him down to the bone. The Mother of Nature was incensed with black earth and grass. James laid helpless, freezing, paralyzed, afraid, and alone in the snow. Just as he did all those years ago.

"Becoming this monster is all I'm good for." James breathed in the ambrosial essence of the Mother as she came closer. "Since the first time I came within sight of Kallahorn, these mountains drew me here. I knew my fate was here. I could never explain it, but I knew I would wind up here for something." He reached around for *Essikah*, but all he found were handfuls of snow. "I didn't come all this way to turn around."

"You're wrong. The Earth made your soul for one thing. Death," she said. A chill ran up James's spine. "In death, you and Maggie can live forever in peace. You don't have to give into the monster inside of you. It will ruin you in the end. It will ruin *her*. You know now what happened last time you let it take over. You killed everyone who loved you. Save the people you love this time, and let the rest die. You don't have to be their hero. If you re-open the Gateway, you will have to deal with the evil in this world. You will have to become a monster to stand up to it, and you will lose everything. I promise you that."

"I will only lose anything if I let *you* live."

"The Creators have thrown the runes for humanity countless times already. If you re-open this door, this will be the last cast. The songs of Yehven will infect the Otherworld and kill the gods. The Creators will eat the earth until nothing remains. The runes of this life will be set, and the world will never have another chance to live when black magics or cataclysms consume this one. Let it die and help the people of the next batch do better. It could be more glorious than Yehven."

The next batch?

"Are you mad? Everyone will die if I don't open that door. There will be no more humanity." James kept searching for *Essikah*, making it look like he was crawling away.

"Some will survive the rotting of the world. Some always do. And they rebuild. The Ailaryan Order will teach them. And the gods will watch as the smallfolk worship us. The Ailaryan Order is above gods. Can't you see that? You can't stop them. I realized that many thousands of years ago."

"You're mad!" James shouted, and his hand touched the cold hilt of *Essikah*.

"You must know the world will die anyway, with the dark Words spreading so freely. You must have sensed it by now," the Mother said. She saw him holding his sword and looked at him with those burning amber eyes. "If you kill me, Adeqor will become unstoppable. Bazal will re-emerge in the body of someone else. The world will die anyway, in a much darker shadow than this."

"I won't let you kill the world."

"But you're very willing to kill the future. And for that, I believe I am better than you are. Nature cannot die. It always finds a way." The Mother was spectacular in her beauty at that moment. She was as serene as a mountain peak or the sunfell—her radiance left James unable to speak. He could only think about Maggie. She could only live if the Mother died. He thought about the life they would have when this was over, if he went through with it. A tough going, hard up kind of life, full of violence and darkness. The Ayelish would avenge their king. *It will be war after war until enough die that one side gives up... but there would be good, too. So much good. You can save the whole world. You can bring back the light. Save Mal Hallow from darkness...* He didn't have to hide from who he was anymore. He could become monstrous. *Essikah* lit up a cold red in one hand, and James smiled and paced forward at the Mother. She was as calm as a still lake.

"This will not end well for you," she said, then seemed to have a peace come over her, like a storm subsiding. Her amber eyes dimmed, and she stuck her twiggy neck out. "Do it then, if you would be so stup—"

James swung *Essikah* with everything he had and cut the Mother of Nature's head off. He didn't think twice, not for Maggie. The surrounding arbor faded into a dark cavern where Maggie and Adeqor stood by. The Mother's severed head showered James in blood.

She was the Mother of Nature, a godlike entity, and she bled just like everyone else. Adeqor opened his mouth and ate her dying soul. The Mother's limp body fell to the ground with a fleshy splat.

Adeqor dropped to his knees and wheezed as he struggled to breathe.

The Mother's soul seemed to wisp right out of his mouth, like it was refusing him. He sucked it up again, as he did the first time. Gasping for air, Adeqor pointed his arm at the silver pool. It was covered over in a purple slime. Pulsing and writhing.

"The Gateway. Open it," he said, sounding strained. The soul seemed to fight him from the inside now, resisting. "Hurry!" he yelled, and he continued to choke and cough.

James walked over to the slimy layer over the pool and thrust *Essikah* into it. The slime moaned as it slid away from the pool. The dead souls poured in the silvery water like a rushing river behind a broken dam. They flowed past James so fast that they created a cold wind.

Adeqor screamed. He was crawling on his stomach, moaning and suffering as green tendrils stretched out from the Mother's throne, roping around his neck and snaking into his nose and ears. The gnarled nytewood chair dragged Adeqor into itself. The roots seemed to suck him in, hold him down.

Then the whole mountain rumbled. The crimson glow of the abyss beyond the silver pool grew brighter. *The Creators...*

"Take this shite off of me, Culdaine. Help!" Adeqor moaned. "Help me, help me!"

James watched hundreds and hundreds of dead souls fill the dank cave and make their way into the pool. The door to their world was open for them once more. They were filling his head with words that weren't just pleas for help now.

"Go."

"Leave."

This many dead would pull him down; he could feel it. Adeqor was laughing now, breaking free from the restraints of the throne, singing songs in crude, dissonant melodies. Maggie grabbed James's hand and pulled him away.

"We have to go. Look." She pointed to the steam rising from the red glow beyond. Wispy hands seemed to reach out slowly for them. James put *Essikah* on his back and followed her away.

Adeqor was singing loudly now. James could hear strange words echoing through the cavern as they ran, giving him a horrible chill. They couldn't find the door.

"It was just like the cave from the backside... I don't remember where..." James muttered. He saw Adeqor still writhing and choking on green tendrils. He was screaming Words instead of singing now, like a chant. Behind him, a blanket of glowing red steam rolled along the surface of the cavern like a wave, and it was picking up speed. Adeqor laughed maniacally as the blanket rolled over him, and he burst into a smoking pile of mush. Still, James heard the Words echoing. The sound of them was vile, making him feel sick. They tore at his ears like sharp rocks and thumped in his head like hooves.

"Here!" Maggie shouted. The whitestone door had stopped glowing.

"Ai'mair!" James screamed. Nothing happened. "Ai'mair, ai'mair darra!"

Nothing. *Only a friend of the Ailaryan Order...* He continued to scream the Mal word for love. The steam was building, and it was almost too hot to bear. Finally, James stopped and looked over at *his* love. Watched her brown hair bounce and her waist move as she searched for another door. As if she knew he was looking at her, she turned around to meet his eyes. One green and one blue, the two orbs he saw in every dream, staring back at him. *We will find each other again, in the next life.* She walked towards him, and they wrapped their arms around each other and squeezed. She was so full of life now. He could feel it flowing out of her, and it filled him. They kissed hard, and James whispered in her ear, "I love you so much, Maggie. I love you so much."

She looked at him as tears fell down his cheek and she said, "We will find each other again. We will always find each other." And they held each other close, sweat pouring off both of them. And it was getting harder to breathe as the red blanket of magics flowed even faster towards them. James closed his eyes and felt Maggie's soul with his. He pressed his nose into her neck and breathed in the smell of her. *Peonies and honey...* He had spent his life running from who he was. He spent his life running from love. Now he could die knowing he faced both. He was ready to die.

"Hey, man!" came a voice that snapped him out of it. James opened his eyes. "Let's go!"

It was Eurick.

James and Maggie ran towards him, and he walked them through the first door.

"You came back?" James said.

"Thought I'd see the world a bit before the Guild catches up with me," Eurick boasted proudly. He had taken his life into his own hands.

"How did you get in here?" Maggie muttered.

"I followed you." Eurick smiled. "And the ravens have always been friends to the Ailaryan Order, man. They created us. It's old blood that runs in our Guild. I knew the door would open for me."

The mountain was shaking profusely now, and rocks broke loose from above.

They ran up the spiralling rock steps and through the rounded tunnel. Eurick whispered a soft word to the whitestone door, and they left the twisted nytewoods of the Mother's shrine. James stepped into the fresh air. The dark clouds were still overhead. He saw a flash of lightning, then heard a rumbling thunder boom. One look back and James saw the corpse of Lord Baleth nailed to the black, oily trunks of the twisted nytewoods, swaying in the strong wind. The red wisp had filled the entrance of the shrine but never left its boundary. To James, it looked like the glow of the sun *. That is the true force of this mountain. The real force of nature that lives in this earth. And that will never die. The power of the Creators.*

Another flash of lightning, and then the rolling thunder. And soon the black clouds pissed down a cold rain. And James thought that he had never been so happy to get stuck out in a storm.

Deep Down Inside

THE SMOKE FROM THE fire got in Wulfee's eyes and burned her nostrils as she dropped a log into the pit. She took a step back and wiped her tears with the back of her forearm.

"I think we've got enough o' that, eh? Why don't you come have a bite?" Tara held out a slab of wood with chunks of steaming venison.

"Just a few more," Wulfee said as she split a log into smaller pieces. *A few more, and I won't ever touch an axe again.* "Just trying to earn my stay."

"Well, you been here a day already. Where you think we're going to send ya if you stop choppin' them logs?"

"You really aint got nowhere else to be, eh?" said Benn.

Wulfee ignored the question and swung. Her axe chomped into the wood with a sharp smack. The smell of wood smoke lingered warmly in the cold air, and it pleasantly burned her nostrils. Wulfee only thought about the spot she was about to strike. She was numb to all else.

"We're happy to have you. We'll need all the fighting folk we can get. It's going to be a long winter," said Tara.

"What makes you think I'm a fighter? I'm naught but an old and broken woman," Wulfee said as her axe smacked another clean bite out of a pine log.

Tara eyed Wulfee up and down, then let her eyes fall on her right hand.

"What happened there?" she said. Wulfee turned to hide the hand.

"Everyone's got scars."

"Not like that," said Benn. He had treated her burns from the drayke when she first arrived. She had walked for at least three weeks to find them in the mountains, and she couldn't believe she hadn't died from the rot in all that time. She reckoned it was some cruel joke from the gods, keeping her alive to stew in what she'd done. But the rot never touched her. The gods had come around to her side. "That's some kind of nasty wound. Some kind of sorcery in whatever burned you. Not even an infection would touch that."

"What happened?" Tara asked.

"The war happened," Wulfee groaned. "To me and to everyone else."

"And it's still happening. So how are you going to put down that axe?"

"It's that old thing called hope," Wulfee said. "It's got power, that, to make you believe it's going to get better. To give you something to live for when it seems like there isn't any."

"I should change his name to Hope then," said Tara, nodding at little Sweyne. "He's all that's kept me going through this."

"He seems like a good kid."

"Aye, he is. He's got my temper, though. And his dad's knack for not hearing a damn thing I say."

Wulfee stopped chopping and stood tall.

"It's like the ugly things we hide deep down inside come out, after all, in our children. It's the gods' way of making you face who you really are." Wulfee wondered if Tara would recognize her without all that hair.

"What'd you say your name was?" Tara squinted her eyes. Wulfee felt a warm tingle in her stomach. An old, welcome thought entered her head, and she remembered a person who she was long ago, before the pain.

"Etta," she smiled. Goosebumps covered every inch of skin.

"Well, Etta, I reckon there's a place for you here. Even if you decide to stop choppin' them logs. You say you ain't a fighter, but I know better. And besides, young Sweyne could use someone around speaking those kinda good words."

"I'd love to stay out the winter. Longer if you'd have me."

"We'll have ya, Etta." Benn shoved a piece of greasy gristle in his mouth. "We'll have ya."

Wulfee smiled, took one last chunk out of a pale piece of pine, and then sunk her axe into the chopping block. When the iron left her hands, she felt the weight of her whole past *thwump* into that stump along with the blade. That was the last time she'd touch a weapon. *A new life now. Another start.*

She picked up one of the logs, dumped it into the fire, and watched the sparks fly up into the clear blue sky. Then Etta packed a fat bowl of chuff into her pipe and lit it up. She sat back and puffed. Somewhere out in the mountains, a wolf howled. It sounded just like that big, grey bitch, and it made Etta smile. She looked at the children playing. She watched young Sweyne throw a rock into a square of sticks. The rock landed inside the bottom corner of the square, and he cheered along with the other children when the rock didn't roll any farther. She watched as they chased each other around in circles with sticks. They played goose and frog, and red gopher come over. And Etta watched them and smiled. They played hoprocks and slings and shoots, and flags, sticks and stones, and touch tag and axe throwing. Etta watched her grandson play. His brown tufts of hair bounced, and his green eyes lit with joy and hope. From here on out, as long as she lived, she would never leave him.

THE STAND

T HE WIND BLEW IN the meadows below Kallahorn, and the long russet coloured grasses swayed and reeled from its push and pull. A sparse canopy of pine and birch, fir, and sentinel stretched out below the mountains in tawny, amber, and copper. The golden blossoms on the nytewood dropped and got caught in the breeze like a hundred-hundred falling stars. James picked a petal out of Maggie's hair and gently stroked the side of her face. He looked into her eyes, and James saw everything he'd dreamed of right in front of him. Itchy played *The Hand and the Heart* on his flute as the last of the people gathered around the nytewood. They laid a thousand candles around the base of the tree. Wax drooled out of them, and their flames danced in the twilight. The sunfell sky was a crisp autumn red and full of chunky grey clouds, fat with rain. A faint silver moon was already visible.

"In the betwixt of day and night, the magics are alive," the shaman said. He was wearing sun-bleached stag's antlers on his head, and he blacked his eyes out with coal. He wore a robe of white fox fur and had painted his bare feet red with ochre. The shaman stood in front of the nytewood and held a stone tablet carved with runes in his hands and recited the words. The same words that had heartbound the kings and queens of the Hallow for all of time. "And so the sun and the moon shall witness the joining of these two souls. I will tie their hands with a hempen rope so they may speak their words of binding."

James and Maggie interlaced their fingers and then crossed their wrists. The shaman tied them together with a clean, new rope that smelled like long grass and dried leaves.

"I will stand by you and do good by you as long as I'm breathing," said James. "Ai'mair darra."

"And I you. Ai'mair darra," Maggie said.

"You're the other half of my soul," James whispered. Tears fell down his cheeks.

"And you're the other half of mine," Maggie smiled.

The shaman pulled out the engagement knife and cut the rope off of their hands. After he broke the bonds, he plunged the knife into the oily black trunk of the nytewood and whispered a prayer to the wind. Golden sap leaked out of the trunk like honeyed blood. The shaman let a good bit of the sap collect on the knife, and then removed it. James licked one side and Maggie the other. When James tried to swallow it, the bitter taste of it made him gag a little, but after a few seconds, he craved more of it. Maggie kissed him hard, and he could taste the piney sap on her tongue. He took the knife and tucked it into her hilt. *Protect her. Always.* The shaman raised his hand and everyone went silent.

"Heartbound!" he proclaimed, and the gathering of people erupted. They had been starting to relax more in the weeks since the world came back to life, and the revelry made James smile. Eurick boomed the loudest, his big beard bouncing. The drums picked up and the flutes and lyre played out to the tune of *The Hallow Queen and King.* Kegs of ale, mead, and shine pulled out of Kallahorn's cellars were tapped now and flowing steadily. All the folk of the Hallow who survived the spring and summer had gathered here. People were dancing and singing, laughing and crying out for joy.

Most of these folks had told James they didn't think they'd see it through the winter. People reached out and touched James and Maggie as they walked away, arm in arm, from the great nytewood. They called out to them in a dozen different northern dialects, but they all said the same thing.

"Thank you."

James could still hear words of gratitude being chanted as he and Maggie walked out towards the grove in the great arbor at the base of the Mountains of the Mother.

The sun had set, and the night had come alive with sound. Crickets and cicadas hummed, owls called out to the moon, and bats squeaked sharply. Bushes rustled with critters, and twigs snapped from predators. A blue jay fluttered down and landed on a thin branch overhanging the smooth dirt road. It made a strange twittering sound and turned its head away when James looked at it. The dark sky was a face and the stars a hundred-hundred eyes watching them.

"What do you see up there, besides stars?" James asked.

Maggie looked at him, her bi-coloured eyes gleaming with moonlight, and smiled.

"Magic."

ON THE NEXT NIGHT, the dining hall at Kallahorn was alive with firelight, conversation, laughter, and crying babies. There was the clanging of silverware and clanking of goblets.

The smells of a feast wafted through the hall: roast pork and honey, roast lamb and mint sauce, roast capon with garlic, and bows of rosemary and thyme, and venison smothered in gravy thickened with butter and flour and seasoned with salt, and thick and syrupy reduced mead to smother all of it. With the meat, they served yellow potatoes with butter and soured cream, orange yams glazed in honey, green beans with pine nuts and maple sap, flamed corn cobs smothered in butter and red salt from Daggland, brussel sprouts and spinach roasted with black vinegar and heads of garlic. Crisped apple pies and glazed pear tarts, spiced poached plums, and candied blackberries.

It was a proper way to spend James's first night in this cold castle. A proper meal for a ruler. Maggie was holding a drink and laughing. She saw James gawking and waved. He smiled back, wiggling his toes in his new leather boots. Everything was just fine. And it made him feel nervous that something would come along and take it all away again. *The Mother told you that you would have to face the darkness.*

Itchy was playing *The God King Rises* for the three hundredth time. James clanked his goblet with Eurick and sang out some words. They had a laugh, and he felt as normal as he had in years.

"I thought I'd feel different," said James.

"Eh?" Eurick slurred.

"You know, like, better," said James. Eurick hiccuped.

"Aye. It's like that old fable, *The Frog and its Pond.* A little frog sits on a rushing riverbank, wishing the water might slow down so she can enjoy the sun on a lily pad. Then some crofters come along and build a dam to turn the new mill. They created a calm, little pond where the river used to be. Couple of months went by, and the frog had found a sturdy lily pad on the calm pond in the sun. But before long, the little frog wasn't happy anymore and moved on to another riverbank. Just to be closer to the sound of rushing water again." James laughed and dropped his head. "What I'm saying, man, is that I think it's just the way it is. Things don't always turn out the way we think they will. Maybe you thought you'd feel better, but you don't. But you *are* better, ain't ya? You saved the damned world. Those fires there are burning because of *you.* These people have found hope again. You did that. Don't forget that, man. You've got the woman you love, and she loves you back. The wizard's off your back. You're the Hallow King, and your people love you," said Eurick. *And I killed the Mother of Nature. How bout that, Eurick?* The words of the Mother stuck with him. *This will be the last batch...* The thought disturbed him. But for now, he had peace. He had love and a full belly, and walls around him. He wasn't sure if that would last, but it was enough for now.

"I want to hire you for a job. We've got gold here in the vaults." James drained his tankard. The ale was going down well this evening. "I can send as much as it takes. We can stop the Raven's Guild from coming after you."

Eurick drained his tankard, too, and slammed it on the table.

"They're probably already on their way for me. They would have known the job ended when the fires came back. Best hold on to it, and we can use it as a bargaining tool whence the Guild arrives to capture me." Eurick hiccuped again. "Might bloody well work, though, man. Might just."

"And if it doesn't?"

"I don't know." Eurick opened his mouth to say more but stopped and smiled. James figured Eurick was alright with not knowing. For now, it was all good. "You don't have to do any of this for me, eh? I wouldn't hold it against you."

"You saved my life. More than once. I'd do more if I could. This is nothing," said James.

"You're a good person, eh? Don't let yourself believe you're some kind of monster now because of all this. You saved the lives of every person on this earth. In every country across the land. You're a hero, man. Don't think any less."

James put his head down. He looked at his tired, cracked hands. The thick veins running up his arms. The scars and the blemishes, and the little hairs standing straight as he thought of what he'd done with them hands and arms. He was a boy running from himself. Became a man running from that boy's trauma. He'd faced who he was deep down and came back up again, alive and well. Happy even. Eurick's words made him feel better, but they couldn't change his mind. He knew what he was and couldn't deny it any longer. He was the World Walker who killed the Mother of Nature. What consequences would come of it he'd yet to find out. But he was ready to live with what he'd done.

Maggie came over, hiding the scarred side of her face with a scarf. The scars meant nothing to James. They were a great honour in the Hallow, but he knew telling her that didn't make her feel better. They meant something different to her.

"I'm going to watch the sunset with everyone," said Maggie. "Meet me out there?"

"I'll be there," James smiled. Eurick patted him on the back.

"You're a bloody hero, man. The stuff of stories. You really lived up to it. Enjoy it, would ya?" He got up and stumbled a bit, nearly falling. Then straightened himself and pulled his dark-winged cloak tight to his chest. "I'm right drunk, man. Time for bed."

James watched Eurick leave for a moment before calling out to him.

"Eurick!" The transporter turned around, hiccuping. James wanted to say a hundred different things but couldn't find the words. This man had become the best friend he'd ever had. "Thank you."

Eurick smiled. A drunken, cheeky old smile if James had ever seen one.

"Had to do it. Never failed a job, man," he said, and stumbled off to bed.

James sat by himself for a while. Many people came to thank him and congratulate him, and swear fealty to him. He gave them courtesies and smiled, and said the things he was supposed to say, but beneath it all, he felt like a failure. He was supposed to feel better.

Itchy finished up and looked at James, then stumbled over to talk to him.

"You're getting pretty okay at that thing." James meant it. If he couldn't feel good himself, he figured he may as well make someone else feel good. The bard had practised damn near every day.

"Oh. Wow, thanks..." said Itchy, rather surprised, then hiccupped. "Say, I... uh, was wondering..." Itchy scratched the back of his head. "Do you like the song I wrote for you? I mean, I've been so bothered that maybe you just hate it, and here I am playing it repeatedly, and I—"

"It's the best song I've heard," said James. Itchy's eyes lit up.

"Oh, wow. By the gods. You're not just saying that?"

"It's been stuck in my head for weeks." James watched Itchy's face blush red. He smiled widely, opened his mouth to say something, and then stopped. Perhaps didn't want to ruin the moment. He hiccupped again.

"Why don't you go on and get some rest? It's been a long day." James patted him on the back. Itchy nodded and staggered off. James was glad to have him stay. It would be a long winter making a stand, and some song and dance would help it be more comfortable.

Mineera stayed too. She'd said she wanted to finish her works on the seers of Mal Hallow and the people north of Ayeland. Said folk would read them aloud all over Edura. The scholar had decided she wasn't going to change her clothes until James did. That made James laugh. She sat alone at a table on the other side of the room, scribbling on her parchment. James was a little afraid to talk to her most times for fear of her saying too many things he didn't understand and making himself out to be an idiot. He figured she was good to have around, though. Perhaps she could teach him words, and he could learn to read runes and tablets. He walked over to her now, and she seemed happy to see him.

"James. It's good to see you back. You wouldn't believe what I've read in some of the books lying around this place," Mineera said, flipping the pages of the book in front of her. "This castle was here before Kelson conquered Ardura—long before. Kelson must have been obsessed with this place—he wrote hundreds of texts in diary fashion."

Dia— what? "What do they say?"

Mineera grinned. "A lot of it is day-to-day personal stuff. Problems with his children. Problems with his husbands and wives. But Kelson spoke much of something else, too." Mineera stopped flipping through the pages and slammed her finger down. "He believed something lived beneath the castle."

"What?" James's stomach turned.

"I don't know. There are hundreds of these. A hundred-hundred maybe. It will take me all winter to read them all. But I've read that he was hearing sounds from below. It was driving him mad, from the looks of it."

James thought of Adeqor for no reason. "Let me know what you find."

"Of course."

James drank another tankard of ale before he got up to meet Maggie. He needed to clear his mind from what Mineera had just told him. The sun would already be set by now, but he hoped Maggie was still there. He needed to talk about that night at the shrine. He hadn't told anybody else that Adeqor still lived in his dreams. That the Words of old Yehven are being sung again, and they would only gain strength the more people use them.

He walked alone through the dark halls of Kallahorn, kicking up a cold echo. *What trouble have you really caused? What is the true price for these people's lives?* He didn't know the answers but knew he'd owe the debt. He remembered the magics of the Mountains that nearly pulled him and Maggie down into its core. The crimson light that Adeqor seemed to control. *The Creators...* James was ready to die with Maggie in his arms. He felt complete at that moment. Like it was all worth it. Now he was left to clean up the mess left behind.

The Ayelish had surrendered Kallahorn without a fight. They had been garrisoned there for nearly a year, and all of them were starved and ready to go home, believing Alder to have gone madder than Baleth Longsongs. When the Ayelish learned the supplies weren't coming from the south and that King Calen Alder was dead, they did exactly that. James let them go with their lives, despite the arguments of Claydon and Brinley, who would have sooner watered the Hallow soil with their lives. But James had seen enough death for that year. He knew it wouldn't be easy to get the rest of their kingdom back, though.

After the elements came back, James had spent weeks tracking down the survivors of the wars and bringing them all to Kallahorn for the coming winter. James had only arrived in the castle himself the day before—his wedding day. Although he felt sick about gathering everyone in that vile castle, it was the safest place for the Hallow to gather and make a stand. He had united the settlements that were near fresh water and had still managed a crop. They put all of their food together, and in Kallahorn, they all lived together. It took nearly a month for the settlements to make the pilgrimage, and some were still rolling in on overloaded wagons, but they made it. They were *going* to make it through this winter. The Hallow would survive another year.

James waited every day for news that Wulfee had come back to Kallahorn, but the news never came. Nobody found her dead or alive. He prayed to the nytewoods for her and asked the Stag to give her strength at every sunset. He hoped she had managed to finally rest easy. Pike said he last saw her during the battle but didn't know what happened to her. He just said he reckoned she was okay. She was a tough old braud. That wasn't good enough for James.

"You didn't look for her during the battle?" he yelled. "You didn't think to save your kihl'dor?"

Pike glared at James in a way that made James feel entirely horrible. Pike didn't even say goodbye when he left with Tess's clan the next day.

The Hallow army and the clans of Feldarra had pushed the Ayelish back across the bridge of Rosen and out of the dead valley. Once they made it known that someone had killed the Wolf in battle, the rest of the Clan of the Severed Head broke into pieces and retreated. James figured there would be hundreds of petty kingships throughout the Hallow, which would cause trouble for the Ayelish lords who had moved in. The brigands would tear the kingdom into tiny scraps and wear it down to the bone. Ockam, Dawning, Lorne, and Fever belonged to the Glennish, though Lord Brynmor was missing and presumed dead. And the Ayelish took everything else that was south of Rosen. James had word that the Ayelish crowned Calen Alder's daughter, Ianna, as the new High Queen of Ayeland. She had made it well known across the lands that she vowed to pick up where her father left off with the conquest of Mal Hallow. She claimed that the indoctrination of the One God Eralis and the destruction of any heathen gods would be necessary to really defeat the Hallow folk.

Along the Fell River, Brinley, Ruwen, and Claydon set up a barricade at each of the crossings. The Ayelish hadn't tried to breach it yet, but they all knew it was just a matter of time. Another war was fermenting, but for now, they were safe. They could gather their strength and live again. *But for how long?*

It was the thirtieth Fell of autumn, as per the Lovasi calendar etched in stone on the ground at Kallahorn. A long shadow showed the date. Tomorrow would be the first Rise of winter, and it was cold enough that James could see his breath. The moon was yellow and chunky in the black sky. In its light, the oily black stone of Kallahorn looked a crude blood red. Maggie looked out over the battlement at the dark valley. James picked up a torch and lit it from the flame of another. A fat blue moth flew directly into the flame. James walked up behind Maggie and wrapped his arms around her. She snuggled in.

"Why don't we just go back out there to the grove, beneath the moon." He kissed her neck.

She laughed and crinkled her neck to resist, and then snuggled back into his arms. "I saw this in my dreams. This and many other outcomes, but I knew I'd be with you again. But I saw many things..."

"What things?"

"Like... this, only there's a dark tinge to it. Like a melancholy has fallen on the world," said Maggie. Dark clouds covered the moon as if to prove her point. *It's me. I'm the dark stain.*

"I feel it too," James said. "But I'll fight for you."

"I know." She giggled. "In life or death, nothing can hurt us."

James carried her to the top of the bannister, and she wrapped her legs around his waist. James whispered, "How do we make sure of it?"

She traced his lips with a finger. "Like this."

Maggie kissed him hard. They stayed there for a while like that with the dead standing around them. Even after the rain came, they stayed and let it wash down over their tired bodies. In the storm, they watched the yellow moon drift in and out of the cover of the dark clouds. James was in no hurry to leave *this*. He would be awake until everyone else was asleep and still longer after that. His nightmares were worse now than ever before, but

James figured he would always have them. And maybe it was worth it to feel the rain again. Maybe it was worth it for *her*.

J AMES KNEW HE WAS the last one awake when the ghosts came back. He kissed Maggie's forehead as she slept, and she stirred only slightly as he left their bedchamber.

"Help." His chest thumped as he followed the blue smoke bodies through the dark halls of Kallahorn. James dipped a torch into the nearby hearth, and it burst to life with flame. He held it up to illuminate the cold basalt walls and kept walking.

"Help." James followed the voice down the stairs, deeper and deeper into the bowels of Kallahorn. *"Please. Help. The gods... slaughtered."*

James walked through the halls, the voices from below compelling him forward. He hadn't stopped thinking of what Mineera had told him. *"There's something below this castle, James. Kelson knew it, and I think many others have known it, too."* His whole life, James had heard his dad speaking of Kallahorn. Its mysteries, its intrigue, its horrors. James was certain that his dad knew more about the castle than he'd told him.

The tunnels went on and on, deeper and deeper, until the cold sunk into James's bones and glossed his eyes with ice. "Where are you taking me?" His breath smoked.

"We're not done with you yet," the bitter voice echoed. James could hardly make out the shape of the souls—faint blue silhouettes in the fire-lit darkness.

"I've done all I can."

"We need you. You're the only one."

"I already opened the Gateway."

"And let someone in."

He trembled in the dark as each step took him closer to the voices. "Who are you?" James cried out, but only his echo answered him. Deeper and deeper he followed. Past iron bars rusted to dust and crumbled stone statues of strange entities. The twisted runes chiseled deep into the black stone walls were like nothing James had ever seen. *Are those...* James traced what seemed to be deep scratch marks from fingers far larger than his. He came to a round, stone door. The door glowed green with runes like the Mother's shrine and danced around like the lights were alive with song. James touched the door, and it stopped glowing. The tunnel behind him flooded with ghosts. James's heart fluttered as he realized the dead had cornered him.

"What is this?"

"Help help help help."

The souls parted like the earth in a quake. From the darkness between them came a hollow voice.

"The Starfall."

"What? What about it?"

"The sky will fall..."

"It's just an old story. Who are you?"

"No." The tunnel lit up in a crimson glow. Eldritch chants swam out of unseen chasms. James vomited from the stench that tore at his nose. And the dead thing that was speaking to him made itself visible through the parted souls. It was the Maw God. He whispered in a low breath. *"It's coming."*

Please Read!

Dear Reader,

We did it. We're here, at the end. I wholeheartedly hope you enjoyed *The First Verse of The Last Ballad, A Memory Of Song.* If you did, and you would like to support the series further, it would mean the world to me if you left an honest review on <u>Amazon</u> and <u>Goodreads.</u>

Honest reviews help books reach a wider audience and give new authors like myself a chance to grow. It's the fans that captain the ship and keep it afloat. I'm merely a nervous navigator, pointing a shaky finger into the fogs of unknown waters, choking up some blind confidence and saying, "This way, everyone, follow me." But I would be nowhere without you.

So, with all of my heart, thank you for trusting me with your time and walking with me on this journey. Let's find out what's down this road together, eh? It'll be safer that way. We've got one hell of a ride ahead of us.

Until the next Verse,

Scott Palmer

Join The Feldarra!

Sign up for my mailing list and be the first to receive news, offers, and exclusive content from *The Last Ballad* series! But that's not all! When you join, you will be in line to receive a free digital copy of *The Sound Of Starfall,* a multi part prelude novella to *The Last Ballad* series, releasing this summer!

I would love to hear from you! Please, reach out. Let's chat about magic, and cats, or whatever...

Join the Feldarra!: https://www.scottpalmerauthor.com/mailinglist
Email: https://www.scottpalmerauthor.com/contact
Facebook: Scott Palmer
Instagram@scottpalmerauthor
X@SPalmerAuthor
Amazon: Scott Palmer / A Memory of Song
Goodreads: Scott Palmer / A Memory of Song

Acknowledgments

T o...

Sydney. Who has walked every step in this world with me. Who endured endless hours of nerdy rants about made up things. Who has climbed every hill and ran through every valley. Who filled me up again when I was empty. Every single time. To put into words what you mean to me would be to sell that feeling short in so many ways. Without you this would still be a dream. *Ai'mair darra,* baby, forever.

Indie. Who taught me priorities. Who forced me to step it up and learn how to push myself. Who stretched my heart to bursting. Who brought me back down when I needed grounding. Whose smile put it all into perspective. It's all for you, baby girl. All of it.

The three who raised me. Mom, Dad (Markabois), and Nan. Who told me stories. Who spent way too much money at Scholastic book fairs. Who came to every game and to every show. Who let me watch Jurrasic Park a little too young. Who watered my imagination and let me explore. Who gave me a chance to succeed in life. I couldn't have gotten this far without you.

My new family. Heartbound not only through marriage, but in truth as well. Thank you for accepting me as one of your own.

My best friend, Jamie, who taught me to love openly and never be ashamed to show what is inside of your heart. Jimmy who judged me in the exact right way at the exact right moment and helped kickstart this whole thing. My bandmates, my first partners in crime, who inspired me to never give up the pursuit of art. Herm, for being there everyday as I make my way through this life, and GX for the time to think at work. And Felix, who once told me, "You've just gotta believe, man."

The ones who helped me make this book into what it is. Max Gorlov at First Book Coaching, who helped me build my toolbox to organize some of the tools I had lying around on the floor, and for enduring the earliest drafts. My beta readers, especially Rob, Elle, Giankarlo, Clarence, Eagle Eye Mike, and Mia. Your feedback was invaluable and helped me to smooth this story out. My editor, Kelley, who poured over this manuscript and chiseled the lump of rock I gave her into something that more closely represents a polished piece of stone. My map maker, Josh, for not only bringing The Remembered Lands to life, but for inspiring the story with his coats of arms. (Especially the big bad wolf) My graphic designer, Brian, for the three hundred emails and counting that resulted in some pretty great art. My cover designer, Stuart Bache, for bringing a vision to life. And all of the friends I made along the way.

GLOSSARY

PLACES AND EVENTS:

Ardura - (ar - dur - ah) The continent of Ardura. One of three known continents in the Remembered Lands, the other two being Edura and Sothura.

The Fells - The northernmost kingdom of Ardura. Mostly inhabited by nomadic, warring clans. Dominated by the overwhelming shadow of the ancient castle Kallahorn and its dark secrets.

Mal Hallow - (mAL hAL - oh) A land of haunted arbors, magic hills, Standing Stones, and rushing rivers. Protected by the great Lovasi castle of Mammoth's Head, built at the crossing of one of few passable fords in the rushing White River. The Mal people have lived here since the start of time. The kingdom is governed by many ruling Lords who have sworn fealty to the king of Ayeland, Calen Alder.

Ayeland - (AIL - ind) The largest kingdom in Ardura. A land of bounty and abundance. Ruled by the Alder dynasty for the last seventy years from the Lovasi castle known as the Bloodwall, in the city of Solace.

Daggland - (dayg - land) An island to the far north. Inhabited by an ancient race of reavers and warriors who once crafted unbreakable steel and have since fallen to a lesser state.

The Glenn - A kingdom in the northwest of Ardura. Known for its contrasting landscape of lush arbors and wide open plains, the Lovasi castle Stone Tree, and the forest city of Elurra. The Brynmor dynasty has ruled the kingdom for the last forty years. The Glenn is also well known for its massive destrier war horses that feed on dead flesh and the speed and strength that the beasts give to their army.

The Starfall - An event that destroyed the great empire of Yehven and left the world in darkness around four thousand years ago. An Abori mage used magics to bring a star down on the Golden City of Ailar, in Yehven. The impact turned the area around Ailar to dust and sent the world into many years of darkness. The seas shifted and the world burned.

CHARACTERS:

Wanderers & Outcasts

James Culdaine - (jaymz kULL – dane) Known as the seer, or World Walker. The son of the usurped king of Mal Hallow. Has been hiding in the Fells with Wulfee and her clan since the death of his family ten years ago.

Bren Culdaine - (bren kULL - dane) Father to James Culdaine. Former king of Mal Hallow. *Killed by Calen Alder.*

Nara of Oster - (nar - ah of aw - ster) Mother to James Culdaine. Former queen of Mal Hallow. *Killed by Calen Alder.*

Eurick - (yurr - ick) A transporter of the Raven's Guild. Hired to track and deliver James.

Adeqor - (a - deh - kor) A Warlock of Yehven. Cast out from The Ailaryan Order—a group of Warlocks that survived the Starfall.

Wulfee - (sounds like wolf - ee) A kihl'dor (leader) of a small clan of Feldarra. Heartbound to Sweyne. Mother to Tarek and Braden.

Sweyne - (sounds like swayne) Heartbound to Wulfee. Father to Tarek and Braden. *Missing.*

Tarek - (tar - ick) Oldest son of Wulfee and Sweyne. *Killed in single combat.*

Braden - (bray - din) Youngest son of Wulfee and Sweyne. *Missing in battle.*

Gen - A youthful Giy'er. Tame from his upbringing with a Human clan.

Pike - An old, chiseled warrior. Karl to Wulfee. Heartbound to Alissa of Lorne. Father to Tess.

Alissa of Lorne - (a - lih - sah) Heartbound to Pike. Mother to Tess. *Mistaken for an intruder and killed by Odhran Ironfist's guards.*

Maggie - (may - gee) A mage of unknown origins. Wulfee's clan took her in after they found her abandoned and injured. Has a mysterious aura.

Folk of the Hallow

Tara - (Tar - ah) Heartbound to Braden. Mother to Little Sweyne.

Benn - An old healer. Travelling with Tara and Little Sweyne.

Little Sweyne - (swayne) Wulfee's grandson (unknown to him). Son of Braden and Tara.

Lew - A stable master in the Hallow Hills

Shaqqa Ro - Also known as *The Green Man.* A shaman, or death stealer, that lives and works at the foot of the Hallow Hills, in the Dark Arbor.

Yule - An albino man who stands seven feet tall. Shaqqa Ro's personal guard.

Rulers of Mal Hallow and Their Followers:

Ockam:

Lord Derudin Deadmaker - (deh - roo - din) Lord of Ockam. Fealty sworn to Calen Alder of Ayeland. Heartbound to Aylee of Oldwood.

Father to Eridan. Former coat of arms is a white flag with a bloody red handprint.

Aylee of Oldwood - (AIL - ee) Former Lady of Ockam. Heartbound to Derudin. Mother to Eridan. *Killed by unknown causes.*

Eridan - (AIR - ih - dan) Son of Derudin and Aylee.

Padraig, The Small - (pa - drayg) A very large warrior. A member of the Blood Company, Derudin's personal guard.

Itchy, the bard - (ih - chee) An old bard who isn't very good.

Mineera Mori - (mih - nEER - a mOR - ee) A scholar from New Lovas. Travelled to Mal Hallow to record the events of barbarians.

Tam, the road smith - A member of the Blood Company.

Gerdey, the cook - (ger - dee) A member of the Blood Company.

Karillin Threethumbs - (kah - rILL - in) A member of the Blood Company.

Berra Coldblood - (bAIR - a) A member of the Blood Company.

Logan TooTall - (loh - gin) A member of the Blood Company.

Arda Honeytongue - (AR - dah) A member of the Blood Company.

Dawning:

Lord Brinley Scareye - (brin - lee) Lord of Dawning. Heartbound to Sessely of Fever. Father to Tilda, Brigid, and Aione. Fealty sworn to King Calen Alder of Ayeland. Former coat of arms is a black crow on a field of gold.

Sessely of Fever - (seh- sih - lee) Lady of Dawning. Heartbound to Brinley. Mother to Tilda, Brigid, and Aione.

Tilda - (tILL - dah) - One of the Three Black Crows of Dawning: (Daughter of Lord Brinley and Lady Sessely)

Brigid - (brih - jid) - One of the Three Black Crows of Dawning: (Daughter of Lord Brinley and Lady Sessely)

Aione - (eye - oh- nee) - One of the Three Black Crows of Dawning: (Daughter of Lord Brinley and Lady Sessely)

<u>Tusk:</u>

Lord Claydon Coldfoot (klay - din) - Lord of Tusk and Castellan to the Lovasi castle of Mammoth's Head. Fealty sworn to King Calen Alder of Ayeland. Former coat of arms is a grey mammoth on a field of green.

Heri Doe - (hair - ee - doe) A mysterious woman who came and went without warning. She disappeared forever after giving birth to Macts. Some folk believe she was a river nymph.

Aron - (ar - on) The oldest son of Claydon Coldfoot and Heri Doe.

Macts - (sounds like max) The youngest son of Claydon Coldfoot and Heri Doe.

Rosen:

Lady Ruwen the Strong - (roo - win) Lady of Rosen. Known as the Old Bear. Fealty sworn to King Calen Alder of Ayeland. Heartbound to Yaren of Rosen. Mother to Gareth and Jon.

Yaren of Rosen - A man of Rosen. Heartbound to Lady Ruwen. Father to Gareth and Jon.

Gareth - (gAIR - ith) The oldest son of Ruwen and Yaren.

Jon - Youngest son of Ruwen and Yaren.

Other:

Lord Richard Brynmor - (brin - mOR) Lord of Elurra, in the Glenn. Former ally of Mal Hallow. A friend to Derudin. Known as the Hammer of the Glenn.

The Rangers of E'daru:

Haro - (hair - oh) Leads a band of Rangers and is a highly respected member of the Fellowship of Rangers. Other band leaders take his word as law.

Florence - (flOR - inse) Leads a band of Rangers. Has a mysterious history. Nobody really knows where she comes from.

Gulla - (gULL - ah) A Ranger of E'daru.

Coal - (kOAL) A Ranger of E'daru whose confidence in himself is unwavering.

Jerrick - (jAIR - ick) A Ranger of E'daru.

Crowseye - A Ranger of E'daru. Master of bow and arrow.

Leatherback - A Ranger of E'daru. Can read the stars and the moon.

Stackhand - A Ranger of E'daru. Wields an axe like no other and only has half a tongue.

The Kihl'dor of Pool & His Followers

Odhran - (ode - ran) Kihl'dor of Pool. Brother to Alissa. Brotherbound to Pike. Uncle to Tess.

Tess - A karl of the Fells. Daughter to Pike and Alissa.

Six-toe Dillon - A karl of the Fells. From a mixed race clan who are known to mate with El'vie.

Killer Jobe - A karl of the Fells. Son of the great kihl'dor, Collen of the Rock.

Tilly One-eye - A karl of the Fells. Daughter of the great kihl'dor, Collen of the Rock.

Golla Grace - (gALL - ah) A karl of the Fells. Known as the She-Wolf of Urum.

Tennit Boneshaker - Kihl'dor of the Bone-Eater clan.

<u>Warlocks, Kings, & Brigands</u>

Ellorin - (el - oh - rin) Known as the Banshee, or the Hunter of Souls. A surviving member of the Ailaryan Order.

King Calen Alder - (kay - lin ALL - der) The King Of Ayeland. Currently garrisoned at Kallahorn. Heartbound to Queen Helen Alder. Father to Ianna, Sammil, Dredrik, Helena, and Sherri Alder.

King Baleth Longsongs - (bAIL - ith) Declared himself King of Kallahorn. Heartbound to Anne of Morland. Father to Fiora. Many say that he went mad in the year before his murder. *Killed by Calen Alder.*

Queen Anne of Morland - Heartbound to Baleth Longsongs. Mother to Fiora. *Killed by Baleth Longsongs.*

Fiora - (fee - OR - ah) Daughter of Baleth Longsongs and Anne of Morland. *Missing.*

The Wolf - A brigand general gathering mercenaries and rebels in the north to fight for the southern army. His true identity is unknown.

Bazal - (bah - zil) A great warlock of the Ailaryan Order, who many believe to have been the most powerful Warlock to have ever lived. His soul has broken free from its confinement in The Otherworld. His location is unknown.

LANGUAGES:

Runish Tongue of the Ancient Mal:

Ai'mair - (eye - mare) means *love.*

Darra - (dar - ah) means *protection.*

Karl - means *free.*

Kihl'dor - (keel-dore) means *leader.*

Nihr'el - (neer-el) means *World Tree.*

Nihr'el nur amo ruso - means *World tree save my soul.*

Lovasi:

Ti arda montë - (tee-ar-dah monn-tay), means *How is your heart?* - old Lovasi greeting.

Ênalia dura - (ee-nah-lee-ah dOOR-ah), means *My heart is home* - Reply to the old greeting; means my heart is happy, safe, warm—feelings of home.

Di ąrda illientë - (dee - ar - dah ILL - ee - en - tay) means *Where is your mind?* - Old Lovasi insult; a way of calling someone stupid.

The Old Tongue (Yehvenki):

Dagdora - (dag-dOR - ah), means *fire*.

NON-HUMAN RACES:

Druids - The old blood of the ancient Mal. Even The Mal know little about the Druids, other than they built the Standing Stones using magics they stole from Old Yehven. Mages and seers were once common amongst the Druids when their blood was pure, but as they have diluted their blood over generations, folk have forgotten them.

El'vie - (Ell-vee) Merrmonsters that live in the Lake of Pool. They are almost more fishlike than they are Human. They speak in a twittering tongue lost on most ears. The Druids said the El'vie have always been there, born out of the waters that surround the world tree. Their souls are bound to it. They pay no attention to others, and they never leave their Pool except to mate with Humans.

Giy'er - (Guy-err) Massive, giant like creatures that live in wide open spaces, usually at the foot of mountains or hills so they can easily catch game animals. Faster than a horse, with leathery skin and rock-like bones. They start enormous bonfires to cook their meat, and they often spread out of control. They are unpredictable.

Hawka - (Hah-kah) Faculative bi-pedal wolfish, moose-like carnivores that roam the mountains and the hills. They eat what they see and they are always hungry. They are afraid of arbors and the dead souls that lurk in them.

Warlocks - The survivors of Old Yehven. A race of folk known to have used dangerous and unpredictable magics to build grand empires. They seem to have used their magics to alter their lifespans and can live for many thousands of years.

Rangers - Descendants of the E'daru—the first skinchanger. (Also known as, greenhoods, skincrawlers, skinchangers, bodysnatchers.) Rangers have the ability to warg into animals. Common folk know little about the details, for most fear going near them. They worship the Maw god and practice sacrifice at full moon.

GROUPS AND GUILDS:

The Feldarra - (Symbol - The nihr'el shield) A group of folk sworn by sacred blood oaths to protect the lands of the Fells and Mal Hallow from foreign invaders.

The Ailaryan Order - (Symbol - The flaming star) A group of Warlocks from Old Yehven who survived the Starfall and established a new world order. They have used their magics to influence the world, and the people in it, ever since.

The Rangers of E'daru - (Symbol - The E'daru, black horse with long human hair and no eyes.) A band of Rangers actively seeking E'daru. They live in the arbors and steal from folks passing through. They are all hoping for a meeting with E'daru. There are many Rangers who are not active in a band and have settled down as a crofter, or in a hamlet somewhere. Because they have already had an encounter with E'daru, or they had simply chosen to walk away.

The Raven's Guild - (Symbol - a spread winged raven) The transporters of Ardura. The Raven's Guild can send one of their ravens to retrieve anything, or anyone, anywhere in the Remembered Lands. And then deliver that thing, anywhere. For the right price, of course.

THE OLD GODS:

The Spirits - Fire, Air, Water, Earth.

Father Tree - Divine justice and ultimate judge of the souls of the dead.

The Hare - Mercy, peace, fertility, childbirth, life - blesses with bountiful harvest (or eats the harvest)

The Owl - Wisdom and foresight.

The Stag - Courage, and strength, fortitude in battle

The Crow - Death, decay, and mystery.

The Swan - Innocence, love, beauty, protects the innocent

The Bluebird Twins - Ayla: Arts and music. Nox: Crafting. Luck.

The Lupin (The Outcast) - Darkness, the moon, and the unknown workings of nature. Referred to as the Maw God.

OTHER GODS:

Eralis - (Eh-rah-lis), The One God. Worshipped throughout most of the Glenn, Ayeland, and the Hesterlands. A religion founded in Lovas by the Prophet Eralis and spread by their empire.

Karaat - (Kah-rat), The Creator God. Worshipped throughout Esher, Lavesh, and most of Edura. A religion that has roots back in the days before the Starfall. Created by the prophets of Ailar for smallfolk and slaves. There are no places of worship for the followers of Karaat. They pray to the sun and the moon below the great sky sea. They usually centre their prayers around sacrifice, morning or night, and fire. Karaat granted his followers with a gift: Words laced with magics. The power of the Words directly relates to how many people worship Karaat.

WHAT'S NEXT?

I have much more in the works for this story and this world. A prelude novella entitled *The Sound of Starfall* will be released in August of this year. This new story will make the reader a witness to the most pivotal moment in the known history of the Remembered Lands: the Starfall.

Next will come the Second Verse of the Last Ballad, which I'm currently working on! The sequel to *AMOS* picks up with James and Wulfee, and expands into the southern kingdoms with FIVE new POV characters. Some that you already know, and some that you don't! We're dealing with the fallout of this book now, and there is a lot of fallout! I hope to have the Second Verse out in early 2025.